LAUGHLAND

IT TOOK A BOY TO FINALLY END A WAR

For Teresa Gill watching the carnival called Laughland spring to life deep in the wasteland of the American West became the exclamation point to a day filled with emotions that reached from wonder and awe to fear and disappointment. The midway blazed with light, the roller coaster car made its steep climb, and at the far end the carousel turned while raising and lowering its horses accompanied by what she felt sure was a Bach fugue rich with its thundering organ cords echoing off the hills.

"It's beautiful," she said.

"Laughland was born at Bong Sat," said Amos Eliot. "The battle was fought because of Nathan Ferry's ambition and heartlessness. My father told me about the jungle, the rain, and the giant cathedral where the organ played while many died."

The carnival glowed, every detail etched in crystalline clarity against the darkness of the surrounding desert while the fugue played on.

"Clyde says Laughland is the conscience of Bong Sat," Amos said. "What happened there was so terrible that God will close the books here on the midway, or if Clyde has his way, in the fun house. Father Harold says Laughland is the moral scab of an evil so profound it cannot heal without an exorcism."

"What do you say?" asked Teresa, feeling the young man's intensity radiating next to her.

They walked down the path in silence until Amos stopped, and said, "I am the heart and soul of all who died. It ends here."

LAUGHLAND

Ken Byers

ISBN 9780983224228
Lloyd Court Press)
Portland, Oregon 97219

Cover photo of carousel courtesy of
Old Tucson Studios, Tucson, Arizona

THIS BOOK IS DEDICATED TO

THE MEMORY OF

MICHAEL W. KASNER (1941-2008)

Soldier, historian, author, and friend.

With heartfelt appreciation for the knowledge, advise, and evenings spent discussing the world – then and now. I miss you.

Thanks,
Ken

1980

Beverly Hills, California

Ned Greene's goodwill, limited at the best of times, vanished before his first cup of coffee cooled.   Greene's bad morning, spent in the foyer of the Four Season's ballroom, brought him face to face with representatives of those who felt slighted not to be seated with Nathan Ferry on the dais of that evening's International Achievement Awards.

"Did your guy win last year?" he asked each supplicant.

The answer always came back no because those who could say yes were already in the seats of honor.

"How about a Noble prize? No? Then get out of my face! Be glad you're here at all."

A few attempted intimidation, but Greene's massive and well cared for physique discouraged most from that ill-chosen path. He didn't see why Nathan Ferry's personal security director – him – got stuck with this pissant job, but every year found him still filling the role. He saw it as a test of how bad he wanted to keep his job. Steady and well paying employment for ex-mercenaries rarely offered as many rewards and so few risks as this one.

This year's banquet had presented a sterner test of his resolve. To begin with his tux and formal accessories got lost on the private jet's trip from New York to Los Angeles. No matter how loud he screamed no one could explain how it happened.

"You put it on the plane before it takes off and you unload it when it lands! So where did it go?"

Since Greene's violent temper was well known, the mad race to find replacements had kept his staff in a state of near panic leaving Greene to do more himself. When, with less than an hour to spare, he learned his replacement tux and accessories had arrived he was ready to explode. The bright spot came when it all fit perfectly although he disliked the large size of the shirt studs and the stiff hinges on the cufflinks. His assistant, Norm Brinks, waited while he dressed and Greene, for at least the hundredth time, demanded an explanation. Brinks still had no answer.

At six o'clock, Greene walked into the ballroom of the Four Seasons, Beverly Hills dressed appropriately. When Nathan Ferry arrived a few minutes later, Greene replaced Brinks and Colin Truax and moved into position two strides behind and to Ferry's right. For the next fifteen minutes he watched impassively, but warily, as Ferry worked the room. Greene wiped the sweat from his eyes and wondered why it was so hot. He waved at Brinks and told him to find out.

"Just did. AC's out," Brinks said. "Hotel says they have people on it."

"How long?"

Brinks shrugged.

When Greene got Ferry's attention he gave him the news.

"Tell them to fix it," Ferry said.

"They're working on it. Might want to relax the dress code."

"No," Ferry said, and turned to another guest.

By dinner all anyone talked about was the heat. After the guests reached their assigned seats, Nathan Ferry took the podium.

"Welcome to the twenty-second annual International Achievement Awards," he said to the five hundred guests. "This year's prizes were hotly contested, and since everyone here has been in the hot seat before I'm sure we can all take the heat for one more night."

He sat down to laughter and applause.

Waiters delivered salads and poured the first wine, a chilled Riesling from the Salinas Valley. It disappeared quickly, and a Chardonnay from a vineyard a little further north intended for the shrimp cocktail filled empty glasses. Unless the courses came faster, the wine would be gone and the guests would either have to drink red with fish or opt for ice water. Anticipating the problem, the staff cranked up the hotel's huge ice makers and raided the machines on each floor of the hotel, but availability lagged far behind demand.

Seated to the left of the head table, sweat ran down Ned Greene's forehead as he nibbled his salad. As he leaned toward his water glass a blow pounded his chest. His first thought was heart attack but then he heard a muffled noise and wondered if the pain or the noise came first. Before the blow he had seen Truax across the table. Now all he saw was ceiling.

"I've been shot," he thought.

This was not the way he imagined he would die. Not in a tux.

Colin Truax saw a small cloud of smoke erupt in the middle of Greene's chest as he heard a sharp pop. He dropped his fork as Greene toppled over backward. He ran around the table and saw a widening red stain in sharp contrast to Greene's white shirt now held in place by three studs where there had been four.

The stud blew up, Truax thought.

"Napkins!" he yelled. He took the first thrust at him and leaned toward the wound.

The second stud exploded.

Greene's torso jumped from the floor. Tiny projectiles hit Truax, one going in the corner of his left eye. He dropped the napkin and covered his face.

"I'm a doctor," a man cried, as he leaned over Greene.

"Stay back," Truax yelled.

The doctor ignored him and reached for Greene's chest. As he did the stud over the victim's stomach exploded. Both the doctor and Greene screamed. Truax tried to imagine the pain

9

ripping into Greene's abdominal cavity. The doctor rocked back on his heels, his hands tending to a cut on his forehead. Somebody else arrived and pushed past Truax and the doctor. People who had seen the explosions, yelled warnings. Truax stared at the bleeding Greene who used both hands to hold his stomach in place. Truax wondered how a charge could be shaped in something as small as a shirt stud.

The cufflink on Greene's right wrist exploded. The recoil lifted Greene's arm, now minus the hand, and spattered those nearby with blood and tissue. The blast, larger than the first three, tossed Truax backward. He watched, immobilized, as Greene bled out.

Norm Brinks toured the ballroom surveying the aftermath of the dramatic killing. The planning and execution of a man Norm thought to be one of the hardest men in the world to assassinate had been brilliant. Greene's tux disappeared, then delays in replacing it. When formal wear materialized at the last minute the relief was so great no one questioned the miracle of clothes to fit Greene's six foot four and nearly two hundred and fifty pound body. Norm had helped close the cufflinks.

As paramedics treated Truax's eye, and Greene's draped body still on the floor, Brinks headed for the elevators. Panicked guests from upper floors filled the lobby as rumors spread. He rode alone to eleven and entered Greene's room. He searched the clothes bag and the boxes the replacement formal wear arrived in, sure he would find something. This had been too perfect for the credit to go unclaimed. After he'd looked everywhere else, he pried out the felt liner of the velvet-covered box that held the studs and cufflinks. Beneath the insert he found a card:

BONG SAT
18 NOV 67

He turned it over:

In Memoriam

Gunnery Sgt Carlos Montoya, USMC Brinks shuddered. Nightmares of pawing through the bodies of Bong Sat's freshly killed still haunted him. Many of the dead had consisted of nothing more than parts, and all the while a raging Nathan Ferry had waved a gun behind him. He even remembered the Gunnery Sergeant Greene had shot. Maybe he'd shot him, too. The two Marines had come around the corner of that church and both he and Greene had opened fire.

Two questions hammered him. Who waits thirteen years for payback? And, would he be next?

Matt Eliot watched the rush of emergency people as he stood in a corner of the hotel lobby. His hands remained in his pockets where they caressed the actuators that had detonated the shaped charges in the studs and cufflink. Earlier in the day, wearing the coveralls of a repair man, Eliot had placed the explosive device and its timer that shut down the air conditioner's control panel. The heat in the ballroom room had forced the opening of the doors allowing Eliot to time his attack, and maximized the panic in the already edgy guests. Screaming security details added to the chaos.

Eliot thought of the two disappointing parts of the evening. He had not seen Greene die, but from the doorway he did see the body lying on the floor in a lake of blood with no one within thirty feet. He had taken a risk getting close, but he owed it to Montoya to see his killer dead on the floor.

Second, he would like to see Ferry's face when he saw the card from the cufflinks box. He had no illusions about Ferry feeling a sense of loss with Greene, but planting seeds of fear and vulnerability in that evil son of a bitch would do. Eliot knew efforts to find him would be stepped up, but pictures from surveillance cameras in the lobby would be of no help.

What no one would see coming was his son. Matt stroked the actuators again as he felt his pride in Amos's handiwork. The remaining cufflink and shirt stud would give testimony to his craftsmanship and ingenuity. Eliot smiled imagining the care the forensics people would use in examining the unexploded jewelry. If the truth ever surfaced, no one would believe they were the creation of a thirteen year old.

Matt walked ten blocks to his car, drove south on La Cienega, entered the I-10 Freeway, and drove into the night toward Laughland.

PART I: BONG SAT

BONG SAT, 17 NOV 67
NEAR VIETNAM'S DEMILITARIZED ZONE

The rain brings both deliverance and misery.

A new drenching downpour delivers safety from the next ambush and leaves the Marines under dripping ponchos as they attempt to keep their dwindling supplies of food and ammunition dry. As long as the rains fall they are left to fight the land, not the North Vietnamese. Two weeks ago, when they jumped from the choppers and into the rain, they numbered twenty two. Now they are fourteen, and the enemy knows more about where they are than they do. They are adrift, and their mission has changed from seek and destroy to avoid and survive.

Their patrol retains a familiar pattern. The sky clears; an ambush comes; and they hold their ground at the cost of more lives until it starts to rain again. The toll from the last ambush is two and would have been higher had not the warning of Xan, their Hmong translator and guide, sent them into cover moments before the enemy could close their trap. After the enemy vanishes, the Marines take personal belongings and dog tags from their dead and bury them in sadly shallow graves. They resume their struggle against the terrain for three more kilometers before the dark stops them.

After a sleepless night they march through the wet dawn. As the rain lets up for the first time since the ambush, Xan hand signals Captain Matthew Eliot who calls his men to a halt. Gunnery Sargent Carlos Montoya sets point and drag while the rest remove their ponchos and sit on the crowns of their steel pots while their bodies steam. Most light cigarettes, some drink from canteens, but all hold their weapons near. While the Marines sit, Xan disappears into the jungle.

"Cap?" *Montoya asks, dropping to a squat next to Eliot.*

"Yeah, Gunny?"

Montoya hands Eliot a gold locket on a chain and dog tags.

"Tubby's," *Montoya says.*

Eliot opens the locket. Inside is the picture of a girl.

"Wife or girlfriend?" *Eliot asks.*

"Tubby wouldn't say. He said the more you talk about something the less likely it is to happen. He never talked about seeing her. All he talked about was how bad he wanted to stay here."

Tubby, real name Ralph Tubman, had been a tall, thin Marine from New Jersey who took a shot in the head and was dead before he hit the ground.

Eliot, as officer in charge, will write to the next of kin of every fallen Marine and wants something personal from each of his dead. There would be many letters. He has never lost eight men on a patrol and they aren't home yet.

"What else you got?" *Eliot asks.*

"Nothing from Lamar Austin."

"Nothing?"

"Tags is all." *Montoya hands dog tags to Eliot.* "Austin thought he was invisible as long as he didn't carry anything personal. He said it was like not being here. Probably find something in his foot locker when we get back."

Eliot pulls his pack around, roots inside, and comes out holding a purple velvet bag with the Seagram's Crown Royal logo stitched in yellow. He opens the bag, drops in the locket and dog tags, and pulls the drawstrings taut. He bounces the bag in his hand, feels the irregular shape of dog tags, lockets, rings, a wallet, a gold pen, along with his most recent additions, then shakes his head. As the bag grows heavier, so does his heart.

"Gunny, this is yours . . . if."

"I know, Cap. No more ifs."

"Put in the picture of Amos."

The first picture of his new son arrived two days before the left.

"Sure. Good picture. Already looks like you."

"Ha, he was two weeks old. You get mail, Gunny?"

"Yeah, the wife's all worried about the roof on the garage. Snowed like a son of a bitch last winter and she's afraid if it happens again the roof will go. Told her I'd fix it when I get home, but until then go to mass and pray for a heat wave."

"How cold's it get up in that high desert?"

"Freeze your ass off. Most people don't think about freezing in New Mexico." He looked at the steam coming off his body. "Not many places could make me miss winter back home. Right now freezing my ass sounds good."

This conversation is not new. It's as close to home as they can come, and like all who have survived, they are haunted by the fear they will never see home again.

Eliot hefts the bag then whispers, "This is it, we're getting out of here."

"Say what, Cap?"

"What have we got left?" Eliot asks, as he puts the purple bag in his pack.

"One good fight and we're out of ammo." Montoya crosses himself. "Hate to say it, Cap, but we could use a miracle or two, maybe a little Divine intervention."

Xan comes out of the foliage and beckons to Eliot.

"Maybe Xan has something." Eliot gets to his feet. "Get 'em ready to move while I take a look."

Eliot follows the Hmong through trees and hanging vines. The way grows steep. His tired legs protest as he steps from root to rock like rungs on a ladder.

"This had better be good," he mutters. "It's gotta be good."

Two more minutes and he emerges out of the bush at the top of a ridge line high enough to see the triangular shaped valley laid out with the wide mouth at the far end. In the middle of the valley, pointing at the sky in defiance of all earthly matters, stand the spires of a huge church.

"Jesus!" Eliot exclaims.

"Bong Sat," Xan says. "Two klicks, less."

"*What is this place?*"

"*'Ville. People come many klicks. Church place, market, many fire fights. No people now.*"

Eliot and Xan hear the chopper before they see it. The American helicopter enters the far end of the valley hugging the tree line. It climbs, circles the spires, then drops near where Eliot puts the church.

"Bring the rest of them up and do it fast," Eliot says. "We need that chopper."

While he waits, Eliot scans the valley with his field glasses. It looks like the top half of an hour glass narrowing as it gets nearer ending in a pass at his feet. A road leads to the 'ville. After fighting the jungle floor for days, the road is inviting but would leave them exposed.

When the Marines stand together, Eliot explains his simple plan to commandeer the Huey.

"Shit, blue sky," a private named Hood says pointing up.

They check their weapons before Xan leads them down the hillside. They parallel the road deep enough in the cover for it to be useful but still make good time. As they draw close to the 'ville, the cover thins and Eliot stops them inside the tree line. They see Bong Sat's burned out shells and tortured buildings that speak to previous firefights. Eliot signals his men to stay put while he moves closer. From his new position he sees the chopper sitting alone with rotors unmoving.

He waves for Montoya and when he gets there, Eliot says, "I'm going to get that bird."

"Cap, I don't like it! Where is everybody? What's going on?" Montoya stares at the church. "Jesus! Look at the size of that monster! Why do they need something that big out here?"

"You're the Catholic. Maybe this is one of those Divine interventions."

"Maybe not, too. Sir, I'll send Traxler to watch your back."

"No, I'm not trying to scare anyone. That's an Air Cav chopper. Move our guys closer to the church then you can all watch my back."

He watches Montoya move the Marines into position, then, keeping a burned out building or a pock-marked wall between him and the square, Eliot cautiously moves forward. As he does, he hears the rotors on the chopper wind up.

"Shit!" he murmurs, and starts to run with his eyes fixed on the near corner of the church. He loses sight of the chopper behind a pile of rubble, but *as he rounds a wall and enters the square he sees a man walking from the chopper toward the church. The man wears some kind of a safari suit with a wide brimmed, khaki-colored hat. The outfit looks new. He appears nervous, walking hesitantly and glancing over his shoulder to the chopper and back to the church. A second man stands in the door of the helicopter and when he sees Eliot he leans back into the shadow. Seconds later Eliot sees a third man, also in civilian clothes and wearing a black baseball cap, standing in the shadow of the church. All three are Caucasians. The one with the baseball cap calls to the walker who moves faster toward him. They disappear into the church, but before Eliot moves the nervous man reappears. He has not seen Eliot, and does not know the Marine is near until Eliot calls,* "We need a lift out of here, sir!"

The man jumps, turns, and Eliot sees his fear.

"Jesus Christ!" *he cries, his voice high and cracking.* "Who are you?"

"Eliot. Recon, 2nd Battalion, 3rd Marines. Who are you?"

"What are you doing here?"

"My men and I could use a ride, sir. Been out two weeks and we're pretty well shot up."

"No way. You picked a bad time, Marine."

"Bad time? We're the ones shot up! What's your problem?"

The man looks at the Marine's soaking fatigues.

"Captain, I got no time," *he says, tapping the face of his watch,* "and I guarantee you do not want to know my problem."

"We're done in. Damn near out of food and ammo. Either get us out of here or you don't lift off. We can all fight right down to the last man."

"Okay, okay, hold . . . just, just hold on." *The man looks at his watch, then asks in a distracted tone,* "How did you happen here?"

"You can see the steeple from the hill," *Eliot said, pointing south.*

The man shakes his head, then stands straight. "Last time, Captain, there is no room on the chopper, and you do not want to be here."

Eliot chambers a round in his weapon. The man sighs.

"Okay, Captain. Wait one." *The man runs to the Huey, and leans in the side door.*

Other than the noise of the Huey's idling rotors, nothing moves and Eliot hears no other sound. Finally, the man breaks from the chopper and jogs back to the Marine.

16

"We're working on it, Captain," he says, as he runs toward the church.

With no cover and none he can reach fast, Eliot feels the hair stand on his neck. He walks quickly toward the front of the church. By the time he sees the two Americans standing in the shadow, he is close enough to hear the second man's exclamation as his eyes lock with Eliot's.

"Jesus, Steerman," he yells, pointing at Eliot. "The escort sees the Marines we got a fire fight! Get them out of sight and make sure they don't get trigger happy."

They argue, lowering their voices and both waving arms and pointing first at Eliot and then toward the far side of the church. The one with the baseball cap says loudly, "Leave Ferry to me." He jogs toward the chopper.

Eliot grabs the terrified man called Steerman.

"Talk to me, Goddamn it!" the Marine orders. In his peripheral vision he sees the man in the baseball cap draw his side arm as he nears the chopper.

"Who is that?" Eliot asks, pointing at the man as the gun comes up.

"Our only hope."

1975

Where The Broken Things Go

In his happiest place everyone called him Amo. When Bill said, "Give us a smile, Amo," his smile came easy; and when Bill said "Grab that spanner, Amo," he laughed as he wrapped his still small hands around the wrench. It took both hands to carry it to Bill, the one who gave him his name. The name 'Amo' carried a smell of its own, too. It smelled like grease and canvas, and almost as good as chocolate frosting smells on cake still warm from the chuck wagon oven. Amo was his name in Laughland's shop tent, where the broken things go.

Not everyone felt happy in the shop tent. Amo's father never smiled there. Bill Tagnut, the maintenance chief and foreman, explained the boss never liked broken things.

"I must be broken, too," Amo said. "Dad sends me here."

"Not so, Amo," Bill replied. "Broken don't happen to people. He sends you here because he knows you're happy helping me."

Things were pretty much the same every day in the shop and Amo liked things the same. For as long as he could remember, he'd spent his mornings in the shop while Bill and the boys banged away with spanners and hammers, blew dust and dirt off this or that, and took apart things with a whole lot of pieces. Pretty soon what had been broken would sputter, then purr. Day after day pretty much the same.

Even when the machines to be repaired changed, the work didn't, although there were different ways of fixing a machine.

"How'd you know to start there?" Amo asked Bill, pointing to what he would soon learn was the air filter on one of Laughland's old trucks.

"The engine couldn't breathe," Bill said. "Kinda like putting your hand over your mouth, sticking a couple of fingers up your nose, and trying to breathe all at the same time. Try it."

Amo tried but soon his eyes bugged.

"No air, you die. Engine's the same way. Soon as we clean all this gunk off, we get the good part. See this here thing? Fuel filter. It plugs, the engine gets no gas and dies. You try going without supper for a week and see how you're doing. Everything needs fuel and air."

"That all everything needs?" Amo asked.

"Nope, gotta be cool. Water for living things, and most of these here trucks need it too. Water's a heat exchanger. Know what that is?"

"Makes hot cool."

Bill smiled and tapped Amo's head. "How come you think you're broken with that smooth running brain between your ears?"

Amo had no answer, but he knew he was broken. He'd seen other kids along the Midway holding hands, and laughing, and riding on the shoulders of their fathers and doing things he never did with his dad. Those kids acted like he did when he was in the shops. Being happy in the place where broken things got fixed meant maybe he could be fixed, maybe he could even fix himself.

In the trailer where he lived with his parents they called him by his real name, Amos, a Biblical name of a prophet no one liked. They didn't talk much about the Bible, but he knew about Amos because someone told him his name was a good Old Testament name and he had to ask his mom what that meant. She explained about the Old Testament and that Amos had been a prophet. His father said no one wanted to listen to the prophet named Amos because he always had bad news. Amos wondered if he had been bad news and that was why they gave him the name. His mother assured him he had been good news, joyous news, and the name Amos came from his father's ancestors.

Out in the shop Mike the Mick, so called because he was Irish, spoke some Latin because he was Catholic, an idea that needed some explanation, because along with the Bible, religion and church weren't a part of Amo's life. Part of being a Catholic, Mike said, was knowing some Latin which was an old fashioned language no one but Catholics spoke.

"Amo in Latin," he said, "means love." Amo noticed the way Mike talked changed when he said the words. It was like he was using someone else's voice. "Amo, amas, amat. I loved, you loved, he loved."

That night Amo, now Amos because he sat in the trailer having dinner, told his mother and father what his name meant in Latin. Jessie, his mother smiled, patted his hand and said everyone loved him so it was the perfect meaning for his name. His father's face grew darker than usual. "No talk of Catholics in this trailer. I'll talk to Mike – and Amos, if anyone tries to talk to you about Catholics, you let me know. That's the law. Clear?"

By the mid '70's the carnival way of life was all but dead in America, but despite dwindling crowds, Laughland traveled the West to small towns and county fairs from Glendive, Montana to Lovington, New Mexico. To earn a living everyone at Laughland had more than one job. Come noon every day the Boys shed their greasy shop clothes and put on clean shirts and hats to earn their keep on the spiel. Bill, the only one not to change out of his coveralls, spent his time dinkering one ride or another that came off the tracks, or patching up "a piece of junk ready to give up the ghost."

Just as everybody had more than one job, many also had more than one life, his folks included who used to be Eliot and now called themselves Caldwell.. His own secret identity was Amo who flew around Laughland on his Lift-a-nator, a platform on wheels that elevated Amo into the action, changing the broken things into "sweet little Jim Dandies."

"Most folk's got a story around here," Bill said to Amos one morning while they made their morning rounds walking the deserted, sawdust strewn aisles of Laughland.

"What's yours?" Amo asked,

"Me? I was a rocket scientist down at that Cape Canaveral."

"Hey, Bill," said Larry, one of the Boys, as he fed long black strings of lube into the gear box of the Ferris wheel, "remember what you told us about not feeding the kid shit?"

"Yeah, Larry, I said I was gonna bust your teeth for using that word."

"It's okay, Bill," Amo said, "I hear it all the time, but I don't say it. Were you really a rocket scientist?"

"More like a jet jockey. Jet jockeys work on the rockets, and, yeah, I did it. Not much different than this damn thing right here. Rockets go up and down, and this here wheel here goes round and round and both wind up pretty much where they started. Cleaner working on rockets, I guess, but that's the main difference. Remember, I told you all machines work the same."

"I remember," Amo said. "Goes in there, comes out here and starts over."

"What's the best part?" Bill asked, still grinning.

"The purr. The purr of a smooth running machine, a sweet little Jim Dandy."

One day Amo asked Bill, "Can I fix a broken thing?"

"I don't know, can you?"

Amo wiggled his fingers. "They're kind of small, but if the broken thing was small, I could fix it. All machines are the same."

Bill stared and laughed, then hugged him. "I do believe you could, yes sir, I do believe. Let's take a look around."

Although the shop tent was an oval, everyone talked in square terms. In one corner, two metal work tables met at a ninety degree angle with a screw clamp on the front of one and a rack with hand tools across the back, while on the other sat a one horse electric motor.

"It's broken, Amo. How come? You figure it out." Bill called over his shoulder as he walked away. "Let me know when you need something."

Amo stared at his first very own broken thing. A cord ending in a three prong plug came out one end and lay coiled near an outlet, while on the other a cord with frayed ends drooped off the bench. With the loose ends wired into place they told the motor what to do. A couple of months ago, he and Bill had changed out a motor just like this one at the Fun House that opened the door when a car tripped the limit switch. He wondered how many boys his age knew about limit switches. Since he couldn't lift the motor, he dropped to his knees and shoved it around. He sucked his lower lip like Bill did when he "cogitated," then wiped his finger across the air vents. They came away dirty. He wiped dirt off the motor with a rag, but the vent holes remained clogged. He walked down the bench and picked up the air hose. He had never used one but he knew what to do. He took the hose in both hands, pointed it upwards, and closed a finger on the trigger. When nothing happened, he used two fingers and the hose jumped. He would have lost hold had he been able to press the trigger harder. This time he trapped the hose between his feet to keep it steady, took a deep breath, and pressed the trigger. He held tight, and made the air go where he aimed. He pointed the hose at the vent holes. The burst of air bit into the choked vents. He loved watching the dirt fly off the fouled screen. Maybe, he thought, the best part wasn't the purr, but the doing.

It got harder cleaning the bottom vents. He used a knee to steady the hose and the rest of the grit flew off. With the vents clean, he put the hose down and plugged the motor in. Nothing. He rocked back on his toes.

"No limit switch, Amo," said Bill. "Good thing, too. That motor would have danced itself right off the bench. That's the bad news. The good news is it would have because it ain't broken no more."

"Why did you do that?" Amo asked, angry.

21

"What's that, Amo?" Bill asked, talking slow.

"You gave me an easy one but I didn't get the good part."

"Good to start on an easy one, Amo," said Bill. "You weren't ready for the good part. What if it had come on? It could have knocked you off the bench along with itself and broken you both."

Bill didn't like the look on Amo's face. It was the face of getting things your own way too damn often. The boy had no life outside the shops, but inside, with all the doting attention, he lived the life of a star. The hard part for Amo would be in the growing up as he lay hands on the broken things, and from time to time met unfamiliar adversity. And what hands! Still so small, but even in Laughland, a world where slight of hand was a way of life and the carnival a refuge for magicians, illusionists, and dips, the boy's flying fingers mesmerized all who saw them.

"You can get heated up all you want," Bill said, "but sometimes there's more than one reason why things don't work. You did good, as far as you did. You used that smart brain of yours, remembered about breathing through your hand, and opened the air vents. That was the reason the motor came off line. Too hard to get to in place and clean it proper. But what do you have to do to make it work?"

Amo pointed at the cords, first the one with the plug on the end and then the other.

"Meaning?" Bill asked.

"No limit switches so it won't work."

"Right, without an actuator nothing happens. What should you have done?"

"Before plugging it in I should have called you. I could have wired a limit switch to the cord and moved the switch with my fingers, but if you'd wanted me to do that you would have told me."

Bill stared at Amo, then smiled.

"That's not a happy smile, Bill."

"You sure you're only eight? Are you one of the midgets we used to have around here?"

"No, I'm eight, but I'm almost nine."

"I can tell you most eight year olds who are damn near nine don't have a notion about what you just said."

"I spend all my time here, I'm nothing special."

"Oh, you're special, you can take that to the bank, Amo." Bill took one of Amo's hands in his, and shook it gently. "These here are a miracle. Fingers on most people – hell, all people – don't move as fast as yours. Got nothing to do with smart. You were born with high test wired into your reflexes. Maybe no voice in your head said, Amos Eliot, go to the shop and use your hands; use that gift God gave you, but you knew this was the best place."

Amo jumped to his feet. He looked Bill dead in the eye.

"How do you know my real name?"

Bill sighed and didn't answer until Amos pulled on his arm.

"From time to time everybody needs a friend," Bill said. "Sometimes they need a friend real bad."

"My dad?"

"Yes, sir. Matt and me go back, way back. When that day came he needed help, I said sure. It was time for me to move on anyhow."

"How come he needed help?"

Bill put a hand on Amo's shoulder and considered a glib answer, but discarded it. The boy deserved the truth as far as the truth was up to him to tell. That, and he didn't think the boy would accept glib.

"That's his story, Amo."

"Dad doesn't talk to me about himself. Mom might tell me, but he would be mad at her. I try to figure out what I did to make them change their names. It must be bad because I don't know anyone else who doesn't use their real name."

"That's a mouthful, Amo, lad. First, how do you know people are using their real names? Around here, there ain't many of us running around answering to the name we were born with. Second, how come you think it's something you did? How much you done?"

"Not much. Why do people change their names?"

"Most people change their names to make it harder to be found."

"Is that the reason my name's not Eliot anymore?"

23

"You're gonna have to ask your dad. I don't tell him about what you and I do because that's our business. I have business with him, that's up to him and me."

"Is business the same as friends?"

Bill laughed. "Not too damn often, but with you and your dad, yes."

Amo dropped to a knee and ran a hand over the motor's gray housing.

"People aren't starts here, ends there, and starts over are they?" Amo asked.

"No, people aren't machines."

"I like machines better."

BONG SAT, 17 NOV 67
NEAR VIETNAM'S, DEMILITARIZED ZONE

Silence settles on the clearing as the man raises his sidearm. *Time stops and Eliot holds his breath. He sees the wind blow high in the trees, smells the acrid edge of the diesel exhaust, and senses his men moving closer.*

A single shot from inside the chopper breaks the silence and Eliot sees the man Steerman has called their only hope stagger back a step, drop to his knees, and a heartbeat later points a finger at the helicopter. Eliot thinks the wounded man has yelled something. From inside the chopper, the passenger who had retreated into shadow steps forward holding a gun. He appears to yell back then shoots again. The impact of the round drives the man on his knees to his side.

Eliot brings up his M-14.

"No!" Steerman yells. "Listen! Two minutes and this place will be . . . gone."

Eliot swings the rifle toward Steerman.

"Save yourself," Steerman says, raising his hands. "Shooting me will do you no good. You might even be doing me a favor."

"What's coming down?"

Eliot feels the danger now, his eyes widening and head turning in an effort to see everywhere at once.

"Bad luck, Marine. If you want to live follow me. I can get you out, if we're lucky, but just you."

"My men."

"Dead and don't know it."

"Bullshit! None of my men die that easy."

"Save yourself or die," Steerman yells, backing away. "No one's supposed to get out of here alive."

"Ambush! Ambush!" he hears Gunny's voice screaming. "Three o'clock!"

Eliot sees the green pith helmets of North Vietnamese regulars running in tight formation toward the far side of the church.

"Last chance, Eliot!" Steerman calls. "You and me, or death."

"Fight with us, Steerman. Tell me what's happening."

"Betrayal, Marine! Betrayal, and it's my fault! I could have killed the devil and failed."

"Fight with us."

Steerman breaks free and shakes his head.

"Marines die once, Steerman!" Eliot yells. "Just once!"

His Marines open fire. One of the NVA falls, but the rest keep going. There is no return fire. Eliot wonders who is in the church. As the Marines make for cover, the Huey lifts off. Eliot sees the man in the doorway throw out the gun almost hitting the body of his victim. The killer raises a hand in a mock salute.

As the Huey passes overhead, Eliot hears, "Nobody get's out of here alive. Nobody but me!"

The M-14 presses into Eliot's shoulder as the chopper gains altitude. Only their limited ammunition stops his pointless gesture of firing at the fading target.

"Who the fuck – ?" he says.

"The devil, Eliot," Steerman calls, running now for the cover of the church. "The devil!"

Eliot joins his men, and with no enemy in sight, squats next to a corporal named Wiggins. He watches as the Huey disappears. For a heartbeat there is silence. Then a deep drone, a sound more felt than heard, reverberates out of the jungle. He recognizes the sound.

"130's!" Eliot screams.

The AC-130H Spectre's *heavy engines are cropped down as low as they can go and still keep the giant airborne. The only time they sound like this is right before the gunship opens fire. Eliot sees the black as death underbelly of the huge plane glide into view as its right wing tilts up. Next will come the rain of fire from the two Vulcans and four mini guns. Combined they will unleash four thousand rounds in less than thirty seconds. The Marines run with Eliot in the lead and no plan beyond survival. They run away from Bong Sat in the middle of the road then veer to the right into the thin vegetation.*

The guns of the death ship open fire. The sound, like ripping canvas, tries to crush Eliot. The earth shakes from the pounding, and still the Marines run. When Eliot thinks they have gone far enough he slows as his men pass him, then turns and drops to a knee, gasping for breath. The plane is no longer overhead, but the 'ville is still coming apart in pieces. Even the front of the church seems to be detaching itself from its prior reality, the masonry flying in larger chunks than the wood of the surrounding buildings. Judging by the path of devastation, the Spectre made an elliptical run, missing nothing in the center of the 'ville, then climbed to clear the closed end of the valley.

He waits two more minutes, then signals Xan, and they all move back to the 'ville. They pick their way through the devastation, approaching the church from its damaged front where the ground is shattered into clods of dirt and rock. The Marines climb the broken remains until they see into the church. There is nothing left of the facade, only irregular piles of rubble, but twenty feet in it appears untouched.

Beyond the far side of the church, he sees the scattered and shredded remains of the NVA patrol and wonders why they left the safety of the church. Eliot jogs to where the Huey lifted off. He rakes the ground with a foot and finds a few remains. He uses a shattered branch to poke in the churned earth. He finds the Colt .45 military issue tossed from the chopper. He slips the gun in his belt, and keeps stabbing the mire. Next, he finds a dented St. Christopher's medal hanging from flesh, and picks it up shaking off the gore. He sees an inscription on the back and after wiping away the blood reads *Luck from your Lady*. He puts it in his pocket and pokes deeper, glancing up every few seconds to check his men. He feels something, drops the stick and rummages in the remains with his hand, touches an edge, and pulls up dog tags on a chain. They read:

Frank Blaine McBride
599-52-8887
7-22-37
15587 99850

The only service numbers like this is for spooks or state department non-combatants.   Eliot opens his purple Seagram's bag and drops in the dog tags and the St. Christopher medal.   He takes the .45 out of his belt and puts it in his pack.

His Marines move toward the church where any survivors will be the enemy who stayed inside.   They move cautiously amid the devastation and absolute silence that creates a dread sense of unreality.   Xan waves an arm and breaks into a run.   Other Marines pull aside large pieces of blasted masonry.

"Sir!" *yells Traxler.* "We got a live one here! A Charlie civilian."

Eliot kneels next to Xan who presses his ear to the mouth of a broken man who miraculously still breaths.   The man's eyes move, but the head stays put.   Xan says something.   The injured man tries to speak, arches off the ground, shouts something in Vietnamese, and with a gasp, dies.

"What did he say?" *Eliot asks.*

"Peace," *Xan says.* "He say no guns, no fight.   Peace."

"See if he's got papers," *Eliot commands.*

"I know him," *Xan says, and rocks back on his heels, looking up.* "Very big man.   I think Ho's cousin." *The Hmong reaches into the debris to look for ID, but stops.*

If the F-4 Phantom jets hadn't approached from the deep, open end of the valley, the Marines would never have had a chance.

"Napalm!" *Eliot screams.*

The Phantoms will sterilize the site.   The first jet passes overhead as the Marines hit what had been the tree line.   The whump of oxygen being sucked into its payload's explosion fills their ears.   The second jet follows close behind.   Eliot has seen the effects of Phantoms dropping Napalm from the relative safety of a chopper surfing in behind the jets.   He's seen the colors of the burning napalm race through the spectrum from red through orange to yellow then settle into black.   As he runs, he feels the heat at his back and waits for his clothes to ignite, or at least the hair and skin on his neck to blister.

27

His men keep running until Eliot waves them to a stop well into the bush where they collapse to the ground with no regard for security. For the next few hours this will be one of the safest places in Vietnam.

Xan tugs at Eliot's sleeve.

"See?" he says, holding up a small square piece of carved wood with a knob on top. "I find before fire plane comes. Ho's chop. He act for Ho Chi Minh."

Eliot rolls it in his hand and sees one end stained with ink.

"What he mean, peace?" Xan asks, looking back toward the inferno.

"I don't know, but he's found it now."

Eliot stares at the chop. What was Ho Chi Min's interest? Why did the dying man scream peace as he died? Not a word often heard this far out. He drops the chop into the purple bag.

He feels lightheaded, and rests on a knee while he watches the flames eat the jungle. He raises his eyes to where the American chopper carrying the man who intended their deaths disappeared. He's been spared a second time this day, and this far into Indian Country no one is spared without a reason. He thinks of his son and pats the pocket with the picture. Eliot has been in the jungle too long to hold any naive ideals about honor and loyalty, but he is a Marine, and God and country, Semper Fidelis, are more than words, more than a code. They are his life, and part of him has just died.

1975

Amo Flies High

After the one horse electric motor, Amo wanted first look at any piece of machinery that found its way into the shop. His determination grew into a problem the day after Laughland arrived in Deer Lodge, Montana. The Monday move from Rexville, Idaho took twelve hours meaning Laughland wouldn't start its run until Wednesday making Tuesday a day to catch up in the shop.

Amo pulled a chair over to a full bench and watched Larry extract the brass filter screen from a valve body, and asked, "What's the valve off?"

"The Dive Bomber."

"That screen looks okay to me," Amo said.

Larry didn't say anything and dipped the screen into cleaning solvent. Amo picked up one of the O-rings that sealed the connection on the input side of the valve and ran it through his fingers.

"O-ring has a nick. That's the problem. Better change it out."

"I checked it and the O-ring's fine," Larry said.

"No, you're wrong," Amo said, and held the rubber ring up for Larry to see.

"Amo, I got shit stacked up to my ass today. I don't have time to baby sit you. Go bug somebody else."

Amo jumped down from the chair and ran out of the tent toward the Dive Bomber. He ran between two red and white saw horses, slipped around a concessions cart being pulled by a tractor, and stopped where the Dive Bomber waited for unloading. It didn't look like much. The twin buckets with the mesh-covered openings at opposite ends of the steel arm, lay on their side. When in operation, the arm rotated from horizontal to vertical whipping around screaming riders tucked into the mesh buckets. It was one of the most popular rides in Laughland, and usually had a line waiting to see if the riders "could keep their cookies in their tummies" as Martha Linnie, the big woman with the red hair who ran the ride, put it.

He saw the Dive Bomber's tarp pulled loose where the leaky valve had been removed. A plastic bag held in place by a rubber band covered the hose end. Under where the valve sat he saw the usually pale leak absorbent now a dirty gray. Amo picked up a handful of saturated absorbent and ran back to the shop. He showed it to Larry who had the valve reassembled and had moved on to an electric motor.

"Larry, this is from under the Dive Bomber. The O-ring leaks bad under pressure."

"No, I already told you that goddamn O-ring is fine."

"You're wrong, Larry," voice rising.

"You're just a little kid," Larry yelled. "You don't know shit!"

"I don't know shit?" Amo shouted. "I know you don't know your ass from a hot rock!"

"Fuck you, Amo!" Larry hollered, and reached for Amo.

"That's enough," Bill said, pulling Amo away from Larry. "What is this?"

"Bill, the stupid kid won't leave me alone – "

"Stupid!" shouted Amo. "I'm not the one who put it back together when it's still broken!"

Larry raised his hands again, but Bill blocked him with a big arm.

"Larry, you first," Bill said. "You wait your turn, Amo."

"The screen on the main hydraulic valve for the Dive Bomber needed cleaning. I cleaned it. The fuck – "

"Larry!"

Larry made a fist, hit the bench, then said, "Amo said the O-ring was bad. I'd already checked it, and told him I was busy. He left. When he came back I already had the valve back together and was working on the motor brushes. He told me I didn't know my ass from a hot rock."

"That right, Amo? You said that?"

"This time he doesn't, Bill." Amos held up the saturated absorbent. "Look at the Quicksorb."

"This from under the valve?" Bill asked. "Let's go have a look, Amo, and Larry, you open the valve while we're gone."

"You're gonna listen to the kid over me?" Larry yelled, his face a bright red.

"I'm going to look at a potential safety hazard. It ain't about the two of you."

Amo ran ahead of Bill who called to him to slow down. When they got to the Dive Bomber, Bill pulled back the tarp, knelt and pushed a finger through the mess under the valve mount.

"Even when you're right, Amo, you gotta know how to get people to do the right thing. Telling them they don't know their ass from a hot rock is not the way."

"You say that, Bill. So do the other guys."

"Okay, but you gotta know when and how to say it. If you say it to someone when you're mad, it just makes them madder than you. What should you have done?"

Amo sighed and didn't look at Bill. "I should have come to you before I got mad."

"So why didn't you?"

"I thought Larry would fix it. I was just trying to help. If I went to you, I'd be a tattle tale."

Bill stood up.

"Laughland's customers ought to be able to have a good time without worrying about the ride. You get what I mean? It wasn't about who was right. It's always about the good part, the purr, the fix."

"I'm sorry I didn't do it right, Bill."

"Right isn't easy, Amo. Come on, let's take a look at that o-ring."

Larry had done as told. The valve lay open on the bench, with the screen and both O-rings out.

"I looked again, Bill, and there ain't a damn thing wrong with either of those rings."

Amo stood on his lift-o-nator. He ran the first ring through his fingers, set it aside and picked up the second.

"Right here, Bill," he said, handing over the ring, "there's a nick."

Bill held up the ring and looked closely, then slowly rotated it.

"I don't see it," Amo."

"See!" Larry shouted. "I told ya'."

"Get the magnifier, Bill," Amo said. "It's there."

"Oh, for Christ's sake!" Larry moaned.

Bill walked over to his own bench, opened his tool box, and came back with a magnifying glass. He held it up, moved the o-ring into the light, and flexed the rubber as he turned it.

"It's there, Larry," he pointed, and beckoned Larry to look through the glass.

"Shit! That wouldn't make no difference," but Larry's voice lacked conviction.

"It would only leak under pressure until it failed completely," Bill answered, "then it would make a big difference."

"You didn't see it either, Bill."

Bill squinted at Amo. "You see it or feel it?"

"I felt it."

Bill nodded. "Okay, Larry, every time we open one of these valves, change the rings. I'll tell the others. Amo, apologize to Larry. You should never have said what you said."

"But I was right!"

"This ain't about right. It's about friends. Larry, you better be practicing saying 'I'm sorry,' too."

After the two exchanged apologies, Bill led Amo away.

"Can I work with the machines without the people, Bill?"

"They sort of go hand in hand."

"I'm pretty good knowing what's wrong with machines. Maybe that can be my job."

Bill put a hand on Amo's shoulder. "You don't have to have a job. Have some fun."

"The only place I'm happy is in the shops with you."

"Don't let your folks hear you say that."

"My mom knows I love her."

"You don't love your dad?"

"I would if he let me."

The next day Jessie kept Amo in the trailer. When he got angry, she sat him in a corner with a book and told him to read. This had never happened before. Just like getting mad at Larry had never happened before. He wondered if the two "never happened befores" had anything to do with each other. Amo didn't know if Bill talked to his dad, but thought it likely, which led to his dad talking to his mom. Being barred from the shop scared him. If the only place where he was happy went off limits, he would be sad. There were looks between his mother and father suggesting he was the topic of unspoken words and it probably had to do with Larry. Wednesday night, after his day in the corner, he did not sleep well. He was afraid.

Thursday morning started better with his mom telling him he could go to the shop after he ate his breakfast. Amos inhaled his toast and Kix, raced out the door and didn't stop until he was in front of the shop tent. He stopped to wonder what the boys would say. Would they be mad? They were Larry's friends, and Amo remembered what Larry had said about baby-sitting him. Maybe the boys put up with him because his dad owned Laughland. As soon as he had the thought he knew it was true. His eyes watered. He wiped them and entered the shop.

Nothing special happened when he came in until Bill saw him. He waved Amo to a corner, and pointed at a bench. Parked in front of a bench, the Lift-a-nator stood with a new second level set to the perfect height. Amo climbed on the new perfect perch, and ran his eyes over the bench top where he saw two small motors and a pump assembly all with their bolts loosened. He also saw tools just for him. He ran his hands over the machines and the tools, and smiled so big his mouth hurt.

"You got a gift, Amo," Bill said, "and we'd be idiots not to put it to use. You were right the other day about the o-ring. You were wrong the way you talked to Larry, but no one else around here, including me, would have spotted what you did. So, this is your bench. When things are small enough, they'll start here. You figure out what needs to be done. If you can't do the fix yourself, we'll pass it on. This ain't the best way, but given the circumstances, it's the way things got to be."

His own bench! He clapped with joy and went to work. After awhile the shop grew quiet. He turned and saw his dad behind him. The boys looked at them, and Amos understood this visit to the shop by his dad was different. He had his own bench now. He was like the Boys, and not just the boss's kid. His dad looked at the others and glared, and everyone went to work except Bill who walked over. When Matt got there and started talking he stared right into Amo's eyes like he always did.

"Bill said you went out to the Dive Bomber by yourself. That right?"

"Yes, sir."

"They were still setting up?"

"Yes, sir, but I waited on the truck like I'm supposed to."

His dad and Bill exchanged looks. Amo waited for the words that didn't mean what they really meant.

"You know why you've got this bench?" his dad asked. The words surprised Amo.

"Because I found the nick in the seal."

"Yes, but that isn't the only reason." Matt nodded at Bill who walked away. "I want Bill to keep a closer eye on you."

"But dad! I'm careful! I don't need baby-sitting."

"Who said anything about baby-sitting?"

"All the guys put up with me because you're my dad."

Matt slowly looked around. The Boys worked with heads down and hands busy.

"They put up with you because they like you. Yes, I tell them to watch out for you, but there's nothing wrong with that. Why do you think we let you come here every day?"

"Because I'm broken!"

Amo saw a look like Bill used, a soft look, slip across his father's face then vanish.

"You are not broken. Here, in the shop, these are men I trust."

"I don't need them. I can take care of myself."

"You do what I say. Bill will make sure you get what you need."

His father turned away. Amo started to say more, but out of the corner of his eye he saw Bill shake his head. Bill walked out of the shop with Matt. Amo wanted to cry. He felt his eyes getting wet but if he cried, standing on his Lift-a-nator, everyone would see him. He turned his back, picked up a screwdriver, and poked at an electric motor. His mother always told him to take deep breaths when he got "worked up" and that's what he did.

When Bill got back, he said, "Let's go for a walk, Amo." They walked out of the shop and turned away from the midway. They walked between the dorm trucks, past the dining trailer, and kept going until they reached the edge of the clearing that was the carnival's home for the week.

"Take a look around, Amo" Bill said. "Go on."

To his left, big mountains ran in a line as far as his eyes could see. Other than the mountains and Laughland, the world was flat.

"I'm looking," Amo said.

"We're in Montana so those are the Rocky Mountains. Biggest mountains in the whole country."

"I know that. Mom always makes me read the atlas on move day."

"Montana's called the big sky state. Know why?"

Amo pointed at the mountains. "Ought to be called the big mountain state."

Bill laughed. "Next week we'll be east of Billings and things are pretty flat."

"When it's flat, you can see a lot of sky. Is that why it's called the big sky state?"

"Right. Out there you can see a whole bunch of nothing."

"That doesn't make sense, Bill. You can't see nothing."

"That's kind of your dad's point, Amo. Just because you can't see something doesn't mean it's not there."

Amo laughed and said, "That doesn't make any sense either. What doesn't my dad see?"

Bill pointed to an old log lying on its side, whitened with age and sun. They sat down, and Bill put his arm around Amo's shoulder.

"Let's get a couple of things real straight. Your dad loves you. More than anything. He just won't tell you."

"Why?"

"Something bad happened to your dad before he ever saw you. He was a brave soldier who almost died. Because he lived, there are people looking for him, powerful people. To hurt him, they would hurt you or your mom."

"Are they looking for you, too?"

"Maybe, but we don't think they know anything about me."

Amo looked at the mountains. "On the map, I saw roads over the mountains. It's a lot shorter to go over the mountains than around. We didn't go over because they were too high and the trucks are old. Right?"

"Sometimes you have to go around."

"That's why we're not Eliot?"

"Yep. Real names, like short roads, aren't always best."

BONG SAT
17 NOV 67

An old Gunnery Sergeant told Eliot the color of the sky decides the kind of day in Indian Country. Contrails running north and south against a stark blue sky meant shit might happen, but you'd live out the day. Clouds with an east-west contrail said keep your head down, but the odds still ran with you. Pure blue, no clouds and no contrails, demanded a grunt at your back. Monsoon clouds were good. Nobody, friend or foe, liked fighting in the rain. White was the next to worst. It was like a hole in reality poised to suck out your life. But the absolute worst was white as a backdrop for billowing black napalm smoke forming a jagged, cracked window into Hell. It is the sky over Bong Sat. Eliot isn't superstitious, but he is flexible. Two years in Vietnam made him listen to every clue, intuition, and old wives' tale. If the sore knee of a motor pool sergeant means a shit storm is on the way, find a hole.

On this day, he is now sure there is a bigger plan in place and he will play a part. He and his men have pulled through as a collateral benefit. At the center is the man in the Huey, the talk of peace, and Ho Chi Min's cousin. And who is Steerman, and where has he gone? Eliot saw him run into the church, but has he survived?

"Cap?"

Carlos Montoya joins him in his pacing. He is a good soldier and the men will follow him if Eliot dies.

"Fucking lucky, Cap."

Eliot nods.

"Got a plan?" Montoya asks. "Sky don't look so good."

"Plan for the worst. Without a radio nobody knows we're here."

The radio took a hit a week ago along with the man who carried it, Private Sam Levine, one of the eight dead.

"Do you want to prowl the burn after it cools, sir?" Montoya lights a Camel. "See if we can find a NVA radio?"

36

"Nothing to lose. Tell you what I don't like, Gunny. That escort. Somebody knows where they are."

"Not my way to whine, Sir, but we're down to fourteen done in, brave sons of bitches, counting you and me."

Eliot looks into the super-heated orange and black of the napalm-fed fires adding to the already supernatural scene of the 'ville burning to the ground. The church remains apart from the fires, a visitor from that old Gunny's other dimension.

"We're going to make a stand right here. I'm sending Xan out on foot."

"He don't make it, Cap, neither do we."

"I'm sending Tagnut with him. Xan shows up by himself nobody listens." Eliot takes his helmet off and wipes his face. "Tell 'em to smoke and rest, then take inventory while I talk to Xan and Bill."

Eliot calls the two men to his side.

"Shit deep?" the Hmong asks.

"I gotta send you two out for help."

"I go alone," Xan said.

"Getting there's only half of it. You gotta get the message delivered, and assets got to get in the air fast."

Xan shook his head. "He slow me down."

"You know how it is, Xan," Eliot says. All the Hmong who help the Americans carry no credentials. Eliot pulls out the map and points. "The closest firebase I know of is there. You two got enough left to run a bit?"

"Cap?" Montoya interrupts. "We got a chopper hovering out there. You want to signal them?"

It is a Huey, but there is no way to tell if it's the one that carried Ferry out.

"Ignore it. If they've seen us they're calling for help. If they don't want to help there's nothing we can do about it."

Eliot sends Montoya back to the tasks at hand.

"You say run," Xan says, and points at the map. "I run not like the wind, maybe, but like a little fish. See river? I ride boat close to where we go."

"Boat?"

Xan shrugs. "Make one, steal one. Boat better than feet."

Their eyes meet, and the Hmong picks up his kit. Tagnut starts to salute, but Eliot shakes his hand.

"Get through, Bill. I want to see my kid."

"Sir! Yes, Sir!"

Eliot watches the two men jog into the jungle.

The remnants of Bravo Company, third platoon, take inventory. Each man has his M-14 and at least four clips of twenty rounds each. They all have side arms with a clip or two. There are a total of 14 hand grenades but no grenade launcher, and no mortar, and no machine gun. Wiggins, their sniper, is out of ammo and his weapon has been damaged.

Eliot waves for his Marines to listen up.

"That NVA escort probably has back-up waiting for the flames to die down, and since we got no place to go this is our Alamo." He watches their faces. "We need anything that'll shoot."

"Cap?" says a lance corporal named Traxler. "That church. It's a big sucker for out here. Over near Da Nang there was a smaller one where they found a whole cache of Charlie arms. Worth a try, sir. They found them in the vestment room where the priests change."

"Where in there?"

"Probably a room to the left of the altar. Far as I've ever seen, they're all pretty much the same."

"Okay, listen up. Montoya will assign the duty. I want two men looking for combustibles to stoke the fire. Lets send the flames high. If Uncle Ho and the boys are waiting for it to die let's keep 'em waiting."

Terry Dawkins, a black kid from L.A. says, "Burn, baby, burn."

Montoya makes Dawkins and a pale-skinned, blue eyed giant from Kansas they all call Meat, the fire stoking detail. Eliot tells Montoya he'll take a look inside the church and find the vestment room. They move out.

As Eliot moves in behind his team, the colors of the sky hit him in the pit of his stomach. The fierce orange flames are dying, but still intermittently black smoke flares against a sky so white he thinks of a shroud.

As if a needle is dropped on a record, organ music blares out the broken front of the church. The notes are tortured like some of the pipes are damaged, but the organist plays on. There are only four classical organ pieces Eliot knows, but he recognizes the opening chords of Bach's Toccata and Fugue in D Minor. The opening notes drive into his heart like a bullet, he catches his breath and waits for the response. It comes, shallower, filled with promise, and then the cascading notes fly through the tortured 'ville.

"Jesus, Mary, and Joseph!" cries Montoya. "Fucking church is ready to fall down!"

"This is freaking me out, man," Meat yells, pointing at the church. "Look at this shit! Fire, smoke and the fucking organ music. What's it mean, Cap? We gonna die?"

Eliot holds up a hand. "That's enough. I got the church, the rest of you keep at hand."

"Hey, Cap?" Traxler laughs, "ask the guy if he knows any Dave 'Baby' Cortez."

Where the big double doors of the church use to be, flames sputter through the scattered rubble. Eliot finds a break in the debris, steps around a fallen door, and enters. Smoke drifting in makes it hard to see, but visibility improves as he nears the altar. Eliot's passage is from rubble to scattered stones, then dust, and finally normalcy. It is as if the building exists in both war and peace. The smoke thins, and he sees the high pulpit slightly left of center although he still can't see the organist. He slings his weapon, starts to remove his pot, but decides to leave it on. This church won't mind a little more disrespecting. As he nears the altar, he sees Steerman at the keyboard of a gigantic pipe organ that Eliot estimates at thirty feet wide and about the same height. The music grows louder and the imperfections stand out. He hears flat notes that should have soared and hissing air leaking from the stops. Steerman sits, head bowed over his hands, body swaying, absorbed in the music. It isn't until Eliot is almost beside him that he turns, his hands continuing over the keys.

"You had the look of a survivor, Captain," he calls, over the thundering music.

"We have a request for Dave 'Baby' Cortez."

Steerman slips into "Happy Organ."

"You're good," Eliot says. "The Bach D Minor is the best I've heard in a long time."

The music stops, Steerman raises his hands and claps.

"Bravo. Culture midst the carnage."

"I had a roommate in college who played. Where'd you learn?"

39

"I grew up in a Catholic orphanage. A priest decided music would save my soul."

Eliot sees a change in the man. He is filthy, with flashes in his eyes like distant lightning.

"Do you have any idea," Steerman begins, opening his arms expansively, *"how much of a miracle it is this organ can breathe a single note, let alone play an entire fugue? Copper pipes and wood stops stranded in this humidity. A miracle!"* Steerman runs his hands lovingly over the keys as he talks, but the light dims out of his eyes. *"Did many die out there?"*

"Unless there's somebody else in here, they're all dead."

"Your men?"

"Still sucking air. You didn't run."

"I had my hidey hole." He turns back to the keyboard and resumes the fugue from near the midpoint. *"My feeble attempt,"* he yells, *"at peace in the midst of my folly, sir."*

"Did you set this up with your buddy?" Eliot asks.

Steerman opens his eyes, and stops playing.

"The blame is as much mine as his, but no, I didn't set it up. I found out about it three days ago. The first day I spent paralyzed by fear; Ferry planned to kill me. The second day I decided to kill him first then abort his plan. The third day, yesterday, I set my plan to kill him where the chopper landed. I had everything but courage, and we have," Steerman opened his arms, *"this."*

"You could have stopped this?"

"If I shot an unarmed man in the chest from point blank range, yes."

"He was doing the same thing to you."

"Therefore I believed I could do it to him. I found that a willingness to kill is not distributed to men equally."

"Was that an NVA escort Ferry obliterated?"

"It was."

"Shit! They never go anywhere alone. When it gets dark, the NVA will send it all."

"Remember today, Captain, as the day the fate of the world changed. I failed and many died. They will continue to die."

"Cut the shit! Who's Ferry? Was McBride from the Company?"

Steerman claps his hands again as Eliot shrugs off his pack.

"*Perhaps God hasn't turned his back quite yet sending in a soldier with a good head. Do you believe in paranoia, sir?*"

"*What?*"

"*Paranoia. A most useful tool for keeping the mind sharp.*" He leans close. "*Listen to me. Remember every word. Because Ferry lived, he will come after you. He will kill you, your family, and anyone who knows what happened.*"

"*Who is this Ferry? I'll kill him first,*" Eliot says with his head down as he reorganizes his pack.

"*Ah, if you only could! He's already in the air back to Washington, and I don't see pursuing him in your future. Don't go after him. If you do, you will fail just as I did.*"

"*I'm no coward, Steerman. What was this about peace?*"

"*This was to be the beginning of the end of the war. The North Vietnamese sent a film from Ho Chi Minh intended for Lyndon Johnson outlining a chance for peace. Peace didn't work for Ferry. He believes war is opportunity.*"

Eliot, thinking of his dead, takes out the purple bag.

"*He could end the war?*"

"*The chance existed,*" Steerman said.

Eliot takes out dog tags on their chain and tolls them like rosary beads.

"*All you can do now is survive and be patient,*" Steerman says. "*Protect yourself and your loved ones.*"

Eliot remains intent on the remains of his dead encased in the bag.

"*What's in the Crown Royal bag?*" Steerman asks.

"*Obligations,*" Eliot replies. "*Memories of my dead.*"

"*Cap?*" Traxler says from behind.

"*Wait one, Marine,*" Eliot says stowing the bag back in his pack, then turns to Steerman. "*Ferry has no way of knowing who I am. We aren't supposed to be anywhere near here.*"

"*The lost patrol, hey? Sadly, I mentioned your name when I tried to get you out. It was a flimsy last gasp to get him to call the strike off. I'm sorry.*"

Eliot swallows hard, then says to Traxler, "*You finished out there?*"

"*Yes, sir. Fuel's stacked but it ain't igniting. Not much luck on the scavenger hunt. You?*"

41

"We need weapons," Eliot says to Steerman. "And a radio. We're down to nothing."

Steerman shakes his head. "I'm sorry. Look around if you want."

"Cap, can I ask a question?" Eliot waves his assent, and Traxler asks Steerman, "What kind of generator runs the organ bellows?"

"Electric," Steerman replies.

"No. Fuel for the generator."

"Ah, yes. Gas, and there's a Jerry can if you need it. Go down the hallway," and he points the way.

As Traxler jogs off, Eliot asks Steerman, "Who was McBride?"

"He will be remembered as the first to die at Bong Sat. He was CIA sent here to observe."

"So why'd Ferry – "

"Cap! Bingo!" Traxler calls from the gloom of the hallway. "All kinds of shit."

"Radio?"

"No, but lots of weapons. AK-47's, some M-14's, a mortar but no shells. Some boxes that I can't read the markings."

"Get Montoya to move all the stuff up front, and start field stripping weapons. If we have firepower, we have a chance." He turns to Steerman. "How do you get up to the belfry?"

Steerman tells him, and Eliot climbs the narrow staircase wrapped around the dangling bell ropes. When he reaches the top, he sees the massive cast bronze carillon of three bells. Spots of green corrosion color the bells, but all in all they look ready to sound the call to mass. From this height he sees the swath cut by the Spectre starts well short of the 'ville, the path marked by shattered trunks. The scattered shreds of green uniforms confirms a heavy toll. He stares across the valley and sees two shallow ridge lines forming a funnel. Peasants coming to worship or trade in the 'ville would have used it for generations. With war driving the worshipers away, the jungle has reclaimed the trail, providing the cover a cautious officer would demand.

He heads down the stairs. Half way, he meets Montoya.

"Got something for you, Cap Bring your imagination."

In the sanctuary, M-14's and AK-47's, are in various stages of cleaning, and rounds of ammunition are being wiped down.

"Wiggins found himself a prize," says Montoya.

Wiggins lovingly wipes down a Marine M-40 sniper rifle complete with scope. He looks up from his cleaning and smiles.

"Not a dent in the chassis, not a scratch on the scope. Got a couple hundred rounds, too."

"Where you want me to set-up?" *Wiggins asks.*

"Where you can do the most good."

"How about the belfry? Should be a full three-sixty field of fire and a mighty nice elevation."

Eliot shakes his head.

"You know what happens if you go up there. You won't last a second when they make you."

"Cap, what if I go up, pick off some officers to buy us some time, then get my ass down? Huh?"

Eliot knows he's right, but if Wiggins waits too long, he's dead.

"I can't spare a spotter," *he says.*

"I love being alone."

"Remember. Don't get comfortable."

"Sir!"

"We got another surprise for you," *Montoya says, and Eliot follows him into the side room.* "Claymores. Two bandoleers."

"Firing device?"

"No, we're going to have to trip-wire them. Oh, yeah, and a case of M-26 grenades. As long as were decorating the tree for the holidays, let's hang a few of these."

"Gunny, you're going to give me some hope you keep this up."

"That's all the real good news, Cap, but here's the imagination part." *He pulls back the tarp on a stack of wood crates.* "Fireworks. Real fireworks. Roman candles, pin wheels, all kinds of shit. Lots of it."

"Rather have a brace of .40mm thumper rounds, but, like you said, what the hell. Flares?"

"A short case of white Para flares."

"White should give Wiggins a good look. Maybe we can spare a spotter after all. You seen Steerman?"

"No."

"Shit, I could have used that guy."

From just off the altar, Eliot and Montoya watch their men work.

"You religious, Cap?"

"No more. Grew up Baptist. It made me tired. You?"

"Name like Montoya? Catholic. I go to confession. You believe in God?"

Eliot looks around the broken insides of the huge cathedral.

"You could say I'm like this church. Used to before the war."

"You ever think about why we're here?" Montoya asks, lighting a cigarette.

"You mean the meaning of life, or why you and me and the rest of us are in Vietnam?"

"You want to take a shot at the meaning of life, go for it, but I was talking about us."

"It started out as an obligation. Uncle Sam paid for my college, and this was part of the deal. I've never been patriotic, you know, flag waving and believing we're always right. Now I'm here for you, me, and the rest of them. I'm supposed to get you guys home, and I'm doing a piss poor job."

"Bullshit, Cap. You're my third officer. The first two are dead. I told the Colonel no more rookies, and he said he'd send me his best. That's you. All the shit we've seen, anyone else, we'd already be dead."

While they talk, Wiggins, with Meat acting as mule, packs the sniper rifle, rounds, and the case of flares up the stairs. They make a second trip for the showiest of the fireworks, the Roman Candles, Star Bursts, and Pinwheels. Dawkins and Traxler, with help from Hood and Kriakopolous, string the Claymores along the trail where they hope to herd the NVA.

"Remember what I said Wiggins" Eliot yells. "Don't' settle in."

"Sir, if I gotta die out here, somebody's going to notice!"

1976

The Death of Amo

Amos loved two things: Laughland's shop and his mother.

Monday was move day as Laughland caravanned its way to the next site. It was while he sat beside her as she drove the Ford truck pulling their trailer that he discovered a third. He fidgeted and to get him to stop she suggested he draw a picture.

"What should I draw?"

"Draw a picture of things that are important to you."

He decided to draw the shop tent because it was the first important thing he thought of. Before committing pencil to paper, he closed his eyes and repeatedly traced the outline of the tent in the air. He then scaled the now practiced motion to the size of the paper and drew. Next he drew the opening of the tent which was big enough for the lift trucks carrying big pieces of broken things. A man stood in the doorway, and even though he was drawn small, and Amos wasn't thinking about Bill as he drew, he knew it was Bill. "Maybe I think about things without knowing I'm thinking about them," he thought. He didn't try to show his mother what he'd drawn because he knew she would never take her eyes off the road. She was a very careful driver, just like she was about everything.

"Who's that in the doorway?" she asked, surprising him. "That's dad isn't it?"

"No, it's Bill. Bill belongs to the shop."

"Is Bill in the picture," she asked, "because he's part of the shop or because he's important to you?"

Amos tried to separate the two ideas, and couldn't.

"Mom, can I say both?"

"If you want."

"Okay, both. I love you, and I love the shop. Does that mean I love Bill, too?"

"It can. It's a good thing to love the people that are important to you, like your father and me, and now Bill."

"I don't love Dad."

"What? How can you say that?"

"I would if he let me, but he doesn't want me to love him."

"Amos, that is not true. There is nothing in this world more important to your father than his only child."

"More important than you?"

"Well, yes. If your father had to choose between saving me or you, he would save you. But so would I."

"If he loves me, why don't he and I do things I see other kids doing with their fathers?'

"Like what?"

"Like holding hands while they walk, and eating cotton candy together, and laughing, and . . . holding me. Dad never holds me."

She let go of the wheel with one hand and placed it on Amos's arm.

"That's just dad. He's had a different kind of life than those fathers you see with their children, but not so different that he doesn't love you."

"What's so different about him?"

Her silence stretched so long Amos gave up and looked out the window at boring old Arizona.

"Your dad saw an evil man doing something terrible. When the evil man found out, he tried to kill him. He is still trying to kill him."

"That's why we have a secret life, isn't it?"

His mom took looked away from the road.

"What?"

"We have a secret life. Our name isn't Caldwell. It's Eliot with one L and one T. My real name is Amos Eliot." He saw her surprise. "I'm pretty smart for my age. All the guys in the shop say so."

"You are very smart. How did you know about your name?"

"Well, Bill called me Amos Eliot, once. It was by accident, but I already knew. I don't remember how I knew."

"Did you tell anyone?"

"I don't see anyone to tell. Everyone around Laughland knows. I guess they do."

"Why?"

"Everyone has a secret life with made up names. Bill says it's harder for someone to find you if they don't know your real name. I always wondered who was looking for us." Amos sat up straight and smiled. "I should have drawn you, momma. You're the one I love the most."

As he lay in bed that night waiting for his mother to read to him, he felt bigger inside than he had that morning. There were more people in there now. They were named Eliot and were not quite the same as the Caldwells, and Bill was there, too.

"Did you brush your teeth," Mom asked, when she sat down on the pullout sofa where he slept. Amos blew toothpaste-scented breath.

"What's the story tonight?" she asked.

"*The Shoemaker and the Elves*," he said.

"You know that one well enough to make your own shoes. We don't need the book."

Amos laughed and held her hand while he said, "I love the book, Momma. It's so big."

Amos's idea of being the unseen magical fixer came after Mom had read the Grimm's fairytale for maybe the third or fourth time. He knew if there were elves at Laughland they would be at the shop. Amos dreamed of floating through the walls of his bedroom, drifting above Laughland's sawdust-covered byways, and into the shop tent. The broken things covering the benches would glow a sickly rusty red in the dark. After he worked his spells they would have a healthy, oily sheen. When everything sparkled, he would float back to bed to become Amos again. In the morning, he would race to the shop, his feet churning up the sawdust instead of floating on his magic elf power. He would beat Bill and the Boys then hold his breath as he waited for their astonishment. Elves were the good guys and he was the best of the elves.

She got the book from his book trunk. "Look at that! It fell open to the very page. Amos, you're old enough to start reading your own stories. Maybe you ought to read to me."

"Kids don't read to their parents. That's silly."

"Maybe not. We're getting behind on your lessons since you're in the shop more. You read to me and we'll count it as study time."

"Mom, I'm doing good. I'm learning new stuff every day."

"You have to learn to think with your head as well as your hands."

He shot up on the sofa, landing on his knees.

"I can think with my hands?" he asked, throwing his arms around her neck. "Wow! I didn't know that!"

"Do you tell your hands what to do, or do they just do it?" she responded. She hugged him before tucking him back under the covers.

He held up his hands and wiggled his fingers. "I told them to do that, but mostly they just do what they want."

"Something's doing all the thinking if your brain isn't," she laughed.

"Wow! Are my hands as smart as my brain?"

"Smarter. That's why you need to read to me so you can use your brain more."

"Do elves have smart hands?"

"Elves have the smartest hands of anyone."

"Smarter than mine?"

"Elves are older so they've had more time to get smart. You'll catch up if you do your lessons."

"How old do elves get?"

"I don't know. Their years are different than ours."

"Older than you?"

"Much older, but they live a very long time."

"How long will you live, Momma?"

She ruffled his head, kissed his cheek, and said, "As long as you need me. Come on, time to sing."

Together they sang his "go to sleep" song, *Jesus Bids Us Shine.*

> *Jesus bids us shine with a clean, pure light,*
> *Like a little candle burning in the night;*
> *In this world of darkness, we must shine,*
> *You in your small corner, and me in mine.*

His Mom always held his hand while they sang. She told him it was as close to God as she could take him.

The day after he and his mother talked about their secret identity he found himself restricted to the trailer. Later, his dad delivered the bad news.

"Your mother told me about your talk yesterday." Amos looked at his mother, but she didn't look back. "I want you to stay in the trailer for a while. That's law. Understood?"

"But, Dad! There's nothing to do here."

"You're behind on your lessons. Now you have time to catch up."

"But the Boys need me in the shop!"

"They'll have to manage without you."

Amos wanted to cry. "Why, Dad?"

"Because I said so."

"No, Dad. I'm old enough to know. I think you should tell me why I can't go to the shop. I don't leave there hardly at all, and never by myself."

"You did when you and Larry got into it."

"I did, yes, sir, but that was the one and only time."

"Amos, I'm not going to argue with you. You heard the law."

"This is about people looking for us because our name's Eliot, isn't it?"

Darkness fall across his dad's face.

"Here comes more law. You are never to say that name. To anyone."

"But why, Dad, why? I can do anything if I know why."

"Matt," his mother said, softly. "It's time."

"No, it will never be time."

"You are changing his life," Jessie said slowly. "He's a boy who doesn't want to be trapped away from what he loves, and his friends. I'm not locking him in here without an explanation.."

Amos would always remember the next few minutes. Matt turned to Jessie, took her in his arms and held her tight. Amos could see the side of his father's face. His eyes were closed. Was he crying? Matt took a deep breath, and turned to Amos.

"The only thing that keeps your mother and you and me alive is that the people looking for us don't know our name. If they find us, we are dead and there isn't anything I, or Bill Tagnut, or anyone else can do about it. This is not a game. We're not on the run for committing a crime. We've done nothing wrong." Matt wiped his mouth and looked at Jessie. Amos thought he might be asking for a chance to stop, but she just stared at him.

"The man after me is above any law. He is rich and powerful. If our real name comes out, he will find us. Fast."

"What if you give him your word you won't tell anybody? You never lie."

"This man lies all the time, and because he's a liar he thinks everyone else lies, too."

Amos didn't like it but if his parents could live in secret, so could he.

"What are you going to do?" Jessie asked.

"I'm going to find out who knows what. Marcus says he'll know if they get close. He hasn't said anything." Matt looked out the window. "I don't know how he stays close to Ferry, because that son of a bitch wants Marcus dead even more than he wants me in the ground." Matt stared hard at Amos, then at his wife. "And, Jessie? When you go shopping, I want Bill to go with you. No exceptions."

"I don't go alone now," she said.

"I know, but Bill knows how serious this is. I don't think I can say the same for the others."

By the time Laughland finished its week in Tuba City, the evenings held a chill in the high desert country of northern Arizona. Their next stop, and the last stop of the season, was Boulder City, Nevada. After that came Laughland's winter home outside Carson City, and the closest place Amos had to a home. If he had to stay locked up, he thought, he'd just as soon be in his own room instead of the trailer.

On move day, the caravan left early. Amos fidgeted and ignored his mother's request to sit still in the front seat of the truck.

"I know you aren't happy," Jessie said, "neither am I. Do you think I want you in the trailer all day fussing under foot? Have you noticed that I'm in there as much as you, and when I do get out, there's always a man getting in the way?"

The next morning, Amos jumped up early, got dressed and sat at the table ready for breakfast when his mother opened the door from the bedroom. "Mom, I need to get over to the shop. It's a down day and the work will be piling up."

"Nice try," Jessie said, with a softness missing of late. "You know we both have to stay in the trailer. Maybe after Dad gets back he'll have some good news."

But when Matt got back he said, "Marcus thinks Ferry has a lead on me. I want you and Amos out of here in the morning."

"Oh, right," Jessie shouted. "You're not sure, but you're sending us away."

"I can't take the risk. Another week and we'll have the whole off season together."

Amos jumped to stand next to his mother.

"Dad, we belong here!"

Amos saw his father's black look he knew so well.

"No discussion. I'm sending Bill with you."

"Bill's going?" Amos asked, feeling better. His father nodded.

"Where are we going?" Jessie asked, still mad. "I'm not going to the winter house without you."

"You're going someplace different," Matt said, "a place Bill and I have been getting ready."

After Amos went to bed, his parents argued outside the trailer's window. Sitting on his knees and pressing his cheek to the screen, he could both hear and see them. Usually when his dad was mad, he got real still. This time, Matt made a lot of arm motions and pulled his mom up against his chest. Amos liked to see his parents hug. It meant they were happy. This time they hugged but he didn't think they were happy.

"Let us stay, Matt," Jessie said. "We're safer and stronger when we're together, just like you always said."

"Not this time, Jess. Please don't cry."

"Why not this time?"

"I can't protect you here, even with Bill's help. What if something happened to you or Amos? It would be the end of my sanity. When I have the dreams, your holding me when I wake up is all that keeps me going. I can manage a few weeks on my own. Not the rest of my life."

The words were more mystery than explanation, but Amos knew his father was a man who did not show his emotions. To show them meant they carried a powerful meaning.

"Stop playing. Tell Marcus to leave us alone."

"I don't like it when you call this 'playing,' Jess, it's no game."

"It's not? I know you two are out there tweaking Ferry's nose. Let . . . it . . . go."

"You're wrong, Jess. We've survived seven years, almost eight, with the most powerful man in the world looking for us. You know why? Because Laughland, this broken down, sorry excuse for a way to live, as you like to call it, keeps us alive. We have a legitimate reason for being on the move. We live in a community where everyone has a secret."

His father's voice get louder.

"We give up Laughland for a picket fence, trade all these people for neighbors with lots of questions and how long are we going to make it?"

"What's more important to you?" Jessie asked. "Keeping us – the three of us – safe, or your revenge? From here it looks a helluva lot like revenge."

"Amos is the most important. He is us. The only thing we have to show for us."

Amos lay down. His parents were sad, but he was happy. He was important to his dad, even the Most Important.

"Alright, Matt, we'll leave in the morning, but tonight is for us."

The first time Amos saw Laughland Valley, the moon started to rise before the sun set.

"Pretty cool, huh?" Bill said, after they stopped at the top of the road into the valley. "Don't often get to see the sun and the moon at the same time. It's a good sign."

"Where's a sign?" Amo asked, even though he knew Bill was talking about the kind of sign that had no words or pictures.

"Is that what we've come to? Omens?" his mother asked.

The trip had been tolerable only because Bill drove and Amos sat in the front. Jessie didn't say much not even when they'd stopped at the small store in Mercy, Nevada, about ten miles away. He and Bill had gone in and bought what they'd needed from a friendly clerk who said his name was Clyde.

Sitting at the top of the hill, Amos rolled down the window and stuck his head out. At the bottom, where the road ended, he saw three wood buildings. "What is this place?"

"Laughland owns pretty much the whole valley," Bill said. "About fourteen square miles. Land's cheap way out here. We bought it from a guy who built a bomb shelter that stays cool in the summer and pretty comfortable in the winter. Our plan is to rig solar panels, but until we do there's a gas generator."

"Is this where we're going to live all the time?" Amos asked.

"No, my friend, we need a safe place to rest up a bit and stay during the off season. Here, we'll have a permanent shop so we can fix things right."

"But what is this place? What's a bomb shelter?"

"You guys bought this because of the bomb shelter, didn't you," Jessie said.

"That's part of it. Not to hide in, but because it's efficient. Matt doesn't expect you to live like a mole."

Jessie leaned over the seat. "I'm not living underground. Period."

"Understood, Jess."

"I still don't know what a bomb shelter is," Amos said.

"It's like a house underground," Bill said.

"You mean like a cave?"

"No, more like a house without windows."

"Let's go!" Amos yelled. "Where's the door to the underground house?"

"We'll find it after we stow our stuff and fix ourselves some grub," Bill said.

Even with food on the table, Jessie's mood persisted. She ate the dinner Bill called a "mixed grill," meaning both hot dogs and hamburgers, fixed on a small, table-top grill. They ate at a picnic table with attached benches. Amos ate a whole hot dog, bun and all, with lots of mustard, and some potato chips. Throughout the meal, Bill kept a steady stream of happy chatter going.

"Can I sleep in the bomb shelter tonight, Mom, can I?" he asked. He thought the idea was so funny it would make her smile.

"If it will make you boys happy, sure, go ahead sleep in a hole in the ground. You can pretend it's a foxhole and you're off fighting a war. Maybe you can find something to shoot at."

"Not fair, Jess," Bill said. "That war was not our idea."

"No, but you did your duty. You know how tired I am of duty? Or hearing about my duty? My duty! I don't have a duty. I have a son and a husband. I have feelings and they are not something to rise above as you boys seem to think. You ever wonder what you two would have been like if you hadn't done your duty?"

"We've all talked about this before, Jess. What good will it do?"

"No good at all, but let's do it anyway. Sitting here not saying a word is not going to get me through the night. Answer my question. Do you? Wonder?"

"We were young and full of can do. Matt had a sweet deal, that's how he described it, getting the military to pay for his college."

"Yeah, helluva deal."

"Sure, I wonder what if. I got a lousy track record for making good personal choices. But being here with the two of you is one of the damn best I ever made. Almost as good as answering the phone when Matt called the first time. Till that call, I figured he was dead, and it was my fault. If he hadn't called, I don't know what would have come of me. Jess, not everybody in that war was messed up."

"You mean the ones that weren't killed, maimed, or living out in the woods smoking dope and making love to their guns?"

Amos didn't want to listen any more. He jumped down from the picnic table and looked out at the flat, scraggly land getting darker by the second. The sun moved faster and faster the closer it came to disappearing over the mountains. He didn't remember seeing the sun set that fast anywhere else and wondered if it had something to do with this valley. He walked slowly back toward the table where Jessie and Bill still argued. He didn't want to listen, but now that it was dark the idea of the desert closing in with all the hungry critters out there scared him worse than riding out his mother's anger.

"I don't like walking away from a fight, Jess, but I'm going to say my piece and if it ain't enough, then walk away is exactly what I'm going to do."

Bill took a breath, looked up, then leaned forward with his elbows on the table.

"Some things you aren't supposed to survive. When you do, life hasn't prepared you. Matt should have died. He wanted to. He told me if Steerman hadn't stopped him, he would have charged those bastards and they would have killed him on the spot. Steerman kept reminding him of Amos and you. Because of Steerman, and because Matt's smart, loyal, and brave, he survived. That CIA guy, McBride, got turned into pulp, and all the rest of his men shot up so bad they never found a trace. I made it because Matt sent me to get help. I didn't get it in time and I live with that failure every day of my life."

Nothing got said for a while. Amos stood still at the edge of the fragile compound and listened. What he heard the loudest was that his dad wanted to see him so bad that it helped keep him alive. It was the second time in two days he knew his father loved him.

"I will do anything for Matt," Bill said. "I would gladly give my life for him, or you, or Amo. It would be meager payback, but it's all I got."

"I don't know how that's supposed to make me feel," Jessie said. "Grateful, I guess, and in a way, I am. You're talking about a war back then, but this is now. My son just asked me if he could sleep in a bomb shelter, and we're hiding here in the middle of nowhere. You know what that makes us? Refugees from that back then war you and Matt volunteered to fight. I got drafted and I don't even know how to describe what that makes Amos."

Amos edged back to the table, and when he was close enough he tapped her arm.

"I didn't really want to sleep in a bomb shelter, Mom. I just said that to make you laugh. I didn't mean to make you angry and mad at Bill. If you want to be mad at someone it's okay to be mad at me."

"Oh, Amos, I'm not mad at you. I'm never mad at you."

"You are when my hands aren't clean. You know, when I have grease on my elbow and under my finger nails."

Jessie laughed. Amos felt better.

"There's mad and then there's mad," his mother said. "Dirty hands are a whole different matter. Little boys don't grow up to be stalwart citizens when they have dirty hands and arms."

She opened her arms and he stepped into them. He closed his eyes and let the feel of her body wrap itself around him.

"We're not going to Carson City for the winter are we?" Jessie asked.

"No," Bill said.

Throughout that off season in Laughland Valley, Amos felt the daily tension between his mother and father. Even though Jessie and Bill told him the problems weren't about him, he didn't believe it. He added his disbelief to the mystery of his "brokeness," a word he now applied to himself. Bill told him if he heard the word one more time he would bar him from the shop.

The shop remained his haven, and he spent most every day there. It began in the largest of the three outbuildings because of the drive-through doors at both ends. They excavated the space under it for stand-up service bays, and built storage areas for all the tools and equipment.

Amos helped Bill measure the underground. The boy did the width times length math of each room which mollified his mother's demands for more time on his studies. Jessie rarely said anything as he ran past her on his way to meet Bill. Amos knew she only had energy for her own problems.

That winter they installed the first phase of the solar panels while they did carnival maintenance. By the time the Boys came in the spring more than half of the electrical energy came from the panels. Another year and they would generate all their own energy.

Amos rarely left the underground. When the others slept, he built tools to fit his hands. It went slow until he talked his dad and Bill into buying a small lathe. One day when his dad got back from a shopping trip to Las Vegas, out of the truck came a wooden crate. When Amos opened the crate, he found the lathe.

It began its life in Laughland as a broken thing, and with only minimal help from Bill, he turned it into a "sweet running little Jim Dandy."

With the arrival of the Boys, Jessie perked up. Her winter lethargy reminded Amos of an electrical motor with worn brushes gradually losing its spark.

As Laughland rolled out of the valley to start the new season, he rode with Jessie as they always did. They talked. She smiled. The world felt better. It felt that way through the late spring and well into summer. Business improved with more and more people coming through the gates, and the Boys made extra change on the spiel. Even Matt seemed to have a sense of humor. Amo spent most mornings in the shop as it became his happiest place again. His prodigious output gave him more time to make tools.

"It's always the right tools," Bill said, admiring the shiny new picks and shims. "You keep getting good, you won't need me around here."

Three weeks later, on a Thursday afternoon without a cloud in the sky, seven miles north of Parkdale, Oregon, Bill and Jessie died. Their car went off a back road that paralleled US Highway 35 where it rolled until it stopped upside down in a river. The Oregon State Police found skid marks indicating the victims might have tried to evade another vehicle, but no other driver came forward.

Laughland cancelled the rest of the season.

Love died for Amos.

BONG SAT

17 NOV 67

By 1700 hours all they can do is wait. Weapons and ammo are set at the best firing stations which outnumber the men. Wiggins and Meat watch from the belfry. The Marines eat sparingly from their few C Rations, backs against the rubble stacked across the front of the church.

"You think maybe they ain't coming, Cap?" Hood asks, a wistful note to his voice.

"Always a chance." Eliot has let the thought wiggle into his mind, but crushes it before it becomes hope.

The last gasp of light winks out and with it comes the first flare and the sound of the sniper's M-40. Eliot leans around a wall in time to see the flare fade closely followed by another. The measured beat of the sniper's bolt action rifle ticks off the dead. Eliot counts seven shots in the time it takes the second flare to die.

"Anybody see out there?" Montoya calls.

"NVA right where they're supposed to be," Traxler calls.

"How come they didn't trip the Claymores?" Eliot demands.

"I don't know, Cap," Dawkins answers. "I wired those myself. The first one goes, they all go."

"They're breaching!" yells Kriakopolous.

"No!" yells Dawkins, and races out of the church. With helmet off and head down, elbows and knees pumping, he races toward the enemy.

"No!" Eliot echos.

Dawkins has a chance in the dark, but when the next flare blossoms it lights him, too.

"Cover him!" Eliot yells.

The Marines open fire. They all see Dawkins spin from a hit high to his left side.

"He's almost there!" Traxler yells.

Dawkins leaps, his arms out-stretched. He sails. He clears the apogee of his flight path and heads down. The first of the directional Claymores explodes followed closely by the rest in no discernable pattern. As they blow, each shattering reddish gold explosion after the other, they kill everyone in their path, including Dawkins.

"Goddamnnn!" moans Traxler. "That was my fuck up, too!"

Eliot tackles him before he can run.

"You live to fight, boy! No more heroes!"

In the belfry the carillon sounds and draws the attacker's fire.

Eliot runs for the staircase and yells into the darkness. "Get out of there, now!"

"Just a sec, Cap," Meat answers. "We're working on a little surprise!"

Eliot runs back to Montoya. "Hit the fireworks. Now!"

Seconds later the first Star Burst lights the sky. The belfry follows with a barrage of Pin Wheels and Roman Candles. The bells continue to toll. From the back of the cathedral, the Bach fugue begins on the giant organ and Eliot feels the bass notes in his stomach. He looks over his shoulder and sees the guttering light of a candle near the organ.

Fireworks explode punctuated with tracer rounds and para flares.

"It's like a carnival from Hell," Montoya yells, "a regular laugh land."

The Marines burn their way through their cache of ammunition. They take loses as the twelve became eight. Three of the eight are wounded, but functional. Eliot does not know about the belfry team. They have not come down, and still lob fireworks. The flares are gone. The single crack of the sniper rifle has slowed, but still sounds.

When the first mortar shell hits the side of the cathedral, the wall shakes. The second and third impacts walk up the wall. The fourth takes out the belfry. The remaining fireworks erupt in a mighty explosion of light, color, and sound. The bells, having rung through the fight, cascade down the belfry's tower until they crash to the floor in a long low clang that when it fades leaves the church in silence.

"Fall back!" calls Eliot, stooping to pick up Hood who is injured but alive. "Gunny, help me!"

Finally, they are four. Eliot and Montoya steady Hood between them, and Traxler scoops up what he can carry as they retreat into the depths of the cathedral. Eliot remembers how Steerman described his men earlier in the day. "Dead and don't know it."

"Helluva fight," Eliot says aloud, and thinks of his son.

"Eliot! Over here." Steerman waves a light at them. "Follow me if you want to live."

It is the second time he has made the offer.

1977

Childhood's End

After his mom and Bill died, Amos hurt inside and out. He had a broken heart. The day after they died, Matt talked to Amos who sat on the bench outside their Airstream trailer. Matt paced in front of him.

"You listen to me real well. Even if you don't get the meaning, you remember every word. You chew on them until you understand and make them your own. Make them your life."

His father's eyes burned into his son.

"Right and wrong have no place in your life," Matt Eliot said, slowly. "Right and wrong belong to other people. You hear me?"

Amos held his breath, but managed to nod.

"When life stares you in the face and screams, what you want to do has nothing to do with what you have to do, you do what you have to do. Survive. That's what you have to do. No matter what. The day you can't make that choice is the day you start to die. When you're done living, then you can think about right and wrong, but not a second before."

His father waited while Amos memorized the words.

"What did I say?" his father demanded. "Repeat it."

"Say it again, please, then I will."

For the one and only time, Amos Eliot heard his father repeat himself. Word for word. Then it was his turn.

"Right and wrong have no place in my life. Right and wrong belong to other people. When life stares you in the – "

"Not you. Say me or I."

"Yes, sir. When life stares me in the face and screams, what I want to do has nothing to do with what I have to do, you – no, I – I have to do what I have to do. Survive. No matter what. The day I can't make that choice is the day I start to die. When I'm done living, then I can think about right and wrong, but not a second before."

Father and son left the carnival, Amos never to return and Matt only periodically. The boy didn't know who would run things, but as they drove away he knew it was no longer his problem. It took seven hours in the truck to reach Laughland Valley. They stopped at Mercy, saw Clyde at the grocery store, bought food and liquor, and finished the trip. While still at the store, Amos saw his father wasn't going to be much help when it came to food.

Amos learned quickly he was responsible for his meals. The last time he was in Laughland Valley, his mother had been alive but she didn't care much about mothering. When Amos looked at that time his memories of his mother were "ghostly," like she was announcing her death to all who would notice her fading life.

He became proficient in the kitchen just as he had in the shop. When he encountered a process that was too complicated he changed it. He made new utensils, like a can opener with a different gear ratio, and he re-plumbed the gas stove so a timer would stop the flow of gas in case he became distracted. He certainly had the time to make the improvements. He so rarely saw his father he counted the times he heard him as seeing him.

It became easier to think of himself as alone.

His emotions progressed beyond grief because he had no one to share them with. He made sure to think about his mother every day. Bill, too. When he didn't know what to do with himself he pretended to ask one or the other what to do. Sometimes he was sure they answered, usually Bill because the voice called him Amo.

Amos learned ghosts could be friends. They couldn't hug you, but they were good for talking to. He liked them putting ideas into his head. He knew the ideas belonged to them because without the ghosts he would never have washed his hands or cleaned his room. It soon became habit and he liked the orderliness of clean. Another time, Bill planted the idea that he needed to keep track of the days. Even in the desert, there were seasons. Winter meant the threat of snow and perhaps running out of supplies.

How supplies came to Laughland was a mystery.

On a sunny Wednesday morning, the 14th of September, Amos sat on a rock that felt good to his behind no matter if he faced east or west. He wondered if the elves brought his food. His father seemed more likely than the elves. So if his father did bring food, what would happen if his father did not come back? Amos had no means of communication with the outside world, and if he did with whom would he communicate? Clyde at the grocery store in Mercy was the obvious choice since there was no one else. But without a telephone and being nine years old, he saw no solution to the communication problem. He remembered what Bill had told him shortly before he died about his "smooth running brain that, before he knew it, wouldn't need anyone." Ready or not, the time had come.

First he went to the garage. He had his choice of a Dodge sedan or his mother's Ford. He chose the Dodge for its smaller size and automatic transmission. He got behind the wheel, determined how much too low he sat and how far to the pedals, went to the shop, and worked on the next part of his problem. Slowly his creation came to life. He found the last component in his mother's belongings which seemed only right since she said she'd be there as long as he needed her.

One week to the day, Amos finished his driving rig and set it up for a trial run. He sat on a booster seat with runners from a rocking chair attached to the bottom of the legs, and strapped on aluminum stilts with his mother's shoes on the bottom and his on the top. Remembering the first electric motor, he didn't try to move the car the first time. Instead, he sat on the passenger's side and simulated the movements he would need to drive, them made some minor adjustments. The second time he turned the engine on but left the transmission in neutral. He applied pressure on the stilt to the gas pedal. The stilt buckled and fell off his foot. He didn't dwell on his failure. He added straps to the tops of his shoes and ran them up his calves. In the shop, Bill had told him the best thing about not getting it right the first time was what he learned.

"Ain't no teacher like oops!" Bill had said.

On the second trial, the stilts with the new straps got the job done. He moved behind the wheel, turned the key, and backed out of the shed. At about thirty miles per hour. The acceleration threw his head back, the wheel jumped out of his hands, and only the lack of something to hit saved a crash. After he turned off the engine and took off his gear, he got out of the car, got to his knees, and leaned into the car to look at the pedals. He moved them with his hands and saw the problem. The metal stilts muted his sense of feel. He practiced until he could feel the pedals through the stilts.

"Okay, I'm ready," he said. He aimed straight and pretty much stopped where he intended.

"Yea! I can do it!"

The road to Mercy offered few obstacles. When he saw another vehicle, he pulled to the side and waited for them to pass.

Clyde did not seem surprised to see him. He didn't ask Amos about his father, or how he got there. The store had no other customers so Clyde helped Amos find the things he wanted.

"Are you sure that's everything?" Clyde asked.

"No, but it's all I can think of," Amos said.

"Might consider a list next time."

"Wow, that's a great idea!"

To his surprise, Clyde said the bill would be taken care of. The answer puzzled Amos, but since it solved a problem, he said nothing. As he lurched and swerved the ten miles back, Amos wondered if a force watched over him. Maybe other elves helped people instead of machines.

A few days after his father returned to Laughland Valley, Amos heard his father going from room to room. When his father was around he spent most of his time in a distant corner of the shelter in a room where he'd built a fort of furniture and blankets. Amos heard the door open.

"Come out, boy."

Amos pushed aside the blanket flap and crawled out. He sat on his knees and looked up at his father backlit by lights in the hallway. Amos hadn't known the lights worked. They weren't very bright, but better than the flashlight he'd been carrying around.

"How do you turn the lights on?" Amos asked.

"At the breaker box. I'm leaving again. Clyde will bring food."

"Dad?"

"Yes?"

"How will I know if you won't be coming back?"

His father walked away without answering.

The morning after his father left, Amos sat on his rock beneath a brilliant blue sky. Even though the sun felt warm, he thought of winter. If his father left for long periods, Amos needed to know how to run Laughland. He thought everything electric ran off the generator, but didn't know if the solar panels provided enough energy to run the generator or if the gas motor ran it as well.

"Fuel, water, and air," he said. "I need them just like a machine."

He planned to be self-sufficient. Taking care of himself meant food, heat, water, clothes, educating his brain, learning how to make a living – there was no hurry on that one – and protecting himself in case *They*, as he had come to think of his father's demons, really did come. Reading Laughland's schematics he saw the way his father and Bill built things always had reasons. He also saw why his father and Bill drew it the way they did because he knew their ways. Would someone know him by his work? He decided to keep it in mind because he almost always thought of more than one good way to do things.

He went to sleep that night with all the lights on and slept all night for the first time since his mother died.

He thought about *They* sometimes. *They* killed his mother and Bill and *They* would come in the dark.

"Wake up, Amos Eliot. Wake up, Amos Eliot."

Amos didn't want to wake up. It wasn't time. Bright light hit his face, and even through his closed eyes the light hurt his head.

"Not time," he muttered, as if arguing with his mother on a move day morning.

A blanket suddenly covered his head. Arms swept him into the air and threw him across a shoulder. He kept his eyes shut, but he knew when they reached the stairs. The arm wrapped around his thighs as they climbed. When they reached the outdoors, they walked a ways before Amos felt himself lowered to the ground on his back.

"Lie still, Amos."

He felt a rope wrap around each arm and leg as the man staked him to the ground. The ropes drew tight. The blanket over his head came away last. A camp fire burned ten feet to the side. A man with his face in the shadow leaned over him.

"You are not to move, Amos. Lie still and listen."

Amos tried to see the features of the face, could not, but thought the voice familiar.

"You are in danger. You will always be in danger."

"Am I in danger from you?"

"No. But I am a danger to you if you fail to escape these ties."

"Why?"

"This is a test. The first of many."

"Why?"

"Do you think this is cruel?"

"My life isn't like other boys."

Amos didn't think his answer needed much thought, but the man said nothing for a long time.

"No, it isn't like the lives of other boys." Another silence. "This is the only life we have. If each of us wants to keep living we have to deal with what comes our way. Your father will not always be here to protect you."

"He doesn't protect me now," Amos said.

"Perhaps, but he makes it easier for you. That will stop some day."

"Why?"

Someday he won't come back."

"Is he after you?"

"No, we are friends of a sort."

"Why are you here?"

"In a way, I am responsible for you."

"No one is responsible for me. I take care of myself."

"You do? Look at you now."

"Did you kill my mother and Bill?"

"No. Despite what your father believes, it's possible their deaths came as an accident." After a pause, the man said, "Trust no one. No one. Do you understand?"

"Should I trust you?"

"This is no time to be petty," the man said. "Do you understand?"

"You told me, I heard you, so I understand. I am very smart."

"So I've heard. Okay, smart boy. Protect yourself at all times. Be prepared for the unexpected. Do you know how I got in?"

Amos didn't, and it bothered him. He knew he'd locked the trap door.

"You got in a way I don't know."

"Yes, and why don't you know?"

"The blueprints show no other door."

"Trust nothing! Always know more than people think you know. Knowledge is power. Protect your knowledge. When you are outnumbered, never tell the truth. A good, reasonable lie always serves better than the truth. If you have the upper hand, always tell the truth. If you are dealing with someone you love and trust, always tell the truth."

"You said trust no one."

"Maybe someday you will find someone to trust. Until then, trust yourself and your skills. Always be honest with yourself. For now I am helping you and I want you to help me. Your father has a purple bag. It belongs to me. Do you know where it is?"

"Why should I tell you?"

"The purple bag holds our safety. Your father has hidden it and I would use it to protect us all. Do you know where it is?"

"No."

"Would you tell me if you did?"

"Not now. I trust no one."

The man got to his feet and straddled Amos.

"Maybe someday I will return and help you again. When I do you might see the wisdom in telling me what I want."

"Are you an elf?"

"I'm a little tall for - . Ah, I see. The Grimm Fairy Tale. No, I'm not an elf. But maybe someday you can be my elf." He looked down at Amos. "Good-bye, Amos."

Amos lay silently until the man was gone. He had already solved the puzzle of the ropes. He elongated his fist and wrist until he could slide them far enough for his fast fingers to touch the knot. His hands came free in seconds. When the ropes fell away, he ran down the ladder, pulled the door closed, but didn't bother to lock it.

BONG SAT

17-18 NOV 67

Marcus Steerman holds the trap door open for the four surviving Marines. They stare down into the darkness.

"Last chance, Captain," he says.

"What is this?" Eliot asks.

"It's called the priest hole," Traxler answers. "The priests would hide there when the barbarians invaded."

"Barbarians?" Eliot says. "Sort of fits if you're not too picky about who's who. Let's go. Easy with Hood."

"Our dead, Cap?" asks Montoya, as he helps Eliot.

"I'm sorry," Steerman answers quietly, "there's very little room."

"They'll have to wait for us, Gunny," Eliot says.

When they are in, Steerman lowers the door. He holds the light while they get settled with the wounded man between them. Hood moans as Eliot and Traxler move him. There is a great deal of blood on his chest, and on the uniforms and hands of the Marines. Besides the men, there is a backpack belonging to Steerman and two film cans Eliot positions under Hood's head. Steerman thinks it will be the most humanitarian use the film will ever serve.

"This man is not dying," Eliot says. "We've had enough death."

Eliot takes off his steel helmet, and asks, "Can we hear anything from up there?"

"Not much," Steerman answers. "Gunfire, maybe footsteps, no voices."

"Can they see our light?"

"No. Not much battery left anyway."

"Kill it."

They sit without speaking in the dark.

"What do you think is happening up there?" *asks Traxler.*

"They're inside by now," *Eliot whispers.* "Keep it down."

"I wonder what happened to that Huey?" *Montoya asks.*

"Don't know, Gunny. Steerman, you sure they can't hear us?"

"The trapdoor's too heavy. What Huey?"

"Not our problem at the moment," *Eliot replies.*

Minutes pass like hours.

"Give me some light," *Eliot orders.* *Steerman turns on the dim light, and sees Eliot leaning over Hood.*

"We're losing him!"

The men look from one to the other for magic or anything to keep Hood alive.

"You guys are Catholic," *Eliot says,* "so is he. Do something. Last rites?"

Steerman looked at Traxler and says, "I know the first line. How about you?"

"I don't exactly go to church."

"I gotta man dying here," *Eliot snaps.* "You going to do something to make his dying easier? Up there, we let the dead down. Not again."

"I'll do what I can," *Steerman says.* *He thinks back to the last time he'd heard the Rite of Holy Unction, something oft heard as an altar boy, but probably not since. He begins, hoping the words will come.*

"Through this holy unction may the Lord pardon thee whatever sins or faults thou hast committed." *He stops.* "We don't have any oil or holy water. It doesn't take without one or the other."

"The fount was still standing when we came down," *Montoya says, pointing up.* "If any priests have been using this place, there's going to be holy water."

"Priests still worship here," *Steerman says.*

"I'll get it," *Montoya says.*

"Sergeant, I don't think that's a good idea. God isn't going to be picky about the details."

A low moan comes from Hood as if he's listening and will accept no substitutes.

"It's not about God yet," *Eliot says.* "You need it, Traxler?"

"It's the ritual, Cap."

"Crack the door, Steerman, and we'll take a look," Eliot says. "Gunny, stay here."

Steerman puts his shoulder to the heavy door. As the door creeps open, he sees a predawn glow dimly filtering into the cathedral. He's lost all sense of time. He wonders if it's still 1967.

He and Eliot climb out. Steerman points to the white fount. They run to it and find it empty.

"Shit!" Eliot says. "Any ideas?"

"We could fake it," Steerman replies.

"We didn't come up here to fake it! There holy water anywhere else?"

"In the storage room where you found the guns. Those closets are where they keep altar supplies."

Eliot starts to walk away, but Steerman pulls his arm.

"How many dead since yesterday?"

After a pause in which Steerman knows Eliot is remembering says, "I lost eight."

"The NVA?"

"Don't know. We put the hurt on. Wiggins, my sniper, was a helluva shot. The NVA got emotional when they saw what was left of the escort."

"How many?" Steerman asks, swallowing hard, but making no move toward the door.

"What are you doing? Making a list?"

"Every man died because I couldn't kill Ferry."

"I told you we don't have time for this!"

Steerman takes his arm again. "I have to know."

"At least a couple hundred since the CIA guy took it."

The windows in the hall where they walk open on a closed courtyard. Eliot sees a light rain is falling from a pale sky. In the Gunny's Rule Book, the combination is a mixed message. Across from the windows is the vestment room. Steerman pushes the empty crates from the guns aside, opens the storage locker, and among the few items remaining he finds two stoppered glass bottles.

"That it?" Eliot asks.

"That's it." They start back, but Steerman stops again. "Eliot. In the hole. One of you said something about a chopper. Is it Ferry?

"*Before the NVA came back, one of our guys saw a Huey hanging a half klick out. No reason for it not to come closer unless it was your boy.*"

"*Did he see you?*"

"*Affirmative. That asshole could have saved us.*"

"*If he knows you're alive, he will be back to tidy his loose ends.*"

"*We'll beat him when Xan gets back. What's he going to do? Kill them, too?*"

"*Yes.*"

Steerman feels a new wave of fear. He had a chance if Ferry thought he was dead, but surviving with Ferry hunting him, he cannot do that alone.

"*You hear that?*" *Eliot asks.* "*Choppers. Hurry.*"

When they reach the trap door, Eliot stops Steerman.

"*That film down there, could it really stop the war?*"

"*Before today, yes.*"

"*How could one man do this?*"

"*Nathan Ferry will do anything to get what he wants, and he doesn't want the war to end.*"

Steerman opens the trap door and they step into darkness.

"*Hood's gone,*" *Montoya says.* "*So's the light.*"

After a long silence, Steerman whispers, "*Add his name to the dead.*"

"*You wanted their names,*" *Eliot says.* "*Wiggins, Kriakopolous, Meat – I forget his real name – Dawkins, Hood, Simms, Paulson, and Gettes. All dead since we showed up here. What did you call this place, Gunny? A carnival from Hell?*"

"*Yeah, Laughland, the carnival from Hell, Cap.*"

"*You said choppers, more than one,*" *Steerman says,* "*What if it's Ferry?*"

"*Not going to know until we look,*" *Eliot answers.*

"*What's the plan, Cap?*" *asks Traxler.*

"*Gotta find out who's up there. We'll split up. Gunny, you and Traxler take the left. Steerman and I will take the right. Stay low, keep your head down.*"

"*Sir?*"

"*Yeah, Traxler?*"

"*Got a weather report? What's the sky?*"

"*Starting to rain. Not much sky.*"

"*Rains good! We going to make it?*"

"Yes, we're going to make it."

While they talk, Steerman gathers his pack and puts the heavy film canisters inside. He opens the trap door and hears the rotor noise. They climb into the sanctuary.

"Can't see much in here," Montoya says. "Maybe we should work the outside. We gotta door over there."

"Get to the front best way you can," Eliot says. "Rule one, live to fight another day. Remember that."

"Sir?" Traxler raises his hand. "How come we can't just hide out here? Nobody's found us yet."

Steerman thinks the plan has merit and is ready to say so, when Eliot speaks first.

"What if it's our guys out there? Xan and Tagnut might have reached a firebase, and got help."

The other three don't argue, but the silence lasts long enough for all to think about Traxler's question.

"Right, Cap," Montoya finally says. "How do we make our move? No sight line, no radio."

"Go with your gut. You'll get to the front before we do. We hear shots, we'll head your way, but don't pull the trigger until you got no choice."

As the four men stand at the altar, Eliot takes Montoya's arm.

"Thanks, Gunny, for always being there."

"Covering your six has been an honor, Sir," Montoya says. "See you up front."

Montoya and Traxler go to the other side of the sanctuary as Eliot and Steerman use the familiar corridor.

"If that's Ferry out there, your Sergeant and Traxler won't see the threat," Steerman says. "You should have put me with one of them."

"You're not a soldier. If you get anyone killed it's going to be me."

"Those two don't make it, Captain, it's on you. I've got no more room for baggage."

The sound of the helicopter reverberates through the wall, but there are no windows other than to the enclosed courtyard. They open the door to the outside of the church, and step out into the rain.

"Oh!" Steerman calls as he sees the dead on the ground.

"Come on, move it!" Eliot calls.

Steerman is frozen. He begins to count the bodies but they are so broken he can't be sure where one ends and another begins. Eliot grabs him and slaps his face. When the first slap fails to break Steerman's paralysis, Eliot hits him harder. He moves.

They run for rain-soaked foliage that will cover their trip to the front of the church. As their cover runs out, they see two choppers and armed men.

"Oh, no!" *Steerman says, and points.* "That's Ferry!"

In front of a Huey, rotors idling, Nathan Ferry holds a .45 automatic like the one he'd used to kill McBride. Two other men in similar outfits and carrying M-14's walk the perimeter of the chopper, while further off, near the second helicopter, are four others in a uniform Steerman recognizes as Air Cav.

"Why would Ferry risk having regular Army guys with him?" *he asks.* "You think your guy got through? Took away Ferry's play?"

Eliot looks at the uniformed men.

"They're not Air Cav," *Eliot says, grabbing Steerman's arm.* "Wrong boots. Your boy's wearing jump boots, the others aren't."

From the other corner of the church, Montoya and Traxler walk into the square. They both hold their weapons pointed forward but muzzles down as they see the Americans. Montoya takes his left hand off the weapon and holds it up in greeting, and Traxler follows suit.

"Kill them!" *Ferry yells.* "Kill them!"

Eliot is about to scream a warning, but it dies in his mouth as the M-14's Ferry's henchmen carry fire a burst from each gun. The Marines fall.

Eliot's weapon now comes to bear on the killers as Steerman throws himself across the Marine's body knocking him to the ground. Eliot is bigger and stronger and throws Steerman aside, but Steerman is determined. He holds himself across Eliot's upper body and covers his mouth.

"Go inside," *Ferry yells.* "There must be more. Kill them, too."

Steerman lies across Eliot, but both see Ferry waving the other men up to join the sweep of the church.

The rain starts.

"No! No!" *Eliot sputters through Steerman's hand as he shakes to free himself.*

"No heroes," Steerman says. "You said that. You go out there, they finish us and Ferry gets away with it. You understand? Ferry gets away with killing your men."

"Bullshit! My men! Gunny!"

"Lie here, Captain, eat your sorrow."

Steerman holds the barrel of the weapon as Eliot tries to jerk if from his hands.

"Listen!" Steerman hisses. "We pull back and wait until after they ride out, then head for Laos."

It starts to rain.

Eliot remains coiled, ready to spring.

"Your call, Eliot. Die now for nothing, or get your revenge."

Slowly, Steerman feels the tension seep out of the Marine.

"Come on, Captain. Let's crawl backwards into the jungle. They won't see us."

They slither, bellies dragging through the mire, then Steerman sees him tense.

"Fuck it. I'd rather be dead."

"A blaze of glory, a pointless sacrifice? Death negates everything you stand for, every chance to avenge your men. You get out of here, will anything stop you?"

"I'll see this every time I close my eyes. I can't live that way."

"And who's going to tell that son you want to see so bad about his dad's wasted death? What's his name?"

"Amos."

"Amos Eliot. Good name. Maybe I could tell him if I lived, which I wouldn't. I can't make it out of this place alone."

Steerman sees Eliot's wild-eyed rage waver. The rain falls harder.

"I might have if Ferry thought I was dead. You guys were alive, so maybe I am, too. He can't afford to take chances. He'll wonder what will happen if I make it out with that film. With your help I will, and you know what I'll do with it? Blackmail Ferry. He might have to pay me for the rest of his life, certainly for the rest of mine." Steerman pauses. "Or until we get even."

"Blackmail?"

"I have him cold. I have voice tape of him telling me to set you up. Get us out of here, I'll copy it then you put the copy in that purple bag of yours. Some day when you feel your resolve start to fade you listen to it."

"*The sky's white,*" Eliot mutters, and Steerman doesn't know if he understood or not. "*White sky means a hole into nowhere.*"

"*We blackmail him,*" Steerman says, pulling Eliots arm, "*and he pays for his own death. We can kill him slow and painful, make it hurt. We have money. I stole enough when I found out he was going to kill me to give us a chance. You listening, Captain?*"

"*If I walk out of here,*" Eliot says, "*I'm a deserter.*"

"*No. You are MIA.*"

Eliot shakes his head. "*I'm a deserter.*"

"*Let go of the book, Captain. Honor is not among the choices. Ferry will do and say anything to get what he wants, and he wants us dead.*"

"*This can't be the end,*" Eliot said.

"*If I promise you this is not the end, will you come with me?*"

"*Promise?*"

"*I promise we will fight on. All we have to do is live.*"

The rain comes with such ferocity it obscures the church taking with it yesterday's deliverance and leaving only misery.

1978

Fuel-Air-Water

After Amos found the unknown entrance he decided he did not want to be surprised again. He collected jugs of water, a couple of bags of chips, and a tin of lunch meat, the kind with a key on the bottom of the can, put everything in a rubberized bag, and hid it in the desert. He would add to it as he could.

One night, while he thought his father was still gone, he heard the carousel start. As he got to his feet, heart pounding, he heard organ music through the speakers on the surface. It was not the usual happy organ music, but slow and sad with sharp loud notes played one and two at a time. Amos hurried to his brand new secret back door and crawled into the night. The carousel lights shown brightly as the horses circled. His dad stood backlit by the ride. Matt Eliot fired a flare then drank from a bottle. The music stopped.

"Gunny, Traxler, Hood!" his father yelled. "I'm sorry!"

He fired another flare. As it burned, Matt Eliot spread his arms and dropped to his knees. Amos saw a purple bag in front of his father. Matt opened the bag and poured the contents on the ground. He stirred them with a hand and began the story of Bong Sat. His son thought this must be the story Bill and his mom said was his father's to tell. Amos heard of gunfire, organ music, fireworks, and murder. In the background the carousel turned, its lights illuminating the terrible tale. After a long silence, the speakers came alive.

"Nobody gets out alive! Nobody but me!"

Amos did not know the voice. The words were hard to understand because there was a mechanical noise behind them, but since they repeated over and over, he eventually understood. When the noise stopped, his father started yelling.

"Goddamn you, Ferry! I hope there is a God. You hear that? I hope there is so he can damn you."

Next he blamed someone named Steerman for not letting him die. The organ music, the sad slow song, started again. Amos saw his dad on his knees, shoulders shaking and he knew his father cried, the purple bag crushed against his chest.

"Ferry, you stole my life. You stole my wife's life, but you are not getting my son."

Periodically through the night Matt sprang to life and fired a flare then screamed, "My boy! Goddamn it to hell! You will not have my boy. Ferry, you son of a bitch! Not my boy!"

Matt finally ran down. He turned off the carousel, but as the horses slowed and the lights dimmed, the music started again. This time it was louder than before.

"You hear that, Johann Sebastian?" Matt yelled over the organ. "You've piped your last dead man!"

Matt fell in the sand. When he didn't move, Amos slipped back into the shelter and went to sleep.

When he went for his noon food, his father collected him.

Matt Eliot stood in the doorway of the kitchen. His hair had spikes, grime streaked his face, and his clothes were wrinkled with dirt at the knees.

"Come with me, boy."

"Why? What do I need?"

"What do you need? Your wits."

His father led him into the desert and pointed at the far side of the valley.

"You will stay out in the wasteland for five days."

Amos tightened up inside.

"Can I come in to get clothes and food and water?"

"No. Don't even think about it. That's the law. When it's time to come back, you'll see a flare."

"Can I get some food and water?"

"No," Matt said. "Get going."

Amos's fear made him shake. "Why, Dad?"

"I thought I could save your mother. I couldn't, and she's dead. You have to learn to take care of yourself. If the desert beats you it's doing us both a favor."

Amos found himself on the opposite side of the compound from his stash. The stash did not have five days of food and water, nor did it have clothes, or anything to make a bed. The stash, when it was finished, was to get him to Clyde's if *They* came. He knew the way over the hills, and if he had to hide out for a few days on the way, he could do it. But not yet.

He dropped into a squat, and cut to his right. He knew this part of the wasteland well, and he patiently worked his way around the perimeter to the hole with his stash. He pulled out the rubberized bag, opened it, and took a drink of water, then checked his supplies. There was food for maybe two days if he didn't eat much, and three 20 ounce bottles of water. He sat cross-legged as he considered his mistakes and vowed to learn from them. How much he could carry determined the contents of the bag, but he could store bags along the way. He smiled at this very smooth running brain solution. He wondered what else he hadn't thought of.

"What do you think, Bill?" Amos asked.

"You got to know what you don't know if you're going to be a good fix-it kind a guy, Amo," Bill said, inside his head.

"That's not easy."

"What you do is play make believe. Grownups call it 'what if.' You play what if this, or what if that. You solve those what ifs, and before you know it there ain't much you don't know."

He needed more supplies. He did have the spare key to the Dodge in the bag. Amos waited for night, then worked his way into the compound.

"You do what you have to do no matter what," he muttered, quoting his dad.

He pulled his driving gear out of its hiding place, got in the Dodge, and drove out of the valley. It marked the first time he'd driven at night. No traffic made it easier, but he could see very little because his headlights showed more where he'd been instead of where he wanted to go. With a sigh of relief, he made it to Mercy and knocked at the back door where Clyde lived. After Clyde helped him with his shopping and on the drive back to Laughland, Amos again wondered why Clyde never asked any questions. Someday he would ask a few questions of his own.

It took three trips to haul his supplies into the desert. He tried to sleep in his shallow hole, he even sang his go-to-sleep song, but instead of making him feel better, the part about burning like a small candle left him frightened. In the desert, he had no protection; nothing to ward off the critters he heard looking for breakfast. He wondered if they drooled when they slithered on their bellies. If he survived the next few hours he needed to be better prepared before nightfall. He sang his song again.

Around mid-day, a flare went off. He thought it might be a trick, so stayed hunkered down near his replenished supplies. An hour or so later, a second flare went off and he heard his father's voice calling his name. He walked slowly back to the compound. When his father saw him, he shook his head and walked away. An hour later, his father's car drove off. Amos wondered if he'd been called in because his father discovered he'd broken the law, or if he had just decided to leave. It made no difference. Amos had work to do. First, he began the process of staging his escape route to Mercy. That took almost a week to stage half the route and every night he went to bed exhausted.

Then he worked on his secret hiding place. It was more like a rabbit hole than a cave. The inspiration came from a book he and his mother had read many times called *Alice In Wonderland,*. Since the main character was a girl, it had never been one of his favorites until he moved underground. Now, as he read the book and applied it to his world, it came alive. Anything can go in the ground if the hole is big enough. He roamed the desert waving his arms, talking aloud, and forgetting to eat. He packed as much stuff as he thought he would need for five days. He took a shovel, tarps, more water, a knife, string, and a cooler. He stored non-perishable food, too, like Twinkies and Doritos.

The second time his father sent him into the desert and he returned to take the car, it wouldn't start. He raised the hood and found the distributor cap missing which answered the question as to whether or not his father knew about his trip to see Clyde. Maybe he had checked the mileage, or the gas level, or maybe Clyde told him. Amos could replace the cap, but he didn't need anything at the store so he sat on the fender and thought. The important thing wasn't that he took the car, but that he could. Be prepared. Learn how to do everything. Always be smarter than the other guy.

On the third day, his father fired the flare cancelling the exercise with no explanation. He drove off without a word.

The three days in the desert put a hole in Amos's supplies. Being prepared meant not taking any chances, so on his second day he decided to stock up. He waited until dark choosing less traffic over visibility. Before he left, he took a reflector to mark the turn for his way home. He saw lights upstairs over the store. He knocked, and waited. Clyde answered, and once again showed no surprise at finding him there.

"Come in, Amos. Maybe I ought to extend my hours. Could be others out there like you with more time to shop at night."

Clyde's appearance and mannerisms reminded Amos of his dad. They seemed the same age and the same thin body. Amos wondered where that thought came from. Could he trust Clyde?

Yes. Clyde had always helped, but the time had come to ask questions.

"Thank you, Clyde," Amos said.

Clyde didn't answer and Amos wondered if he'd spoken out loud. He talked to no one other than himself and very rarely his dad.

"Thank you, Clyde," he repeated and made sure he spoke loudly. "I'm running kinda low. Bottled water, lots. Potato chips, jerky, and Twinkies."

Clyde walked around with him and handed down the items out of Amos's reach.

"Clyde, who pays for all this?"

Clyde added a six pack of Twinkies to the cart.

"I don't know if I'm supposed to tell you. What's next?"

"Bread. How come?"

"I got my instructions." A loaf of Wonder Bread with the red and blue balloons landed in the basket. "One loaf? I mail the bill out once a month and a week or two later a cashier's check shows up. There's a running deposit so I'm never out of pocket, although that wouldn't be a problem."

"What's a cashier's check?"

"Good as cash and safer to mail. Gotta get them at the bank."

"Where do you mail it?"

Clyde stopped the cart and looked down at Amos.

"At the post office," he laughed. "Why all the interest?"

"I'm getting pretty old not to know how things work. When my mom and I went to the store, she always paid before we went home."

"That's the way it's usually done, no doubt. But stores out in the country, like this one, have regular customers who open accounts and pay once a month."

"So I'm like most people?"

"Well, I wouldn't go that far. For one thing, you're a helluva lot shorter than most. And most come to the front door during regular hours. Another thing is most pay in person even if it is once a month."

"I'm sorry, Clyde."

"Don't be, Amos. I like you. I will always open the door to you."

As Clyde packed Amos's goods into paper bags, Amos asked, "Why do you like me?"

Clyde opened the shiny cap of a big glass jar holding things that were colorful, translucent, and on a stick. He offered the jar to Amos.

"What are they?"

Clyde almost dropped the jar. "Candy. Never had a sucker?"

"My mom didn't let me have candy. What's a sucker?"

"What's your favorite color?"

Amos thought for a second, and choose the color of the sun. "Yellow."

Clyde took out a yellow sucker, peeled off the plastic wrapper and handed it to Amos.

"Put it in your mouth and suck on it. Sucker, see? Yellow tastes like lemons. You know lemons?"

Amos took the sucker out of his mouth and said, "I'm ten, and I'm not dumb."

Clyde chose a purple one for himself and laughed. "Any guesses on what purple oughta taste like?"

"I don't know any purple food. Maybe I am dumb."

"Not dumb by a damn sight. A little limited is all." They shared their suckers in silence until Clyde said, "Why do I like you? I could say you are a kid with a lot of pluck, and let it go at that. It's true, you got loads of pluck. But if you're smart enough to ask the question, you deserve a thoughtful answer." A loud crunch came from Clyde's mouth followed by a powerful pucker before the stick came out clean. "People in these parts live on secrets. Soon as anyone's got a secret, everybody else's got rumors and gossip. Got more gossip going over this counter than cash." Clyde waved the bare stick at Amos. "Never hear a word about you or your pa. It's like nobody knows you're here, and if they do, they know better than to mention it. That's powerful strange. I got my reasons for not talking, client confidentiality and all that stuff, but how come nobody else gossips, guesses, or just plain lies about you?"

Amos considered what he'd heard, then said, "Do you know where I live?"

Clyde took a green sucker out of the still open jar, and peeled it while he talked. "Green is lime, and I do know where you are. And I admit to a delivery or two, which, no doubt, you had already figured out. Time gone by, your pa asked me to keep my eyes open for land."

"You knew my dad?"

"We shared a bad patch and lived through it. Builds pretty powerful friends, and," Clyde pointed the new green sucker at him, "loyal. Loyal to you both. You want someone to trust, you come on by."

"Tell me about my dad."

"Can't do that. Loyal means no gossip, and no talking behind your friend's back. You two come in here together, we can swap some stories about a place far, far away in a time best forgotten. One thing, though. No way you can be too careful, Amos. It takes juice to keep people quiet and you got juice. People with your kind of juice got it for a reason and the reason's never a good news."

"What's juice?"

"It's always either what people want, or what they're afraid of, or both. You gotta wonder where your juice is coming from."

"I do wonder."

"Keep your head down and your eyes open. Do that and when the answer comes it won't bite you on the ass."

Amos stuck a red sucker in his mouth for the road as they loaded the supplies.

"Remember what I said about a friend to trust," Clyde called.

Amos drove away thinking trusting anyone meant taking a chance. To others, even Clyde, trust was a word. To Amos trust meant risking his life.

He stopped at the turn-off for Laughland Valley and picked up the reflector. As he came down the hill and drove into the garage, his heart stopped. His father leaned against his car, waiting. Amos closed his eyes and felt like he would cry.

"No!" he whispered, "I do not cry!"

SAN FRANCISCO

19 NOV 67

The private plane that carried Nathan Ferry across the Pacific landed in San Jose, California. A limo picked him up and drove him north on 101 into San Francisco. The forty five minute trip ended as the long, black car entered the gates of a house in the Seacliff district. He had not seen the home of his early childhood in nearly two years.

"Welcome home, Sir," Martin, the butler, greeted him.

"Thank you. Is my mother here?"

"She knows you're expected, but is engaged, sir. I've drawn you a bath and laid out fresh clothes. Your father will be called when you leave for his office."

An hour later the limo took him downtown and dropped him at the entrance of a high rise on Montgomery near the corner of Bush. He used a key in the elevator that stopped the car at the thirteenth floor although there was no button for it. He waited twenty minutes before his father called him in.

"Nathan is here," Albert Ferry said into a phone then sat back to look at his son. "How long has it been?"

"Eighteen months, sir."

No one would take the two as father and son. Where Nathan stood tall, Albert did not. Nathan's patrician features contrasted with Albert's round face and blunt nose. They shared the same eyes that held the object of their stare captive with their blue intensity.

"Yes, I remember. At the board meeting that approved your entry into public service."

A side door to the office opened and Nathan's uncle, Jacob, entered. Jacob and Nathan did look like father and son. Theirs were the traditional Ferry look that photographs proved went back four generations. Nathan knew the similarity between himself and his uncle formed the heart of his estrangement with Albert.

Nathan stood and extended a hand. Jacob was the only Ferry that shook hands.

"Report," Albert directed when the three sat.

"There is no risk of peace," Nathan said. His tone revealed his elation.

"Was the offer sincere?" Jacob asked. "We had serious doubts."

"Yes. They carried a film intended for Johnson of Ho offering to pursue peace."

"My God," Albert said, "that would have set us back years."

"Yes, once the film became public the war would have ended much sooner," Jacob said. "I trust there is no chance of that."

"None," Nathan said. "The slaughter of their envoys will infuriate the North. Expect an escalation. Prepare our people to move ahead."

Jacob and Albert agreed.

"Are your actions hidden?" Jacob asked.

"Yes."

"What about that McBride fellow? The one who wrote the paper?"

"He is no longer a problem."

"His paper?"

"There are no copies other than the one in the archives at Yale. It will disappear."

"How did he divine out intentions?" Albert asked.

"Our plan is logical once the audacity and scope is imagined. His envisioning was academic while our practical actions will change the world."

"A coincidence then?" Albert asked.

"Yes," Nathan agreed.

"The book is closed. No loose ends."

"None that we foresee. My staff is ready to deal with the unforeseen."

Jacob stood and smoothed his trousers.

"You have acted well," Nathan's uncle said. "The board will be pleased."

"Burn no bridges," Albert Ferry said. "We may have to do this again."

Nathan left without good-byes.

1978

"Nobody Wants to be Dinner"

Amos drove into the slot for the Dodge, jerked to a stop and opened the door. By the time he had the stilts unstrapped his father stood at the door staring at his driving gear.

"You made these?"

"Clyde doesn't sell them so I must have."

"Do not sass me. You earned respect with your resourcefulness. Spend it wisely. What else have you made?"

"Nothing, sir." He couldn't risk showing his father his tools and other supplies.

"I don't believe you, You see me as the enemy and a thoughtful lie works better than the truth. I respect that. Get out of the car."

Amos fell as he got out. His knees hit the dirt. He opened his mouth to shout, but caught himself.

"It is 0330 hours," Matt Eliot said. "I'll see you in ten days. Not a moment sooner. There will be no flare, no recall. This is it. Live or die, it's up to you. You can forget your sack of goodies. You've probably got rations stashed around the desert for emergencies. You'd better, boy, because this is an emergency."

"Are *They* coming?"

"Maybe. If not now, some day. You can forget sneaking in through the perimeter. I'll be here and I'll be watching. This is not a game to see if you can outsmart your old man. Believe that."

Amos walked into the moonless night. He took the most familiar path away from the compound. He saw the familiar outline of his rock, fitted his butt to the stone and decided to sit there until morning. He heard night noises and wondered what made each sound. He felt no wind and wondered what made the sagebrush rustle so loud. Things that crawled and slithered and ate boys. There must be a lot of them to make so much noise. Would they fight over him? He doubted critters shared.

"Are there ghosts out here?" he called.

"Jessie and me's about it for ghosts, Amo," said Bill.

Amos heard it so clear he stood and made a complete circle of his rock. He saw no ghosts, not even Bill.

"Bill, I'm scared. Real scared."

"Fear short circuits the brain, Amo. Stuff the fear and you'll feel better."

"I can't tell fear to go away."

"Why not?"

"It won't do it. Will it?"

"You answered your own question. Will it. Focus that smooth running brain on survival."

"That's pretty funny, Bill. Will it. Okay, I will will it."

The fear didn't disappear but it did fade. By the time daylight etched the tops of the eastern mountains he had a plan.

He had entrances to the shelter not on the blueprints. He'd dug holes in the soft earth over unfinished tunnels, letting the debris fall. He then erected a false end to the tunnel that would pass in bad light. Next he built a lightweight hatch cover at ground level and covered it with dirt.

His father would not know about the hatches. Amos could get inside, get his tools, and get out. Since Amos would be expected to sneak in at night, and not even his father could stay awake all hours, he waited until mid-afternoon to make his move. His father said not to think of his plight as a game. Amos knew it was no game. If he lost he died. He wondered what his father won. As the sun moved past midday he wondered how many other ten year olds worried about winning or dying.

He made it as far as his room. He had the bag with his tools in his hand when his father came in.

"Bravo," Matt said. "Again I'm impressed, but again you got caught. Anyone else and you'd be dead or dying."

Amos fought back his disappointment.

"You know what gave you away? Trip wire. You know what a trip wire is?"

Amos shook his head.

"You know what a trip wire is, boy?" Matt barked.

"No, sir."

"A length of string or piano wire under tension. When you step on it an alarm sounds. When it's set up right you don't even know you've done it. I have it all around the compound."

Matt held out his hand for the bag. Amos wanted to run, but couldn't get around his father in the doorway and couldn't outrun him even if he did.

"I think you still consider this a game," his father said, taking the bag.

"No." Amos shook his head. "A game is something you win. I lost maybe my life."

"Maybe so," his father said, and stepped aside.

Amos went up the main ladder and out of the shelter. The afternoon sun, even this late in the year, burned his skin. He reached to adjust his hat, but felt only his hair. He must have left the hat in his room, and started back into the shelter. His father blocked the way.

"My hat, sir."

"Your hard luck. You should have thought of it earlier. Get on your way."

Amos looked at the wasteland then over his shoulder at his father.

"You never walked the midway with me. You never held my hand."

Father and son went their separate ways without another word.

The light, the heat, and the emptiness of everything entered him through his head. He felt a "chug" or a "clunk" in his head as his brain overheated and then seemed to slow. All he thought about was dying. He wondered if people over-felt right before they died. He wondered if he would see his mother as he died, or if Bill would be waiting for him, and together they would find Jessie. It just seemed right that at the end his life they would be there.

He liked the idea, but even his slowed down brain ran well enough to remind him death made no promises. Maybe he should decide to save his life on his own, or lie down and let the sun dry him like a raisin. Raisins. He was hungry. He wondered if they made raisin flavored suckers. What color would they be? Black? The loot his father confiscated included the bag of suckers Clyde tossed in "on the house." A sucker, any flavor, with a swig of cold water. Umm! He smacked his lips.

"This ain't getting it done, Amo," Bill said. "You remember that saying of Larry's?"

"I remember, Bill. Wish in one hand and poop in the other and see which one fills up first."

"Bingo. Looks like you got your buttooski in a bit of a bind."

"Buttooski?"

"Your butt. You're a big boy now, so we might as well call it by its real name. You got your ass in a sling."

"You're talking, funny."

"Not really. Just talking to you man to man. Regardless of age, when your life is on the line, you're a man making man-sized decisions."

"Like living or dying?"

"You're not thinking about dying. Not seriously. Just lonely and thought you might make some new friends over here on the dead side."

"What is it like being dead?"

"Can't really tell you. It's nothing until you think of me, then, here I am. Maybe that's why I don't want you to die. If you did, who'd wake me up?"

"It's like taking a nap?"

"It's like nothing. If I had to put some words to it I'd say I only live inside your head."

"If you're only in my head, how can you be standing over there next to that rock?"

"Good question, Amo. Don't be thinking I got all the answers. I'm just a regular old dead guy that fixed broken things back in the world. Speaking of broken things, this still ain't getting it done. You through deciding about living or dying?"

"Living. I don't want you to go away."

"I'm for that, but you gotta live for yourself first and that's still a challenge, ain't it?"

"What should I do?"

"Get out of the sun before it dries up your lube. How about working at night?"

"That's when the critters drool over the smell of little boys."

"I doubt if you smell much like a boy anymore, and old guys don't smell so good. Cooler at night, too, and that's a good thing, and so is not seeing so much that it scares the hell out of you. Now that we have that clear, what's the problem?"

"Same old, same old," Amos said. "Fuel, air, water."

"One down and two to go. No shortage of air. What's the plan?"

"I gotta get my supplies out of the shelter."

"Tough. Your old man's waiting for you. Remember when your ma read you *Jack and the Beanstalk?*"

"Sure, but I don't have any magic beans."

"Your pa is like the ogre hoarding his gold, only he's keeping a better eye on it. He caught you sneaking in, so maybe you need another plan. You can keep trying to figure out a way in, sure, but unless you can solve your own fuel and water problem, it won't go so good for you."

"He has everything. I'll be out of supplies today. I guess I could walk to Clyde's. I've got goodies stashed on the way. Maybe Clyde would let me hide out for a few days."

"You think Clyde's is the only place to get food?"

"The only place I've seen."

"Look around! Put your head in gear, Amo."

Amos looked.

"I don't see anything."

"Where does Clyde get the food you buy?"

"That's a good question."

"World's a big place and it's never too soon to get a grip."

"I'm pretty small."

"Even when you're full grown and your brain is full up, you'll still be pretty small. The trick is to think about the part of the world you need to understand. You like hamburgers, right?"

"Sure. Who doesn't?"

"So where does hamburger meat come from?"

"From dead cows. Mom told me all about meat."

"There you go."

"There I go where?"

"You don't think Clyde kills the cows, do you?"

"I guess not. Who does?"

"Somebody with a need to. Every guy has to eat. Why do you think the Boys worked the spiel so hard? They had to put food on the table. They earned money so they could give it to somebody who sold the food that somebody else killed to earn a living."

"So I should kill my own cows and make hamburgers."

"Good idea."

Amos looked around.

"I don't see any cows."

"Just as well. What would you do when you saw one? I gotta believe they feel the same way about you eating them as you do about the critters who drool in the night. Nobody wants to be dinner."

"So what do I do?"

"Every challenge starts with understanding. What could be dinner and how do you catch it?"

Bill started to leave. He didn't walk away. He just started not being there.

"Are you a ghost, Bill?"

"Let me give a thought here." Bill became more "here" while he thought. "When that guy had you tied up, you asked him if he was an elf. Remember?"

"You were there? Are you always there, or here?"

"I think I'm always close. Anyway, remember what he said?"

"He said he wasn't an elf. He said something about my subconscious, whatever that is."

"You know what it is. Come on, figure it out."

"Okay. Sub means under, like a submarine is under water. So subconscious is under conscious. Make sense?"

"Sure. What are you right now, standing out here talking to me?"

"Conscious?"

"Right-o. That submarine can float on the surface, too, so it must be a lot like your brain. There are thoughts on top we always know about, and then there are those below the surface we don't know we're thinking."

"So I'm talking to myself while my brain is figuring out what to do."

"You got it. What are you going to do?"

"Fuel, air, and water. Got air so water's next. I don't think there's another place to get water other than from the shelter or the garage. You know anything about trip wires?"

"They're just what your pa said. Here's something for you to chew on. He said they're all around the compound. Did you see him out there stringing them?"

Amos shook his head, and as he did a light washed over his brain. His father lied to him! But there had to be some trip wires, so how did he find them?

"Don't rule out luck," Bill said.

Amos stared back at the compound.

"Here's the plan," he said to Bill. "I'm going back right now. I'll watch the ground real good, but I'm getting to the garage. There are water jugs there. I can carry two. Then the only problem will be fuel. Time I stop relying on Clyde."

Twenty minutes later, as he lugged the two one gallon bottles topped off with water from the above ground tank, he knew his father had lied. He had seen no trip wires. Maybe he'd lied about more than that.

As Amos stowed his water, he told Bill, "Down to fuel. Guess I'm gonna have kill a critter. Rabbits look about the right size for catching. They're faster than I am, so I have to get them when they aren't moving. What if I use a rope tied in a loop with a slip knot that tightens when the rabbit steps inside?"

"You're a good man with a knot, no doubt."

"Lots of good stuff in the dump."

In the last light of day, Amos scavenged the perimeter of the compound. He carried away dirty and frayed ropes of various lengths, pieces of wood, busted up sheets of plywood he had to drag, and the real treasure – a utility knife with fresh blades. He slept that night, and awoke to the dawn of the day that marked the true end of childhood.

He caught the rabbit on his fourth try after the first three failed.

First, he used a trap with a rope loop next to an upside down plastic lid with water for bait. The first rabbit must have seen the rope because it shied away with a longing look at the water, so Amos covered the rope with dirt and smoothed it to invisibility. The second rabbit looked him right in the eye.

"Bill, Larry would have called me a dumb shit."

"Forget it, Amo. What you need is called camouflage. It's doing to yourself what you did to the rope."

Amos freshened up the water then set to the dirty business of making himself as invisible as the rope. When the job was done, Bill whispered to him.

"You got the fastest hands I ever seen, Amo. Going to need them. That rabbit doesn't need to see the rope closing on him. He'll sense it. Just like you, he loses he dies."

Fast as he was, the third rabbit was gone long before the rope touched him.

"He got shot in the ass by the will to live," Bill said.

It was a long wait between rabbits. He had learned from the last one he'd left too much slack, so he looped the excess rope around his wrist. When the rabbit stepped in and he jerked the noose, the panicked animal's reaction almost separated Amos from his arm. The rabbit jerked pulling Amos out of his dirt camouflage. It squealed. He stabbed it. It took many cuts to bring the small body to rest.

Amos cried with no words for his tears. He knew he would have to get much better at killing if he hoped to survive. Despite the tears, he discovered a mental toughness as he prepared the rabbit. He built a fire, and cooked the whole rabbit. He cut off pieces when they were hot. He cut other pieces and cooked them like marshmallows on a stick. He ate what he needed, and washed it down with lukewarm water. He put the leftovers in a plastic grocery bag.

When life stares you in the face and screams what you want to do's got nothing to do with what you have to do, you do what you have to do. Survive. No matter what. His father must have had this moment in mind.

He used his rabbit hole at night, but changed the name after his kill. At first light he crawled out. He jumped around to warm himself and decided to heat the leftover rabbit. He built a fire and went to get the plastic grocery bag. He found it in shreds. A trail of small bones led into the desert.

"Bill? You there?"

"Sure am, Amo."

"You know the 'F' word I'm never supposed to use? I'm going to use it. I am such a fuck-up!" He screamed the last words. "I still don't think anything all the way through."

"You're learning, Amo. It takes time. It's not like you're forgetting to do things you already know, you're not thinking of things you don't know."

"What?"

"There's a whole lot you don't know so it takes time to think about what might happen. If you'd thought about it you would have known a critter would take the food. If they'd eat you, they'd eat a dead, already cooked rabbit. They should have given you a big old wet kiss for being so damn good to them."

"Yuck. I know you're just trying to make me feel better, but if I knew the critters would take it why didn't I do something about it?"

"Two parts to knowing about something. First, you gotta know there's something there to know, and second, is a plan. Remember all that stuff about the subconscious? Well, that's where you store stuff you're not using. You need a way to get that knowing up to the top of your brain."

"The more I know the better off I am."

"Right-o."

"If what I know is in my subconscious and that's where you are, why don't you take over knowing what I know?"

"Seems fair. What do you want to know?"

"I want to know how to stop making mistakes."

"Simple. Takes two things – a smooth running brain and patience."

"I have the first one."

"Get the second. It's the easiest."

Amos saw the critters always ate the same thing and spent all day finding it. If he caught and ate a rabbit every day, then gave the leftovers to the critters, everyone would be happy. The rabbit trap he'd used last time pitted his speed against the rabbit, and rabbits were very fast. He needed another way.

"I remember seeing a picture of a box propped up by a stick. When the rabbit went in to get the bait, it would tip the stick and get trapped in the box."

"What if the rabbit takes the bait and doesn't hit the stick?" Bill asked.

"See?" Amos said. "I hadn't thought of that. Any ideas?"

"Tie the string to the stick and pull on it while the rabbit's under the box."

Amos revisited the dump for material to build his traps.

"The only thing good about this is the idea," he said, surveying the sad collection of waste he had to turn into survival gear.

"You can build anything if you have the will," Bill said. "Kick that brain into gear and before you know it you got a miracle."

When he finished the first box, he cut and shaped a stick with a shallow-tined fork on the end to prop up the box. He refined the prop until it took no more than a nudge for it to fall.

He baited the trap with water, set it up about fifty yards from where he worked, and started on a second trap. He'd noticed the critters watching him. None got close, but neither did they seem put off by the noise he made. By dusk, he had three traps set.

"I'm going to call it a day, Bill."

"Good idea. You going to see if you caught anything?"

The first trap had been sprung, and his heart beat faster.

"Sprung doesn't mean caught," Bill said. "How you going to know? Peek?"

"The rabbit would run. Thought I'd hit the side of the trap and scare it."

"Rabbits are pretty smart when they're scared. How about running a stick under the lip?"

"Good idea."

Amos got down on his knees and pried up the lip far enough to run a stick under it. The trap was empty. He pulled up the box and saw the hole the rabbit had dug to escape. The trap had worked, but the rabbit had outsmarted him.

"That's one we didn't think of," said Bill. "He did the same thing you would have done. Give you any ideas?"

"Yes. Put myself in the place of the quarry." He examined the prop stick and the rest of the trap. It seemed to be fine. "I'm not discouraged. The idea of thinking what I would do if I was in the trap is a good one."

"Learn from experience, Amo lad. If you're the one worried about a trap always make yourself a way out. If you're doing the trappin' then close the doors tight."

The second still sat open. Amos moved the trap onto a rock shelf and reset it. The third trap had been tripped. He tapped the side of the box. He heard the panicked scurrying of a critter. It sounded bigger than a rabbit.

"Here's a thought, Bill. What if it's not a rabbit?"

"Can't be bigger than the box if you're thinking lion or tiger."

"Very funny."

"Maybe it's one of those long-eared rabbits. The ears would scrap the box."

"Maybe. The trap's too small for one those prickly pig things. Could be one of those lizards, but they usually don't move when they see me."

"What's the plan?"

Amos sat cross-legged near the box and stared at it while resting his chin on his fist. Out of the corner of his eye he saw movement, and leaped to his feet in a flash.

His father stepped out of the dark.

"Time for us to talk, Amos. Sit down."

Matt sat facing him and offered a bottle of water.

"No, thank you, sir. I'm not thirsty."

"You've been in the sun all day and drunk nothing. You are dehydrated. Drink."

Amos took the bottle and drank. He wiped his face on the back of his hand and saw the dirt come away streaked.

"Keep it," his father said, when Amos tried to hand it back. "I want to talk about these."

Matt held out the leather case Amos had made for his homemade tools. What he would have given to have them the last few days.

"You made these?" his father asked.

"Yes, sir. Mom helped with the case."

"Did you make the tools in the shop?"

"Sure. Bill helped me get started, but I did it."

He said you had great hands. You miss him, don't you?"

"Kinda, but I talk to him all the time. He lives in my subconscious. That's what he said. He's been helping me."

"That's who you been talking to?"

"I was having a hard time thinking of everything by myself so he keeps track of the hard stuff." Amos got to his knees. "You're a good hider. I didn't see you watching me."

"I have experience. How you going to kill what's in the box?"

"Why are you here?"

"You didn't answer the question."

"If I'm going back to the shelter, I don't have to kill it. I'll have Clyde's food. If I'm not, I haven't decided. I'm not a good killer yet."

"How do you feel about killing?"

"It's not what I want to do, it's what I have to do."

His father smiled.

"I'm here to take you home," he said. "It's time to work together on our problem. So, what are you going to do with what's in the box?"

"I'm going to look inside." He stood and reached for the trap. His father held up a hand while he got to his feet, then stepped back and nodded. Amos tipped the box up, open end pointed away. A grey blur exploded out.

"Antelope rabbit," Matt said. "The cotton tails are better eating. Impressive, though, that you trapped it. Let's close the other traps and head back."

They closed the traps then walked back side by side.

"Dad?"

"Yes, son?"

"Would you have let me die?"

Matt said nothing, but he took his son's hand as they walked. When they entered the compound, he stopped and looked back into the desert.

"Would I let you die? Out there? No. But I don't know if I can prevent it in the rest of the world. I couldn't save your mother." He squeezed Amos's hand.

"I had to know if you could save yourself. By God, you can. Come on. Let's get cleaned up and have some dinner out of a can."

"And a sucker!"

PART II: The Diemaker

1981-1986

1980

Father & Son, Inc.

At the end of Laughland's season the carnival returned to the valley. Matt kept Amos out of sight until the Boys finished dismantling and dead-lining, and left for the winter. When they were alone, Amos and Matt started on repairs to the equipment. Several weeks later Matt left with the promise he would be back soon with a surprise.

Amos worked long hours. When he didn't work beneath the ground, Amos came to the surface to ride the carousel on his golden palomino named Streaker. Sometimes he left the music on. He liked happy organ music, not the Johann Sebastian music that had made his dad sad. Sometimes he rode in silence. He mainly liked the carousel for the way it made him feel. The horses went up and down and around and around and always left him right where he started. When he traveled with Laughland, it always moved on Mondays and even if the trailer was the same, it stopped someplace different. Now Amos rode the carousel and clapped his hands when he got off Streaker and yelled, "I'm still here!"

When Matt returned, the surprise came in a large wooden crate. Amos watched as his dad unload the box from the truck with the fork lift, and when Matt handed him a pry bar and pointed at the box, the boy flew into action. Inside he saw a brand new, shiny lathe.

"You're growing up, Amos. Time for a man sized machine for man sized projects. Like expanding the underground shop."

"We're going to make it bigger?" Amos asked, eyes wide.

"Yes, and you will help plan how we do it."

Amos again stayed out of sight of the construction crew working on the expansion. He slept during the day despite the construction noise and at night father and son evaluated the progress. Each morning the workers found new instructions. Some left the foreman skeptical because things weren't done that way. Matt insisted the designs and methods be implemented exactly as laid out. By the end of the project, the foreman thanked Matt for new ideas he'd use in the future. In less than eight weeks the workers left and father and son settled into a new routine.

Matt spent at least two or three hours each day watching his son work. He also created mechanical problems for Amos that required both dexterity and inspiration designed to move Amos from repair to design then implementation. Most of their time together Matt said nothing. Sometimes his son's solutions made him shake his head in surprise, and other times he patted Amos on the back. Amos still missed Bill in the flesh, but they talked every day. Between them they came up with great ideas that Amos made real.

When spring and the Boys arrived to put Laughland back together, Amos remained underground. He had little to do since all the machines now worked. He worried he'd be bored, but his dad promised new projects.

"What kind?" Amos asked.

"Fuel, air, and water problems," Matt answered.

One day Amos found manuals and pictures on his bench. One of the pictures showed a big man wearing a white shirt and a black coat. Amos knew sharp contrasts made things look bigger, but even so the man was big. The manuals immediately fascinated Amos because they explained explosives. They warned explosives could be hard and dangerous.

"Hard and dangerous are my specialties," he told Matt.

"There's more than one kind of hard and dangerous," Matt said. "We want to know how small you can shape an explosive charge and detonate it with a radio signal."

While Amos studied, the carnival left for the season, and his dad left a few days later. Right before he did, Matt gave Amos a small box. Inside Amos saw four small, highly polished black rocks on short pins, and two larger ones on hinged metal posts.

"Can you fit a shaped charge inside the studs and the cufflinks," Matt asked, "detonate it, and blast a hole one inch in diameter in a half inch piece of plywood?"

The next morning after Matt loaded his car, he found Amos kneeling on his stool, elbows on his workbench, and his chin in his hands. The studs, cufflinks, small wads of the plastic explosive Semtex, electrical wire, and a piece of plywood lay spread out on his bench top.

"What do you think?" Matt asked.

"It's three problems – size, shape, and trigger."

"Keep the Semtex upstairs in the safe until you're ready to shape the charge, and then do it outside."

"Yes, sir."

"I have to go. I'll be back in three weeks. Clyde will be out on Tuesday nights with food and to say hello."

"What's today?"

"Monday."

"Tell him to bring suckers."

"I did. Think you can have a demonstration when I get back?"

"Sure, Dad."

98

The next day Amos sat cross-legged on the ground looking at a length of detonator wire running thirty feet to a one foot square piece of half inch plywood. In the middle of the plywood sat a five gram ball of Semtex with a wire inserted in its side.

"Remember that first motor, Amo?" Bill asked. "The one that got away?"

"Think I'm too close?"

"Too far and all you got is a long piece of leftover wire. Too close and you got wood splinters in your head."

"Okay."

Amos picked out a place another sixty feet away.

"Think of anything else?" he asked Bill.

"Bombs away, Amo."

He squatted on his haunches, and turned the handle.

Dirt landed on his head and the boom echoed faintly off the mountains. The board lay in three larger pieces and lots of splinters. The plywood had split along the glue lines, but when he put it back together he found a three inch hole in the middle. The next charge weighed one gram.

The explosion did not split the board this time. The plywood bounced and rolled six feet, and shards of plywood poked out of the hole. This had not been a shaped charge, and if all the explosive force had been guided in one direction it would have been more than enough to do what his father asked.

Days passed. Clyde came and went. They talked, not for long because Clyde always had to get back and Amos was usually distracted. They did talk about food, but by now Clyde knew he needed to check supplies and make his own list. He listened to Amos tell him what he wanted, and for the most part, he filled the requests. Gradually, Clyde replaced junk food with fresh.

Amos read everything his dad left, and decided that detonating the Semtex with a radio signal made the most sense. He learned how to send a signal, but assigning frequencies lay beyond his grasp. He decided to ask Clyde for help.

Since it was Tuesday he sat on his rock and watched the sun go down as he waited for Clyde. As he sat, he noticed his butt didn't fit the rock the way it used to.

"I'm growing," he said, out loud.

"Speaking of," Bill said, " your mom sends her love. Says she's damn sorry to be missing you getting old."

"My mom said 'damn'?"

"You know she can swear up a storm if need be, Amo."

Amos laughed. "Tell her I love her, too. How come she never comes to talk to me?"

"She said it's better if the boys talk together and leave her to take care of the rest of the managing you need."

"She manages me?"

"Sure she does. Who do you think whispers in your brain while you sleep and tells you to wash your clothes and take a bath?"

"That's her?"

"Damn straight. Imagine how much of a mess you'd be without her."

"Sometimes I wake up thinking those thoughts and I don't want to do them. I'll bet that makes her mad!"

"If you want to ease her pain, you ought to do what she tells you."

"I promise, Bill. You tell her, okay?"

Amos saw headlights come over the ridge.

"Tell her, Bill," he said again, and went to meet Clyde. When he came around the corner of the building, he saw Clyde bent into the trunk of the car.

"Hi, Clyde."

"Wow!" Clyde yelled, jumping and hitting his head. "Ow!"

"What's wrong?"

"You scared the holy hell out of me, Amos! What are you doing above ground?"

"Waiting for you. How come I scarred you?"

"Boy, it's been months since I seen you outside that damn hole. I know your old man's gone, so when you sneaked up on me, I thought it was a ghost."

"There are ghosts, well one ghost, but you wouldn't have to worry about Bill. He helps me."

"Bill? Bill Tagnut? He's your ghost?"

"Yeah, he helps me think of things. We're a team. Bill says he's my unconscious."

100

"I think that's subconscious."

"Yeah, right. Do you know Bill?"

"Remember, I told you your old man and I go back. Bill was around then, too. How often do you see Bill?"

"It's more talking than seeing, but he and I talk all the time. We were just yakking while I was waiting for you."

"Say hi if you would, Amos."

Clyde got the box out of the car, rested it on the bumper, and handed Amos a bag. Together they carried everything it. On the way, Amos asked, "What do you know about radio?"

"Know there ain't many stations around here, and if you don't like Johnny Cash you're out of luck."

"Who's Johnny Cash?"

"Right on." Clyde opened cabinets and drawers, and began stowing food. "Radio, you mean how it works?"

"Yeah. Can you read a manual and tell me the parts I don't know?"

"Probably. What you got going?"

"I want to explode Semtex with a radio signal."

Clyde stopped his putting away.

"Guess we'd better take a look at the manual. You don't have any Semtex down here do you?"

"No. That would be dangerous."

"Right you are."

Amos led Clyde to the workroom.

Wire, transistors, and other electronic components covered the table along with two partial assemblies. Clyde picked up the largest.

"Your dad help you with this?"

"No. I can make the signal go from the transmitter to the receiver, but I don't know how to do the frequencies. There are a lot of things I don't know."

Clyde spent ten minutes picking things up, and glancing at the manual and papers.

"Where's the Semtex?" he asked.

"In the old safe in the shed."

"Matt give you any of the other munitions he's got stashed around here?"

"What are munitions?"

"Weapons. Guns, mortars, a couple of rocket launchers, plastic explosives. He's a good one for scavenging. He figures Ferry's going to show up one day and he plans on being ready."

"No, this is all he gave me."

Clyde nodded, poked around, then looked at Amos.

"How big a piece of Semtex you want to detonate?"

"Very small. About one gram, probably a little less."

"Not going to do much damage with that."

"If it's shaped right it can punch a hole in half inch plywood."

"You're shaping charges?"

"It's not hard."

"No, but you shape charges for a reason. What's yours?"

"To blow a hole in half inch plywood."

"That's all?"

"For now."

"Then what?"

Amos shrugged.

"You doing this with your dad?"

"Yep. We're working together."

"Sort of father and son incorporated."

"What's incorporated?"

"Amos, most people know what incorporated means long before they know how to shape Semtex."

"I don't."

"True. Incorporated means a type of business. Gets shorted to I N C, so it would be Father and Son, Inc. Ever think about playing with a ball or reading about flying saucers?"

"No. Why?"

"It's what boys your age do."

"I do what I have to do, not what I want to do."

"Where have I heard that before? Tell you what. I'll come back Thursday about noon and see what we can put together."

Thursday, right at noon, Clyde returned. A few minutes later Clyde held a small piece of explosive in his hand.

"Do you know about explosives?" Amos asked.

"I do. I was in EOD, Explosive Ordinance Disposal. I was the guy that defused bombs that didn't go off."

"Why didn't they go off?" Amos asked.

Clyde set the Semtex down gently and looked at the boy.

"That's not what people usually say," he said. "They say, Wow! that sounds dangerous."

"Don't people say what they think? I do."

Clyde put the Semtex in the safe, then closed and locked the door.

"How about you and me go downstairs and have a chat?"

Five minutes later Clyde poked around the sink and the stove, and looked in the fridge.

"What are you doing?" Amos asked.

"Minding your own business and taking risks."

"That sounds funny."

"I hope you think so. Amos, I've got a conscience and it's putting some pressure on me. Before we talk about blowing things up, we need to talk about keeping you alive and well." Clyde took a deep breath. "It's a damn shame losing your ma the way you did, and your pa ain't exactly a piece of cake. Seems to me, and this is the trouble part, you could use some help growing up. If you were going to school, they would teach these things in a class called Home Ec."

"Teach what?"

"Personal hygiene, how and why you wash your food and how to prepare it. In general, how to take care of yourself."

"Thank you, Clyde, but I do a pretty good job on my own. My mom may be dead, but she watches out for me and whispers to me in my sleep. That's what Bill told me."

"You do a much better job than any other kid would, but that don't change the fact you're a kid. You're thirteen, right?"

"Yes, Clyde."

"No one your age is supposed to know how to do these things. You do what you know how to do, but it's the damn things you don't know that kill you. What if you get food poisoning? You could lie here long enough to die."

"I don't want that to happen. I can make sure it doesn't if I listen to you, right?"

"I don't want to be a butt-in-ski, or no pain in the ass – "

"A what-in-ski?"

"A butt-in-ski. Means someone who sticks their nose in where it ain't wanted."

"I like that word."

"All I'm trying to tell you, take some help from someone willing to make things a little easier because you're a worthy kind of guy."

Amos thought about it and asked, "What would I call you?"

"How about a guardian?"

"Guardian. Okay, you can be my guardian. Will you help me with my project? I only need help once, then I know how to do things."

"When's Matt get back?"

Amos added up how long his dad had been gone. "A few days I think."

"He and I need to visit a bit before we get carried away. I'll help you blow up a piece of wood, though."

Man and boy spent two and a half hours together, with Clyde talking and Amos doing.

As Clyde got ready to leave, he said, "Watching your hands is something close to a miracle."

"Bill says I'm wired with high test."

"Don't mean much since high test can't be wired, but . . . it makes perfect sense."

1981

Nathan Ferry

After ten days of treatment and observation, the full extent of Colin Truax's eye injury sustained when Ned Greene's second shirt stud exploded remained undetermined. The specialist released him to a New York doctor, and said it was too soon to predict any permanent loss of vision. Truax left L.A. wearing an eye patch and spent his first two days in New York with his new doctors.

The local cops were done with him when he left L.A.. The incident still received a lot of space in the media, but with nothing new it had already faded to the inside pages. Truax and Brinks had held back the card in the box and without it, he knew the case would die in the cold file. None of the hotel's surveillance cameras had a good shot of the tailor's face, and there were no prints on the clothes bags or boxes. The unexploded stud and cufflink yielded only Greene's and Norman Brinks's prints. Truax wound up with the card when Brinks refused to deal with Nathan Ferry.

"He scares the shit out of me when he turns all red," Brinks had said, handing over the card.

Colin Truax arrived for his first meeting with Nathan Ferry since Greene's death and wondered how Ferry would react to the tie to Bong Sat.

The east coast offices of Sierra Terrace Holdings occupied the entire fifty-eighth floor of the building on the Avenue of the Americas. After leaving the elevator, Truax turned left at reception, gave a curt nod to the receptionist, and walked down a hallway to the office that sheltered Ferry's inner sanctum. The male secretary pointed at a chair.

Truax had worked out of New York most of his first year working with Greene. Truax had gone into Vietnam as an advisor. On a night drop four months into his tour he broke his leg in two places. Greene had found Truax in 1966 not long after he got out of a V.A. hospital.

"I'm looking for a good operations man," Greene had said to him while Truax leaned on his cane. "No field work."

After a year Truax lost the cane but the limp persisted.

From the beginning, Truax worked only with Ferry. He became proficient at dealing with the unexpected as Ferry led a dual existence between the State Department and his private sector interests. His job amounted to an appointment secretary with a gun. In 1967, Greene, with Truax doing the work, arranged security for Ferry's travels outside the public sector. This brought Truax into contact with Ferry's executive assistant, Marcus Steerman, who did Truax's job at State. He got to know Steerman, and they occasionally met to deal with the overlap in their duties. Truax soon realized Ferry did little more than tolerate his role at State. His real passion was the Ferry family businesses under the Sierra Terrace Holdings umbrella. Truax had met Nathan's father and uncle and knew some of the family history including the great-grandfather who famously said there are two kinds of people: those who say that's mine, and those who agree.

Ferry expected precision in everyone but himself. In his wake floated loose ends, incomplete schemes, and failures never intended to see the light of day. If they did, they were someone else's fault. At times Truax felt like the guy at the end of the parade with a shovel.

Because Bong Sat was considered field work, it had not included Truax. During its execution, and for months afterward, he knew nothing, not even that Ferry had been out of the country. Ferry disappeared from time to time, and Truax remained in the dark. All he knew was that Steerman had disappeared without explanation. Truax first heard of Bong Sat when he walked in on Greene talking on his secure line.

"We still don't know what happened," Greene said, as Truax entered his office. Greene waved him out, but as Truax closed the door he heard, "There are no answers at Bong Sat, especially about Steerman."

Steerman's position remained unfilled, and Truax took on more of the job. He discreetly attempted to find out what had happened at Bong Sat and to Steerman. He got nowhere.

Then Steerman contacted him.

The first time had been a carefully worded phone call at home. From then on the few exchanges they shared happened by mail and all dealt with Bong Sat. Truax wanted to know what happened, and Steerman wanted to know if Ferry got close to finding him.

When Ferry's secretary waved him in, Truax passed through both doors to the sound proofed inner office. The furnishings consisted of a desk and functional chairs. The walls held an original Bierstadt and three photographs Truax knew were all of Ferry's family.

Ferry sat behind his desk and did not look up, leaving Truax standing at military ease with his hands clasped behind his back. Ferry finally pointed at a desk.

"Your vision?" Ferry asked.

"Will get better, sir."

"Report. The official version first."

Truax recited how Greene's garment bag disappeared, the search for a replacement tux, and the fruitless search for the man who provided the clothes.

"You don't think this man will be caught?"

"Correct, sir. Somebody wanted Greene dead."

"Did it need to be so public?"

Truax thought how much the question said about Ferry.

"Greene was not an easy target. Other than that dinner, it would be hard to predict where he would be."

"You are convinced the target was Greene and Greene only?"

"Yes."

"Explain."

"The weapon. They went to a lot of trouble to make sure Greene would wear the studs and cufflinks."

"Tell me about the weapons."

"Tiny amounts of Semtex detonated by radio signal. The timing of the detonations made sure no one would help Greene until it was too late. Very effective for creating panic. The L.A. forensics people say they haven't seen anything like it. I know a guy at CIA and they talked exploding cufflinks for Castro almost twenty years ago, but he doesn't know if it was ever done. Anything that small is not very reliable, but these worked. All of them. Perfectly. We may have someone new on the scene."

"A serial killer?"

"The guy who built them. Everybody's checking their files. I called around this morning and no one has a lead. They've seen tiny explosive devices, but after the fact when there isn't much to see. This time they have the stud and cufflink without the charges. It gives everyone a good look. They could have come out of a Tiffany's box was the way the FBI put it. Our guy left no prints, and there's no chance of tracing components since they all appear to be homemade."

"So no idea?

"I didn't say that." He placed the card on Ferry's desk with the place and date side up. "It was inside the box with the studs and cufflinks."

Ferry picked it up, glanced at it and pursed his lips.

"There's more on the back," Truax said.

Ferry turned the card over slowly, and read.

"Do you understand this?" Ferry asked.

"I wasn't part of it, sir."

Ferry nodded. "I'm through with you for the moment."

"Do you want me to wait around?"

"If you wish, but not in this office."

"Yes, sir," Truax said, and went down the hall to Norm Brinks. Truax knocked once and entered.

"He'll be calling," Truax said.

"Shit! You know what this means? He's going to put me in charge!"

Truax nodded, and smiled.

"You were there, Norm. I wasn't."

"I saw that smirk! You know as much as I do about it. Shit, we've talked about it for years."

"And nobody knows we did," Truax said. "Go to the meeting. You know what he wants."

"Yeah, that fucking Marine. Who else could it be? Shit, man, all these years and all of a sudden Greene blows up! Who waits that long to get even?"

"Not only does he wait, but he tells us." As he said the words, Truax saw an explanation. "I don't believe it."

"What?"

"He thinks we've been looking for him."

"Why would he think that?" Brinks asked.

"That's a good question," Truax said, then added, "Do you remember the Marine's name?"

"Hell, no. Colin, I don't get it. He's got to know if we'd been looking all these years we would have found him."

Truax did not mention they'd been looking for Steerman for just as long. Then the second inspiration hit. The Marine and Steerman were together.

"By noon you'll be digging for the name."

Truax opened the door.

"You gonna leave me on a limb?" Brinks asked.

"No, Norm. Lunch at the sandwich shop on Fifty-third. I'll help, but if Ferry finds out we're comparing notes, we're both done."

"I owe you, man," Brinks said.

As Truax walked away he felt sure Steerman had let the Marine think they were looking for him.

Nathan Ferry stared at the final page of the quarterly report that concluded eighty-six corporations now owned or controlled seventy-five percent of the world's necessities defined as food, energy, and precious metals. When Sierra Terrace Holdings first commissioned the report at the end of World War I, it had been an annual and the number had been over four hundred. Ten years ago it had been two hundred and sixty-one, but technology and consolidation reduced the number. Add arbitrage, and the weak and vulnerable fell faster. Six years ago, Nathan predicted the shrinkage would go as low as fourteen corporations ruling the world that mattered.

Sierra Terrace Holdings masked the activities of eight of their core companies known internally as the Pacifica alliance. Of the eight, Ferry Precious Metals of San Francisco, run by its visionary leader Ambrose Ferry, had led Pacifica from the beginning. Formed in 1935, Pacifica correctly anticipated corporations rather than bloodlines would eventually rule the world. The eight also shared the Pacific Rim.

During the first half of the twentieth century with its dying monarchies, depression, and world wars, the opportunistic corporations saw that chaos bred opportunity. In the mid 1930's they foresaw the onset of a truly world war that would involve Japan, China, and all of Southeast Asia including Australia. A world in upheaval would reward the bold.

The two most important events in Ferry family history after they became wealthy in 1848 was U.S. Admiral Perry's visit to Japan in 1853 with its subsequent unlocking of the Orient, and the bombing of Pearl Harbor. The twentieth century saw the world shift power toward the Pacific Rim with the Ferry legacy profiting heavily from the shift. With Nathan at the helm, the end of the twentieth century and the beginning of the next would see the Ferry reach its magnificent potential.

The bedtime stories of Nathan's youth featured wealth and power and never opened with once upon a time. He sat at grandfather Nathaniel's knee and listened to the tales of a new elite emerging from a war-torn world to offer direction and sanity. He heard how pivotal decisions would now be made in living rooms and private clubs from Palo Alto to Tokyo, decisions to adjust the course of wars, alter political courses, and decide who would prosper and who would not. Nathan Ferry learned of a much larger stage than the one the rest of the world aspired to or could even grasp. His grandfather often finished the stories with the moral that War is Opportunity.

During World War II, Pacifica began planning its involvement in Southeast Asia where its gigantic population would one day be the world's greatest concentration of consumers. The abrupt end of WWII with the nuclear bombing of Japan surprised Pacifica and left it short of its long term goals.

The Fifties frustrated them. Korea showed promise taking Americans back to Asia, but the McCarthy years served as a serious distraction that cancelled out Korea. Eisenhower started as a promising "war president," but in his second term became another unpleasant surprise. The old soldier went so far as to warn against the growth of the military – had even coined the phrase "military industrial complex." It appeared America would return to a form of isolationism that threatened Pacifica and its ambitions. But years of careful work, much of it done by Nathan, saw troops begin their slow insertion into Vietnam. With its proximity to China, both geographically and ideologically, Vietnam would serve as Pacifica's spearhead.

In the mid '50's, a vote of the board put Nathan into civil service to work from the inside. He had trained for this possibility while attending Vanderheigh, Wharton, and Princeton, where he met and cultivated the right people. It didn't take long to identify the real enemy – the Kennedy's with their preoccupation with the Soviets and Cuba. Had JFK been reelected, he planned to get Americans out of Vietnam, but Pacifica had dealt with that rich brat and his Pulitzer Prize. In comparison, the note from Ho Chi Minh threatening peace should have been a mere hiccup.

With America fighting in Vietnam, it created a second front for the Chinese, with the Soviets being the other. The combination kept the Chinese focus away from events within their own borders as vast portions of Chinese agriculture began restructuring. Pacifica trained key personnel so that when the communist hold inevitably weakened sensible voices – Pacifica bred voices – would encourage a form of free enterprise to feed the masses and make the products they desired.

Nathan's phone buzzed bringing him back to the present.

"Yes?"

"Norman Brinks, sir, as you instructed."

"Two minutes."

Nathan looked again at the card Truax had handed him.

BONG SAT
18 NOV 67

He ticked the card with a finger. Bong Sat, from Marcus's annual call to reminders like this, lingered as his worst mistake. Not a mistake really; he had been decisive in the face of the totally unexpected and dealt with it. He'd planned well, but events outside of his control turned against him. Greene had said with that many people involved, events often do not go as planned.

He cleared his desk other than the card from Truax. When the door opened, he looked at Brinks and saw a gray man. Hair, skin, and clothes, all gray. Its was not the look of a leader. He waved Brinks to a chair.

"You've seen this?" he asked, extending the card to Brinks who took it.

"Yes, sir," Brinks said. "I found it."

"What is your conclusion?"

"It means the Marine lives," the nervous Brinks said.

"Yes. The Marine. His name?"

"I don't know, sir. Greene would remember, but . . . "

111

"Go through Greene's papers. See what you can find. I want the Marine's name and I want to know what happened to him."

"Sir, I know Greene had no paperwork on Bong Sat. He made sure I didn't have any either. He said never talk about it, and I didn't."

"What does Truax know?"

"He knows something happened. Steerman disappeared, and Greene imposed a gag order. If he knows any more, I don't know how. He and Greene were kind of close, so maybe Greene talked."

"Norman," Ferry said, softly, "either I put you in charge of finding the Marine or I bring Truax into the picture. I don't want anyone else involved that does not need to be. Do you understand?"

"Sir, I'm not a good leader, but I understand. I can find the Marine. Give me direction, and I'll do my best. I always try to do my best."

The funny thing is, Ferry thought, Brinks always tried.

"**I hate what** a weak ass I am," Brinks hissed, as the men ate their sandwiches in a hole in the wall sandwich shop. "I backed out of his office, I didn't bow or scrape, but damn near. I hate that guy!"

Truax wrapped up what was left of his ham and Swiss, and finished his coffee. "He wants the information in the morning?"

Brinks nodded as he looked at his pastrami, and then threw the soggy rye bread into the red plastic basket in front of him.

"I don't even know if it exists. I guess I could start with the order of battle records."

"Don't bother. Remember, Greene said those Marines had been in the bush for weeks. They could have been from anywhere. Check graves registry. Find out how many Marine Captains died or went missing about that time. Get a list. Ferry might be impressed with how much you came up with even if it doesn't answer the question."

"How about AWOL's and MIA's?"

"Fine, but we know the Marine's not dead. Who cares if he's listed as AWOL or MIA. Let's hope Ferry doesn't raise that troublesome point."

"You got any ideas?"

"I can tell you what not to do. Do not come at this through Bong Sat. If the man discovers there's general info about Bong Sat - if there is - he'll shit himself."

"Hey, what about hitting the rumor mill? There's always some conspiracy thing about Bong Sat, some of it pretty close to the truth."

Truax shifted in his seat and leaned closer.

"Greene told me if I ever got tired of my job I should take some of those rumors to Nathan. There are safer ways to spend our time." Truax unwrapped the wreckage of his lunch. "Do what you can. The lists are good. If Ferry isn't satisfied then tell him there's nothing more. He isn't going to fire you, and you don't want Greene's job anyway."

"That's going to make him happy?"

"No, but emphasize the nothing about Bong Sat." Truax brushed his shirt front, stood, and put on his overcoat. "Maybe the dead Marine on the card had a brother who heard the rumors and was willing to pay for Greene's death. Think about it. Why would the Captain act now?"

Later that day Truax placed a classified in the international edition of the *New York Times*.

The Captain has been heard from, it read.

The convoluted method Truax used to communicate with Marcus Steerman took time. He placed the ad and waited. Five weeks later a letter arrived. In the envelope a single piece of paper read: *Impossible. The Marine died at Bong Sat.*

You lying sack of shit, Truax thought, as he lit the paper with a match. He had neither seen Steerman nor talked to him since that first phone call. Steerman lied to him and sometimes he lied to Steerman, but the lies Truax told all prompted Marcus to keep sending him ten thousand dollars a year. The motives for Steerman's lies often defied discovery. The man was slick and totally without conscience. Truax felt confident the Marine lived and would strike again.

1982

The Death of Norman Brinks

The details of Ned Greene coming apart one small explosion at a time filled the national press for almost a week as each witness surpassed the previous for providing bloody detail. Murder as theater, as one article put it, sharpened the media's pencil. When the second very public killing took place they were ready, even if it was six months later and half the world away. Sir Douglas Treblehorn also died wearing a tux.

While most of Britain rebuilt itself in the aftermath of World War II, Treblehorn headed for South Africa to reconstruct his personal prospects. His family had a long history of making fortunes in far off lands. Sir Douglas became adroit at brokering precious metals for surplus arms to outfit one rag-tag chieftain after another to help them successfully wage war on their neighbor. Part of the deal always included mineral rights once the chief won his battle. The practice earned Sir Douglas enemies at the same rate he accumulated wealth.

On an extended visit to London, the profoundly hard of hearing Sir Douglas purchased new hearing aids. Part of his London routine included dining formally each evening at his club where the food was dependable and his fellow members cared little he was no more than an arms dealer.

On a Thursday evening, over leg of lamb with mint jelly, boiled potatoes, Brussels sprouts, and twelve year old bottles of Cabernet, his table mates heard a soft *plop* followed immediately by a great gush of blood out of Sir Douglas's left ear. He fell face first into his plate. Thirty seconds later everyone, but the already dead Sir Douglas, heard a second plop as the other hearing aid detonated. No one approached the body for thirty minutes.

114

The media connected the deaths of Greene and Sir Douglas. Both featured multiple explosions and impeccable workmanship. It had to be the same guy and he needed a name. A writer for *Time* came up with The Diemaker, and it stuck because it married machine precision with lethal inevitability.

The Diemaker story carried great legs and when the International Achievement Awards arrived without a new victim, the television news shows and magazine writers settled for the retelling of Ned Greene's death. When the event came and went without incident, the disappointed media's legs got tired and The Diemaker faded from sight.

Not all of The Diemaker's inventions were high profile. Father and Son, Inc. remained busy with Amos doing design and production and Matt handling the marketing. In the first year Matt banked a half million dollars.

Amos glowed with excitement. The challenge and joy lay in the doing. He knew nothing of The Diemaker.

After the uneventful International Achievement Awards, Ferry remained in California. Five weeks later, Ferry agreed to speak at a formal dinner celebrating a new Pacific rim business alliance. The dinner would be in San Francisco at the Mark Hopkins. Ferry told Truax the security arrangements would be the usual, meaning Colin and Norm Brinks would have to dress for dinner.

"Jesus, I just got my breath back from the last time," Brinks said.

"Norm, let it go. Nothing happened then, and nothing is going to happen in San Francisco. Is your tux clean?"

"Yeah, I sent it out right after the dinner so I could lock it up." Brinks took Truax's arm. "You know what really pisses me off? This fucking guy - I know it's that Marine - used Greene to build a reputation. Did you see those ads in the merc papers about weapons made to order? "

"I saw them."

"Didn't that piss you off? Then the media turns this guy into a hero. The Diemaker. What a bunch of shit!"

"Yes, it pissed me off, for all the good it did. Did you check your tux when it came back?"

"Sure. I sent it to the same place I always use. I trust them."

"It's your life."

"Okay, I'll check it again. What's the plan?"

"We take the jet, fly into Oakland, and chopper to the hotel. You can dress here or on the plane."

"Good. The last thing I want to do is let that fucking monkey suit out of my sight."

Matt Eliot almost missed the article announcing the dinner in San Francisco. He smiled when he read the dinner would be black tie. Matt had already done the hard part breaking into the cleaners and replacing the victim's boxed shirt and black tie. Two days before the event, he put the transmitter into his bag, marveling once again at his son's work, and drove away from Laughland Valley toward San Francisco.

When Norm Brinks dressed for the International Achievement Awards, he noticed his tux fit tighter than he remembered. Now it felt tighter still.

"If I don't get serious about the weight, I'll have to get a new tux," he thought, trying to fasten the collar button. Heavy starch made it more difficult. As he tried to fasten the cummerbund around his middle, Truax walked into his room without knocking.

"You heard of Giancarlo Gianetti?"

"No," Brinks said, biting his lower lip as he fought the hooks.

"Norm, fasten it in front and then slide it around."

"Then it gets all wrinkled."

"Here," Truax said, "turn around and I'll do it."

"Thanks, so who is this guy?"

"Gianetti was a liberal politician in Italy. The Mafia hated his guts, but the guy was so heavily guarded they hadn't been able to get to him."

"I'm not going to like this, am I?"

"No. He's dead. His black plastic comb killed him."

"His comb?"

"I talked to a friend in Paris who got it from someone at Interpol. The tips of the tines were sealed with wax. After the guy used his comb a week or so, the wax wore off. When it was gone, teeth dipped in curare scratched the guy's head. Killed him."

"Maybe it's not our guy. Nothing exploded. The vic wasn't wearing a tux was he?"

"Pajamas. He was vain about his hair, even combed it before he went to bed to hide his bald spot."

"First guy I ever heard of getting killed by a comb."

"The good news, if it's the Marine, he's been too busy to fuck with us. We're going to be fine." Truax pointed at the still open collar. "You going to finish getting dressed?"

"On the plane. It's tight. I've gained weight."

"We're all gaining weight sitting on our asses. Maybe we need to start group runs or something. We can talk about it tomorrow."

Right before they landed, Brinks got his collar closed. He asked Truax to fasten the tie in back.

"Can you breathe?"

"Yeah, no problem," Brinks said, then faked a cough and stuck out his tongue. "Diet or die, eh, Colin?"

They reached the Mark Hopkins on schedule, and Ferry walked into the usual crowd of men that either knew him or wanted to know him. Truax recognized most, and none of those he did not recognize looked out of place. He milled about on the periphery of the scrum that held Ferry at its center.

Matthew Eliot sat in the lobby reading the paper. In his pocket he held the transmitter that would send a signal to the receivers built into Norm Brinks' black tie and dress shirt. The signal caused a vibration in the very high frequency range to activate the specially treated high tensile wire in the tie. The heat would fuse the tie's metal clasp then the wire would lose thirty percent of its length.

Ferry, as the keynote speaker, sat at the raised head table. Truax and Brinks stood to the side and behind him at stations visible to the rest of the room. As desert appeared, Truax heard Brinks cough. He looked and saw his face a bright red and his right hand pulling at his collar.

"Can't breathe!" Brinks gasped, then fell to his knees. His face turned to purple, and his eyes started to pop as his tongue pushed through his teeth. The gagging got louder. Brinks jumped to his feet and staggered toward the speaker's table. He shouted a tortured, high pitched scream and pitched forward almost hitting Ferry from behind. Truax pulled Brinks away from the table and let him fall as the crowd panicked. Truax tried to hold him, but Brinks broke free.

"Norm," Truax yelled, "unfasten the tie!"

"Can't!"

Truax wrapped an arm around Brink's head and reached for the clasp. He singed his fingers then grabbed a steak knife off the nearby table and tried to cut the tie, but the blade snapped.

Truax watched Brinks die. Norm stopped moving but as with Greene, death did not end it. As the shrinking around the neck continued, Truax wondered if it would decapitate the corpse.

1983

Matt Eliot Reclaims His Honor

The carnival sat on the same field it used every year when it came to Bishop, California. Matt figured it was the eleventh year old Micah Crenshaw welcomed them to his farm. Micah and his wife, June, always invited them to park the trailer next to the farm house and share meals inside. The childless couple loved the week with Amos, and Jessie was happy to get out of the trailer. Four years ago Jessie died two days after they received a wire from Micah with word June had died. Micah buried her under a tree where she could see the carnival when it came.

Matt and Micah still shared a drink. Micah would drop by the office wagon while Matt counted the day's receipts. Matt welcomed him, but the talk was desultory. They drank a cup or two and did their best.

Micah knew Matt's routine, especially the part about the loaded gun he kept on the table. When he came to call he knocked and announced himself, and still waited for the invitation to come in. This time Micah brought a fresh bottle of Johnny Walker Black.

"You ought to lock that door, Matthew," he said, twisting off the cap and digging in the usual drawer for glasses. He found two and held them to the light.

"If you don't learn a few more housekeeping skills, I'll start bringing my own glasses along with what goes in them."

Matt didn't look up as he counted.

"I'm turning over a new leaf, Micah. Clean glasses for the next toast. I promise. You want to ride along tonight to that Wells Fargo cross town?"

"Nope. I'm not much good after dark anymore. June did my night time seeing, and since she's gone, well, I pretty much stay in. Why don't you step on it and get there before it's all the way dark."

Matt picked up the .45. "I don't worry about it."

"Maybe you should."

"I sleep better after the money's in the bank."

"You sleep, my friend?"

"Some. More than I used to. Amos is safe in that school, and I'm thinking about parking Laughland for the last time. There's no money in it and I'm getting old."

"Ah! – not so old. But if you park it, I'll have it easier telling you I'm selling the farm."

Matt looked up. "Yeah. I saw the houses right up to your fence line."

"The farm's worth more growing houses than alfalfa. I have to move June. She and you are the reasons I haven't sold before."

his drink. He picked up the .45., and said, "Nothing lasts forever, Micah."

Bishop had two Wells Fargo branches with night depositories, but Matt didn't like the closest because a hedge blocked the view from the street. As he drove to the further one he thought he saw a tail. He made an unnecessary turn a few blocks from the bank

119

and the vehicle, a van with a side door, kept going straight. He felt uneasy so he took a spare clip for the .45 out of the glove box and slipped it into his windbreaker.

He got to the bank and turned into the lot. By the time he saw the van waiting in a dim corner he was off the street. He looked in the mirror to back out, but an old station wagon screeched to a stop blocking him. The side doors on the van slid open and two men jumped out. Matt heard doors behind him. He chambered a round, took off the safety, and slid low on the seat. He wondered why he hadn't rammed the car behind him. He felt the sweat pooling on his side against the seat, and his mouth went dry. He had not felt this way since Bong Sat. As soon as the thought formed, he knew why he had not backed up.

"I love you, Jess," he said, aloud. He closed his eyes. "Gunny, all you guys, I never forgot you. I should have done more."

He took a deep breath and as he did, the rear window exploded. Glass made it to the front seat, but the car's body was old enough to have real Detroit steel that took the hits well. He felt a sharp bite at his cheek and blood flowed.

"No matter," he whispered.

The majestic chords of the Bach fugue filled his head. He pulled the door latch on the passenger side until he felt the catch disengage. He pulled his knees back then shot them at the door which flew open under the impact. He came out low and rolled on the ground. He caught his attackers from the station wagon in the open, and emptied the clip into the two men.

Matt looked under the car. He saw feet coming from the van.

"All this for a carnival night drop?" he muttered, and knew the money did not matter. "Ferry!"

The approach of death transported him back to Bong Sat and the rain soaked jungle outside the church. He felt the mire on his back and the smell of the vegetation in his nose. He saw Gunny and Traxler dead on the ground, but now no Steerman held him back.

"This has been waiting," he thought, feeling the awe of a second chance.

He slipped in the new clip.

He came out in a crouch, zig-zagging, running at his attackers, and shooting until the clip was empty. At least one more man went down before the shotgun blast from the last attacker took him in the chest.

1983

Marcus Steerman Returns to Laughland

Marcus Steerman stood in the international calls alcove of the Metropole Hotel in Macau City and tried to breathe deeply. There had been no messages for a week which could mean only one thing. Matt Eliot was dead. When Matt put Amos to work as The Diemaker, Steerman knew the end would come. This matter of fact acceptance hid his feeling that he had lost his only friend. Before he started dialing he amended friend to partner, but the change did nothing to soothe the sense of loss.

He reached the carnival in Carson City, Nevada and talked to Jack McQuarry, the acting manager. Steerman heard what the police had told McQuarry of the robbery. Matt lay buried in Bishop, and McQuarry didn't like it, but didn't know what else to do. Micah Crenshaw volunteered his farm and a grave next to his wife's, but said he couldn't guarantee the body a permanent home. To make it worse, they'd found no contact info on Amos so the boy didn't know. Steerman said he was out of the country but would get there as soon as possible. He would notify Amos.

He caught the carnival outside Sparks. He and McQuarry decided to shut Laughland down at the end of the stay. Six stops remained, but without Matt doing his advance work there would be little business. Anyone not needed to close down the carnival would receive three weeks severance pay. When McQuarry asked about next year, Steerman told him he doubted there would be a next year. He told him three months ago he and Matt were approached by a company interested in buying Laughland primarily for the valley. As far as Marcus knew they had no interest in maintaining the carnival. He would sell if the offer still stood. He was sorry.

Steerman, racked with jet lag, slept late in Sparks then drove to Las Vegas. With two hours left on his drive, he tried to focus on the years ahead, but he drifted back to Bong Sat. Panic flared, but Steerman freed enough of his mind to ask questions never before asked. Why had Ferry done it? War as opportunity was a very large umbrella for assigning motivation, but what was the precise opportunity? Who was Frank McBride and why did he have to be at Bong Sat? Ferry had made the arrangements himself ao it was important. At the time when Steerman asked, Ferry told him as long as the CIA had to be involved he wanted someone he could trust. Since Ferry had lied about everything else who was McBride and why did he have to die?

For answers to Bong Sat he realized he'd always counted on Eliot for answers. He still did. What Steerman sought lay in that Purple Bag. He'd watched Eliot drop items of his dead into the bag and would never have let it go. Marcus smiled. The most amazing thing he knew to be in the bag was Ho Chi Minh's chop. With the film it would be a powerful indictment of Ferry.

He spent the rest of the drive imaging the other contents of that Seagram's Crown Royal bag. When he reached Las Vegas he went straight to the deposit boxes at the Stardust. He hadn't been there in three years, but he knew by the weight of the box Matt had been there. He opened it, lifted out the papers, and on top of the film canister at the bottom of the box he saw a .45 automatic sealed in a plastic bag. It had not been there the last time he'd visited the box three years ago. He set it aside and went through the papers.

He found the insurance policy on Matt. It was for two million dollars and owned by the Laughland Corporation which now was Marcus. He also found the deed to Laughland Valley, indispensable given all the shortcuts they'd used to get the land. What was not there was a method for contacting Amos. The one reference to Amos was a letter addressed in Matt's hand that told Marcus the letter was confidential and to give it to Amos in the advent of his death. Marcus opened the letter. It read:

Dear Son:
I am dead. It's been a long time coming for no good reason.
Settle the score with Ferry. Find a fate worse than death. Find one of
your elegant solutions from The Diemaker days. The gun is the gun that
fired the first shot at Bong Sat. Ferry killed a man named McBride. His
dog tags are in my purple bag. Perhaps the gun will end the horror that
ruined our lives.
    Also in the bag is the whole story of Bong Sat. You deserve to know
what happened. Marcus says he had the chance to kill Ferry soon as their
chopper hit the ground. He failed and everything else followed.
    At Bong Sat I couldn't stop Ferry's evil from killing my Marines.
You will find the names of my dead in the bag. They, like you, need more
respect than I gave them. I beseech you to make my amends the best way
you can. When Nathan Ferry lies dying, you tell him the ghosts of Bong
Sat are waiting.
    Amos, there is no right or wrong. Only what must be done. You
remember that.
    Do not trust Marcus. He will tell you anything to get what he wants.
    Use my purple bag to get Ferry. Do not let Marcus have it. It belongs
to the memories of my Marines, the ones who died because of him. Use
your smooth running brain to find it.
    Shed no tears for me. I am better off dead be it heaven or hell or the
worms. The two best things that ever happened to me were your mother
and you.

Your father,
Captain Matthew Eliot, USMC

Steerman's hands shook as he read the letter. Under no
condition should Amos see what his father had written. Steerman
couldn't believe Matt had spelled out his failure for the boy, but
the letter also placed the balancing of the scales squarely on
Amos. He picked up the gun that had killed Frank McBride and
marveled at its existence. He didn't know Matt had kept it. He
wondered what Matt envisioned Amos would do with it. He
returned the letter to its envelope and placed it in the box. Before
leaving the repository, Marcus removed the Caldwell name and

changed his name on the account. He also changed the password and recorded the new information in his notebook.

The next day Marcus drove to Laughland Valley. He stopped at Clyde's store and broke the news of Matt's death.

"Does Amos know?" Clyde asked.

"No. How is he?"

"Fine as far as I know. I deliver every other week. Even figure out what he needs since his communication skills are pretty close to zero." Clyde shook his head. "Damn! I'm sorry about Matt. There hadn't been any good times since Jessie died. When she did I thought he'd go straight to hell, but he pulled back. We can thank Amos for that. What's going to happen to the boy? He's damn near a train wreck now."

"It's way too late to send him to a regular school with other kids."

"You talking about leaving him?"

"I'm going to ask him what he wants and if that's it, so be it. If he stays, I'll let you know. I hope we can keep the arrangement."

"Is he a genius?"

"I don't know. He could be."

"You wouldn't believe all the magazines I get for him. Electronics, mainly, but lots of mechanical stuff. Gets a Granger catalogue every time it comes out." Clyde reached under the counter and came up with four corrugated mailing tubes. "Might as well take them. If I read all this stuff, I'd be too damn smart to run the store. Probably just as well I don't."

"Do you see Amos?"

"Not often. I spend time with him when I can. Sometimes he forgets to talk out loud, and I remind him. Make things a damn sight easier if you put a phone out there."

Communication was near the top of Steerman's agenda. The problem was not calling attention to Laughland.

"When I leave, I'll stop by."

"I ain't going nowhere."

As Marcus headed for the door, Clyde said, "I was wrong what I said about Matt. It wasn't losing Jessie. After that Goddamn war he didn't know how to get what he wanted."

Steerman waited for more, one hand on the door knob.

"He only knew how to be a Marine. The Marine died at Bong Sat. Now you want to leave his boy out there alone."

Steerman found nothing to say and opened the door.

"I was you, showing up near dark," Clyde said, "I'd take Amos a bag of suckers."

He parked his car at the bottom of the hill, and walked into Laughland. He saw the house Matt had lived in. Beyond the house were the original clapboard shacks. He stood in plain sight with his hands in the air, one of them holding his hat and the other the bag of suckers.

"Amos! My name is Marcus. I have news of your father."

The shadows grew longer as his arms grew heavy. He had not known a silence as deep since his last visit. When the voice came from behind him, he jumped.

"I know who you are," Amos said.

Having the boy behind him made him nervous.

"I'm afraid I have bad news."

"My father is dead," Amos said.

"Yes. I'm sorry." Steerman waved the hand with the suckers. "Clyde said you'd like these."

He waited but there was no response.

"Amos? Please, we need to talk. You are in danger here. I want to help you."

Steerman worked up his nerve and turned. No Amos. He saw no way for the boy to disappear, but he had. He walked back to the car where he wrapped himself in a coat. Sleep came and went. As the moonlight slowly tracked across the valley, he had an idea.

Shortly after dawn, he again stood on the valley floor.

"I mean you no harm," he called. "You are a fearsome, mysterious figure to the outside world. You have an alter ego called The Diemaker. A reporter for a magazine gave you the name."

Marcus waited for a sign.

"The Diemaker name came after the fourth victim. Did you know that precise acts of violence are the most terrifying? A doctor wrote a book about The Diemaker and how his targets could do nothing to avoid their deaths. What impressed the FBI and the Secret Service the most was The Diemaker killed only the intended victim. No bystanders. Between the exploding cufflinks, the hearing aids, and the dress shirt that strangled the victim, you put a real crimp in formal dinners. There were even jokes on television. Why did you decide to use clothing items as murder weapons."

"I knew they would be used."

Again the voice startled him. Steerman turned and saw Amos holding a large dark blue umbrella over his head, and wearing a broad brimmed, black slouch hat with a black cape that nearly touched the ground.

"I have a message for you from my father."

"A message?"

"He knew you would come when he was dead."

Amos's voice broke, but Steerman doubted from emotion.

"He called you a reaper. You harvest dead people."

"Was that the whole message?"

"No. 'My death is now final.' That is the message."

"I see. I'm sorry."

"Don't say that. No one has believed you for many years."

Steerman's nervousness increased. "Are you angry?"

"Why are you frightened of me?"

"Because you might be mad from the last time I was here."

"I wasn't mad you at then. You said I have an alter ego called The Diemaker. I don't know what that means."

"Yes. The Diemaker. A die maker is someone who fabricates shapes. In your case death."

"Is an alter ego someone other than who you really are?"

"Yes,"

"What if you don't know who you are? Does that count?"

"No," Steerman whispered, "it doesn't count."

If Steerman's resolve to carry on ever weakened, these last few moments would bolster him.

"The Diemaker." The voice broke again. "I like the name."

"Why are you holding an umbrella?" Steerman asked, eager to change the subject.

"I don't like daylight."

"Then invite me in. There is much I want to talk to you about."

"Why would I want to talk with you? My parents are dead because of you."

"Amos, your mother's death was an accident that had nothing to do with me. Well, almost nothing. She was where she was because your father survived the war and I am responsible for that. I could have let him die at Bong Sat but then you would never have known your father. Even with all that has happened, I think you're better off for knowing him. I was an orphan. I know what it means to have no parents. Your life may be tough. So was mine."

Marcus watched the boy for a reaction, but Amos stood as still as a statue, the umbrella steady over his head.

"Why would I want to talk to you?" the boy asked again.

"I pay for the groceries you eat and the land you live on. What I don't buy directly, I provide the money for. Your father and I were partners. It wasn't easy, and we weren't happy, but he was my friend and I'll bet I've shed more tears over him than you have. With him dead, what shall we do now?"

Time passed in silence. The umbrella slipped lower in Amos's hands until it appeared the spokes rested on his hat.

"I had a friend," Amos said. "He died with my mother. I still see him. We talk. I loved him. I drew a picture of him. It upset my mom that I drew the picture of him instead of my dad. I don't know what I felt for my father."

"Your father and I tried to protect the people who are important to us and failed. Because we failed, our secret became the most important thing in our lives. The day will come when I will need your help. Until then I can help you survive. But now I'm very tired and very thirsty so if you don't invite me in I will leave you on your own."

"Then you can come in after you swear an oath of secrecy."

"Oath of secrecy?"

"Not to tell anyone about Amos's Underground."

If there had been any doubt as to whether Amos was a genius, it vanished in Steerman's first minutes below the surface. Each room centered around a motif. The most elaborate motifs were in the work rooms, where instead of greasy work benches Steerman saw rectory tables free of clutter.

"*Alice in Wonderland's* first name was *Alice's Adventures Underground,*" Amos said, as he led Marcus through the tunnels.

In one work room, the table lay set with six settings each with a white plastic chair. Each setting had a tea cup on a saucer, and at least one spent sucker stick with traces of color embedded in the stick. Steerman walked around the table and saw each saucer had its own color. The most sticks showed traces of purple, while yellow ran a distant second.

"The Mad Hatter's Tea Party?"

"The Mad Sucker Party," Amos answered, his voice cracked, he cleared his throat, and said, "What's 'mad?'"

"Mad is a mental instability," Steerman said, as they walked back into the hallway. The Underground was the collision of a child with his adolescence that shuttled his approaching adulthood onto a siding.

In the next work room, track lighting coolly lit the space. Steerman saw a maze of tangled electrical wires, circuit boards, and exotically shaped components he didn't recognize. Schematics lay draped over many of the benches. A chair on castors sat parked at one of the work benches near stacks of electronics magazines.

"Clyde sent more magazines," Steerman said.

"Yea! Where are they?" Amos jumped up and down. "Come on! Where?"

"In my bag."

"Yea!" Amos yelled, as he ran out.

On the bench, Steerman saw a small television connected to a box with three tape players wired together. A thick manual lay open in front of the assembly. He poured over the manual and the contraption comparing what he saw on the table with what he saw in the book.

"No! No! Don't touch anything!" Amos yelled as he returned with the magazines still in their shipping tubes.

Steerman backed away with his hands in the air. "You're building a computer?"

"Yes, but mine will be better. They," Amos pointed at the manual, "aren't very smart. Soon I can build a really good one. You know what a modem is? You use the phone for talking to other computers. I need a phone."

"There are many things you need. May I make a suggestion?"

"Okay, what?"

"I would like to shower and change clothes. I'm hungry, too. Let me clean up and eat, and then we can talk."

"Cleanliness is next to Godliness. My mom said that, even though she did not believe in God. My dad said that if you live clean you live longer. He was clean and he didn't live longer."

An hour later Steerman sat in the kitchen eating a bologna sandwich on white bread with lots of yellow mustard, and a snack pack of potato chips with a Twinkie chaser. A folded napkin sat to the left of the sparkling clean melamine plate. A knife and fork he probably wouldn't use were equally clean.

Steerman guessed Amos at about five foot nine and overweight. He wasn't fat like a round person, but rather a thin person who carried too much weight. His fair hair grew over his collar. Steerman guessed his father had cut his hair, and he added that detail to his Amos Worry List. The boy had blue eyes and pale skin be-speckled with acne. It wasn't to a point where it would scar, but if it got much worse it would.

"Amos?" The boy sat across from him reading *Popular Mechanics*. "There are things to talk about. Changes are coming."

Amos ignored him. Steerman reached across the table and pulled the magazine away. Amos yelped.

"I forgot you're real," he said.

"What do you mean?"

"I'm not always alone. Ghosts."

"Ghosts of whom?"

"Bill, usually. My mom. Do you think my dad will visit?"

"Do you?"

"No. He didn't like being alive."

"So you believe in life after death."

"I believe in what I see. What do you believe?"

"I don't believe in religion."

"What's religion?"

129

"A religion, and there are many, is a system of beliefs that includes an entity or entities greater than a mortal human."

"Like God."

"Yes, although God has many names."

"My mom said if there was a God it did a piss poor job of taking care of the world. Is piss a swear word?"

"No, piss is not a swear word. Do you believe in God?"

"You didn't answer my question. Is there more to religion than a god?"

"Yes. The problem with religions is not what they believe, but the people who practice them. Some of the most devout live in religious orders. Most people who say they know what God wants, only want power over you. If you want to know what they know you have to do what they say."

"Is that why they call God 'father'? My father said if I wanted to do what I wanted, I would have to do what he wanted first."

"I don't know. Maybe it is. I've never thought of it like that."

"What are religious orders? Who gives them?"

"Orders are groups of people, usually men, who believe the same doctrine. Doctrine can be narrowly defined as a collection of rules. You might actually fit in to some orders. They live secluded, regimented lives as they practice their beliefs."

"I believe in what I can touch," Amos said. He held his hands up and his fingers flew. "Did you know I have special hands?"

If Steerman attempted to do what he had just seen, his fingers would look slow, stiff, and clumsy.

"I would love to visit with you for hours, Amos, but there are things we have to talk about."

Amos started reading again. It was like throwing a switch. Steerman no longer existed. Marcus slowly reached across the table, pushed the magazine a few inches to the side, then laid his fingers gently on Amos's arm.

"I am here, I am real, and I can't go until we talk. Please pay attention. Amos, are you good at math?"

"I am very smart."

"Yes, I know, but you might be smart at only one or two things and know nothing about everything else."

"There's a name for that isn't there? Savant?"

He pronounced it with a short "a."

"Yes. Savant." Marcus repeated the word with a long 'a.' "Do you know about money?"

"I said I am very smart."

"I don't know what you are smart about."

"Money is what we give Clyde. Everything has a price. You add up all the prices and that's how much money to give him. See? Money."

"How much money is a lot?"

"Enough to buy everything I want." He held up the magazine. "There are lots of things I want."

"What stops you from buying them?"

"Time. It takes time to build things. Will I make more Diemaker things?"

"Do you know why you made Diemaker things?"

"Dad and I had a problem that needed a solution so I made them."

"What problem?"

"After Mom was killed, Dad said we had to protect ourselves. We were partners."

Steerman heard Matt's words and way of speaking flowing out of his son's mouth. He found it unsettling.

"He picked the targets and you made the weapons."

"Yes," Amos said. "Tell me about The Diemaker."

"The Diemaker remains a mystery. He – you – was responsible for at least eleven deaths. The Diemaker had an air of calculated inevitability where the victim became the walking dead. That scared the hell out of people who thought someone might want to kill them. The Italian guy, the one killed by his comb, started the scare. If a comb could kill, anything could and no one felt safe. People went to extraordinary lengths to protect themselves. They paid more attention to *things* than *people*, but nothing stopped The Diemaker."

Marcus felt sure Amos had never connected the death of a human with each problem his father presented. He wondered how the boy perceived the act of murder.

"The Diemaker never gave warnings. Some victims bragged they were beyond reach. Many died in public and in agony. A psychologist said a messy death in public is something most humans fear the way they fear being eaten by a wild animal. Whose idea was The Diemaker, yours or Matt's?"

"We tried his ideas, but I told him they wouldn't work."

"Why wouldn't they work?"

"They were not elegant solutions."

"What do you mean elegant?" Marcus asked, thinking of the letter in the safe deposit box.

"Elegant solutions to fixing machines or killing critters always come down to Fuel, Air, and Water. You have to fix what's broken without breaking something else. When you do, it's elegant. It's harder than it sounds. Bill told me all about elegant."

"What did he say?"

"That only the real smart ones can do elegant. My father said I could find the elegant solution to anything."

Marcus thrilled at Amos's explanation. Maybe Ferry would pay after all.

"I don't understand the fuel, air, and water," he said.

"Easy. To fix a machine, give it all three. To kill a critter, take one away. Very simple. Very elegant."

Steerman suspected Amos included humans with the critters.

"What do you know of morality?" Steerman asked.

"What is it?"

"Simply put, it is right and wrong."

"Right and wrong belong to other people. What I have to do is survive. When I'm done living, then I can think about right and wrong."

Steerman didn't think Matt had ever phrased his life that succinctly, but that was the way he had lived and died.

"There are a great many books written about what you said," Steerman said. "Life is more complicated than any absolute."

"Why are you telling me this?"

"To know what you know. Change is coming."

"I don't like change."

"Another element of life we can't always control. You have done far better than most."

"I want to stay in Amos's Underground and build elegant."

By all means, Marcus thought. For the next two hours Marcus talked and Amos listened as long as Steerman talked about what interested him.

Questions about life on the surface usually came down to Clyde, who held an almost God-like station. The return of the carnival made no difference because Clyde would continue to come and bring Amos what he wanted. Steerman asked if he ever got lonely, and from his reaction Marcus decided loneliness, like The Diemaker, no longer existed.

"Amos, your father did not die by accident."

"The Enemies killed him and my mom and Bill."

"That's what we must believe. There can be no indication above ground that Laughland is inhabited. Phone lines, power lines, people coming and going all need explanations. Do you have any ideas?" Amos said nothing, so Steerman continued. "Laughland will need a caretaker. We can't leave it unattended, can we."

"Clyde!"

"Yes, Clyde."

"Great idea!"

"We can make Clyde a watchman."

"He's already my guardian."

"Well, then, maybe he can stay until you're ready to live above ground."

Amos shook his head.

"I don't go up."

"You did when I got here."

"I had to."

"You would live the rest of your life down here?"

"Yes!"

"It is a very large world, Amos. There is much to see and do."

"I live inside." He tapped his head. "I have everything I need and Clyde will bring more."

"What if the enemies come?"

The question seemed to surprise Amos.

"Why would they?"

"I don't know, but I believe it's possible." Steerman leaned back in his chair. As he did, he felt Amos's attention drift away.

Reality, to Amos, had to be within arm's reach, so again he took the boy's hands. "I want you to be content. If staying here does that, then so be it. But, you must promise me if I learn you are in danger, or if Clyde becomes convinced there is danger, you must leave."

Amos yanked his hand away, and leaped to his feet. The boy could go from dead still to full tilt instantly.

"How would I survive up there?"

"I can't tell you," Steerman said, then motioned for him to sit and take his hands. "You will have to make a plan and be ready. When that day comes, tell Clyde where you're going, and I will help."

"Are there more fallout shelters?"

"Not as nice or as big but there are places underground. There are underground houses or cave houses built into the side of a mountain where only the front has windows."

"No windows."

"Fine, no windows."

"I don't want that day to come. I never want to leave."

Steerman let go of the hands. Oh, yes, the day will come and he could hardly wait.

1983

They

Not long after Clyde assumed the role of caretaker he closed the store and moved into the house where Matt had lived. Steerman said it was to keep an eye on things and to help Amos prepare for the day he would have to leave Laughland either because Ferry would find him – in Clyde's opinion more an Eliot family myth than reality – or because it was neither human nor healthy for the boy to spend his life in a hole.

As for Ferry, Clyde thought it remotely possible he looked for Amos because The Diemaker killed two of his goons, but doubted the guy really cared about some vague threat that only killed other people. The second reason, Amos's health, Clyde took as his responsibility. The boy's diet of mostly suckers, Spam sandwiches, and Twinkies found him in sorry shape. Clyde told Amos once the only green he ate was mold.

"I'm not exactly Betty Crocker," Clyde told him, "but I know enough you might malnutrition yourself to death. I'm going to put fresh vegetables in the grocery box and you damn well better eat them."

The first couple of weeks of this new regimen saw the broccoli and lettuce wilt either on the counter or at the back of the fridge. Catching Amos face to face always presented a challenge, so Clyde called into the depths of the Underground that he'd left fresh vegetables on the counter and not much else. Two days later he went back. The veggies sat right where he'd left them and looked none too appetizing. He figured Amos had a stash, a habit formed back in the bivouac days.

Amos had no other way to get food, so Clyde waited him out. Then Clyde's own supply of goodies took a hit.

"Lesson learned," he muttered, and moved his food, other than vegetables, to a fridge in the storage shed with a lock. Amos picked the lock and cleaned it out.

"Goddamn," Clyde muttered, "he thinks it's a game."

Clyde made the trip to restock, but bought only enough for himself for a couple of days. Two nights later, Clyde sat in waiting. About three a.m. Amos showed up with a flashlight and his toolkit. Clyde watched as Amos started to pull the pins on the hinges.

"Goddamn," Clyde thought, and waited until Amos started to lift the door off.

"Nutrition is no game, son. You need the right food. You ever hear of brain food?"

Amos did not jump. He stopped and turned to look at Clyde, then flipped on the overhead lights.

"No. There's no such thing."

"How do you know? You don't know a damn thing about nutrition."

"Maybe, but there's no such thing as brain food."

"I'll make you a deal. I'll bring you an article on general nutrition and one on nutrition for better mental health. You see for yourself. Then after you've read it, you eat what I bring you. Deal?"

"Can I have some suckers?"

"Yeah. For now. But in a week or so you better hope they make broccoli flavored suckers, or they're a thing of the past."

Clyde got the magazines on his next trip to the city. He read them first and wondered how he was going to get enough fish down that boy when there wasn't a fresh one for fifty miles. Good thing tuna came in cans. When he finished his reading, he left them in the kitchen for Amos.

Within a week Amos demanded more "brain food." That meant more eggs and less sugar, both of which suited Clyde just fine, and he promised Amos he would buy omega-3 supplements the next time he did the shopping.

In the next few weeks, sharing dinner became common place. Vegetables and other fresh foods needed the right preparation, meaning cooking, and Amos didn't know how. He liked tuna casserole enough to learn how to fix it himself.

Eating right was half the problem.

"How you going to keep that smooth running brain healthy if you smother it in fat?" Clyde asked.

"There's no fat up there," Amos said, pointing at his head.

Clyde threw some more magazines on the table and said, "Read these."

Two nights later when Amos came in for dinner, he said, "I need to exercise."

He placed a picture of a gym layout on the table and said, "That one."

Clyde got Steerman to spring for the gym gear and together Clyde and Amos set up a workout room in the Underground.

When the exercise program began, Amos became compulsive. He demanded more books and magazines on nutrition and exercise, and even got into body building. Next Clyde talked to him about balance in his life. Amos ignored him and just kept on exercising and lifting weights. He wore out a treadmill in less than three months. When the new one came he rebuilt the motor to turn the belt faster, then ordered a belt that would last longer. Next he wanted sun lamps for Vitamin C. When they came he attached them to an arc-shaped frame so the lights tracked across the ceiling like the sun travels across the sky. Clyde didn't know if Amos did it because he could or if he thought it was the best way. It sure as hell wasn't because he missed the outdoors.

Because Amos only slept a few hours each day, it gave him time to indulge his compulsiveness. He told Clyde he didn't sleep more than about four hours out of every twenty-four, and rarely more than ninety minutes at a time. The combination of compulsive behaviors, not sleeping, and his generous aptitudes, gave Amos a prodigious output. His interests encompassed everything mechanical. He didn't care about the arts other than his own drawings of stars and rockets which he kept making on the ceilings and walls of the underground and which seemed incongruous with the rest of his pursuits.

"What's with the space travel theme?" Clyde asked, after helping Amos clean the kitchen and bathroom. General sanitization had slipped since other compulsions forced it out of Amos's list of priorities.

"Why?"

"You seem to have jumped over something between the Underground and outer space."

"What?"

"Where damn near every other human lives."

"Oh. Nothing there interests me."

"How do you know? You've never seen it."

When Amos burnt out the second treadmill, Clyde brought up the outdoors again suggesting he run on the surface of the planet. The idea met with silence.

"Amos, you can't spend your life down here."

"Why not?"

"You know why. We've had this discussion a hundred times. It's a big world and you've got a lot to offer."

"What's that mean?"

"The world would be damn glad to have you and that brain of yours."

"That's flattery, isn't it? Flattery means you say something nice so I'll do what you want. I only do what *I* want, Clyde."

"Why won't you go out?"

"I don't like it."

"Why? It remind you of bivouac?"

Amos's face turned red, he balled his fists, and he screamed. "Get out! Get out of Amos's Underground world!"

He picked up a book to throw. Clyde was glad they were in the library and not the kitchen where he could have found something more lethal. Clyde pointed his finger in Amos's face.

"You stop right there, young man!" Amos threw the book. He missed high and wide which Clyde took to mean Amos's heart wasn't in hitting him. Clyde pushed harder. "You are a spoiled brat, boy! Spoiled!"

Amos reached for another book.

"Go ahead and throw it, but don't miss this time. Either have the nerve to do it right, or put it down. Before you make up your mind though, listen. Because of me, you get every damn thing you ask for. You get to stay down this damn hole and pretend you're king of the world. What would you be king of if I weren't here?"

"You wouldn't leave Laughland," Amos said, making it as much a question as a statement.

"I would. I would because I am just as guilty as you are. You are a wonder boy. You got a miracle for a life, and it's slipping by while you hide from your own shadow." Clyde walked closer and held his arms open. "You have the kind of brain that can work anywhere. Most folks, their brains work just fine in their own little world, but take them somewhere else, they do poorly. If you gave yours a chance you'd see I know what I'm saying."

Amos put the book down, but the angry look remained.

"I got no family," Clyde said. "Nobody, but you. Don't know much about love either, but I have to say I love you. I ain't your dad, but I was proud to step in when offered the chance. But if I let you stay in this Goddamn hole, I'm letting him, your mother, and most of all, you, down. No sir."

Clyde dropped his arms, but kept his eyes on Amos.

"An anywhere brain?" Amos asked, the anger draining away and replaced with the look Clyde recognized as the one he used when entranced by a new idea.

"That's what you got."

1985

Clyde and Amos

One night nearly two years later, Amos came into Clyde's kitchen and sat at the table. Clyde put more food on the counter and started changing dinner for one into dinner for two.

"What's the difference between right and wrong?" Amos asked.

Clyde kept at his chopping until he said, "Right and wrong's a moving target. Sort of depends on who wants to know and why? You?"

"Yes. My father told me right and wrong doesn't apply to me."

"Seems I remember hearing that. You believe him?"

"He said the day I start worrying about right and wrong is the day I start to die."

Clyde put his knife down and leaned a hip against the counter top. "How do you feel about that?"

"If I stay here I don't have to feel about it."

"So the underground is a hideout."

"No, it's where I want to be, but I don't have to think about right or wrong either."

"Everybody has to wrestle with right and wrong. Don't think that your weird upbringing got you off the duty roster on that one. Right and wrong is totally dependent on how bad you want something and what you're willing to do to get it. There are a whole bunch of fancy words to put a different spin on it, but that's what it always comes down to. You don't want to die. You will defend yourself. That's what most people would do. You're just better prepared to do the protecting."

"It's a hideout, son," Clyde said, as he turned the fire off under the pan, "because every day in your life is pretty much the same and completely under your control."

"I like it that way."

"I know, but that ain't the way of the world. Change and the unexpected makes you faster on your feet and faster in the brain. You learn how to prioritize. Some right and wrongs are no big deal. Choosing comes easy. Others are harder. Ferry comes at you and it's kill or be killed, right and wrong get pretty blurry. That would be true for anyone. How come you want to talk about this? The Diemaker?"

Amos dropped his fork. "You know?"

"Helping you shape charges of Semtex down to a gram and reading about that guy getting blown apart makes the one plus one pretty easy."

"You asked my dad."

"I did, and you may recall I didn't help you anymore."

"I didn't ask."

"Okay, but I wouldn't have helped if you had. What you guys were doing was wrong. He told me you didn't know how The Diemaker things were used and against whom, but you ain't no dummy. How did you feel killing people?"

"I didn't know them."

"That is so wrong, since we're talking about right and wrong."

Amos pushed his plate aside and clasped his hands together.

"Yes, I know that. Now. I'm not a kid anymore so I think for myself, but I don't know many of the answers."

"I'm sorry to tell you those answers ain't going to find you down here."

"I'm not leaving. How much bigger am I than when I was a kid?"

Amos had changed the subject. Clyde knew the futility of pursuing a conversation if Amos didn't want to talk about it.

"A helluva lot bigger than you were when you drove the Dodge down to the store."

"I wouldn't need the driving gear, would I?"

"Nope. I figure you're six foot. Weight? I don't know. You want some scales?"

"No. I don't need to know. Just tell me what you think."

"I'd guess a very solid two hundred pounds. Why?"

Amos looked at himself. He exhibited no pride as he rippled the muscles in his chest and shoulders.

"You were right about a healthy body building a healthy mind. I'm smarter now than when I ate Twinkies and suckers. I kind of miss the suckers, though."

"You can have one every now and then. You know where they are." Clyde finished dicing and slicing and put the pan on the stove again.

"Marcus was here," he said, while he poured oil into the pan.

"You give him my list?"

"I did. He doesn't even ask what you want all this stuff for anymore. He just looks at it and nods. I added some stuff."

Amos stopped flexing. "What?"

"Identity papers. Two sets with driver's license, credit cards, and passports."

"Clyde, you can forget it. I'm not leaving here. Not now and not later."

"What are you going to do if They come?"

"There is no They. It's a boogeyman to scare me."

"Who's trying to scare you? Me?"

Amos went to the drawer with the suckers and sorted them until he found a purple one.

"You think your dad lied to you to scare you? Was The Diemaker a trick to get you to do what he wanted? *They* are going to come. There are people out there looking for you. I don't know how hard, but since The Diemaker, and killing your dad, they are there. But if they don't find you, somebody else will. The sad part is they won't even be looking for you."

"I don't get it," Amos said.

"What are you going to do when I die?"

"You aren't going to die.

"Not tomorrow, but I am going to die. Then what? Who's going to bring food and guard the carnival?"

"Marcus won't let me stay here alone.""

Amos finished the first sucker and reached for another. Clyde saw his anxiety when he took the first one he touched.

"Why not? Why do you think he watches out and buys all the stuff you want?"

"Because he owes it to me."

"He owes you nothing. Marcus Steerman is like you, he only does what he wants. He keeps you in gadgets and grits because someday he's going to have you kill Nathan Ferry. He doesn't have the balls to do it himself. Maybe that's okay. Killing that son of a bitch might actually be too good for the man who ruined so many lives. But if you can't come out of this damn hole, Steerman will see you are of no use. He won't provide any more money. Then what?"

"We have lots of Diemaker money."

"But you won't have me to get it or what it can buy. Down here you are the invisible man and you know what happened to the invisible man when he crossed the street."

"What ?"

"He got run over."

"That's because he went outside."

"You're missing the point. The world is changing. This land has water and sooner or later someone will want it. Steerman is the registered agent and he'll get an offer. I'll be dead and buried, and you'll be alive and buried, so he'll think what the hell, and sell. *They* are coming, and as long as you're afraid of outside you ain't got much to look forward to."

Amos finished the sucker and his fingers started moving faster.

"I'm not afraid."

"Yes, you are, and don't throw a fit."

"I don't throw fits! Don't say that."

"Don't raise your voice."

Amos turned to leave the room.

"You walk out, I'm gone," Clyde said. "I wasn't kidding about letting you and your folks down."

Amos stopped in the doorway. A minute passed while Clyde watched his back. It didn't quiver. It didn't move at all.

"My own way, Clyde." Amos turned to face Clyde. "I'll figure it out, but please don't yell at me again. Remember when you said you loved me?"

"I do."

"I love you, too. I loved my mom and Bill, and I guess my dad, although I'm not sure. I love you because you are here. You care enough that you would go away from me to help." Amos wrung his hands. "I don't want to leave. There is no one anywhere else I know. I believed you when you said I had an anywhere brain, but other places are scary. Worst of all, none of them have you."

Clyde felt the moisture on his face. He reached across the table and took Amos's hands. The boy looked at him.

"I promise you, Amos, if you leave I will be here when you come back."

"That's a real promise?"

"As real as it gets. If I'm alive and if Marcus doesn't sell Laughland, I will be here. I promise."

They sat in silence, and Clyde tried to think of a time in his life when he faced a more difficult path. He didn't want to be lonely any more than Amos did.

"If you had some identity papers, you could start building legends, you know what a legend is?"

Amos shook his head.

"It's a secret identity only you and the people you trust know. You wouldn't be Amos Eliot, you could be anybody you wanted."

"But Clyde, my brain doesn't work outside."

"How come?"

"I don't know."

"What do you guess?" Clyde asked.

"Everything I want is in the Underground."

"What about the carousel?"

143

"Yeah, but it has a hat."

"So you don't like the sky."

Amos shrugged again.

"I'd be lying to you if I said there was an easy answer," Clyde said. "The only way it will get better is enduring it. Most people couldn't live in the Underground. They'd get what's called cabin fever. Sort of the flip side of you."

"There is no way to leave without going outside."

"You're this way because of what happened to you, not because it was the way you were born. Make some new happenings, and you'll change for the better."

Amos thought about it with his head down, then met Clyde's eyes.

"*They* is me," he said.

Months went by, but Clyde knew Amos worked on the problem as the compulsive behaviors disappeared and more measured and diverse activities took their place. He saw evidence of Amos in places around Laughland he'd never noticed them before. Alterations in several of the rides, not their movement, but their frame defied explanation. Several other places Clyde saw stakes hammered into the ground. One day Clyde found Amos sitting on his golden palomino, Streaker. His feet nearly touched the ground. It was the first time Clyde had seen him in over a week.

"What is a safe deposit box?" the boy asked.

"A place where people keep important papers and valuables. Why?"

"Is the Stardust a place?"

"There's a Stardust casino in Las Vegas."

"Do they have safe deposit boxes?"

"Could. You gonna tell me what this is about?"

"No. Tell Marcus I want two more identity sets. Do you know what I'll need to change them?"

"You mean paper or pens, or what?"

"I don't want Marcus to know my secret names. And I'll need money, too."

"Okay."

"Turn the horses on, please. Clyde, I'm sorry not telling you my whys."

Clyde didn't see Amos much after that. After Steerman sent the identity sets, Clyde got what Amos had requested and left it in the Underground.

One day, a few months later, it occurred to him Amos was gone. He looked through the Underground, mindful of not getting lost, and finally looked on the tool bench of the work room with the most recent copies of *Popular Mechanics*. He pushed things around and found an envelope with his name on the front. He read the letter. Amos was gone, but he would be back. Perhaps it would be years, but he would be back. Clyde turned the page to his to do list. He smiled. He would be busy..

PART III: HELL

1986-1989

Nathan:

After all these years I believe in very little. Not religion, not government. The priests denied me one, and you the other. I have learned both are constructs empowering the few to control the many. Now I look for the way for the one – me – to control the few – you and yours. I have a plan now. I will stop you without firing a shot, well, maybe one. I will give you a clue: What do Maine, Louisiana, Colorado, and Montana have in common with the timely (for you) death of a Minnesota congressman?

What you are doing is not new, but it is audacious. Your attempt to gain simultaneous control of the world's five strongest economies is bold

145

even by your standards. Are you surprised I've foreseen your play? I'm sure you remember Frank McBride. I found his paper at Yale. The paper that foresaw your plan and sealed his fate. He called it Four Justifications for War in Southeast Asia. You no doubt know that, since I can find no copy other than the one I uncovered. The paper is brilliant, and that's not my opinion alone. I've shown it around. Did you know that? If you didn't, you must question the quality of the people you have looking for me. Perhaps, like with Eliot, you aren't looking at all.

As always in my annual report, I state my return on investment earned on the money I stole from you almost twenty years ago. The money did well with all the emerging technologies. (It amuses my sense of irony to invest in the very technologies you plan to employ.) I could have done better, but you know how conservative I am. My ROI was 17%.

This remains the one time a year I tell the truth.

Yours in perfidy,
Marcus

1986

Prison

On October 2, 1986, not long after darkness and under a full moon, Amos Eliot walked away from Laughland. He carried papers identifying him as John Patrick Nelson, an alias known to no one, and a backpack with three quart bottles of water, a change of both underwear and socks, and his handmade miniature tool set. He walked nineteen miles in less than six hours. He reached Highway 62 with three hours of darkness remaining, and since the prospect of standing under the sun surrounded by wind and highway noise frightened him, he decided to hitchhike while he walked despite the dark. As the sky started to show color, he saw a big truck along the road with its engine bonnet raised. The driver stood by the front bumper thumping his hand with a long-handled flashlight.

"If you got tools," Amos said, "I can help."

"What makes you think so?" the driver asked. "You ain't even looked."

"I can fix anything. After I fix it, will you give me a ride to Las Vegas?"

"I got tools, but I ain't going to Vegas. Make you a deal. You help me out, I'll make sure you get there."

Thirty minutes later, Amos sat in the front seat while the driver listened to the smooth purr of the engine.

"I'll be damned," the driver said.

"Best part is the purr."

The driver pulled the big rig out on to the highway and shifted carefully up through the gears until he reached cruising speed.

"I have never seen hands move as fast as yours," he said. "How do you do that?"

"A friend said my fingers are wired with high test."

The driver looked at Amos out of the corner of his eye.

"A guy I know in Modesto could use you. He's got a repair business."

"No, thank you. There are things you should do to make your truck run better."

Amos told him what they were and the driver said he'd never heard of such things, but he'd do them.

Soon their road met an Interstate highway. Amos saw lots of lights and parked trucks at a fueling station with a café where the driver bought Amos breakfast. The driver also asked around and found a truck headed for Las Vegas. As Amos left with his new ride, he saw the man talking to several others. From what he saw, he felt sure they talked about his hands.

As the sun came out, Amos felt the oppressive weight of day. The driver didn't have much to say, instead he listened to music on a dashboard tape machine. Amos had heard very little music other than organ music on the carousel. He didn't like this, whatever it was, but he was glad to have it to divert his attention. When the truck stopped on the outskirts of Las Vegas at a truck plaza with a motel and a café, Amos rented a room. He slept, left the motel at midnight, and walked into the artificial lights of the city. He asked directions and soon found the Stardust where he went to the safe deposit box repository.

More than Clyde's insisting he leave the underground, the contents of the box motivated Amos. When Steerman came to tell him of his father's death, Amos searched Steerman's bag for the magazines Clyde had sent, and found a notebook. Later, while Steerman slept, Amos took the book and read it. He found the name and password Steerman used at the Stardust. and even though the boy didn't know what all the entrees in Steerman's book meant, he deduced the safe deposit box most likely held the deed to Laughland Valley.

"My father has a box here," he said, standing at the window to the repository. "He is in the hospital. He sent me to get papers from the box, but I don't know what to do."

The attendant laughed.

"If your name isn't on the account there's no way you're getting in. Your father should know that."

"I know the number and the code," Amos said.

"No matter. Your name has to be on the account."

"Okay. How can he put my name on it? He's very sick and can't come here."

"He should have planned ahead. Most accounts have two names so the other person can get in."

"Maybe there are. Would you look?"

"What's the name?"

"Delbert Pickens."

Amos told him the number, and the man said he would check. He came back shaking his head.

"That's the only name."

Amos thanked him and waited for a shift change. When a different person came on, he went back and told the man he wanted into box 285557, signed a card using Steerman's false name, and was admitted. In the viewing room, he opened the heavy box. On top were papers and beneath them he saw a gun in a plastic bag sitting on a film canister labeled BONG SAT. He set the papers and gun aside and used both hands to remove the canister sealed with duct tape. Next he held the gun up to the light and saw rust and sand on the metal.

He turned his attention to the papers, and smiled when he found the deed to Laughland. He read the document and learned upon his father's death the land reverted entirely to Steerman. The next set of papers said Laughland was owned by a Canadian company. He was too late. He forced himself to read on and almost cried with relief when he saw the real owner of the Canadian company was Steerman. There were other legal documents regarding the partnership between his father and Steerman he didn't understand beyond knowing Marcus

Steerman, with these papers, controlled his future. In the bottom was a bound paper called *Four Justifications for War in Southeast Asia*. He set all the paper and the gun on the film canister.

Finally, he looked at the front of a white envelope with instructions that in the case of his father's death the envelope be given to Amos. Steerman had opened it. Amos read the one page letter.

Even though his father told him not to, Amos cried. He wiped the tears, read the letter again, and understood why Marcus had not given it to him. He then reread the part about the elegant solution to Nathan Ferry. To find it he would have to live above ground with people. He would also need his father's purple bag. He looked at the bound paper again and saw the name of the author. Frank McBride. The same name as in the letter.

He sat in the viewing room considering what he must do, then rang for the assistant.

"Do you care what name I use to open another box?"

"No, sir."

Thirty minutes later, Amos rented a box under an assumed name. He back-dated the rental papers two months. The new box held the tool kit, the film canister, the gun, and the deed. After returning the box, he left the Stardust and went to the library. He read about crime and punishment and prisons. After two hours of reading, he left the library, walked three blocks and held up a convenience store. He did it badly and two hours later sat in jail. Booking made the police mad because the John Patrick Nelson identity led the authorities nowhere. He possessed no social security number, and his fingerprints were unknown. At one point in the process of getting Nelson to trial, his court appointed attorney suggested the prisoner be sentenced to a mental ward, or at least a state hospital. When "Nelson" learned of this possibility, he assured the attorney of his sanity and that he deserved to be in jail.

"If you want to go to jail, you're crazy, and if you're crazy you belong in a hospital," the attorney said. "And what's this thing about going outside? They told me you go nuts in the exercise yard."

Amos said again he would not go to a hospital. He could pass any sanity test. The attorney shrugged and said going to prison could be arranged with a guilty plea. Since John Nelson had such strong feelings, how long did he wish to be in prison?

"I have a choice?" Amos asked, surprised.

"You could get off with parole. You have no record, which in itself is a little odd, because I mean no record of any kind."

"I want to go to jail."

"Why?" When Amos said nothing, the lawyer said, "Anything you say to me is in confidence and I am legally bound not to repeat it."

"I belong in prison. If I don't get sent there, I will rob another store and use a weapon."

"You'd probably get shot. How long?"

"Three years at Crocket State Prison," Amos said.

Crocket State Prison, an aged, medium security prison located many miles from any town and many years from the idea of modernization, was a throw-back to Nevada's territorial prison system of the previous century. When Amos arrived he appeared to be easy and desirable pickings. Young, buff, and shy made him perfect. Despite his papers giving his age as twenty-one, Amos was nineteen, and measured in street years, no more than an infant. Crocket put new inmates into single cells until they could be evaluated. The prison evaluated for work and discipline while the inmates made judgments for less pleasant reasons. The segregation lasted long enough for the new inmates to fear what would happen when they joined the general population. For Amos it didn't take that long to find out.

The first three days he spent at Crocket, Amos, with his usual analytical thoroughness, watched the flow of the prison, a task made easy by the severe regimentation. By the end of the second day he saw the inmates needed the help of the guards to get what they wanted. Even though the inmates were to have nothing of value, most did and arranged with guards to get and keep more.

On his fourth day of incarceration, two inmates cornered him in a utility room. The two bracketed Amos front and back without Amos recognizing his peril. Each attacker took an arm.

"Time for a pretty boy like you to learn the ropes," the one to his left said as he slid his hand down the front of Amos's pants.

"Yes, my man," the other said, his grip tightening as Amos flexed, "a little lesson in humility will get you off on the right foot."

Amos had never been in a fight. The men tried to push Amos to his knees. When he realized they meant him harm, he reacted without hesitation. Using his speed he spun away from their grip. His body building and exercise regimen included martial arts moves, but he had never tried them on a human. He felt clumsy and inexpert, but even so he had both men on the floor gasping and bleeding when a guard stumbled on the aftermath. Later, when the guard reported the fight, he said the kid stood over his victims – that was the word he used – wringing his hands real fast and muttering "fuel, air, water," over and over.

Amos landed in solitary confinement. Solitary, also known as the hole, with its continuous darkness, fit Amos nicely. Its comfort exceeded his bivouac hidey hole and had no slobbering critters waiting for him to go to sleep. The slobbering critters in prison lived on the other side of the door.

At Crocket, solitary meant just that and to hell with the quaint idea that every prisoner must do a hour a day in the exercise yard. Amos, already an expert in how to exercise in a limited space, scaled his regimen down and maintained a minimal, by his standards, level of fitness. When his thirty days ended, the guards led Amos to the showers and a change of clothes. Then he was taken to the assistant warden's office by Captain Crane, the head of the guards. Crane carried a baton and slapped his hand as he walked.

"Move it, Convict," Crane said, and hit Amos across the back of his thighs.

Amos stopped and started to turn as Crane hit him again.

"Move it. I love hitting losers like you."

Amos swallowed his anger. He entered an office with letters on the glass that read *LaVoy McDaniels, Assistant Warden*. After entering, Crane told him to stand at attention with this toes on a red line.

"That will be all, Crane," LaVoy McDaniels said, from behind his desk.

"This one might give you trouble. I had to encourage him so I better stay."

"I said, that will be all. There's a man posted outside the door."

Amos saw the dislike on Crane's face. The door closed hard behind him.

"Stand at ease," the warden said.

Amos didn't know what "at ease" meant. McDaniels told him.

"Who are you?" McDaniels demanded.

"Nelson, John, sir."

"So it says on your paperwork." McDaniels punctuated the statement with a finger jabbing the contents of a file on his desk. "Where are you from?"

"Nebraska, sir. Small town."

"So I see. Name of Polk. What did you do there?"

"Nothing, sir, so I left."

"Yes, and robbed a store. In your file the arresting officer said it was the most inept robbery he'd ever seen. He wrote," McDaniels read from the file, "that he thought you wanted to get arrested. He wondered if you were running from someone or something. Is that true?"

"No, sir."

"What about this wanting to go to jail?"

"No one wants to go to jail, do they?"

"Listen up, boy, do not answer a question with a question. I expect a civil and forthright response. Is that understood?"

"Yes. Yes, sir. I did not have any money, I was hungry, and I thought robbing the store would be easy. When I told the clerk to give me all the money, she looked scared and I felt bad. I didn't know what to do."

McDaniels looked at the file again.

"You turned down parole and insisted on coming to prison. Normal people don't do that. Why did you?"

Amos shuffled his feet and wiped his face.

"I didn't say you could move!"

Amos snapped back to the position.

"Yes, sir. What was the question?"

McDaniels repeated the question.

"I did the wrong thing. I could have found another way to get food without scaring the girl."

McDaniels closed the file, folded his hands on top of it and looked at Amos.

"I don't believe a word. You are a babe in the woods here, son, and the woods are full of wolves."

"Little Red Riding Hood!" Amos said.

McDaniels looked at him for a long time, then leaned back in his chair.

"What level of school did you finish?"

"I am very smart," Amos said.

"I'd never know." McDaniels tapped his desk before saying, "I am going to have you sent to the infirmary for a few days. While you're there, we're going to do some tests. If we can't figure out who you are, maybe we can figure out what you are. Any questions?"

Amos shook his head, realized his mistake, and said, "No, sir."

"The guards said you didn't mind solitary. They even said you could do another thirty days. Is that right?"

Amos started to move his feet, but caught himself.

"I am not afraid of being alone in the dark, sir."

McDaniels nodded, then opened the file again. "They told me you exercised a couple of hours a day in the dark."

"It made me feel better, sir."

"While they're running those tests? I think we'll try to figure out why you don't like the outdoors. County lockup says you," he put his finger on the page and moved it across the sheet, "became agitated outdoors. You stayed in the shadow as much as possible. Umm. They called you 'Vampire.' You afraid to go outside, Nelson?"

Amos kept his eyes on the floor, but raised them to meet those of the assistant warden.

"I am very good with my hands, sir, and would rather work inside. Sir."

"I asked you a direct question, boy! Answer it."

"Sir, I am very good with my hands!"

"Do you want to get sent back to the hole?"

"Yes!"

McDaniels stared at him.

"You wouldn't be the first to hide out in the hole, no sir." McDaniels tapped the fingers of both hands on the file. "I want to know *what* you are. Forget solitary."

The door opened, and McDaniels instructed a guard to take Amos to the infirmary. As Amos left, McDaniels called to him.

"Those two guys you beat to a pulp? They both lived." The guard stopped Amos as McDaniels continued. "One was transferred to a medical facility, but the other is still here. He will want to settle things with you, probably with the help of a few friends. Just a word to the wise. Prison is hell and don't forget it."

Amos and the guard left. As they walked through the hall, the guard said, "They deserved it, what you did to those two. They've done worse to other guys. They won't touch you in the infirmary, but soon as you get sent back to the block they'll come for you. Understand?"

"Yes, sir."

Assessment tests of all kinds filled the next few days. When he finished them, Amos returned to the warden's office. This time he knew how to stand.

"You don't seem to fit any of our round holes, Nelson." A file lay open in front of McDaniels again. "Manual dexterity so far off the chart the doctor thought you were on speed. When he made you do it again, you were faster. Your handwriting is very poor, your reading comprehension is very high – we think it's pretty high because getting what you know out of you isn't easy – but the doctor agrees. He thinks you're very smart."

McDaniels turned a page.

"Your psych evaluation is a mess. One shrink says you should be in a mental hospital, and the another says just because they don't know what you are doesn't mean you're crazy." McDaniels looked at Amos. "The one who thinks you aren't crazy says you should read the Bible an hour a day, and after you've read it cover to cover, he wants to test you again. Now why would he say that?"

"I don't know, Sir."

"You must have some idea."

"He asked me how I decided what needed to be done and I said I did what I had to do."

"There's more." McDaniels looked at the file again. "Go on."

"I told him what needed to be done was the only thing that mattered. He asked me what I thought of right and wrong, and I told him right and wrong belonged to other people."

"Yes, that's what it says. He says this means you are 'amoral.' Do you know what amoral means?"

"It means I have no morals."

"Does that bother you?"

Amos did not speak. McDaniels nodded slowly in the face of the silence.

"How old are you?"

"Twenty-one, sir."

"No, you're younger. I don't really care, because your ass is here and not even God can get you out. Do you believe in God?"

"No, sir."

"Did your parents?"

"No."

"Why?"

"Before my mother was killed she said if there was a god it was an evil god and she didn't want to know it."

"Your mother was killed. Your father?"

"He was killed, too."

"At the same time?"

"No, five years apart. Sir."

"What happened?"

"I don't talk about my parents."

"Were they criminals?" McDaniels held a hand up. "You and I are alone so we can talk. I want to open a meaningful dialogue with you, but if you keep that look I will call the guard – my finger is on the button under my desk – and I will have you shackled. Is that what you want?"

Amos took a breath, and said, "No, sir."

"You don't want to talk about your parents, okay, I will respect that for now, but at some time we will talk. I will ask you what I want, and you will answer. If it isn't me you talk to, it will be a shrink, and maybe that's what's called for, psychiatric work and lots of it." He drummed his fingers again. "But, I'm not ready to write you off."

McDaniels closed the file on his desk.

"I'm sending you to the general population. You will work in the machine shop where we can put that manual dexterity to work and – for the time being – you can stay inside. You will have a cell mate. He has no history of violence, and as far as I know, will not side against you. Neither will he defend you. Do you know what I am saying, Nelson?"

"Yes, sir. I'm on my own."

For the first time in his life Amos knew he was alone. He didn't have Bill to help remember the hard stuff, and no Clyde. Already a bad sleeper, his first night of sharing a cell on the block gave Amos more reasons to be awake. It remained noisy after lights out. He didn't know he paced until his cell mate, a man named Crimmins, told him to lie down and stay down.

"In a couple of weeks you'll get used to it," Crimmins said. Later, he hissed, "Stay on that fucking bunk. If you wake me up one more time I'll make sure you stay there."

Amos could not lie still so he got up, and stood at the bars. The door, like all those on the block, could be unlocked and opened as a group, but each had a manual override that required a key. The system, like much at Crocket, was old. He thought the large keyhole would be an easy lock to pick, but he would need two stout picks. Even if he got out he didn't know where he would go and what he would do, but standing at the door and visualizing how the lock worked was better than lying on the bunk or making Crimmins mad. When morning came and the doors opened, Amos heard the screech of the rollers. They would need fixing, too.

He swept the floor his first day in the machine shop. The old lathes, metal cutting saws, drill presses, and other machines all needed tuning. As he pushed his broom, he watched the inept inmates turning, drilling, and grinding. If he worked here he would stand out. In Laughland it had been alright to be a showoff, but it would not be good here. He wondered if his hands could ever move that slow.

As he swept the floor, he moved around the shop and learned where to find the things he would need. He wanted two picks for the lock and something he could use as a weapon. He knew he would be assaulted and wanted to be prepared.

The attack came right after lunch and he wasn't ready. The guard who watched the section looked at him, looked into a hall masked by a partition, and walked away. Amos worked near a corner out of sight of the rest of the machine shop. As soon as the partition hid him, four men moved out of the hall.

"Hurt him," said the survivor of the first attack, and pointed at Amos. Before the three could move Amos leaped on the speaker, wrapped his arms around the man's shoulders, spun him and hit him three times in the face so fast the punches blurred. The man was unconscious before he hit the floor.

"Next," Amos said.

The men stepped closer, fanning to encircle him.

"I will not hurt you if you go away." Amos's spoke calmly. He moved on the balls of his feet. "If you don't, I will hurt you just like him. I am faster and smarter and don't care if you live or die."

The men charged.

Amos started with the one behind him. He stepped aside and took the man's lowered head as he charged. He choked him, stopping short of cutting off all his air, then used his body as a shield until the guards stopped the fight. Amos let go and the man fell at the guards' feet. The guards looked at the bloodied body on the floor and demanded an explanation.

As the guards moved apart, the attacker Amos had held in a headlock whispered, "You are a dead man. I will kill you myself."

The men were taken back to their cells and left there without dinner.

By the time Amos ended his second day on the job he had a weapon in his pocket, picks for the lock, and a small, flat can of lubricating oil. Because word of the fight had spread, Amos was the center of attention. He felt the stares and heard some of the talk. He learned his attacker's name was Tidwell and rumor said the man had killed before. Two men laughed and pointed at Amos.

"You're next," one of them called.

Returning from dinner, he saw Tidwell's cell was on the same tier as his.

In the middle of the night while his cellmate slept, Amos oiled the door, picked the lock and slipped down the walkway. He hugged the rail to keep as far as possible from the cells. No one stood at the bars of their cell to see the phantom moving where no man walked between lights out and reveille. He found the cell he sought, oiled the track, picked the lock, and opened the door far enough to slip through. When he was done, he reversed his steps, and lay down on his bunk and waited for morning.

An inmate named Lester Tidwell lay dead in his bed with his neck broken, and breakfast had to wait. The guards led Tidwell's cell mate away screaming that he'd done nothing. McDaniels stood near the bridge that crossed the atrium on each tier, and watched as they took the prisoner away. He held no doubt as to *what* happened. *How* remained something else. As far as he knew, no inmate had ever left his cell, entered another, committed a crime and then gone back to his own. He had not believed it possible. He signaled to Captain Crane, and the population queued for breakfast. He watched Nelson walk by and noted the man made no eye contact, not that any of the others did either. After the convicts left the block, McDaniels entered Nelson's cell. He examined the lock, and decided if there were any scratches he didn't want to find them. He knelt and felt the track where the door slid. At first he felt nothing, but as his hand slid along the portion of the track nearest the door, he felt a light oil. He pulled his hand away, rubbed his fingers together, then went to the dead man's cell. He found the same thing.

McDaniels had not anticipated the murder, and even though he knew no one else would have either, he hated the feel of the guilt. In a cold moment he acknowledged the dead man was no loss, perhaps even deserved it, but the Angel of Death did not visit as another inmate. He took a handkerchief from his back pocket, and walked away wiping his hands.

LaVoy McDaniels was born in northwestern Louisiana into what he later identified as a family with limited money and high expectation. His parents met in high school, something none of their parents could have said. Education became a priority, and despite the hardships of the deep south in the late 1940's and '50's, his parents made it through twelfth grade. Even though black universities offered inexpensive classes, incomes from jobs came first. Both his parents used the pain of education interrupted as impetus to send as many of their children to college as would go. LaVoy worked hard at a state school, and carried a 3.2 GPA through his undergraduate studies.

Growing up, he faced life's basic conflict of Good and Bad. The church was the glue of the Good folks, just as the jukes and roadhouses sat at the heart of the Bad. Every day of LaVoy's childhood he learned about the one and only Good, the same way he learned of the one and only God. Choices, manifesting as shades of gray that inevitably slid to black, could not be trusted.

LaVoy McDaniels finished his undergraduate degree, earned a master's degree in corrections and psychology, then moved west. He had been at Crocket six years, and assistant warden the last two. He looked for prisoners who offered hope they could be converted from Bad to Good, and then he tried to help in the transformation. When he was successful, the inmate re-entered the world. McDaniels was not above using God in cases where he thought it would help, but believed more in the self-help approach. Prisons were for the pragmatic. He added the interesting cases to his doctoral thesis research.

In his experience, John Patrick Nelson stood as an original. He had seen true psychopaths who did not distinguish between Good and Bad, and others who couldn't be bothered by the distinction, but Nelson's uniqueness came from his absolute lack of a moral infrastructure. At the moment though, LaVoy McDaniels filled his thoughts with how Nelson accomplished the seemingly impossible.

The Locked Cell Murder Mystery dominated the prison. In the prevailing wisdom, no one could match John Nelson for motive, but opportunity defied explanation. For the authorities the dead man's cell mate met the need for an answer. The two had barely tolerated each other, but no one could explain why all of a sudden one would kill the other. For the inmates, one other seemingly implausible explanation captured everyone's attention.

After the discovery of the body, Amos went about his proscribed activities. He had done what needed to be done, and promised himself he would remain wary.

In the machine shop, he taught himself to perform at a slower speed, although still substantially faster than anyone else. He made slight changes in the gears of a lathe, and cleaned the teeth so it ran smoother leaving no machine marks on a properly mounted object. He wanted to make other improvements, but decided not to call attention to himself. He made no friends, and didn't mind. He and Crimmins became easy with each other, although Crimmins had been leery when he heard the stories of the Locked Cell Murder Mystery. Amos knew how not to bother Crimmins in his sleep, and even began to sleep better himself, due, he decided, to the set schedule of prison life.

Two weeks passed before his next summons to Assistant Warden McDaniels' office. A straight back chair faced the desk with its front legs on the line. A second man sat near the desk to his right.

"Sit," McDaniels said, and Amos did. "Put your hands on your knees. Leave them there. Move and I'll call the guards. Understood?"

"Yes, sir." Amos sat at attention, hands on his knees.

"This is Mr. Reynolds, he manages the machine shop."

Reynolds leaned slightly forward when he talked.

"You modified the number eight lathe," Reynolds said. "Why?"

"It turned out of round, sir."

"How could you tell?"

"I . . . I could see it. Sir."

"You could see it?"

"Yes, sir, and I could feel it."

Reynolds looked at McDaniels, then said, "I put a micrometer on shafts turned before he made the adjustments. Less than three thousands of an inch out of round." He looked back to Amos. "I don't believe you could feel a difference that fine."

"And the difference after Nelson made the adjustment?" McDaniels asked.

Reynolds gave his head one hard shake.

"May I ask what the trouble is, Sir?" Amos asked.

"Inmates are not permitted to change the settings of the machines," Reynolds said. "You broke a shop rule."

"I didn't know. Machines are always supposed to do their best."

"Like people?" McDaniels asked.

After an uncomfortable delay, Amos said, "Machines and people are not the same, Sir."

"What do you want this inmate to do, Mr. Reynolds?" McDaniels asked, not taking his eyes off Amos.

Reynolds leaned even further forward.

"I want him to calibrate the other lathes."

"So, he would work under your supervision?"

"Yes."

"Nelson?"

"I will do what I am told to do, sir."

When warden and prisoner sat alone, McDaniels said, "You are adjusting."

"Yes, sir."

"Did you know there is a mystique that you have special powers." McDaniels rocked back in his chair, staring hard. "Nobody wants to pick on someone who can get them in their sleep."

Amos relaxed.

McDaniels thumbed the pages of a file on his desk without looking at them. "One of your tests was an IQ test. Do you know what that means?"

"Intelligence Quotient. The higher the number the smarter you are."

"They told you before the test?"

"Yes, but I already knew."

"Did they tell you your score?" When Amos shook his head, McDaniels said, "People aren't usually told their scores. What you are is what you are, but I'm going to tell you. You tested over 190. Part of the reason you scored so high is the speed you do things, but that aside you still had to know what to do."

"Why are you telling me, sir?"

"Any idea what percentage of the world's population has an IQ over 190? A number so small we don't need to discuss it." McDaniels' closed the file. "Why are you in prison?"

"I broke the law."

"Are you asking me?"

"I broke the law."

"What else is against the law?" McDaniels waved a hand. "Generally speaking."

"I don't understand the question, sir."

"Let me rephrase. Why do we have laws?"

Amos did not see where the questions led because he had never lived as part of a group. Yes, he had! The shop. Bill had rules so the Boys didn't fight.

"Come on, Nelson, the question isn't that hard."

"There are laws so people don't fight. Laws are like rules."

"Fair enough. Who makes the rules?"

"You do, sir."

"Does that make me right? Truth, Nelson."

"No, sir. It means you have power."

"Does that make you angry?"

"I'm not like most people."

"You believe it would make most people mad?"

"I don't know most people, but it would make some mad."

"How mad?"

"They would want to kill you."

"For telling them to stand? For making the rules in this room? This prison?"

Amos sat frozen. For the first time, he saw prison might be more than a hiding place, and that the problems of right and wrong could apply to him.

1986

Marcus Steerman and The Search for Amos

Clyde did not miss Amos for over a week and didn't think much of not seeing him for nearly another. When he did decide he was gone, Clyde tried to reach Steerman, but waited another week for a reply. By the time Marcus got to Laughland, the boy had a month's head start.

"He didn't say anything?" Marcus asked.

"I don't give a Goddamn how many times you ask, the answer is still no. He didn't say nothing. Next you're going to ask why I didn't miss him sooner. Well, the answer's the same there, too. I didn't. He didn't come up, and I didn't go down. I missed him because the fridge stayed full. Satisfied?"

Steerman ran his hand through his thinning hair.

"Amos would not walk away without a reason."

"It doesn't mean he told me. If you want to point fingers, how come you didn't call sooner?"

Steerman held up his hands, whether in surrender or frustration Clyde didn't know.

"So you think he walked out to Highway 62?" Steerman asked.

"No other way."

"How about over the hill and down the road to Mercy?"

"You see many cars on that road? Next to none. If he left right at nightfall, he could walk to 62 in about six hours or so. He's in good shape, so maybe faster. Then he'd hitch."

Steerman shook his head harder.

"This is crazy! Amos knows nothing of the world. How would he even know to hitchhike? Where would he go? What would he use for money?"

Clyde had no intention of telling Steerman about his talk with Amos and about The Diemaker bank accounts.

For two days Steerman searched the Underground looking for clues and found nothing. Next he poked around the corners of Laughland Valley, not the carnival grounds, but the surrounding desert. Clyde grew tired of watching Marcus stumble around jabbing a stick in the ground. The effort revealed Steerman's desperation.

On the third day Steerman asked, "Did Amos have any favorite spots, you know, above ground?"

"Are you kidding? You know how he felt about daylight."

"I still can't believe he would leave!"

"The boy is nineteen." Clyde doubted Marcus ever considered Amos more than a brilliant curiosity. "There ain't nothing around here he really needs, if you get my drift."

Steerman stared off to the west apparently hoping some trail would appear. Clyde shook his head and walked slowly back to his house.

By the time Steerman left the next day, they decided Clyde would stay on as caretaker of Laughland. Amos might have left, Clyde thought, but he'd be back. No Goddamn doubt.

Marcus left Laughland after dark and picked up Highway 62. The closest city was Las Vegas, but if imagining Amos out of his Underground was difficult, imagining him in Las Vegas sent a chill down his back. When he had visited years ago with news of Matt's death he had suspected Amos of going through his bag, but no harm could come from that. No harm as long as Amos stayed in Laughland.

Traffic was light, mostly eighteen wheelers, and when he got to the Interstate and saw the truck stop he took the exit, parked, and went into the café.

"I'm looking for a young man who might have come through here about a month ago," he said to the cashier. "I'm his uncle and he's a runaway. His mother is sick and I need to find him."

"A penny for every time I've heard that story," the woman said.

"Sometimes it's true. He had a gift that someone might have noticed."

She waved him to step aside so she could do her job.

"A gift?"

"A talent. He could fix anything."

She looked at him, and he knew he'd scored.

"Anything?" she asked.

"Yes. Any help would be appreciated."

She took the check from the next man, rang it up, then glanced at Steerman. She shook her head. Frustrated, he headed for the door and stepped into the night.

"He got fast hands?" a voice from behind asked.

Marcus stopped and looked back at a man.

"Very. Did you see him?"

"No, but I heard a story about some kid who fixed a truck stuck in the desert. Don Koontz, the trucker, told this story all over these parts."

"How can I find Don Koontz?"

"Don't think it'd do you any good if you found him. He brought the kid here and found him a ride to Vegas."

Steerman headed for Las Vegas convinced Amos had gone to the Stardust. The downside to using a casino's vault was if you had the name and password anyone could get in. He wondered what Amos hoped to find. Answers, just like Marcus wanted at that age.

Marcus had grown up in a Chicago orphanage. The sisters at St. Catherine's told him his mother left him in a basket on the front porch of the church with his name pinned to the blanket. After a college education made possible by a Catholic scholarship, he returned to the orphanage to look for his mother. He saw the piece of paper where his mother had scrawled his name. MARCUS STEERMAN, no middle initial. At St. Catherine's, in the absence of a middle initial, they always inserted "J" for Jesus, and so he became MARCUS J. STEERMAN.

After all his efforts to find her failed, he had held the piece of paper to his forehead to learn its secret. It said only that he was checked baggage at the lost and found. He envisioned his mother standing on the orphanage steps, tears streaming down her cheeks as she pinned the paper to his blanket. It could have been worse. She might have chosen a fate worse than St. Catherine's. He never fantasized a father.

Amos had been an orphan for years, but Marcus was sure the boy had not given it a thought. Marcus knew being an orphan had more to do with where you lived than whether you had parents. He knew if he had to choose between St. Catherine's or a hole in the ground in the desert, he would have chosen the hole. He had never felt sorry for Amos.

By the time Marcus had been a sophomore in college he knew he wanted a secure future with career and friends. A secure job, he decided, meant a government job so he switched his major from music to Political Science. The pay in government jobs was good, he would work with many people, and he would be stable enough to provide for his children. He won the job he sought, advanced quickly, and then his life took an unexpected turn. He met Nathan Ferry. It was the perfect pairing of the starving underdog and the ultimate champion.

When he reached Las Vegas, he parked at the Stardust, entered and went directly to the vault. He signed in, and as soon as he held the much lighter box he knew the boy had been there.

Behind the curtain, he sank into the chair and raised the lid. The missing film came as a shock. This was the original he and Matt had carried out of the jungle. Copies existed in Macao and Buenos Aires, but this was the one made in Hanoi by a man who felt his desperate plan was the right thing for his country. Marcus shook his head and felt the loss in his stomach. If Matt knew that his son had the film he would call it a good thing saying Amos would put it to better use than they had.

The next shock was the missing deed to Laughland. Without it he had no way to sell the land. Too many corners had been cut to sell it without the deed. He thumbed through the rest of the box. The gun was gone as was Matt's letter. Depression hit him like a fist. He had no hope of killing Ferry without Amos. He could not stop looking. He rang for an attendant.

"Sir?"

"Would you look and see when I was here last?"

"Yes, sir," the attendant said, taking the box.

Marcus's last visit had been thirty-one days ago.

"I have a rather curious request," Marcus said, and took some currency out of his pocket. "Would you look and see if any new accounts for boxes were opened on that date?"

The man took the money. "As you wish. It will take a few minutes."

The answer came back negative.

He checked into a room and pondered a course of action. He had no idea where Amos had gone. The missing deed need not be bad news. If Amos didn't want Laughland sold it implied he meant to return. The bigger question was what would Amos do with the purple bag? Would he return to Laughland to claim it? He fell asleep wondering. When he awoke he knew he had to return to Laughland. He needed the boy and the bag.

Tired of body and dull of mind, Steerman drove down the hill into Laughland Valley. The light elongated the shadows cast by Laughland's tents giving the carnival a larger than life look. The pennants atop the tents flapped in the wind like distant applause. He had come upon the carnival in many strange places. He supposed that thousands of people had laughed and shared joy on the midways and rides, but the happiness had always been lost on him.

Clyde came out of his house buckling his gun belt to his waist, and adjusted his cowboy hat lower on his forehead.

"Back," Clyde said, slipping his thumbs into the belt.

"There's no trace of Amos out there," Steerman waved his arm at the outside world. "There's nowhere else to look. How about above ground? Some bunker that he and Matt might have made?"

"That's quite the idea, but if he was out there he'd still have to eat." When Marcus didn't answer, Clyde said, "What are you really doing here?"

"I couldn't think of anything else." Steerman looked around, then walked slowly down the Midway. "I feel it coming apart. This is all that's left. Matt's gone, Jessie's gone, and now Amos."

"The boy's alive, don't you fear about that."

Steerman nodded, surprised at Clyde's emotion. "Oh, yes, I'm sure he is, but he's gone to me as surely as if he was dead."

"Well, now who's fault's that? Don't tell me you had delusions of fatherhood after Matt was killed."

"No, nothing like that," but Marcus wondered if there had been a paternalistic urge. What did he know about fathers? He had acknowledged his financial responsibility for Amos, but did not assume it was synonymous with fatherhood. Yet the idea lingered. "Well, maybe."

"You got any idea what a father does?"

Steerman heard the sharp edge to the words, and understood Clyde now saw himself as the father.

"Do you?" Marcus shot back.

"Yeah, I got a clue about fathers," Clyde said. "They're there when they're needed. They give encouragement and support. They don't turn their backs on their children, and don't send them out to do a man's job."

The words rocked Marcus because he had expected Clyde's condemnation to be directed at him, not Matt.

"It's not fathers that fucked up that boy," Clyde said, as he pulled his gun and pointed it at Steerman. "It's you and that goddamn Ferry, and all the others who send boys out to do their fighting for them. You steal lives. You're no better than thieves."

The winds of change whistled loudly as Marcus stared at the gun. He had not had a firearm pointed at him since Bong Sat. He saw Bong Sat in the darkness of the barrel with all of its dying, and none of it his.

"Are you going to kill me?" Steerman asked.

"Kill you? I don't think so."

"Tell me about soldiers and fathers then."

"I'm not telling you about fathers, either. What the hell do I know? But," Clyde dropped his aim and cocked the weapon, "I will tell you about soldiers."

The gun slowly came up, passed over Steerman's chest in a precise re-enactment of Steerman's infamous moment of failure with Nathan Ferry. He felt no relief, but saw a glimmer of hope. If Clyde didn't kill him, it would be a rebirth.

"Soldiers sent into battle," Clyde enunciated clearly, "are sent to break things and kill people. They ain't fighting for you, and they ain't fighting for a flag, or for the folks back home, or a piece of paper. Maybe those ideas got them there, but when the bullets are flying and the flames are roaring up their backs they ain't thinking about that. They're fighting for themselves and for the man next to them. It is the sharpest test with the highest stakes."

Clyde's gun reached the perpendicular and he fired a shot into the air. Steerman flinched. With the recoil, Clyde lowered it back to his side, and the barrel started another slow trip up.

"I've had years to look for the right words. I ain't found them. To a Marine, to a fighting man who was there, you ain't got to tell him nothing. If you're trying to tell someone who didn't fight, he ain't never going to get it, but, here I am, trying anyhow."

The gun passed over Steerman's chest again and kept going. When the gun reached apogee, Clyde pulled the trigger. It dropped and started up a third time.

"You know why so many fighting men don't take to life state side? It ain't no life at all. Just one nothing day after another. Not like war where your life can end in an instant. Out there the heat of living burns you."

Again the gun traversed his chest, made the climb to the perpendicular, and fired.

"You know the craziest part of war? It ain't personal. There ain't nobody out there calling your name. It's just some guy about as scared as you are shooting in your general direction. He gets lucky, well, you're dead and he's alive."

This time the gun stayed pointed up.

"No sane man wants to die. Fighting is the ultimate high, and you want to live to do it again. Covering the man's back next to you, working together, both feeling so much life racing through your bodies it's like a miracle you don't burst. Then word gets to you some asshole who never shared a risk, never missed a meal, never shed a tear is perverting what you did. He talks about your sacrifice as if it belonged to him. Know what?"

The barrel stopped dead center on his head.

"You want to shoot him between the eyes. You want to savor the moment the life goes out of that son of a bitch."

The aim jumped right as Clyde fired and the bullet missed. Steerman did not flinch.

"I suspect fatherhood has its own risks," Clyde said. He holstered his gun, turned away and called over his shoulder, "Hunt to your heart's content."

Steerman held his ground. "Not so fast," he said, "my turn." He stared at Laughland. "I'd never been to a carnival, never even knew there were such places as amusement parks. I was never part of anything. All I ever dreamed about when I was young was a day without fear. Fear of damnation or fear of hell on Earth. No one watched my back, no buddy depended on me, and no one died in my arms grateful for a friend to hold him at the end. I've never fired a gun in reality or metaphorically to release my tension. The only thing I had to do was watch my own back and take what I could get."

Steerman wondered why he was telling Clyde his story. Maybe it was time to talk of failure, and Clyde was here.

"I had no training for what happened at Bong Sat. I was a desk man. I worked with the North Vietnamese setting up the meeting. Being part of an ending to the war and seeing my name in the history books excited me, but I didn't think I would have to kill somebody. Then, twenty-four hours before the fact, I learned Ferry's plan. I dreamed of being a hero. All I had to do was kill Ferry."

Marcus wiped his mouth, then used his finger as a gun.

"When the time came, he stood there. I held the gun but lacked the courage to pull the trigger. In one second of cowardice my dreams changed from being a hero to wanting nothing more than to live. Then I met Eliot, covered in dirt and blood, and full of the pieces of life I lacked. I wanted to be like him."

Steerman looked down the midway past the rides and tents.

"I came out of my hole in the ground after Ferry had tried to kill us all, and I played Bach. The majesty! Johann Sebastian would have been proud. It was the sound track to the battle. Men fought and prayed and died and tried the most heroic steps to save their comrades. When Eliot wanted to avenge his men and die in the doing I stopped him. I needed him to show me how to live, to help me out of the jungle, and I promised him revenge. But revenge takes courage and I failed him."

Steerman waited for judgment from Clyde but none came.

"Sometimes I think Matt was right and we both died at Bong Sat, but it's not true. I'm here because I failed and set the world on a path God never intended."

"Are you that important?"

"History always comes down to two men, or two sides. Right and wrong. Good and Evil. The world turns on the result. Ferry wants to take over the world's money markets and he might now that he's had another twenty years to make it happen."

"Why would he do that?"

Steerman walked slowly down the midway and felt Clyde follow.

"Every man has a dream. You did, I did. Mine was to have another day of life. Pretty modest but I didn't have anything. Ferry was born to it all. Maybe someone asked him when he was a boy what he wanted now that he had all the money in the world. Maybe that boy smiled and thought that would be nice."

"What are you going to do?" Clyde asked. "Keep looking for Amos? You want that boy to hold your hand and walk you down the midway to make you feel better? Ain't going to happen. Let's get one thing damn straight. I ain't that boy's father, but I'd take the job in a heartbeat. You got the slightest idea what a remarkable human that boy is? Don't answer because you don't. He would have been remarkable no matter what hand fate dealt him. A different hand though and he wouldn't have been shaping Semtex at twelve, or figuring how to kill people to keep his old man in spare change."

"Matt never needed the money."

"How do you know? You gave him what he asked for, sure. At least I assume you did. Maybe you hassled him about expenses and that's why he had his stash."

"He had a stash? Does Amos know?"

"Who do you think earned the money?"

"All from killing people?"

"Most of it, but Amos, or at least a dummy corporation, holds the patents on a handful of gadgets. You want to know more, go find out. You should know who you're dealing with."

If Amos didn't need him for money, and he had the deed to Laughland, Marcus held no leverage over the boy. He felt Ferry drawing nearer.

"Did Matt tell you about Bong Sat?" he asked.

"He did."

"Why?"

"Who do you think he drank with?"

Steerman had spent sleepless nights wandering the streets of cities around the world wondering to whom a drunken Matt Eliot might be spilling his guts.

"I came out here one night with a delivery. Matt sat right over yonder howling at the moon, cursing you and your buddy, Ferry. He had an M-16. He hosed you guys down pretty good until he ran out the last clip. Then he tossed the weapon, and picked up a bottle of Jack. He sat on his heels and bawled. I waited until some composure settled in, and walked in on him. It broke my heart. He thought I was his gunny, a guy named Montoya. It lasted until the bottle was as dry as that clip."

They reached the carousel and turned around.

"We had a little chat about not drinking alone," Clyde said. "He knew it was hard on Amos, so some nights he'd pull up out back of the store, and honk. I'd take a quart off the shelf and we'd sit in the desert. I heard all he had to say on Bong Sat. I don't think he told anyone else."

"I was there when Montoya died," Steerman said. "Traxler, too. It wasn't Matt's fault. It was mine."

"One of your men dies, it's on you. This time they all died."

"When he thought you were Montoya, was that before The Diemaker?"

"Yes. I didn't see The Diemaker coming."

"You have a great deal of influence. What did you say to Amos to make him leave?"

"I don't know nothing to help you find the boy."

"What did you tell him?"

"I told him the world could use a brain like his."

"And that sent him away? Why?"

"To learn what he doesn't know."

They reached the mouth of the midway where the ticket taker's booth used to stand, but it was gone along with the fence. Laughland sat open and unprotected.

"How cannot killing someone have been so wrong?" Steerman asked. "What am I to do?"

"Yeah." Clyde pushed the hat back and hooked his thumbs in the gun belt. "I figure what you and Ferry done at Bong Sat was so terrible that if God decides to balance the scales he'll do it right here. This place wouldn't exist without Bong Sat. It lives and breathes that perversion. It's the conscience. You get a second chance to shoot Ferry – you better do it."

1986

Teresa Gill

"**How come no one** caught The Diemaker?" asked Teresa Gill, reporter.

"Knock, knock," replied her editor, Edgar Chiswell, whose office she had invaded.

"I don't knock anymore. You tell me to go away."

"Oh, right. Go away."

"Too late. How come?"

Chiswell sighed and dropped the tear sheet he'd been reading. "I give. Why?"

"Edgar, don't be a twit. I'm serious. The guy - assuming it is a guy - was all over the news and now, a year or so later, no one cares."

"Why is this the business of the *Los Angeles Times?*"

"Nathan Ferry. He's local and the paper doesn't like him."

"The paper neither likes nor dislikes. That's official. Go away. Cover your beat. Or do you miss the valley and want to go back to - what was it? - the Kiwanis Club luncheon circuit?"

"Ha, ha. San Fernando Valley business. I'm qualified. I had a double major in college. Business and economics."

"Not journalism?"

"I could already write, and besides, I'm a genius. In separate incidents, more than a year apart, two of Ferry's security guys get killed in front of hundreds of witnesses. End of story. The first one is the highest profile murder in L.A. in the last five years open or closed. And here we are with our thumbs in our butts."

"Colorful. You may have been a genius in college but you aren't here. Here you are missing a huge chunk of reality. We do not get to write fantasy in the guise of news. Good-bye."

"Why those two guys, Edgar? Somebody hired The Diemaker to kill those guys. Who would want to do that instead of Ferry himself?"

Chiswell leaned back in his chair and clasped his hands behind his head. He said nothing.

"That's the question no one's asked. The Diemaker didn't make mistakes so Greene and Brinks were the intended targets. Who pays tons of dough to knock off the hired help?"

"If that's a rhetorical question, I'm interested."

"Nobody. The Diemaker himself wanted those two guys dead."

Chiswell put his arms down and tapped a pencil on his cluttered desk. "You're saying those two guys can lead to The Diemaker."

"That wasn't so hard, was it Edgar?"

Chiswell scribbled on a desktop calendar. "I'll put somebody on this."

"Oh, no! You got somebody on it!"

Chiswell pointed at a chair, but Gill shook her head and paced.

"You want a civil reply, then sit." She sat. "This paper will not turn you loose on Nathan Ferry, nor on anyone else rich and powerful enough to do us in. Those kinds of people do not take third year reporters seriously. They would be insulted. I admit, you have a good idea. I will send it on and perhaps someone will do something about it. Of course, you could always quit your job and go to work for someone who doesn't mind pissing off guys like Nathan Ferry."

Teresa Gill smiled and stood.

"I'll go away now," she said.

As she left, she knocked on the door frame. Walking toward her distant desk, she silently thanked Edgar for a very good idea.

1986-87

Prison Life

Nine months into prison life, Amos roamed the shop fixing what he was told to fix and going where his job took him. Because no one talked to him and he saw little reason to talk, his passing went largely unseen. He knew some guards brokered what inmates wanted, and knew they did it for gain, but he wondered why some did and others did not. He decided some cared more about rules than others. As time passed Amos slowly materialized.

LaVoy McDaniels followed Amos's adjustment to prison life. Warden and inmate still shared periodic visits, and Amos submitted to more tests. Amos became curious about the test results and wondered if other people knew as little about themselves as he did. McDaniels assured him they did, and few cared, or even wondered. Most people, McDaniels said, accepted the way they were and never gave it another thought. Because Amos wondered and believed he could change, their meetings continued.

It was the combination of Amos repeatedly walking in on prison commerce and his trips to the warden's office that brought trouble.

The last time, four men jumped Amos and one had held back. Six attacked this time and no one held back. Two men held his shoulders before he could move, and two held his legs as he fell. Of the two remaining, one knelt on Amos to use his fists and the other kicked Amos in the mid-section.

When the surprise wore off, Amos fought back. He yelled from deep in his diaphragm. He bucked, then again and on the third thrust he found room to twist and throw off one of the men holding his arms. With one arm free, he drove a fist into the crotch of the man hitting his face, and twisted so the kicks hit his hip. He contorted to reach the man holding his other arm, caught him by the hair and threw him over his body to crash into the man he had hit in the balls.

Amos saw the wrench coming just enough to duck part of the blow. He lost, then regained consciousness.

"Jesus! Did you kill him?" one of the attackers said.

"I fucking hope so! He's not human."

Amos listened as his attackers caught their breath. He let the strength fill his body before he moved. When he did, it appeared he levitated to his feet in one motion. As he stood before them, blood dripping down the side of his head, he saw two on the ground, two on their knees gasping, and the other two on their feet ready to charge. One of them still held the wrench.

"Run or die," Amos said. His voice was the same level tone he always used, and showed no shortness of breath.

The one with the wrench said, "You fucking snitch."

Amos held up his hand.

"Your business is your business. Mine is mine."

"Hold off, Ray, hold off," one of the others said.

"Not till he's dead."

"Are you crazy? He's ready to kill you, maybe rip your head off like he did Tidwell."

In the months since Tidwell had died in his cell, the story had grown more grotesque. In the current version his head had been ripped off and then desecrated, the desecration changing with the teller.

Ray's eyes flicked to Amos's right at the moment one of the men on the floor rallied to attack Amos's legs. Amos fell. Ray attacked, swinging the wrench as he threw himself at Amos. When Amos fell, he pulled the man on the floor between him and the wildly swinging Ray. The blow from the wrench took the man in the face. Blood spurted onto Ray as his momentum sent him sprawling. Amos rolled free, and got to his feet on the bloody floor. When the attacker saw the blood covered Amos coming, he ran. Two more followed close behind.

Ray lay still on the floor. When he tried to stand his feet slipped in the blood. The third attacker stood rooted to the spot with his eyes wide and his mouth hanging open.

"You tell everyone," Amos said, pointing, "never, never, come at me. My business is mine. I don't care about yours. Run."

The man did.

Ray gave up trying to stand. The wrench lay on the ground out of reach and he made no move to retrieve it. He raised his hands.

"Please."

"Do not move," Amos said.

Amos found two guards in the hall. Their astonished looks told him they had acted as lookouts.

"Ray has something he wants to tell you," Amos said. "Bring a doctor."

One guard left to bring a doctor. As he ran off, the other called, "You'd better bring Crane. He's going to be pissed."

The remaining guard reluctantly walked with Amos, his eyes never leaving him, his stick at the ready.

Ray admitted he had hit the injured man, but it had been an accident. Captain Crane arrived as Ray finished his story. He pointed at Amos.

"Get him in restraints," Crane commanded, "then I want him hauled off to the hole. Wait until I get there before you lock him in."

"Not that fast, Crane," said LaVoy McDaniels, as he came around the corner from the administration wing. "Nelson and I are going to talk first."

"Want the latest from your little snitch, McDaniels?" Crane asked.

"That's irresponsible, Crane. You spread talk like that and more men will die. Maybe that's what you want."

"As long as they aren't guards, I don't give a shit."

More guards came and a pair of orderlies arrived from the infirmary. They took the prisoners and the wounded man away. McDaniels demanded to hear the whole story. Amos told it, keeping it simple and minimizing the fight. The remaining guard had heard Ray's version, and when Crane questioned the chain of events, Amos looked at the guard who confirmed his telling.

"How is it possible that six men can be unaccounted for in the middle of the work day, Captain?" McDaniels asked, emphasizing the word captain.

"Don't give me any of your enlightened bullshit, McDaniels," Crane said. "You and your projects are nothing but a pain in my ass, always dragging inmates off to a class or some crap. This is a prison, no matter what you do."

McDaniels and Crane shared a hard stare until Crane said, "If you're done with this prisoner I'll send him down to solitary."

"I'm not done with him, but I am done with you. You may go," he paused, "Captain, stop by my office."

"Why should I?"

"*Quid pro quo*, Crane. Let's talk in private, shall we?"

McDaniels went with Amos to the infirmary to have his cuts treated. Other than the cut to the side of his head, they were not deemed serious, although the bruises from the kicks were already starting to turn color.

"How do you beat six men?" McDaniels asked.

"Because I could. They were slow."

"But how? Even if they were slow, they were big, and they were afraid of you."

"They hadn't decided to kill me."

McDaniels stared and felt the same chill he'd felt before when Amos talked of death.

"And you had?"

Amos shrugged.

"I do what I have to."

"Yes. So you've said. You're going to solitary for that fight. One more thing. Watch out for the guards. I'll do what I can about Crane, but it's not always possible." As the assistant warden went to the door to call the guard, he turned to the prisoner and said, "Don't think there's anything special about your treatment. If anything happens to you Crane wins a battle with me. It makes me look bad in front of my boss."

Crane paced outside McDaniels's office when the warden returned from the infirmary. Once inside, McDaniels pointed at a chair, but Crane chose to stand.

"So what's your *quid pro quo*, McDaniels?"

"Simple. You leave my interests alone and I reciprocate. Clear?"

"You got some kind of sick interest in these guys?"

McDaniels did not respond to the baiting.

"Since we're alone, let's put it on the table. My professional interest is rehabilitation. My personal interest is my own education. You, on the other hand, are a sadistic petty thief who belongs on the other side of the bars. You have some protection from Warden Stathem, but last time I looked at the job descriptions, I hire and fire your ass. I inherited you. I'm under no obligation to keep you." McDaniels leaned closer to Crane. "No one will cover your ass when your drug trafficking comes out, which I promise you it will. If you think your little slaves will cover for you, they'll sell you for immunity in a heartbeat."

"I doubt that."

"You should have shared the wealth." McDaniels saw he'd scored. "You leave Nelson, and my other projects alone, and I do the same for you. Simple enough even for you? If you slip, there are plenty of convicts here who would love to see you locked up with them. If you get convicted, I can be sure you are sent here than make it look like an administrative error. Picture this." McDaniels held his ups to frame his words. "I would work frantically to have you reassigned, but my feeble efforts would turn out to be too late. And don't think about trying to get at me. I have a lot more friends than you do."

After leaving Clyde, Marcus gave himself the drive to Las Vegas to think of a plan for looking for the boy. With no picture and no way of predicting what Amos would do, he gave up. He returned home to Singapore where he spent months seeking inspiration, and then out of sheer perseverance, he thought of prison. Indoors and regimented, it fit Amos to a tee.

He called a detective agency in San Francisco and told them to track down crimes perpetrated by Caucasian juveniles in and around Las Vegas near the date Amos accessed the box at the Stardust. He gave the agency the aliases he had provided. He suggested the detectives look for a culprit who was promptly caught, tried, and imprisoned. Marcus told them he wanted copies of the charge sheets and mug shots.

Three days later the detective agency said they found no juvenile crimes during the specified period. Did they want him to check adult crimes? Marcus considered writing the exercise off as a bad idea, but no other ideas lurked. He told them to go ahead.

Business took him to Macao where the casino expansion craze had created enough demand for his expertise that he added staff. A few months earlier he might have turned down the extra business, but with Matt dead for nearly five years and Amos gone, he found himself worried about his future. This glimmer of normalcy both surprised and diminished him.

Twenty-four hours later his fax machine came to life. He tossed away the first sheet with no more than a glance. He looked a little closer at the next, but discarded it, too. Amos looked at him from the third. He faxed instructions for all available information on John Patrick Nelson.

The Nelson identity surprised him. Either Clyde helped Amos secure new papers, or Amos had altered what he'd been given.

The latter choice irritated Marcus because he had not suspected it right away. He spent an anxious two days waiting for additional information. When it came, he devoured it. John Patrick Nelson served a three to five year sentence for theft in Crocket State Prison. At the time of the report he was in solitary confinement where he would remain until the end of the month. Marcus, despite his eagerness, saw no reason to go back to the states until Amos left solitary.

LaVoy McDaniels paced while he awaited the meeting with his boss, head warden Jack Stathem. He felt on edge and forced himself to think of something more pleasant. He didn't have to look far. He liked his office. He liked his diplomas framed and precisely centered and leveled so no inconsistency distracted the visitor's eye from his achievement. The only thing he did not like was his window. It was tall and narrow and looked onto one of the exercise yards and at the gray wall of B block. After the euphoria of having an office wore off, he found blinds that raised from the bottom to block the grim gray and showed only sky.

A single knock on his office door sounded, and Stathem stuck his head in. McDaniels followed him down the hall to the warden's office.

"What's the story?" Stathem asked.

"Around three o'clock, prisoner Ray Dressler woke up – "

"Dressler?"

"Fifteen to twenty-five. Armed robbery. He's a two time loser on C block."

"Go on."

"He says, and this is shaky because he was close to hysterical – "

"Close to what?"

"Hysterical. Screaming, beating on the bars."

"Jesus! What set him off? Are drugs getting in here again?"

"Not drugs. He was scared, terrified. He said he woke up with something wet on his face. He opened his eyes and the wet was blood from a decapitated rat on his pillow."

"And that made him hysterical?"

"Yeah." McDaniels paused. "How did it get there?"

"Who's he in with?"

"No one last night."

Stathem sat straight. "Tell me about it."

McDaniels had not told Stathem any of the Nelson problems.

"Six months ago, Robert Tidwell was killed in his cell."

"Yeah, his cellmate did it."

"That's the way we handled it."

"What's that mean?"

"Earlier the day Tidwell died, he and three others assaulted a fish named John Nelson. Two inmates tried to rape Nelson weeks earlier, and Nelson beat them up pretty bad. I sent Nelson to the hole. When he got out, Tidwell volunteered to help with the payback. Somehow Nelson turned the tables and one of the attackers was nearly killed. Tidwell told Nelson he'd get him next time." McDaniels paused. He didn't like the way what he was about to say would sound. "That night Tidwell was alive at lock down and dead at roll call. The block went nuts."

"Was Nelson in the hole?"

"No. I should have sent him, but when he was in the first time, I swear, he liked it. I figured he used the hole to hide out."

Stathem shrugged. "It happens."

"Nelson was in his cell all night," McDaniels said, and paused before adding, "The guards all swear to it."

"What's that supposed to mean?"

"Just about everybody believes Nelson killed Tidwell."

Stathem wrinkled his forehead. McDaniels picked up the pace.

"I checked Nelson's cell. The tracks for the door's rollers had fresh oil for the first twelve inches. Tidwell's cell door did too. I do not believe Nelson opened the door to his cell, sneaked past fifty cells, opened another door and killed a man while his cell mate slept four feet away. That is not human."

"I don't remember how Tidwell died."

"Broken neck. Whoever did it twisted his head until it broke the neck. The story got around that Tidwell's head got twisted off."

"Jesus Christ! The rat?"

"Yes. The population believes Nelson killed Tidwell and we're covering up. They already thought he was some kind of a ghost."

"This is crazy."

"Five days ago six men attacked Nelson. Dressler tried to kill him with a wrench and hit another inmate instead. Those are facts. A guard said he heard Nelson warn Dressler to leave him alone or else. That's all we know."

"Where's Nelson?"

"In the hole. I wasn't taking any chances."

"What happened during the night? How did the rat get in there?"

McDaniels shook his head. "No idea. I moved Dressler's cellmate out after the fight."

"Maybe Dressler did it himself."

"He wasn't playing games. The orderly said it took three shots to knock him out."

Stathem shook his head.

"It had to be a guard."

"At this point the general population isn't going to believe anything we say."

"Then let them have their spook story," Stathem said. "I'll talk to Crane. Any of his guards turn out to be behind this they're fired. Crane will be too if it happens again. Tell me about this Nelson. Who is he?"

"He's a three to five for burglary. No priors. Young. I was surprised when he showed up here. He seemed more fitted to minimum security."

"Why did he get sent here?"

"Courts assigned him. There's not much on him. Says he's twenty-one, but looks younger."

"Did you send his prints out?"

"Yes, but there was nothing. I ran some assessments on him. IQ so high it's nearly off the charts. The shrink looked at him and couldn't decide if he's a psychopath, a religious zealot, or just seriously screwed up. I don't know either."

"What's his job?"

"That's the other thing. He's got hands like you wouldn't believe. He can fix anything so we put him in the shop working for Reynolds repairing machines. Reynolds is disappointed he isn't a lifer."

Stathem stood and walked to the window. Unlike McDaniels's office, the view did not include the prison, instead showing the long road that led to civilization. The windows weren't the only difference. McDaniels hung his diplomas on his wall, but Stathem displayed pictures of himself with the governor and a state senator.

"Move him," the head warden said. "There are lots of other sites where he would fit in better."

McDaniels could drag the process out, but the star of his research project would be gone long before his parole date.

Two days after John Patrick Nelson rejoined the general population, a man named Larry Zoeller signed in as a visitor. The processing guard, following instructions, routed the paperwork to McDaniels's office. The guard told Mr. Zoeller to have a seat. Twenty minutes later the visitor entered a room where the assistant warden waited for him.

"Who are you, Mr. Zoeller?"

Marcus Steerman looked around the room. Bars covered the outside of the windows. A large mirror hung on one wall.

"Two way?" Zoeller asked, pointing at the mirror.

"When a convict answers a question with a question, he gets sent back to his cell."

"Not as easy with visitors."

McDaniels smiled and leaned back in his chair. "No, not as easy but just as final. Who are you?"

"I have an interest in John Nelson."

"Are you family?"

"Oh, no. Not that kind of interest. Do I have to be family to see him?"

"No, but we like to know who's coming and going. Part of our program is to separate the past from the future."

"I was a friend of his father's. I am not an unofficial uncle, or anything like that, but when his father died I tried to keep an eye on John."

"Where did you keep an eye on him?"

The interrogation found Steerman unprepared. He had planned to slip in, see Amos, and let him know there were no hard feelings about the items taken at the Stardust.

"Why should I answer your questions? Am I obligated? If I don't, I don't get in?"

"Why shouldn't you answer? We have a lot of questions about John Nelson."

"I have a question." Steerman held up his hand acknowledging he once again answered a question with a question. "How does a nice boy who never got in any trouble wind up in prison?"

McDaniels leaned forward and folded his hands on the table and held Steerman's eyes.

"I don't think we are going to let you in," McDaniels said. "You either don't know Nelson or you're part of the lie."

Steerman stood slowly, took a handkerchief from his pocket and wiped his hands.

"Don't bother wiping the table and chair," McDaniels said. "We have the pen you signed in with."

"I am not a criminal," Steerman said.

"What's your name?"

"I will not tell you that." Steerman pointed at the mirror. "Two way?"

"Yes, but there's no one in there. If I push the button under the table there would be in seconds."

Steerman wiped his forehead. He should have foreseen this, but his desire to see Amos trumped his inherent caution.

"The boy and I are being sought by people who will kill us if they find us."

"That's a start. Don't think I accept it, but it's a start."

"It's a pity you don't know me. If you did, you would know how unique the truth is coming from my mouth."

"Like you said, I don't know you. Tell me about Nelson."

"Has he told you about himself?"

"Not a word," McDaniels said.

"How is he? He was in solitary confinement?"

McDaniels's now appeared to be the uncomfortable one.

"Your John Nelson presented an inviting target when he arrived. It took a while for people to learn it didn't pay to harass him."

Other than Matt and Clyde, the warden was the first person Steerman had met who knew Amos.

"What do you think of him?" he asked.

"He is like the stone thrown in a still pool. Before the stone is cast skeeters, dust motes, and bits of grass float on the water. When the stone hits the water, the ripples threaten to sink them all. If the stone had never been cast they would still be floating in the sun."

Steerman felt moved to applaud. As one of the surface creatures still tossing in the ripples of Bong Sat, it was as eloquent an explanation for himself as he had heard.

"He is not the stone," Steerman said. "I won't tell you his real name. It would mean nothing and be just as invisible as the name John Nelson. The stone that still rocks his world hit the water when he was an infant. His father and I survived a betrayal in Vietnam by people who still have a great deal to lose."

"Why would he come to my jail?" McDaniels asked.

"I don't know. I'd say he's here on purpose."

"But who goes to jail to hide?"

"Answer that question and you will understand him. Start with his fear."

"No!" McDaniels slammed his hand on the table. "That boy has problems, but he's afraid of no man. You know what he says?"

Steerman nodded, and said, "He does what he has to do."

For the first time McDaniels felt this man actually knew Nelson.

"Would he be happy to see you?"

"I don't know."

"How about I talk to him first? What could I say so he would know it's you?"

"His mother's name was Jessie. If that isn't enough, tell him Clyde misses him."

"Okay. Come back tomorrow."

Steerman stood again, and shook his head.

"No, I won't be coming back. No offense, Warden, but I can't do that. I don't trust anyone that much." He started for the door, then stopped. "Give him a message. Tell him I know what he did. Tell him I don't blame him, and it's as much his as mine. Tell him I'll see him when he goes home. Make sure it doesn't sound like a threat."

"You won't be coming back?"

"No. Please don't run my prints. I'll be gone, but the boy will still be here."

"His prints don't show up."

"Mine do."

"I'll give him the message. Oh. The head warden wants him transferred."

"That's your problem if he doesn't want to leave."

1986

Teresa Gill Makes a Name

During her sophomore, and part of her junior, year at the University of California at Berkeley, Teresa Gill shared a dorm room with Jasmine Harris. Jasmine liked older guys. The first year they were room mates Jasmine's man of the year was a graduate student named Oscar Mason. Oscar was the motivating force behind a weekly paper sold on street corners and record stores around the east bay. He called his magazine *Mother's Own* and mother was Mother Earth. In their junior year Jasmine left school to make Oscar more than her man of the year. Teresa still saw Jasmine and Oscar because they moved no further than across the bay to San Francisco. For alternative presses, no place offered more opportunity than Northern California.

Five years later Oscar Mason, no longer assisted by Jasmine, still ran *Mother's Own*. The weekly had not lost its environmental emphasis. The lead story still dealt with ozone or spotted owls, but its growth lay in its willingness to tackle stories no one else wanted to print. Mason got away with it for two very solid reasons. First, all their stories were extremely well written and airbrushed with an unmistakable patina of truth, and second, no subject of one of their stories wanted to sue the small press for fear they would morph the piss ant into a raging lion. It helped that Oscar's brother was an astute attorney with an uncanny ability to spot the early stages of libel or slander. *Mother's Own* continued to build its circulation as people in the Bay Area finished their educations, moved away and subscribed by mail. With time a few stories got picked up by the national press and *Mother's Own* saw its reputation grow.

"We don't do much crime," Oscar told Teresa on the phone. Teresa had called with her idea regarding The Diemaker. It was Friday night and they were both home, one in Los Angeles and the other in San Francisco.

"It's not crime," she said. Nearly a year had passed and nothing had happened at the *Times,* but she'd researched her topic and written a draft. "Oscar, Nathan Ferry is the kind of guy you should have on your dartboard."

"We don't have a dartboard, but if we did he'd be there. Sierra Terrace Holdings funds more anti-environmental lobbyists than anyone else in the country."

"Let me write a story naming companies who spend big to protect their polluting. Then I say guess who they have in common – Nathan Ferry and Sierra Terrace. Oh, and by the way, guess what other little known fact has Ferry in the middle. These two guys killed by The Diemaker."

Teresa drummed her fingers on her desk as she waited for an answer. The longer she waited, the more she feared the response.

"I don't know," Oscar said. "It would be touchy. You're really out to skewer Ferry for non-environmental reasons. Editorially, that's okay, but we don't want the story to appear to be one thing then turn into something else."

"Sort of rests on the skill of the writer, doesn't it?" Teresa said. "How about I write a draft and send it to you. I'll do it for nothing. I don't want to use my own name, either."

"No money, no fame. What's that leave?"

"The truth. It makes me nuts that a guy as brilliant as The Diemaker just disappeared. Smart people fascinate me. I want to know the end of the story. Sticking pins in Nathan Ferry is a bonus."

"What name are you going to use?"

"I was thinking Louise Lake. Sort of Lois Lane-ish."

"Let's use Lois Lake. It's been awhile since Superman flew. No point in being subtle."

"Then I'll use Lois Lane."

When LaVoy McDaniels put out the word that Crocket had a prisoner they wanted to transfer to a lower security facility, the official word came back beds were tight. Unofficially, beds could be found for anyone other than John Patrick Nelson. Between the Locked Cell Murder Mystery and the Case of the Headless Rat no one wanted Nelson.

Two weeks later, McDaniels reported the situation to Stathem.

"Let's keep him," McDaniels said.

"You studying this guy?"

"Yes, but Reynolds wants him because the shop machines are better than new. Productivity is way up."

The head warden bounced the retractor of his ball point pen on his desk. "So we keep him and make you guys happy. What if somebody else dies?"

"I was wrong, and it's my ass."

"You're willing to stick it out for that guy?"

"We know nothing about him. I still think he's in here to hide."

"That's ridiculous. Who goes to jail to hide?"

"Exactly."

"I want to know how you became you," LaVoy McDaniels said, as Amos and he walked near the Machine Shop. "I doubt you have ever had any formal schooling. Students learn by what they study and from whom they study with. You with me?"

"Yes, sir."

"The prison school will teach you subjects you've never studied and will help you learn how to interact with others. If you were under twenty-one, the state of Nevada would compel me to educate you. Since you aren't you will have to apply for schooling. Are you interested?"

Without hesitation, Amos said yes.

"I expected you to resist," McDaniels said.

"I want to know why I am the way I am, too."

McDaniels snorted and shook his head. All of this head tripping and he had but to ask.

At first Amos did not speak in any of his classes. He sat, listened, did both the in-class assignments and the homework, but remained silent. Gradually, he overcame his silence. For the first few weeks he feigned ignorance when asked questions, but then he started speaking when he knew the answer. Usually, others knew the answers, too.

He was very good at math, but after six weeks he advanced to geometry and found it more difficult. It made him think he did not know everything, which shook his belief in his smooth running brain. In the Underground, he decided what he wanted to learn. Here others decided.

His reading skills rated below average. He found reading a whole book more difficult than reading *Popular Mechanics* one article at a time. His homework included enough reading for his skills to improve. He won library time with good job performance and with practice he learned how to read faster.

McDaniels made sure he visited the inmate no more than once every two weeks, and sometimes stretched it to three. When Nelson first arrived at Crocket his face was an expressionless mask that never changed. With school and socialization, the mask softened. A guard said he'd seen Nelson smile, not laugh, but smile. Learning how to interact with others was a big part of McDaniels's plan. He had to get Nelson out of the familiar and into situations – non-threatening situations – where he would solve his problem without violence. The process, he hoped, would help learn about Nelson.

One day, McDaniels called Nelson to his office. "I'm sending you outside for your scheduled exercise."

Nelson stiffened.

"What's the problem with you and the outdoors?" McDaniels stood, walked around his desk, and leaned on an edge. "Nelson?"

"Sir, nothing good has ever happened to me outside. I want to stay in."

"No. You're going out. What kind of nothing good?"

Nelson's feet moved restlessly against the red line on the floor. His hands locked waist high.

"I was at risk outside."

"How so?"

"There were things that wanted to eat me, and men who would kill me if they found me."

The force of the childhood memory shocked McDaniels.

"You were afraid of being eaten?"

"I was small. I was afraid. My mother was dead and my father sent me into the desert with no food and no water. He told me he would let me know when I could come in."

"How old were you?"

"Nine."

"How many hours did he expect you to stay out there?"

"Days. The first time five days."

"Your father expected you to survive for five days in the desert?"

"He said it was time to find out if I could survive. I had to learn to take care of myself because someday he would be gone."

"Did you know what he meant?"

"My father believed powerful men wished to kill him. They had already killed my mother and my best friend."

How did you survive in the desert? Was it a real desert?"

"Yes, we lived in a real desert. The first time I stole one of his cars and drove it to the town to get food and water."

"You drove a car at nine?"

"Yes, but not very well. I made driving stilts so I could reach the pedals. I do what I have to do."

"Where was this desert?"

"I won't tell you."

"Why?"

"I won't tell you."

"Okay. How many times did your father leave you in the desert?"

"Three."

McDaniels had seen the results of many cases of child abuse and Nelson's was not the most remarkable. Nelson himself was remarkable, but John Nelson would be remarkable at whatever he pursued.

"When you go outside you are not at risk here. The guards see everything." McDaniels saw a pleading look. "Your father is dead?"

"Yes."

"How long?"

"Five, no six, years."

"Did the people looking for him kill him?"

"Yes, one way or the other they killed him."

"How do you know he died?"

"The man who came here told me, but he's a liar."

"Would you like me to find out?"

"Sir, for you to find out means trusting you. I have never trusted a real person since I was nine." He thought of Clyde. "Well, one."

"Nelson, I promise to help you if I can."

Amos nodded, and told his story of the carnival and his father's death as it had been told to him.

"Bishop, six years ago," McDaniels said as he wrote in the file. "I'll see what I can find. Who did you live with after your father was dead?"

"A friend, but we didn't see each other often. He didn't like the Underground and I didn't go up."

McDaniels was afraid to interrupt the flow of the story, and let the "Underground" comment go.

"This was still in the desert?"

"Yes."

"Did you have friends? Did you see other people?"

Nelson shook his head, his hands starting to move faster.

"Do you believe that you are still in danger?"

"It doesn't matter."

"Why?"

"We all believed in the danger. Believing makes it true."

McDaniels returned to the back of his desk.

"The first day, I asked you if you were hiding in prison. You said no. Is that true?"

Nelson stopped fidgeting.

"Yes."

"What are you doing here?"

"I need to learn about the outside world."

"In prison?"

"Yes."

"What do you want to do in the outside world?"

"I have to learn how not to be afraid."

"What are you afraid of?"

"If someone makes me angry, I can't control myself."

"Okay, you'll go you out with the maximum security people. They are confined to one section of the yard. There will be plenty of room for you to be alone. You get acclimated, gain your control, and then I'll send you out with the rest. You have two weeks."

"Thank you, sir."

"Dismissed."

Nelson turned away, but McDaniels stopped him.

"After you learn not to be afraid of the outside world and you leave here, then what?"

Nelson stopped. He faced the door and did not turn as he spoke.

"My father gave me an order."

"What?"

"I don't think I should tell you."

"Whatever you say will stay between us."

"That's a promise?"

"I said so. Don't insult me."

"Sir, what does a fate worse than death mean?"

"Why do you want to know?"

"He told me to find a fate worse than death for the men who ruined our lives. If I couldn't find one then I am to kill them. I don't know what a fate worse than death means."

The cold chill that gripped him every time Nelson visited this office, clutched McDaniels again.

"Come back here! Toes on the line! Let me get this straight. You came to prison- of all places - to learn how to exist in the outside world so you can kill people. Right?"

"You promised, sir."

The chill turned to ice and he swallowed the anger in a gulp.

"God help me, I did," McDaniels whispered.

The buzzer on his desk rang. He ignored it as he tried to think. The buzzer rang again, and he answered.

"What?"

"You're late for your meeting with Warden Stathem, sir," his secretary said.

"Okay, I'll be right there. Send the guard in."

He hung up the phone.

"This conversation is not through. It appears I have twenty months to talk you out of this idea. In the meantime, I'll see what I can find out about your father. "

Later in the day, he called the Bishop, California police and inquired into the shooting death of a man named Caldwell. He made it an official inquiry and the detective he was transferred to wanted to know the reason for the call.

"Rumors. You know how it is. Inmates looking for leverage."

"What did you hear?"

"Only that there was a killing over a payroll from a carnival six years ago and the victim's name was Caldwell."

"I'll get back to you," the detective said. "We're going to want to know who this inmate is. This is still an open case."

"Are you working it?"

"I just said it's open. Three people died. Caldwell took two of the shooters with him, and we figure a couple more got away. We still don't know why it took four shooters to steal three thousand dollars."

"And you know nothing more?"

"That's right."

"I'll see if I can find anything else," McDaniels said.

It took a week for Bishop to call him back. It gave him time to come up with a story.

"So who was this inmate?" Bishop detective John Lowenson asked.

"His name was Ellis Wietz."

"Was?"

"He died a few days ago of lung cancer." McDaniels had looked for a convict with vague ties to Southern California. Wietz, even before he died, was perfect. "He knew he was dying. We hear this kind of stuff all the time in the hospital, and no one paid any attention until it was too late. Whatever he knew went with him."

The long silence that met his story surprised McDaniels.

"What's the deal?" he asked.

"Thanks for the call," Lowenson said, and hung up.

He called me, McDaniels thought, now completely convinced of the validity of Nelson's story. He left his office and went to reception in the Visitors Center. He found the visitor's record for the day "Larry Zoeller" visited, removed the entry, and updated the directive that all inquiries regarding John Patrick Nelson must go through him.

On the first day Amos went into the yard for his hour of exercise the sky was overcast. A cold wind sent dust swirling into the corners. Amos went out as the rest of the general population came in. No one commented on his hat pulled low on his forehead and the collar of his coat turned up higher than the corner of his eyes. After the door locked behind him, he kept his head down, his hands in his pockets, and shuffled when he walked. Mentally and physically he slowed. By the time he finished his second lap, he felt a thumping in the middle of his forehead that grew louder with each step. His vision blurred as his headache intensified. He stumbled to the locked door, and saw no guards inside. He tried to walk away, but the throbbing and blurring grew worse.

At the end of the hour, the guards found him with his elbows, knees, and forehead on the ground. Unable to answer questions, and unable to stand, the guards helped him to the infirmary where he received aspirin. He sat on a straight-back chair with his eyes closed and waited for his headache to recede. When he returned to his cell the headache still blurred his vision.

The second day brought more of the same, but this time the guards offered no help when he came in. They enforced the rules and the rule said the inmate shall be active outside for one hour. They saw Nelson's antics as malingering.

On the third day Amos pushed against the pounding and blurring. He picked a point across the yard and paced the distance. When he could no longer cope, he closed his eyes and set himself on the line, then counted steps. In a few minutes, even with his eyes closed, the feeling spread faster than either of the previous times. With no warning, he threw up violently. He waited for the spasms to pass and opened his eyes. His field of vision had shrunk to the size of a small tube. The distorted input sent his stomach spiraling, and he retched even more violently than the first time, then fainted. He awoke on the floor inside the door to the exercise yard. The guards had to help him back to his cell, dragging him past the other inmates of C Block.

LaVoy McDaniels received reports of Nelson's trips to the yard. At first he made the decision to leave the condition untreated to speed Nelson's acclimation. When told of the vomiting and Nelson being led past the prisoners in an obviously weakened state, he moved Nelson to the infirmary and went to see him. When he got there, he found Nelson asleep and on a drip.

"He's dehydrated," an intern said.

"What's happening?"

"Don't know," the intern said. "His temperature is 99.6 but that can be agitation. His heartbeat is irregular and his pulse high. The doctor won't be here for a couple of days. Maybe a shrink could do more."

"I'll find somebody," McDaniels said.

1987

Bird Shit to Bullion

Teresa Gill's first outing for *Mother's Own* appeared under the headline "Boss Ferry – Man in the Middle" and the byline read "Lois Lane." The story followed the general idea Teresa had laid out for Oscar Mason, but together they added a third man-in-the-middle component. They focused on Ferry's business interests under the family name. It was more a history lesson, but it filled in the back story for what she'd write next and disguised her non-environmental motivations. Under the head was a 19th century style cartoon depicting Nathan Ferry as Boss Tweed with tentacles reaching into all kinds of nefarious anti-green businesses.

"Don't you think this is kind of pathetic," Gill said into the phone, "that we always talk on Friday night because neither of us has anything better to do?"

"What do you know about bird shit?" Mason said, ignoring her question.

"It pisses me off when it hits my windshield," she answered. "What's that got to do with my next Diemaker story?"

"Nothing. Unless you can prove the guy's next victim is going to be Denis Puleston, or he intends to blow up the Green Peace boat, we aren't ready. Speaking of Puleston, what do you know about bird shit."

"Obviously not what you want me to say. Give me a clue."

"Read up on W. R. Grace's phosphate empire and then take another look at Ferry. I got a killer idea for an editorial cartoon so make this good. I'll even pay you because you didn't want to do it."

"Will whining do me any good? I want to do my Diemaker stories."

"Soon. I promise."

The good news about talking on Friday nights was that it usually gave her Saturday and Sunday to do her research. It didn't take long to discover that W.R. Grace and Company was founded in Peru in the 1850's on bird shit, or guano, bird droppings rich in phosphates and nitrogen that made excellent fertilizers and explosives, both in demand at the time. Their success eventually led to Grace National Bank. The Grace interests lay far to the political right. Teresa wondered if W.R. Grace and Ambrose Ferry had known each other.

The Ferry's may have drawn inspiration from Grace's bird shit deposits in Peru with a similar enterprise in Malaysia, or Borneo as it was known at the time. She wondered if the Grace foray into banking was prompted by the Ferry's horning in on a good deal, though there was no evidence the two were ever direct competitors. The Ferry's kept their guano in Asia converting it to gold before bringing the bullion home. She wondered how all of this played out with the British who still called the shots in southeast Asia. Her master's degree in economics told her it seemed unlikely the Ferry's could have pulled this off without support from England. It took time to find her answer, but when she did she pumped her fist in the air before slamming the library table, a gesture that got her booted from the reference room. Ferry's English angel was a vice consul named Sir Bartholomew Treblehorn, whose great-grandson, Sir Douglas, was The Diemaker's second victim.

"What's all that mean?" Oscar wanted to know.

"I don't know. The Diemaker was a history major, or a closet environmentalist?"

"Teresa, forget The Diemaker. Write me the story I want. That cartoon I told you about? I'm dying to use it. It's Nathan

Ferry with mutton-chop whiskers squatting in a bird nest shitting gold bricks. Is that great or what?"

"Okay, Oscar, but then it's my turn."

"Deal," Oscar said.

1986-87

Prison Learning

For Colin Truax, San Francisco beat the hell out of New York. In the five years he'd lived in the City he had grown used to the cool summers, the crystal clear days of both fall and spring, and even the chilly, damp winters that made your teeth chatter. He stood at the window of his twelfth floor corner office of the building on Sacramento Street. He smiled at the deep blue sky on this autumn Friday afternoon. The Forty-Niners played the Packers on Sunday and he had tickets. He heard the door open behind him and saw the reflection of Thomas Wilford in the glass.

"Remember the incident a few years ago with a guy named Caldwell?" Wilford asked. "He ran a carnival."

"Bishop."

"Right. There's a cop there who watches for anyone asking questions."

Truax felt a constriction in his chest.

"Go on."

"An assistant warden at a Nevada prison called. He wanted details."

"Why?"

"Supposedly a convict had a death-bed clearing of the conscience."

"We know that's not true. Find out."

"I pulled the file," Wilford said. "It's orange."

"Yes, I know. Go out there yourself. Where is the prison?"

"Crocket State Prison, about an hour and a half out of Vegas. Why not use our people there?"

"Because orange means Steerman, and Ferry's all over my ass about not catching Steerman." Truax shook his head. "Twenty years. It makes me crazy if I think about it too much. Show his picture that we aged."

"He'll be long gone. I guess he could be the prisoner."

"He'll be gone, but maybe who he went to see isn't."

"I'll leave first thing Monday."

"Go now. You do remember who Caldwell was, don't you?"

"The Marine. Eliot."

"Ferry's going to shit if this isn't tied down fast."

"Don't tell him until we know."

"I like this job. I like telling you to go to Nevada while I go to the Packers game. That means keeping Ferry informed. Get going."

As Chief Executive Officer of Vesta Corporation, Truax told other people to do what he used to do himself. Vesta had been his idea, born less than a year after Greene died. At the beginning, he and Norm Brinks spent all their time hunting for Steerman and for the Marine without result. But they did find people on the run, and some had rewards on their heads. About the same time, two of Greene's mercenary friends asked if he wanted any help looking for his killer. Truax said no. As they left, the mercs said they'd keep their ears open and maybe they could help each other. They were always looking for men, any men. It didn't take long for Truax to discover when you turned a man in for a reward there were all kinds of questions, but in the merc world there were none and the money better.

Vesta settled profitably into the Ferry stable of financial interests. Colin loved his townhouse in Sausalito with its view of the bay and the weekend sailboats, the ferry back and forth across the bay to work, weekends in the wine country, and season tickets to the Forty-Niners. Life was good other than Ferry's rants at four a.m. Truax still collected his five grand a year from Steerman but at no time in the twenty years since Bong Sat had he ever had the chance to lay his hands on the man.

During John Nelson's visits to the yard, his school work suffered. Each day the prisoner spent one hour in English comp, an hour in beginning geometry, and on three days a week an hour in a class called Civilization. LaVoy McDaniels had written the syllabus for Civilization. The hour included twenty minutes of lecture on topics ranging from philosophy to political science, and forty minutes of group discussion.

After school, Nelson went into the yard for an hour where his exercise area was visible from LaVoy's office. On the third day he looked down and saw Nelson cowering against a wall and wondered if his plan had any chance of working. He decided to talk to George Hillard, the teacher of the Civilization class.

"Is he participating? No. Not a peep. There's life there, I can see a light in the eye, but that's it."

"You saw his assessment results?" McDaniels asked.

"Yeah, but it doesn't show. He's getting by, not much more."

McDaniels took the long way home that night, and stopped on a bluff overlooking Crocket in the middle of its valley. The usual afternoon winds eddied dust around the walls like the prison was under attack. He got out of the car and worried about his decision on Nelson. As he paced, LaVoy decided it was more important to work on Nelson's brain than his phobia.

The next day McDaniels found Nelson in the shop.

"Try harder in school and we'll forget about yard," he said. Nelson smiled. It was the first time McDaniels had ever seen it.

By his third day free of the yard, Nelson's performance in the classroom improved noticeably. By the fifth, George Hillard told McDaniels a different story.

"Hard to believe it's the same guy. The quick intelligence? Well, it's there. It shows in his body language, but until a few days ago, he was like a puppet with his strings cut."

"Now?"

"He hates to sit. He does, but he's ready to launch. When he's thinking, he sways."

"What else?" McDaniels asked.

"I think his intuitive skills are exceptional. If I'm making an argument, he gets there way ahead of everyone else. When he stops swaying, I know he's got it. We call it a fast brain. It's hereditary, and he makes the most of his ability – now that he's indoors."

LaVoy saw the name St. Thomas Aquinas printed on the blackboard.

"The Five Proofs of God?" he asked.

"Yeah, it's an interesting exercise," Hillard said. "Where did that come from?"

"Baptist school. I went to church school three afternoons a week after public school. Baptists believe in God, period, but the good reverend who taught the class thought faith was enough but proof of God wouldn't hurt. He taught Aquinas."

"Most of the guys in this class have some religion in their past. More religion than math, of course religious proof is far less rigorous. Your boy loved the first proof of God."

"The argument of the unmoved mover," McDaniels said. "Aristotle."

"I'd like to get him alone. I think he's holding back."

"Let's see how he does for a few more weeks."

Saturday afternoon found Thomas Wilford driving back from Crocket. Coming from New York City left him unprepared for the oppressive emptiness that surrounded the prison. If anyone escaped it wouldn't be on foot. His car phone got no signal until he neared Las Vegas.

"No luck," he told Truax, "but they have two shifts."

"When's the shift change?" Truax asked.

"Tuesday."

"Call me then. While you're in Vegas show the Steerman picture around the hotels. If he went to the prison he had the same problem you have. And, Thomas, I've haven't called Ferry yet. Get me something."

The yard became the first time Amos had set his mind to something and failed and failure left him vulnerable. The "vampire" nickname returned, and he heard laughs behind his back. When he came to Crocket he didn't care what other people thought, but now he did. He didn't want friends, but he wanted to be able to pass as normal. In school he learned discipline and restraint by not speaking out every time he knew the answer. When he did answer, he was always right.

He needed a victory after the setback in the yard, and decided a normal conversation would bolster his confidence.

Near the end of the second week, a con named Chuck Duggan walked out of the classroom with him.

"How come you're so smart?" Duggan asked.

Amos remembered practicing a conversation like this during his last stay in solitary.

"I'm not so smart. Kinda smart about some things, and know nothing about others."

Duggan walked slower, Amos slowed too, until only a guard trailed them as they headed for the cell block.

"You tear the head off that guy?"

"How could I? I was locked up same as you."

He had practiced this conversation, too.

"Can you walk through steel?"

"Nobody can do that."

"So how'd you do it?"

"I didn't," Amos said, voice even. "People are afraid of me for things I can't do. How could I tear the head off that rat? I was in the hole. Maybe I could have picked the lock on my cell, but in the hole there is no lock on the inside. No way to get out."

"You can't walk through walls, either?"

"Why would I be here I could? Would you stay?"

"That's what I told those humps! If a guy could do that he'd just leave!"

"I'd have to be invisible, too."

"You know what I would do if I was invisible?" Duggan asked, then laughed. "I'd hang out in the girls' dorm. Shit!"

That same day a guard took Amos to McDaniels. A chair sat with its front legs on the line and McDaniels waved him to it.

"I've heard back from Bishop. A man named Caldwell was killed by four gunmen, two of whom were killed in the shootout. The other two got away. The police say the case is still open."

They existed. He closed his eyes, then thanked McDaniels.

McDaniels closed the file on his desk. "School is better since we stopped the yard."

"Yes, sir."

"How do you feel about not going out?"

"I'm disappointed."

"We can keep trying," McDaniels said, "but I don't see much point."

"I want to go out."

"Why?"

"I want to be normal."

McDaniels leaned back in his chair.

"There are doctors who might be able to help. There may be a physical reason, or something else. Either way there will be questions. Where do you want to start?"

"The physical."

Thomas Wilford took Sunday off to tend to his own needs, and on Monday started the hotel search for Steerman. He reached the Stardust in mid-afternoon. The desk clerk said he'd been off the week in question, but the person who had taken his shifts would be in at eleven. Something in the clerk's wording caught Wilford's ear.

"You recognize the photo?"

"I wasn't here on those dates."

"Yeah, right, but have you *ever* seen this guy?"

"Yes. He's kinda of a regular."

"How regular?"

The unexpected success caught Wilford by surprise. The clerk saw his interest.

"I'm afraid I couldn't say, sir."

"How much do you think it might cost so you could say?"

"I'm off at four. Meet me in the coffee shop."

Wilford went to a pay phone and called San Francisco.

"No luck on the juice," Truax said. "Looks like you'll have to stay over."

"Is there a plan in place for actually finding Steerman?" Wilford asked.

"There is a protocol. It's never been used."

"Dust it off. The desk clerk at the Stardust says he's a regular."

Truax opened a folder with an orange tab, and spread the contents on his desk. He called the number – a Los Angeles 213 area code. A beep sounded followed by instructions for the message.

"Quarries name – Steerman," he said. "Information confirmed. Colin Truax, Vesta, 415-555-1588."

He wondered to whom the call would go.

LaVoy McDaniels talked with the outside doctor who'd examined Nelson.

"Okay, here's my best guess," Dr. Marshall Peters said. "Receptors in the eye are distorting light in the UV range and sending messages his brain interprets as acute anxiety. It explains his closing and shading his eyes. Even then he gets sick. Probably because it's already too late and the brain has flooded him with panic."

"You're sure about this?" McDaniels asked.

"Not at all. It's a theory. Nothing more. The only physical support is that his pupils are a little larger than normal. Is that enough to cause the rest? I don't know."

"How did it start?"

"He says he spent the last ten years literally underground. That covers all of puberty. When he saw the light of day, he was scared. Think of all the body's changes during those years." Peters took LaVoy's arm. "Our experiences become our input and his input was radically different. It's kind of a miracle he isn't more of a mess."

"What do I do?"

"He told me he doesn't sleep. Probably from a distorted body clock that normally sets itself with daylight. I'll start him on Melatonin. When he's rested he should deal with the anxiety better. I'm sending you some wrap around shades treated to reduce ninety percent of all UV light. Make sure he wears them in the yard. It will reduce his vision, but he'll be ahead of the game." Peters held up a hand. "If I'm right."

"Will he get over this?"

"I don't know. I doubt it, but let me know what happens." The doctor started to leave. "Oh, what might work is to gradually increase the amount of UV and see if the brain adjusts. I'll send you some more shades with reduced UV filtering. Nothing to lose as long as he's in here."

"As long as he's in here?"

"He can't control himself when the attacks hit. Physically, he's one hell of a specimen so he could do a lot of damage." He turned toward the door, then stopped again. "Let's say what Nelson told us is the truth. We know about the light problem because he couldn't hide it. God knows what else is wrong with him. Going outside, school, he's being challenged. It's all very upsetting."

"How upsetting?"

"I'd say extreme."

Wilford called Truax back an hour later.

"The clerk definitely remembers him but not his name," Wilford said. "He says he's seen him two or three times in the last year."

"How long since the first time he saw him?"

"About a year."

"Thomas, find out if Steerman went to that prison, and if he did, who he saw. You got it?"

"Yeah, the new shift comes on tomorrow."

As Amos went into the yard, he put on the oversized dark sunglasses. Everything dimmed, but he could see. As before, he had this corner of the yard to himself. Seventy yards away the maximum security prisoners lifted weights, kicked a ball, or sat on bleachers. He forced himself to keep his eyes open, and walked slowly toward the far side of the yard. He picked out a spot and counted steps so he could find his way back if he had to. He reached his goal, took a breath, and started back. Five laps later, he felt an increase in his heart rate. He pushed the glasses tighter and walked faster.

The phone woke Truax at four a.m.

"Tell me what you have," said Nathan Ferry.

Truax shook off the surprise, told Ferry everything, and waited.

"Call me when you have more. Get me what I want."

The Civilization class met every Tuesday, Thursday, and Friday. John Patrick Nelson, Chuck Duggan, and three others known only as Vern, Cannon, and Theo made up the class taught by George Hillard.

"What's the purpose of the Ethics section, Vern?" Hillard asked.

"So we can learn to think for ourselves."

"Okay. Specifically, Theo?"

"Learning how others learned to think and how they built value systems so we can too."

"Care to expand on that, Cannon?"

Cannon who sat slumped in his chair and rarely spoke, shook his head.

"Anyone? Duggan?"

"Studying Thomas Aquinas and his philosophy about God."

"Specifically, Nelson?"

"What we can know and how we come to know it."

"And?"

"Aquinas said all humans gain knowledge by natural revelation – human nature – or special revelations that could come only from God."

"Okay, more or less. What was this special revelation called?"

"Supernatural."

"What does supernatural mean? Anyone?"

"Ghosts, spooks," Vern said.

"Sure, but let's take a look at the word. Super. What does 'super' mean?"

No one replied.

"Come on, people. Anyone?"

"Anything that exceeds every day," Nelson said.

"Yes, good way to put it. So, to Aquinas, supernatural revelations exceeded natural revelations because they were above everyday life. Way above, as in coming only from God. Today, as we talk about what Aquinas believed, think about your own situations. Thomas Aquinas said you can learn from your human reasoning, but you can also learn by taking other things on faith. Questions?"

No one raised a hand.

"All humans possess human nature. In psychiatry, there is a term – semantic memory – that describes shared memories we all have that form a context for our individual experiences. Then there is knowledge that Aquinas said came only from God taught by the Catholic Church and the Scriptures. This supernatural knowledge could not be deduced from the simple application of our human reasoning. Returning to our psychiatric analogy, and this one doesn't work as well, we each have episodic memories that define our individuality in the context of those shared memories. So why raise the ideas of Aquinas's human nature and semantic memory in the same breath?"

"Because all humans are the same," Nelson answered.

Hillard looked at him with interest. "Do you believe that about yourself?"

Nelson squirmed, and Hillard saw him start to stand, then fall heavily back as if tied on a short tether. The other four students looked at Nelson.

"The definition of universality is always open to discussion," Hillard said. "Now, given that leeway, do you believe you are the same as your classmates?"

Silence stretched, then Nelson said, "Do they think I am the same as them?"

"Let's find out. Vern, are you and Nelson the same?"

"No."

"Why not?"

"Because he can do things none of the rest of us can do."

"How do you know he can?"

"How come you're picking on me?"

"I'm not. Cannon, do you agree and if so, why?"

Cannon sat up and licked his lips.

"He can do weird things like walk through bars and be invisible."

"Does this make you nervous, Nelson, your peers believing you are supernatural?"

Nelson's agitation grew, and as it did, his chair started rocking.

"Easy, Nelson," Hillard said. "How do the rest of you know Nelson is different? Somebody told somebody who told somebody else and pretty soon it's common knowledge. In the context of what we're describing, what is this?"

"Supernatural!" Duggan said.

"Right. You took rumor on faith and now everyone believes it. Can you walk through bars, Nelson?"

Nelson shook his head.

"Or make yourself invisible? No, but if you could what would change? You could walk out of here and no one could stop you, but only *your* reality would change."

Hillard looked around, inviting comments, but none came.

"What's this mean? That sometimes human nature trumps the truth we all see with the supernatural we take on faith. We all know we can't walk through walls and make ourselves invisible, but here we are believing Nelson can."

Hillard stopped, leaned forward inviting a response, but even when none came he saw they were all into the topic.

"We're trained to accept supernatural knowledge as soon as we learn about religion. Religion teaches there are wonderful, mystical things in existence that we cannot see, and if we want to find out for ourselves we have to take it on faith. The same with Nelson. Think of all the speculation you've shared with your friends talking about how you wish you could do what you believe he can."

Duggan laughed and nodded.

"Why are we talking about this in prison? Theo?"

Theo didn't reply.

"What do you talk about the most?"

"Pussy."

Laughter, and then Hillard said, "Second most."

"Getting out."

"Right. And once you're out, how many of you want to come back? No one, right? But, statistically, two of you will. Forty percent become repeat offenders. Now, Theo, what are we talking about?"

"If we are going to take anything on faith it should be we can get out and stay out."

Hillard looked around and was gratified to see five faces staring back.

"Questions before we call it a day? None? Okay, so until Thursday, think about what we talked about. And, Nelson, we all know you can't just disappear. Right?"

Four of the five faces did not meet Hillard's eyes.

Thomas Wilford met the shift change as they reported for work. No one recognized the photo until the next to the last guard. The double take told Wilford the guard recognized the face, even though he denied it.

Wilford waited until break time and followed the man to the smoking porch.

"You recognized my guy," Wilford said. "There's money in it for some help."

"How much?"

"Names and dates, five hundred. Information on who he came to see another five hundred."

"Show me the money. I can give you both right now."

Wilford peeled off five one hundred dollar bills and let the man see there were more.

"The guy's name is Zoeller, Larry Zoeller. You want the exact date? I can get it, but somebody will know if I look. Your call."

"Who'd he see?"

"He came to see John Nelson, but he never saw him."

"How come?"

The man held his hand out for the rest of his money.

"Nelson still here?"

"Yep."

Wilford counted out five more hundreds.

"Anybody who wants to see Nelson has to go through a warden named McDaniels. Zoeller saw McDaniels then left. He did not come back. That's like four or five months ago."

"You don't know why they're screening his visitors?"

"It happens."

"You know anything about Nelson?"

"Scary."

"He's scary?"

"I heard he's killed a couple of guys."

"How's he getting away with it?"

"Self-defense. The chicken hawks came at him. Word has it Nelson sneaked out of his cell one night and tore the head off a guy in his cell. Now no one fucks with him. Having McDaniels looking out for you doesn't hurt, either."

"What's with McDaniels?"

The guard shook his head.

"Can you get me Nelson's prints?"

"It won't do you no good. The guy ain't got no prints on file other than Vegas."

"How do you know?"

"How much you think we got to talk about? This guy is one never-happened-before after another. Can't go outside, either. He's like some kind of vampire."

"If this is bullshit, you're jerking off the wrong guy."

"Believe it or not, up to you."

"What if I want to see this guy?"

"Sign in. You'll get held until McDaniels screens you."

"What if I don't want to see McDaniels?"

"Try asking for Wilbur Crane, he's the captain of the guard. He's approachable, if you get what I mean." The guard laughed. "He'd help you get at Nelson. He'd love an excuse to lose that guy."

"There a phone here?"

It didn't take McDaniels long to hear about the inquiries into Nelson. He knew the interest was his fault.

"How much you get paid?" McDaniels asked the guard who had taken the money.

The guard didn't answer.

"I can't fire you for this," McDaniels said, "it's not illegal, but I'd start looking for another job. There are people in here we're trying to protect from their pasts? Did he ask anything else?"

"He wanted to see Nelson. I told him he would have to see you. He went off to use the phone and didn't come back."

Thomas Wilford decided not to talk to Truax on a phone from the waiting room, and this was no conversation for a car phone. The call waited until he reached Las Vegas.

"Any ideas who the kid is?" Wilford asked.

"None, but I want to know. I don't like the warden screening our mystery man,. Get out of Vegas. I'll take care of this with local people. It will be easier for them to get inside than us."

"There's a captain of the guard they tell me is on the take."

"If he can be bought by one he can be bought by two. I don't like leaving a trail."

"What about the warden?"

"I haven't decided. It's the same guy who called Bishop, but I've got a call to make first."

Truax called the number in the Steerman file. Ferry called him back three hours later.

"Identify the prisoner and get rid of him," he said. "If Steerman is interested, we should be as well."

"The warden?"

"No one will care about a dead prisoner. They'd care about a dead warden."

LaVoy McDaniels heard about the hit on Nelson from one of the snitches he had salted through the inmate population.

"Who took it?" he asked.

"No one yet. They all know what will happen if they miss."

"Let me know," McDaniels said.

"I might not hear in time. New guys who don't know Nelson might take it. It's a lot of money. For that much it could even be a guard. If Crane takes it I won't hear nothing."

"Get word to Nelson," McDaniels said.

Duggan found Amos toward the end of his shift in the machine shop.

"There's a hit on you."

Amos stopped pushing his broom, and asked, "Who?"

Duggan shrugged. "It's out, that's all I know. Nobody's picked it up, but be ready."

"Thanks," Amos said. He didn't want to leave prison, he liked school, but it was time. Before he left the machine shop, he armed himself. He made a crude garrote and wore it like a belt.

The glasses weren't perfect. Each day in the yard he kept his mind busy feeling himself move as anxiety feelings wiggled at the edge of his attention. He started with his feet, and by the time he reached the neck, he forced himself to look up. Never at the sun, but at the sky. Even on the bluest of days, it looked gray through the filtered lenses. He never relaxed even though the yard was the one place he considered himself safe.

He wondered if McDaniels knew about the hit and that he'd started it with his call.

The yells from the maximum security cons carried across the yard. He looked up as the yells grew louder. The glasses blocked his peripheral vision. He heard running steps and more yells. It took seconds to see the men who chased a ball directly toward him. He debated whether he should kick it back, or pick it up, or perhaps simply step aside.

When the man closest to the ball kicked it again to keep it coming, he recognized the threat.

The man ran fast, two others lagged behind. Amos threw the glasses aside. The man held a shiv.

Light sliced into his eyes, but he could see. Anxiety raced through his body. Amos threw himself at the attacker's feet, rolling sideways as he fell and freeing the garrote. His repressed fury fueled by the daylight ignited. He grunted as the man's feet kicked his ribs, then fell across him. The attacker lunged, missed as Amos continued to roll, and lost his balance. Amos threw himself across his downed enemy, and snaked the garrote around the man's throat. The slack disappeared as Amos crossed his wrists and pulled. The attacker's mouth opened, but no sound escaped. The wire drove the tongue out of his throat.

Amos's exultant roar echoed across the yard. The other two men had hesitated giving the first a chance to do his job. When he failed, they leaped. Amos fell backward, still holding a death grip on the garrote. The pain in his head, released by the exertion, disappeared, and he roared again. He let go of the wire, rolled free, and leaped to his feet, arms stretched to the sky. He faced the other attackers. Saliva trailed from the corners of his mouth and his eyes stared so wide the muscles hurt. His attackers cowered, then ran. He caught the slowest, and bellowed again as he wrapped his arms around the man's neck and made ready to snap the neck. As his eyesight dimmed, he saw guards running toward him. He let go of the neck and sank to his knees. He wrapped his arms over his head as if protecting it. He thought of the glasses, looked through eyes now no wider than slits, and saw his shades ten yards away. He crawled toward them and put them on. Too late. The fire of the attack had evaporated. He lost consciousness.

LaVoy McDaniels stood at attention across the desk from where Warden Jack Stathem yelled at him. Wilbur Crane leaned a shoulder against the wall and McDaniels sensed his enjoyment as Stathem's anger rained down.

"You wagered your ass that you could keep Nelson off my radar. You lost!"

"Yes, sir."

"What's the body count since Nelson joined us? Just the ones he personally killed."

"Two, sir."

"I thought it was more."

"Yes, sir. Some were hurt pretty bad."

"I want a permanent solution to this problem," Stathem said. "Permanent and quiet. I think this is a matter for you, Captain."

Crane pushed off the wall and saluted, the smile growing larger as he said, "The pleasure is all mine."

"Are you going to share the contract money with the warden, Crane?" McDaniels asked.

"What contract?" Stathem asked.

"You didn't know, sir?" McDaniels asked. "The hit out on Nelson. None of the cons wanted it except the clowns Nelson threw around the yard. Crane let it go down so we would have this conversation."

"That true, Crane?"

"No, sir. McDaniels is just whining because he's losing his favorite toy."

"It's a damn shame," McDaniels said. "You get rid of Nelson, sir, and your profits in the shop go up in smoke. Crane wants him gone because Nelson sees all the contraband Crane smuggles in and out, plus Crane takes a fat payoff for following your orders. Crime pays. Right, Crane? What's *your* body count while you've been working here?"

Stathem looked back and forth between the two adversaries.

"We all have our reasons for being here in this hell hole, and I'm willing to let a few things slide." Stathem stood. "I'm sick of you two bickering. Crane, I think we'll leave you out of the solution. If Nelson goes missing you and I are going to take a long hard look at how drugs are getting into the prison. You follow what I'm saying?"

"Sir! Don't believe a word this fucking guy says."

"Shut up! You get away with the shit you do because it keeps things in balance, but don't think you have any secrets." Stathem shook his head. "I know about the contract and who holds it. I wrote the book on keeping snitches in play. Either do what I say, or I replace you."

"You're making a mistake."

"Fuck up again, Crane, and you'll be the one who gets lost. Now get out of here. McDaniels, stay put."

After the door closed behind Crane, Stathem turned to face McDaniels.

"You won this one, LaVoy, but I wouldn't savor the victory."

"Yes, sir."

"Take care of the Nelson problem." Stathem looked at the closed door. "It would be nice to take care of both Nelson and Crane at the same time. You could say we share those problems."

"I'll take care of Nelson. He's off your radar. I'll see what I can do about our other problem, sir."

"Good." The warden went back to his view of elsewhere. "Be glad your passion is tied to your intellect, and not your purse. Dismissed."

McDaniels went into the hole to see Nelson. McDaniels signaled the guard to open Nelson's door then waved him off. Nelson sat on the narrow pallet that passed for a bed, and came to his feet. In the dim light he appeared older.

"I am told to make you disappear. Around here, that means you get taken out in the desert and killed – unless you have a better idea."

"I am a legend," Nelson said quietly. "I should fulfill everyone's expectations and disappear."

"How?"

"With your help. No one will ever hear of John Nelson again other than as a myth."

"What do you need?"

"There is a steel door off the shop that leads to the utilities tunnel."

"How do you know?"

Nelson looked at him, and didn't answer.

"Okay, yes," LaVoy nodded.

"Does it end outside the prison walls?"

"I think it goes outside to a substation and the backup generators. I'll check."

"How many doors?"

"I'll find out."

"I can walk four miles an hour at night, faster if there's moonlight. How long will it take me to walk to a town?"

"Two nights, maybe three."

"Are you willing to leave me a change of clothes, a map, water and food for three days?"

McDaniels nodded.

"Tomorrow, release me from here. I will go to my first two classes, and then disappear before Civilization."

"Why then?"

"Hillard told the class it was impossible for me to disappear."

"He'll report you missing."

"I'll tell Duggan I'm going to the infirmary. Hillard won't check. It will buy a few hours."

The next morning, a guard led Amos to the mess hall. Everyone stared as he filled a tray and sat at his usual table. No one spoke to him until Duggan came over and sat beside him.

"You okay, man?"

"Thanks for the warning."

"What happened? I heard you killed three guys, but that can't be true. You'd be in solitary forever."

"Two were hurt. The other ran."

"No shit! They had to be crazy to take a hit on you."

"Please don't talk about this. I just want to fit in."

"Fit in?" Duggan laughed, and slapped Amos on the back. "No chance, man! You going to class?"

"After the infirmary."

Amos walked to the checkout and told a guard he had an appointment in the infirmary. He waited twenty minutes before being led to an examining room. McDaniels came in a few minutes later.

"There are three doors in the tunnel," he said, and handed Amos the keys.

Amos looked at them, ran a finger over their surfaces, and accepted two.

"I can pick the first lock. You might be asked to account for that key later."

"The two doors in the tunnel won't open after the alarm sounds for an escape."

"I'll be out by then. What about the substation?"

"Manhole cover. I don't have a key to the gate, but you can pick it. I buried a pack just north of the substation. Your glasses are there, and a second pair just in case. There's a candy wrapper with a rock on it to mark the spot."

The men looked at each other in silence.

"Where will you go?" McDaniels asked.

"I don't know."

"I'm sorry you're leaving." McDaniels shook his head. "First time I've ever said that to a prisoner, but then it's the first time I've ever helped one escape."

"I wanted to finish school. I want to know how people think."

McDaniels took a prescription tablet off the desk. He tore out a page and scrawled on the back.

"Go here." He handed the slip to Amos. "It's in Oregon. They will help you learn what you want."

"Thank you, for everything," Amos said, and put the paper in his pocket. "You believed in me."

"It scares me, turning you loose."

"You have nothing to fear, from me anyway."

"I have a favor," McDaniels said. "When you disappear, Crane will tell the people who put out the hit he took care of you and try to collect. It would be nice if he failed."

Amos nodded.

"Go to Oregon," LaVoy said. "You will learn more about God and man."

Before Civilization, Amos picked the lock on the steel door near the machine shop and slipped through. He followed the tunnel, then used the keys McDaniels gave him. At the end, he checked to be sure the manhole cover was loose before waiting for nightfall.

After dark he raised the manhole, exited the tunnel, and picked the lock on the door. He found the pack McDaniels had left for him, changed clothes, then started walking. Two days later a young man with a large back pack waited at a roadside stop for the night bus to Las Vegas.

After he arrived in Vegas, he went to the Stardust. He visited his safe deposit box, and took out a thousand dollars. He also retrieved his tool case and the letter from his father. Later, he sat in the lobby and read the local paper as he waited for the library to open. Buried on an inside page he found a small story saying the hunt for prisoner John Patrick Nelson continued. At the library, Amos used a typewriter, scissors, and the photocopy machine, then researched his next step. On the way to the bus depot he bought stamps, better fitting clothes, and mailed two letters.

A few days later, LaVoy McDaniels received a letter in a white envelope with a return address claiming to be from the Baptist Relief Fund of North America, in Medford, Oregon. He opened the envelope and inside were three one hundred dollar bills and a typed note that read:

Thank you. Since I have means and you were very generous with your supplies, please consider this a repayment.

LaVoy smiled at the money, then burned the letter and the envelope. He picked up the phone, called a friend in the Clark County Sheriff's office and collected on a debt that necessitated the friend changing a photo in a prisoner's file.

Finding John Patrick Nelson became harder.

PART IV: HEAVEN

1987-88

Monastic Life

Amos's bus arrived in Medford at dawn. Following the instructions McDaniels had written in the note, he asked the clerk at the bus depot how to find St. Mary's Catholic Church. She told him and he started walking.

Downtown Medford had few trees and the low buildings created little shade from the harsh glare of the morning sun. Even with his glasses, his headache started before he'd walked a block and grew rapidly worse. He wondered if fatigue weakened his resistance. He kept his head down and pushed the frames tighter to his forehead. He turned onto a street that took the sun out of his eyes. Up the block, he saw trees rich in shade. When he reached them, he knelt at the base, closed his eyes, and waited for the thickness in his head to thin.

"Do you need help?" a man asked.

Amos looked up. He saw a man in a black suit with a white collar.

"Are you a man of God?" Amos asked.

The man laughed softly.

"No one has asked for a long time. Yes, I am a man of God. How may I help, my son?"

"Would you help me to St. Mary's Catholic Church?"

"Yes, I will help you."

"Do you know Father Harold?"

"I am Father Harold."

"I would like to go there, please. I have a message for you."

"Take my arm. Are you ill?"

"Only for a moment. It will pass, and once I'm inside I'll be fine."

"What is your problem?"

"The light hurts my eyes."

"Are you blind? Partly blind?"

"No, sir. Ultraviolet light hurts my eyes. It's worse when I'm tired. I was on the bus all night."

"I see. If you want to close your eyes, I can lead you. I have led the blind before."

"But I'm not blind."

"A figure of speech, my son. Here, take my arm."

Two more blocks brought them to the church. Father Harold led Amos into the main sanctuary where morning mass was being said.

"Are you Catholic?" Father Harold whispered.

"No, sir, I'm curious."

"Sit here until mass is over, then we will talk of your curiosity."

Amos put his bag and pack on the bench as Father Harold left through a side door. At the front of the church, Amos counted eighteen people who walked to the altar and knelt. A priest wearing a white robe offered each something from a silver tray and then each drank from a silver cup. Amos heard words spoken to each by the priest but he did not recognize the language. He wondered if it was Latin. At the end, some of the people left, and others waited to visit a small room behind a

222

curtain. In the dim, quiet, church he yawned, and fell asleep. He awoke with Father Harold gently shaking his shoulder.

"Shall we talk quietly?" he asked, when Amos sat up. "What is your name?"

"John Nelson, sir."

"The standard address to a priest is father."

"Even though we are not related?"

"We are all related in the eyes of God. As a priest, God shares his wisdom with me, and it is my responsibility to share it with you, the way an earthly father shares his wisdom with his children. Why are you not religious?"

"There were no churches where I lived."

"Didn't your parents talk to you of faith?"

"My parents are dead, Father. My mother said that if there was a god it was an evil god."

The priest frowned.

"After she died who took care of you?"

"Father, it is not good for me to talk about this. I'm sorry if this is rude. Could you help me find St. Peter in the Woods?"

"St. Peter in - ." The priest leaned away and frowned. "Why?"

"I wish to stay there."

"But if you are not religious, why would you want to live at a monastery?"

Amos reached for his pack. "These are questions I don't wish to answer. I'm going to leave."

"Just a moment, my son. Stay seated." When Amos sat, the priest asked, "What is the message you have for me?"

"It is from Horatio. That's the name he said to tell you."

The priest nodded. "What is Horatio's message?"

"St. Peter in the Woods needs my skills. I can fix anything."

"I see. Well, that's different." Father Harold leaned back against the pew, and closed his eyes. He worked his lips in and out, then said, "Did Horatio tell you anything of St. Peter in the Woods?"

"No, Father."

"It is a place where only the most religious of the men of this faith go. It is a very long way from the rest of the world. They are not welcoming."

"But I can fix anything, and I want someplace a long way from the world where I can learn about St. Thomas Aquinas. You know the teachings of St. Thomas Aquinas?"

"I am familiar with them."

"I want to know more. I want to know how he thought."

"Why?"

"Where I was last, I was in school and we studied how Aquinas thought. I had to leave before I could learn more."

"I will have to think about this." Father Harold stood, and offered Amos a hand. "If you've been traveling all night you must be hungry."

Being in no hurry to admit failure to Nathan Ferry, Colin Truax omitted the color code on his next message. The response came from someone Truax did not know and instructed him to fly to Los Angeles. He was to report the next day at precisely one o'clock.

In the past, corporate jets carried him to meetings with Ferry. Not this time. He left Sausalito early enough to avoid traffic delays through downtown San Francisco, and made it to the airport in time to buy coffee and read *The Chronicle*. His flight boarded on time.

The plane sat on the ground for no explained reason for over an hour, and took off within minutes of their scheduled arrival in Los Angeles. After a smooth flight, they circled in a holding pattern for another hour. By the time Truax rode the escalator under the "Welcome to Los Angeles" sign, he was two hours behind schedule. He rented a car, drove out of the airport, and made it two blocks before coming to a complete stop on Century Drive. He tuned the radio to traffic information where he learned there were "incidents" in both directions on the San Diego Freeway and to expect lengthy delays. He looked at his watch and knew he would never reach Ferry by one o'clock. Allowing seven hours for door to door had seemed adequate. He sat, motor idling, and seethed. When he arrived at the gated mansion high on a ridge west of Brentwood offering a spectacular view of the ocean on the rare day without smog, the guard at the gate shook his head.

"He's pissed, man. You were supposed to be here an hour ago."

"Yeah, well tell it to United Airlines. They don't give a shit about Ferry's schedule."

Colin Truax worked on suppressing his anger as he cooled his heels outside Ferry's office for the fourth completely wasted hour of the day.

"Where have you been?" Ferry demanded, when Truax was finally admitted. "Your instructions were to be here at one."

"I've been sitting on a runway, sitting on a plane watching Los Angeles circle under my ass, sitting in traffic, and sitting right outside that door."

Ferry looked up from the papers on his desk.

"Kindly put a civil tongue in your head, Truax."

"Civil? This report could have been made in three minutes on the phone. Instead, you waste a complete day of my time. If that lacks respect, sir, then it runs both ways."

Ferry, who wore half glasses, peered over their top before removing them.

"Well, Colin, this is a side you've kept hidden."

"Sir, I was raised to respect authority. I try. I was also taught to stand up to its abuse."

"Abuse?"

"Yes. We have a more important issue than me standing here for your amusement."

"Amusement? Make your report."

"John Patrick Nelson is either dead in prison, or not there at all."

"Care to guess?"

"I don't like guesses, but thanks to John Nelson I've learned if you're resourceful there are few better places to hide than prison."

"Tell me."

"We have no proof of who he is – or was – or even if we should care. His clumsy robbery should have drawn probation but instead led to prison, and not just any prison but a prison as primitive as Crocket. The warden who called Bishop has been at Crocket six years. He's working on his Ph.D. and uses prisoners for his research. There is no reason to think there are other ties."

"Where is this going?"

"Absolutely nowhere. It just shows how pitifully little we know."

"What do you know?"

"Crocket reported John Nelson escaped, but no explanation as to how he escaped, no sightings, and the story petered out without word of his recapture. A prisoner either died, or almost died – we don't know which – in a brawl the day of the reported escape. Maybe there was no escape. Maybe it was just cover for an inmate's death, and maybe the inmate was Nelson. Our man who took the contract on Nelson, says he thinks his guy inside is the dead, or nearly dead, one, but he's still trying to verify it. To make it worse, our contact paid out on Nelson's death to an undisclosed hitter I think is either a complete hoax or maybe a guard. I wish I could say that's as weird as it gets, but there are stories so wild about Nelson I don't know what to believe."

"That's it?"

"No. I'm sure Steerman tried to visit Nelson. He didn't see him because the warden screened Nelson's visitors. It is the first hard information on Steerman in twenty years."

Ferry sighed, and waved Truax to a chair.

"What do you surmise, Colin?"

After adjusting himself carefully in the seat Truax said, "Sir, I know far more about Bong Sat than I have let on."

Mrs. Rafferty, the housekeeper at the manse, placed fried eggs and pancakes in front of Amos as long as he would eat them.

"I was hungry, Father," the young man said, with his mouth full.

"So I see. The fastest way to Mrs. Rafferty's heart is to pay due respect to her food."

"As respectful as there's been here for a bit, Father," Mrs. Rafferty said.

When Nelson set his fork down, Father Harold applauded. "Let the dishes sit, Mrs. Rafferty, I wish to speak to our sated guest."

Father Harold found himself in a precarious position. The Trappists at St. Peter's were hard core Benedictines a long way from Rome. In their view, they were much closer to God and he was far more real than a prelate half way round the globe. Exercising their freedom over the last hundred and forty years created inconsistencies compared to other Trappist orders, as well as yawning schisms with Rome. They constantly teetered on the brink of losing their charter.

He had intimate knowledge of St. Peter in the Woods which, by local standards, was very old. The first structure, not much more than a log cabin, started in the mid 1850's and gradually grew to its present size in haphazard leaps of questionable quality. The ceiling leaked, fixtures broke, the water system failed, and repairs relied on duct tape and prayer due to the expense of skilled workers. The monks desperately needed a man who "could fix anything."

The monks had another problem and this is were Father Harold came in. The brothers learned sharing their innermost thoughts with God through one of their own sometimes reached the ears of their fellows. The normal hostilities common to monastic orders escalated until the abbot at that time decided that once a month a priest from the outside would hear confession. Father Harold had listened to the monthly confessions for the last four years. In between his visits the brothers shared their more mundane sins with their abbot.

"I can help you find a welcome at St. Peters," Father Harold said to the young man.

The priest prided himself on being a good judge of people. He had listened to their sins, miscalculations, failed plans, and misdeeds for nearly twenty years. He believed the young man to be honest, but needed to be sure he wasn't turning a wolf loose in the close confines of St. Peter's. "But first I must be sure of your good character."

He saw Nelson erect his walls the way he had in the sanctuary.

227

"Look at me and answer my questions. Without my help you will never reach St. Peters."

Nelson folded his hands on the table.

"Are you a truthful person?" Father Harold asked.

"Yes, father, I am, as long as the truth does not prevent me from doing what I have to do."

"What do you have to do?"

"Survive."

"I see. Has your survival been tested before?"

Nelson took a deep breath, and sat up straighter.

"Yes."

Father Harold decided he did not need to know more since nothing at the monastery would pose a threat.

"If your survival is left unchallenged are you truthful and peaceful?"

"I am. Father, if I go to the monastery, can they help me learn about Thomas Aquinas, and the proof of God, and right and wrong?"

"Is this so important?"

"Yes, Father. I grew up where right and wrong belonged to other people and all that mattered was what I had to do. Now I want to find a place where I can learn about right and wrong because that is what I have to do."

Father Harold sipped from his coffee and parsed what the young man said. They talked for another hour, then he excused himself to make a phone call. He returned and said, "I will help you."

Nelson insisted they leave separately. Father Harold picked him up two blocks from the church.

"Until the night he died," Colin Truax said to Nathan Ferry, "if anyone had asked me to name the hardest man in the world to kill, I would have said Ned Greene. But that night, he wasn't just killed, his death humiliated him. He was blown to pieces bit by bit by the Marine for what he did at Bong Sat. The way I heard it Greene and Brinks gunned down a couple of Marines including the guy named on the card. Brinks was an easier target, but his death was just as public and just as sensational. Choking him to death in front of a room full of people amounted to another piece of sweet revenge."

"What's this have to do with . . . Vietnam?" Ferry asked.

Truax stood up, and pointed at a wet bar on a side cart. "Water, sir?"

"Help yourself."

Truax poured and looked around the room done in dark wood and lined with bookcases holding leather-backed books. Heavy drapes hung at the edge of the windows. A large oil portrait of a man wearing 19th century clothing hung above the mantel of a wood burning fireplace. French doors opened onto a patio where a pergola dripped profuse green leaves and small white blooms.

"Greene and some of his merc buddies would swap war stories, and Bong Sat came up from time to time.

Ferry's face turned red with anger, but Truax held up his hand.

"Your name never got mentioned. Greene was too much the pro to talk names out of class. When he died and the Marine left his calling card, I looked into it."

"How very enterprising of you," Ferry said. "I still want to know where this is going. I have a meeting.

"By then it was my job. Anyone who could kill Greene and Brinks amounted to a risk to you I didn't know if I could stop." He went back to his chair and sat. "What pissed me off is that Greene and Brinks became the Marine's marketing plan."

"What kind of marketing?"

"He bragged if I can kill these guys and walk, I can kill anyone. Creative death gets noticed. The Marine, let's give him a name, Matthew Eliot, set up The Diemaker. We can attribute at least eleven hits to weapons The Diemaker made. Personally, I think there were at least seven or eight more that were declared accidents, or suicides, or happened places where no one looked too close. All the killers, just like Eliot, walked." Ferry stood and went to the fireplace, but Truax felt sure he hung on every word. "I've come up with an estimate of what The Diemaker earned selling weapons and stay out of jail cards."

"And?"

"Over four million. Dollars."

"And you are willing to give Eliot, an AWOL ex-Marine, credit for all this? Why would he run some third rate medicine show if he had a little money?"

"Eliot was the front man for The Diemaker. He traveled all over the West with that carnival. He was their twenty-four hour man – the advance guy. Laughland stayed off the main roads and played to small towns. No one paid any attention and carny people never talk out of school. Living that life gave him all kinds of reasons to be anywhere and meet all kinds of odd people. He was on a mission. He was after you."

Ferry stiffened. His chin came up, and Truax recognized the look Ferry wore when challenged. "So if Eliot was the front man, who was The Diemaker?"

"His kid. His military records list a wife and a dependent, no mention of gender. The kid would have been thirteen when The Diemaker first made the scene."

"This is becoming quite fanciful, Colin."

"Bear with me. It'll be worth it." Truax finished his water and set the glass down. "We snared a small time crook named Larry something or other. He'd been in jail three times and was looking at a forever bounce. We gave him a choice. He could take the fall, or we could find him a spot out of the country. Easy choice, but to get it he had to tell us everything about every grifter, crook, and lowlife he'd ever known. Standard procedure. He was so eager we started to discount what he said until he mentioned he'd worked in a traveling show run by an AWOL jarhead. Said the guy's name was Caldwell but it was an alias. He didn't know the real name, but he was sure about the Marine and the AWOL part. Then he mentions this Caldwell had some kind of genius kid who could make anything. Seems sweetheart Larry had a run in with the kid and the kid won. We kept the guy on ice until we got a picture of Eliot. He ID'd him. That's how we got the Marine. We never found a hint as to the kid. Word had it he was in school in Europe, but we didn't buy the story."

"Colin, you are suggesting the prisoner in Nevada is the younger Eliot." Truax nodded. "The one that got away from you."

"Clean, without a trace." Truax said.

Father Harold drove west out of Medford, through the pioneer town of Jacksonville, then north over a two lane highway along a river. They passed orchards and fields as they traveled roads with little traffic. Beyond the town of Cave Junction, Father Harold turned off the highway and drove up a steep dirt road cut into the side of a sharp cliff. Near the top, Father Harold suggested Amos walk the rest of the way while the priest prepared the brothers.

Amos walked deep in the shade of the huge trees. He had never been in a forest before. He liked the shade, the silence, and the aroma of old trees and damp vegetation. He liked the feel of fallen trees and their crumbling bark, and even though the trees were dead, their fiber felt alive. He heard the tolling of bells from up the mountain. The sound, coupled with his surroundings, pleased him.

He stopped at a creek where the water made a noise like none he'd ever heard. He ran his fingers in the dancing water as it bounced on, over, and around rocks. He drank from his hands and then refilled his water bottle. He resumed his walk to the monastery.

"I was getting worried," Father Harold said, outside two doors made of wide, vertical wood planks. On each door hung a rusted iron circle.

"I have never walked in a forest before," Amos answered, and looked back down the hill. "Wow! We're a long way up. I heard bells."

"The bells sound across the valley to the mountains. I told the brothers you can fix anything."

"Good. Everything has a reason it doesn't work."

"Then you are a prayer answered," the priest said. "I'm sure you will win the brothers over."

"They don't want me here."

"No, but don't take it personally. They don't want anyone, but that's no longer practical." Father Harold opened the car door. "Brother Donato will be out in a minute. He's been granted a dispensation to be your . . . mentor. I am here once a month. We will talk each visit. God be with you."

Amos watched the car leave him to his future.

231

The pale plaster outer walls of the monastery stood ten feet tall by one hundred and fifty feet wide. Visible above the wall a belfry sat astride the peak of the tallest roof. He knocked with his fist and waited, but no one came. He walked toward the valley. The monastery sat on the edge of a precipice with a sheer drop of hundreds of feet. He had never stood so close to such an edge, and felt dizzy. To the northwest, in the otherwise clear blue sky, puffy white clouds obscured the top of the highest peak in the western mountains.

He walked the length of the front wall to the other corner where a cord disappeared through a hole in the wall. He pulled it and the tinkle of a small bell came from inside. Since there appeared to be no other door, he returned to the gate. When it opened, the hinges screeched and raised the hair on the back of his neck.

A man wearing a brown robe and a rope belt stepped out. Wire-rimmed glasses sat on his nose and a straw hat with a very wide brim covered his head.

"I like your hat," Amos said.

The man looked him over, then used both hands to pull the door closed behind him. The hinges squealed again.

"You are John Nelson?"

"Yes. Brother Donato? Father Harold said. . . I don't know what to call any of you. Are they your friends?"

"I am a monk. To address us you would say brother."

"And I should call you 'brother' because we are all part of God's family."

Brother Donato gave a small smile. "You could say that. We don't."

"What do you say?"

"We are a Trappist order. An order refers to a group that share a belief different from others who share the same broader belief."

"I don't understand."

"We are a segment of the Catholic Church of Rome that adheres to the teachings of St. Benedict, but we differ from other Benedictines because we think they are too worldly. Trappists are a contemplative order because we spend our time contemplating

God and the teachings that come from him through the scriptures."

"Contemplative means thinking," Amos said. "So you spend all your time thinking of God."

"Not all, but most. We have to eat."

"What else do you do?"

"St. Benedict said we must live by our hands. We make things to trade and sell for food and the necessities we can't make for ourselves."

"I live by my hands, so I guess I'm a monk. Is that why I'm being admitted?"

"You are here because you can do something we can't," Brother Donato said, hands out of sight in the sleeves of his robe. "We are not a practical order. We can not meet all of our needs, so we must ask for help. We would rather remain out of sight, pursue our beliefs and not be interrupted."

"Wow! That's what I like. I did it for five years. I had one friend who brought me food and left me alone. I was very happy building things and thinking about what interested me. Did that make me a monk?"

Brother Donato stared. "You saw no one, talked to no one other than your friend for five years?"

"Yes. I never talked. I almost forgot how, so I started talking to myself. I used different voices to pretend I talked to other people, but I always agreed with myself and got very smart."

"If you had talked to God and thought about nothing other than God, you would have been like a monk." Brother Donato watched Amos closely. "Inside the walls, we do not talk other than to God in prayers and as part of our rituals."

"Who is God?"

"If you spend the rest of your life behind these walls contemplating nothing but that question, you might – might! – find an answer. Without understanding we do not achieve the kingdom of God and life everlasting."

Amos looked across to the mountains. Clouds still hovered over the tall mountain.

"I understand the words, but not their meaning."

"We will help you in return for your work." Brother Donato put his hand on Amos's shoulder and said, "There have been decisions made regarding you. We are accepting you as a lay brother. Each morning one of us will spend an hour outside the walls with you then show you what needs to be done. We will pray with you."

"I'm not good with prayer."

"You will be. Each evening, before vespers, another brother will spend a second hour with you here teaching you the way of St. Benedict."

"I am more interested in St. Thomas Aquinas."

"So I understand and you will not be disappointed." Brother Donato took his arm and guided him toward the gate. "Do you have questions before we go in? Inside you may not speak. I will show you to a cell with a pallet where you will sleep. Someone will lead you to supper when it is time."

"Are the cells locked?"

"This is not a prison." Brother Donato looked across the open spaces at the world, then said, "not the way you mean."

After the screech of the gate faded, the quiet of St. Peter in the Woods enveloped Amos in a silence unknown since leaving Laughland. Between the wall and the inner buildings, he saw trees in neat rows with small, bright green fruit he thought might be pears. Nearer the building and out of the shade of the orchard, he saw straight rows of plants of various kinds.

They entered the building through double doors. Candle-lit wall sconces provided the light as Brother Donato led him deeper into the cool interior. Doors lined the hall, but all were closed. At a wide arch Brother Donato stopped. Amos saw a long room with a high ceiling and wooden tables set for meals. Two candelabra with their many candles burning hung suspended on rope pulleys. Two monks moved about setting out utensils while a third straightened benches. At the far end, on a raised dais, a short table sat perpendicular to the others. A huge fireplace big enough to walk into dominated the far wall, and he smelled a vague aroma of food.

Brother Donato pulled his arm and they continued their walk. Two more turns and they stopped at a door. Brother Donato opened it and waved Amos in. On the narrow bed Amos saw his bag and his pack. Brother Donato nodded and left Amos alone.

"Why haven't you told me this before?" Nathan Ferry demanded, still standing at the fireplace as he glared at Colin Truax.

"It's taken years to put this together. We still don't know for sure about the kid. I believe he was The Diemaker but there's no proof. And lots of questions like how come you're still alive?"

"Because of you," Ferry said.

"I doubt it. Eliot wanted your head, but here you are. What's your relationship with Steerman?"

"That's none of your business."

"But it is my business. Maybe Steerman and the Marine were in cahoots. In the beginning Greene thought they were. By the time I entered the picture, I believe Steerman held Eliot back. Why?"

Nathan Ferry mulled the question. "Are you sure you want the answer, Colin?"

"No, but if I'm to do my job, and Vesta aside, my job is to protect you, I need to know."

Ferry pointed at the bar cart, and said, "Scotch."

As Truax poured the drink, Ferry cancelled his appointments.

"Do you read Coleridge, Colin? Samuel Taylor Coleridge?"

"No, sir."

"Coleridge wrote a poem about a man who, while on a sea journey, shot an albatross, and is haunted by the act the rest of his life. Bong Sat is my albatross." Ferry sipped his drink, then carefully put it down on a corner of his desk pad. "Coleridge's ancient mariner did not regret his journey, only the shooting of the bird. I do not regret Bong Sat, only its execution, and like the albatross, it haunts me."

Ferry finished his drink and waved off a refill.

"Carrying out the responsibilities of power requires courage. During World War II, Churchill knew the Germans were going to destroy Coventry. If he fortified the city the Germans would know their codes had been broken and the Allies would lose their advantage. Churchill decided the dead at Coventry would number far less than the dead if his enemies learned the truth. He said nothing."

"Bong Sat?"

"The world is changing and few see what the changes bring. Bong Sat was necessary." Ferry stopped, picked up his empty glass and rolled it between the palms of his hands while looking at Truax. "Churchill was vilified for his decision. Had he sought more power after the world learned of Coventry, a power that required the goodwill of his people, he would not have won it. Dispassionate history has shown he made the right decision. History will not make its judgment on me for many years, and long after I seek power only the goodwill of the masses can give. If Bong Sat is made public, I will not win what I seek. Marcus Steerman has the means of making it public."

"And this knowledge also protects him?"

"To a point, but removing him is only part of the challenge."

"The rest?"

"Marcus and the Marine escaped Bong Sat together. I suspect Marcus used revenge as an inducement to win the Marine's aid which Marcus, a city boy, badly needed to survive. Marcus, while still in the jungle, had no idea I would submit to his blackmail, and took the Marine on as a partner." Ferry noticed his empty glass and waved it at Truax. "Another drink, Colin. Recollection is a thirsty exercise."

After Truax returned with the drinks, Ferry resumed.

"Marcus and I are very much alike despite our vast differences. I come from an old family, Marcus is an orphan. I grew up in wealth, Marcus in the poverty of a Catholic orphanage. I have the imperative of my history to guide me, and Marcus is blown by the winds of chance. Yet we both do remarkably well with what we have. You know me, but think about Marcus. His whereabouts and his movements have remained a mystery for twenty years. He has moved about the world unseen despite all the resources we have to find him."

"Do you admire him?"

"Admire? No. Appreciate? Yes. Let's return to the moment. Greene's death was as much of a shock to Marcus as it was to us."

"How do you know?"

"It rocked the equilibrium we share. How could I interpret this as anything other than a threat?"

"This was revenge for Greene's killing Montoya at Bong Sat," Truax said, angry with Ferry's casting aside of Greene. "Brinks was there, too, killing people. Eliot would have eventually gotten around to you if we hadn't gotten to him first."

"Your tone is approaching insolent."

"Sir, there is no greater threat to my personal safety than knowing about Bong Sat. My tone is irrelevant."

"So you and I are concerned with the same thing – ourselves."

"I still have a job to do, which is to protect you. How did Greene's death impact Steerman?"

"Our communications are limited. He threatens to expose me and I pay his blackmail. The price is affordable, and he knows it. From my perspective, it is a slight premium for knowing Bong Sat will remain out of the public eye. I know it will remain there because if it comes to light, there is no reason for me to pay him. Like I said, equilibrium. Then Greene was killed."

"Eliot had gone rogue."

"Exactly. Remember when you finished the Marine that wasn't there? I forget his name."

"Yeah, Tagnut. We found out about him from our guy that hears most of the rumors that get passed around on Nam. It went down smooth."

"Apparently the woman he died with was Eliot's wife and the boy's mother."

"We didn't know. The hit was housekeeping. Our guy that gave us Tagnut set up the hit. We paid off on it and didn't give it another thought."

"It started Eliot out on his own. A few years later came The Diemaker. Marcus raised the blackmail because I could never be safe if he decided my death was desirable. It shook me. The choice of the seemingly impregnable Greene was inspired, but I suspected Marcus had nothing to do with it. He is a coward and would never choose a messy death over continued income. Then Brinks died under similar circumstances despite our preparedness. Marcus again upped the stakes and I paid, but I told him I wanted some assurance that I wasn't next."

"And?"

"He said I was paying to keep him silent, not for protection. Then he reminded me about the goose that laid the golden egg."

"You talk on the phone?"

"Once a year."

The two men sat in silence as Truax tried to assimilate all Ferry told him.

"I have to find out if the prisoner was Eliot's son," Truax said.

"It was," Ferry said, eyes meeting Truax's.

"How do you know?"

Ferry stood, walked back to the painting above the fireplace, and pointed. "My great-grandfather. He found great wealth and knew what to do with it. I am still carrying out his design." Ferry faced Truax. "Colin, don't you find it the least bit surprising that I have spoken so candidly about a subject you know I guard zealously?"

Truax had.

Ferry returned to his desk where he opened the top drawer. He withdrew an envelope.

"I have not played fair with you in this conversation, but I wanted to find out what you knew. You know a fair amount and much of it gained with your wits."

Truax watched Ferry withdraw a folded sheet of paper from the envelope. Ferry scanned it before handing it to Truax.

Dear Son:

I am dead. It's been a long time coming for no good reason.

Settle the score with Ferry. Find a fate worse than death. Find one of your elegant solutions from The Diemaker days. The gun is the gun that fired the first shot at Bong Sat. Ferry killed a man named McBride. His dog tags are in my purple bag. Perhaps the gun will end the horror that ruined our lives.

Also in the bag is the whole story of Bong Sat. You deserve to know what happened. Marcus says he had the chance to kill Ferry soon as their chopper hit the ground. He failed and everything else followed.

At Bong Sat I couldn't stop Ferry's evil from killing my Marines. You will find the names of my dead in the bag. They, like you, need more respect than I gave them. I beseech you to make my amends the best way you can. When Nathan Ferry lies dying, you tell him the ghosts of Bong Sat are waiting.

Amos, there is no right or wrong. Only what must be done. You remember that.

Do not trust Marcus. He will tell you anything to get what he wants.

Use my purple bag to get Ferry. Do not let Marcus have it. It belongs to the memories of my Marines, the ones who died because of him. Use your smooth running brain to find it.

Shed no tears for me. I am better off dead be it heaven or hell or the worms. The two best things that ever happened to me were your mother and you.

Your father,
Captain Matthew Eliot, USMC

"When did this come?" Truax asked.

"Day before yesterday."

Truax reread the letter.

"Um. . . the ghosts of Bong Sat. Do you have nightmares, sir?"

"Of Bong Sat? No, why should I? It needed to happen. Imagine the adventurous course this country would have followed had the North capitulated in 1967. We needed to find out for ourselves that war in Southeast Asia was a poor investment."

"And you were responsible for that lesson."

"Be careful with your sarcasm, Colin. We will talk of this now, then not again. Stand up and take off your shirt. If you are wearing a wire you will be dealt with. Want to change your mind?"

Truax took off his suit coat, tie, and dress shirt. He slowly turned, arms out to his side.

"Fine. Get dressed. Marcus wore a wire that day. The clarity of my words is remarkable."

Ferry waited until Truax finished dressing.

"Here comes the one and only time we will discuss November 17, 1967. That day lingers with me as intensely as the day I lived it. Are you ready?"

"Yes, sir."

"When I learned of the North Vietnamese offer to negotiate peace, I was shocked. A U.S. victory at that moment would have insured America's growing presence in Southeast Asia, a move not in the interest of this country, and - Colin, this is most important - not in the interest of my family's ambition and those with whom we do business."

"Why not?"

"The inevitable consequence of peace in Vietnam in 1967 was the destabilization of the Asian subcontinent. The United States would have been strong and gregarious, and would have posed a threat to the Chinese, possibly a greater threat than the Soviets. If that was the case they might have worked a treaty and joined forces. A confrontation of that magnitude for the third time this century was not acceptable. But if we were busy fighting and losing a guerilla war, the Chinese were free to continue their efforts against the Soviets, luring them into the poor decisions that led to their downfall. Better them than us."

"So Bong Sat was a humanitarian effort and the Marines got in the way."

"Sarcasm again, Colin, but you are still on your free pass. Yes, they were in the way." Ferry looked up at his ancestor. "My family's business interests and those of our partners are food and vital consumables - the items people must buy. By the 1960's we had worked tirelessly for nearly a century to consolidate our interests. The Vietnamese conflict was the next crucial step."

"You created the Vietnam War?"

"Oh, no, Colin, we can't take the credit, but if not Vietnam, it would have been Cambodia or Laos. The old colonialism was giving way to Communism, an economic order doomed to fail given time. A victorious United States in Vietnam would have bolstered the French, and, to a lessor degree, the English. We preferred Communism. It would take several decades to reach its certain failure, and when it did the region would be desperate for our help. All we needed was Vietnam to wend its natural agonizing course then we would implement our plans."

"Which were?"

"A regional distribution of efficient production carried out by companies best suited to the task. We would stabilize food supplies. People who are well fed are less contentious and more inclined to be consumers. That regional success would then serve as a worldwide model."

"You would provide these global efficiencies?"

"And my partners."

"The world owes you a great debt."

Ferry took another look at his great-grandfather, then leaned his elbows on the back of his desk chair.

"To the victor goes the authoring of history. Others would not spin it as I have."

"So, Steerman unleashes his tapes and your spin is gone."

"Succinctly put and painfully true. The focus would be on ruthless personal gain rather than the humanitarian."

"You could claim fraud."

"Yes, but his package is compelling."

"Do you care?"

"The time will come when I do."

"When?"

"Soon."

"Why?"

"Not now."

"Who was this McBride guy you killed?"

"It was self-defense."

"Okay, but who was he?"

"A nobody. A CIA agent sent to snoop."

Truax studied Ferry's face and knew Ferry had lied to him. He also knew there was no point in pursuing the subject.

"May I see the envelope?"

Ferry handed it to him. In the upper left corner it read *Eliot.*

"The name's an attention grabber," Truax said. "Postmarked Las Vegas. Your address?"

"Listed in *Who's Who.*"

"Simple. I guess we can quit worrying about the prison. Our friends in Vegas will be disappointed, perhaps even vengeful, since they paid out on the hit."

"Notice he is warned off Marcus meaning Marcus has no control – if he ever did – and the boy is sent on a mission to kill me."

"You and anyone else connected to Bong Sat."

"Welcome to the club. Any thoughts?"

"Find the boy."

"I'm sure you will. When you do, bring him to me. Alive."

"Why?"

"He has something I want, and I want to meet him. Do you remember the months following Brinks's death?"

"Vividly."

"What do you remember the most?"

"All the questions about why two of your people were hit by The Diemaker and you weren't. Then a cult grew up around the victims. Why them?"

"My aspirations suffered more during those months than at any other time. Cover stories, as Greene enjoyed telling me, are shallow graves hiding the truth and every question washes away more of the cover." Ferry picked up the letter. "I wonder why he sent it."

"Payback. He's been living in fear most of his life. Your turn."

"You think that explains it? I wonder. I want him alive, Colin. I want to know who he is. I want to know if he works alone. I want to know his timing. Is there an unseen grand design? So many questions only the boy can answer. Bring him and make it fast. I want this over and I want everyone dead when I'm through with them."

Late that night, with the French doors open and a pleasant breeze carrying the aroma of the well-tended garden to his chair by the unlit fireplace, Nathan Ferry reached a decision. In the twenty years of their balancing act, Ferry had never used the protocol for reaching Steerman. He always showed his disdain for the blackmailer by accepting the annual call without emotion or evident concern.

The afternoon session with Truax and its trip through history upset him. Ferry did not want to believe a child killed Ned Greene, but he had. Truax told him to worry. If the purple bag, the film and the recording existed, worry came easily. The Ferry's grand hundred year plan could not be consummated until Bong Sat was dead and buried.

The next morning he placed a call to the classified desk of *The New York Times*. The weeks passed while he waited for Steerman's reply.

1967 -- BONG SAT

Marcus Steerman and Nathan Ferry

The Huey rushed over the many shades of green of the Vietnamese jungle, every thud of the helicopter's rotors bringing him closer to Bong Sat. Looking out the side door, Marcus Steerman saw the midday sunlight penetrate the jungle canopy creating shadows as distinctly defined as the light of hope and the dark of fear. As his moment approached he questioned his resolve. If he failed, he doubted he would survive Ferry's infamy. If he pulled the trigger after he sighted down the barrel, Nathan Ferry's chest would explode and the world would rejoice. His head fell into his hands. He was a bureaucrat, an economist, not a killer.

The tallest spire of the cathedral at Bong Sat sliced through the roof of the jungle, its cross the sole sign of humanity. Steerman turned away from Ferry and held his hands out palms down. He saw a tremor, but nothing like the shakes of yesterday when he had scouted the site and made his contingency plan. It was a coward's plan that if needed meant many would soon die instead of just one.

Forgive me, Father, for I am about to sin, he muttered, eyes on the cross.

"Right Hand, time for action!" yelled Ferry.

Time slowed and he imagined pointing the .45 right in the middle of Ferry's chest. Even he could not miss from ten feet.

"Steerman, Goddamn it, move it! Time for action!"

He had never fired a gun. He did not look the part of a warrior with his glasses hanging from a cord so if they slipped off his nose he would not lose them. He wore a long-sleeve, long-pant khaki ensemble still creased from the Ambercrombie and Fitch box, and a soft hat with a broad brim to protect his pale skin.

"Right Hand?" Nathan Ferry shouted.

"Yes, sir," he yelled, as he reached under his shirt to activate the miniature tape recorder plastered to his skin.

"You did well, Right Hand, choosing this place," Ferry yelled, over the rotor noise. "Did you pick it because of your Catholic upbringing or because of the symbolism of the cross? Or was it your devilish sense of irony?"

It was as if Ferry read his mind, as if he had divined his intention and now challenged his fortitude. With an epiphanic clarity, he knew this day would define the rest of his life.

For the sake of the tape recording, Steerman slid closer to the man who planned his death.

"Last rehash, Right Hand," Ferry said. "Make sure who you're dealing with, get the film, bring it to me, then return and keep them on task until plans are firm. I want it all done in less than thirty minutes. This close to the DMZ we are vulnerable to both sides."

Negotiations for the meeting and the setting of the protocol, had taken six frenzied weeks. Steerman's role was to set up the meeting with the North Vietnamese, then make sure everything went as Ferry planned.

Three days ago everything changed when an Air Force major Steerman had often dealt with failed to read the security routing and copied him on directions for an air strike that Steerman saw would kill him and everyone at the meeting. Only Ferry was to have received the confirmation. Steerman rerouted it with no indication he had seen.

The Huey banked hard to port as it descended.

"The plan is clear, is it not, Right Hand?" Ferry asked, staring into Steerman.

"Absolutely, sir."

"The CIA coverage?"

"The one you requested. Some guy named McBride."

"Good. Keep the agency close, but not included."

Steerman mentally set aside Ferry's plan for his own. After he pulled the trigger, and Ferry lay dead, he would go into the church, get the film, come back and head for home. He would cancel the air strike, everyone would live. Later, over the jungle, he would kick Ferry's body out never to be seen again. The war would end and he would be a hero.

Forgive me, Father . . .

The helicopter made a quick sweep of the clearing where it would land. The huge cathedral dominated the center of the small 'ville. Beyond the cathedral, there was little left of Bong Sat. The few buildings that survived the earlier fighting were heavily damaged. Steerman saw two in the old French Colonial style, but most were burned and broken shells defying architectural definition. Two minutes later, the Huey was on the ground. Seconds later, Steerman's feet hit the dirt.

Forgive me, Father . . .

Steerman removed the .45 automatic from his belt, and, just as he'd practiced, pulled the slide to chamber a round. He looked up at Ferry standing in the hatch. It was just as he had envisioned.

"Follow the plan, Right Hand!" Ferry called. "Remember, you have thirty minutes."

Time to change the world.

"Are you sure you want me to bring the film out as soon as I have it? Don't you want to wait until we're done?"

He was in control! No break in his voice. The barrel came up. In seconds it would be over.

"Follow the plan," Ferry called. "There is a reason for everything. Focus on all the lives saved by ending the war. You will be a hero."

The gun passed across Ferry's chest. At the precise, perfect moment, when humanity caught its breath, Steerman saw a flash of fear in his target's eyes, but it vanished into a smirk as the gun traversed beyond the chest with the bullet still in the chamber. Steerman, weak-kneed with failure, walked meekly toward the cathedral.

Forgive me, Father, for I have failed.

1987

Teresa Gill Verses Lois Lane

Her excitement at finding a third victim of The Diemaker tied to Ferry, Sir Douglas Treblehorn, lasted no longer than her next conversation with Oscar Mason. His question, "What does that mean?" stuck in her head. She still didn't know.

The bird shit story sold out faster than any previous issue of *Mother's Own*. The story was good, but in her opinion the cartoon, inspired by Thomas Nast's skewering of Boss Tweed's Tammany Hall gang in the 1870's, fueled newsstand pickup. With the issue's success came Oscar's green light on The Diemaker. He had already commissioned a cartoon of Ferry patting his still intact body parts while people around him lost theirs. Oscar had found a winning format and intended to run with it. *Mother's Own* would run The Diemaker story in two weeks – *if* she had it written.

Her favorite place to sit and think in Los Angeles was Griffith Park at the picnic table uphill from the carousel. She sat facing the carousel, close enough for the calliope music to soothe her while the up and down sailing of the horses kept her focused. She sat with her elbows on the table and her notebook open between them. The next day was Halloween, but she wore shorts and a T-shirt. At home, in Montana, her mother told her they had six inches of snow. Teresa knew she would never leave California.

She'd begun The Diemaker story tracing the victims to Ferry, but she would need a "why" to go with her "what." Ned Greene, the first victim, and Norm Brinks, the fourth, both worked for Ferry. Greene had been a mercenary who started his own bodyguard business before Ferry took him on full time. Brinks worked for Greene after Greene recruited him in Vietnam. There was nothing too remarkable in that. Mercenaries hire soldiers and they go to wars to find them. Brinks was not the only American soldier Greene hired with Vietnam experience. The other was Colin Truax, an injured Special Forces guy who replaced Greene after The Diemaker finished with him. She'd read the police reports and everything in *The Times* morgue, meaning she had the same stuff everyone had on The Diemaker.

Truax still worked for Ferry. He showed up in pictures of Ferry standing where a bodyguard would stand, and was listed as an attendee at functions where Ferry made an appearance. But when she ran a search for Colin Truax she found a match in the state corporation division as the president of something called Vesta Corporation. Vesta listed the nature of its business as "fugitive recovery." She checked and it appeared that made them bounty hunters. As for who owned Vesta the trail disappeared off shore in a manner that no legitimate company ever used. She'd found that last morsel yesterday, Saturday, and a sunny Sunday meant a day in the park.

She read the three headings on her open notebook: The Diemaker, Nathan Ferry, and Vesta Corporation. Only the third column had an entry. She stared at the paper and told herself it would become clear, that her life in warm Southern California was not at risk, and that she was too smart not to see the connection.

Teresa Gill jumped when a folded copy of *Mother's Own* landed on her notebook.

"How you doing, Lois?" asked Edgar Chiswell.

"Edgar! What are you doing here? Stalking me?"

Chiswell wore a blue polo shirt over denim pants, and pointed toward the carousel.

"Family outing. The wife and kids are in line."

"You always carry the alternative press to the park?"

Chiswell sat across from her and drummed a finger on the magazine.

"Good story, Gill."

"Byline says Lois Lane."

"Small presses can't afford world class editors like me. You make the same mistakes no matter what name you use. So what's next?"

"You mad?"

Chiswell glanced over his shoulder as the carousel started to turn and the calliope music grew louder.

"No. You did what I told you to do. What have you got?"

"Why?"

"Gill, we can't print stories about Ferry but that doesn't mean we aren't interested. Big papers count on small presses to stir the shit."

"I need a bigger spoon because I'm stuck."

She filled Edgar Chiswell in on the Treblehorn connection and got a raised eyebrow. From there she went to Greene and Brinks, then to Truax.

"You heard of a Vesta Corporation?" she asked.

"The bounty hunter Vesta?"

"Yes."

"You found them looking at Ferry?"

"Yeah, Truax is listed as president. Their ownership is pretty well hidden off shore. Why?"

"And you'd never heard of Vesta before your Ferry research?"

"No, no, and no."

Chiswell licked his lips and drummed his fingers. When the calliope music slowed and the carousel with it, he looked at her.

"Vesta is something the paper is interested in. Come see me at end of day tomorrow."

"Will I get my own byline on Ferry?"

"No way. Best case they'll let you play and be mentioned at the end as a contributor."

Two boys, she put their ages at five and six, ran up the grassy hill toward Chiswell. The one behind tackled the leader and they rolled on the grass yelling.

"Do I have to knock tomorrow?"

"You always have to knock, Gill." He turned toward the scuffling boys, then stopped. "The L.A. *Times* can't put much stock in rumors."

Gill watched him hurry down the hill to separate his sons. When he had a boy in each hand, he joined a woman standing near the rail of the carousel. Edgar handed off one boy and the family headed for the parking lot.

She drove to her desk and spent the rest of her Sunday on the computer looking for the rumor the *Times* couldn't place any stock in. At least once an hour she reminded herself she was smart enough to figure it out. When she finally went home she didn't feel very smart.

1967

BONG SAT

Marcus Steerman enters the Bong Sat cathedral and stands inside the door as his eyes adjust. When they do, the church appears even larger inside than out. Pews stretch row after row toward the altar. It is a distance that nearly exceeds the light from the doorway. He sees the Vietnamese grouped near the altar. Marcus walks down the aisle, and stops fifty feet from the group. One of the Vietnamese walks to meet the American.

"No guns, Mr. Steerman." The speaker is Dang Li Phan and speaks in nearly accent-free English.

Steerman lays his weapon on a pew, then wipes the sweat off his face.

"It is symbolic," Dang says. "Here we are unarmed and surrounded by war." The voice echoes in the vastness of the cathedral. "These are *very impressive surroundings, Mr. Steerman. Do you think the organ plays?"*

"*If there's air to the pipes,*" Steerman says. "*It would sound – imperfect. See the rust and dents on the pipes? The stops are probably fouled, too.*"

"*You are a musician?*"

"*When I was younger.*"

Dang leans closer and says softly, "*You are nervous.*"

"*And you aren't?*"

"*Do you trust your Nathan Ferry?*"

Steerman feels ice form on his spine.

"*Do you trust Ho?*"

"*Power serves no greater good. We are pawns.*" Dang points over Steerman's shoulder. "*Who is your helper? The CIA man we requested?*"

Steerman had seen no one. He looks over his shoulder. He is surprised, but recovers and excuses himself.

"*You the CIA guy?*" Steerman asks.

"*McBride, Frank B. Who are these guys? Why wasn't I briefed?*"

"*It's all need to know, McBride.*"

"*I'd say a company of NVA outside the door and this close to the DMZ is need to know.*"

The sweat on Steerman's face runs faster. He had not seen the North Vietnamese Regulars either.

"*How did you get here?*" Steerman asks.

"*Need to know,*" McBride retaliates. "*I'll give you a clue. A ride out would be nice.*"

"*Hang tight, Frank B. and you'll get your need to know.*" Steerman turns away. "*Time's a little tight.*"

McBride points behind Steerman. "*Looks like time's up.*"

"*Is that your CIA?*" Dang asks, standing at Steerman's side. "*Identification, please.*"

McBride passes his Company ID to Dang. Dang takes it to his people.

"*Okay, here it is,*" Steerman whispers. "*They have a film of Ho Chi Minh offering to negotiate the end of the war. The film is to be delivered to Johnson. They don't trust the Company so they want some assurances.*"

McBride stares. "*Is this for real?*"

"As real as it gets."

"How come this is happening out here? This is crazy."

"You're here because Central Intelligence doesn't know what's at stake."

"Who are you? State?"

Steerman nods.

"Mr. Steerman," the interpreter calls, "it is time. My people wish to return over the border."

"Just a moment, please," Steerman says.

"Who else knows?" McBride asks.

Steerman slowly shakes his head. "This is it."

"No one? Jesus! Who's in the chopper?" McBride asks.

"Nathan Ferry," Steerman says. "He requested you."

"Then this is all bullshit! The last thing that snake Ferry wants is the end of the war."

"What are you talking about?"

"Ferry's betting on a nice long war. How do you know this isn't a trap?"

"I don't," Steerman says, indecision raging. "Let's get the film and then we both take it out to the chopper."

Steerman looks at his watch again. In 16 minutes this place will be bombed into oblivion.

"What's with the watch?" McBride asks. "Expecting somebody?"

"I'm a desk man. This scares the shit out of me."

Dang starts toward them. McBride speaks harshly in Vietnamese. Steerman stares in surprise.

"What did you tell him?"

"I told them we'd be with them in a minute. It's not the words. It's the tone. You see it? They're scared, too. How'd this get set up?"

"I've been working with Dang for six weeks. They're afraid if we bomb the North like we did Germany in World War II they can't win."

"We didn't think their doves had the nerve for this kind of move," McBride says. "Come on. They're out of patience. Tell me you were lying about nobody but Ferry."

"Sorry. There's just us."

"Jesus!" McBride shows his nerves by shaking out his hands and arms. "What's the plan?"

"Get the film, get back in the helicopter and fly out of here. Everyone lives happily ever after."

"Dreamer," McBride said, shaking his head. "We have to get hold of that bird."

"I'll go out there," Steerman said, "and blame the delay on you."

"Yeah, okay. Tell Ferry I'll bring the film out in a couple of minutes. Be sure and tell him I have the film and I want to hand it to him personally. That should piss him off."

McBride places his weapon on the pew, then walks toward the group. Steerman makes the introductions.

"The film," Dang says.

"Allow me to update my superior, first," Steerman says. "Give the film to my associate."

"No. I will not hand this to your CIA. You take it."

Steerman and McBride look at each other, then Steerman says, "Sure."

The general waves at an aide who, with a slight bow, hands him two large canvas-covered film cases. The general holds them an extra heartbeat before stepping forward and handing them to Steerman.

"Make no mistake," the general says through his own interpreter, "this is not a sign of weakness. It is a humanitarian gesture. Accept it, and we all win. Reject it, many will die. Tell your president, it is a war he cannot win."

"I will tell him," Steerman says, accepting the cases. "Why two?"

"It is not a short film. Clarity is important."

"Thank you," Steerman says. "I will confirm the film with my colleague and return in a moment."

He hurries up the aisle and stoops as if tying a shoe to set the film canisters on the floor behind the last pew. As he goes out he squints against the glare and jogs to the helicopter. Ferry stands in the hatch and turns his head at Steerman's approached. The rotors turn slowly.

"Problems," Steerman said.

"There is no time for problems. Where's the fucking film?"

Steerman's hopes climb. Ferry never swears unless under stress. Steerman chooses his words carefully.

"They don't trust us. The CIA guy, McBride, will carry out the film when we get it."

"What's the hold up?"

"They want you inside. It's about respect."

"Out of the question. Tell them I will meet with Ho, but not with them."

"Then send your ID."

"No. Show me what you're made of, and get in there and get your job done."

"I can do it, but it will take much longer. I thought you were in a hurry."

Ferry tensed at the tone of Steerman's voice, then relaxed.

"Yes, time is important, so get to cracking."

"That's another problem. They have an escort." He pointed into the jungle north of the cathedral. "It's a full company. McBride – the CIA guy – says they're armed for a full fire fight. No trust around here."

"Forget the distractions! Do what you have to do to get that film. Soon as you get it to me you can worry about smoothing their feelings. Do you copy?"

"I'll do what I can, but you can forget the plan." Time for a lie of his own. "There's another copy of the film."

"What?" Ferry nearly screams.

"They didn't want to risk it out here in the jungle so it's going through the Chinese to Washington."

"To whom, for God's sake?"

"I don't know. I'll find out. Hang tight."

With that Steerman turns and jogs to the church. He had done what he can to keep Ferry on the ground. As he nears the cathedral's entrance, a Marine Corps Captain dressed in dirty jungle camo and his weapon slung on his shoulder, steps out of the shadows.

"Who are you?" Steerman asks, startled.

"Eliot. Recon, 2nd Battalion, 3rd Marines. Who are you?"

Time accelerates. McBride comes out of the church. Steerman talks to him before the CIA man strides to the chopper who Steerman placates the Marine. Ferry shoots McBride. As the chopper lifts off, Steerman hears Ferry's voice with a near supernatural clarity, yell, "No one gets out of here alive but me!"

Time has run out.

1988

Right and Wrong

At the end of his third week at St. Peter in the Woods, Amos met Father Harold outside the abbey and its veil of silence. They stood on the rocky promontory that looked across the valley to the Coast Range and the mountain peak lost in its perpetual cloud cover. Below to the right a large waterfall poured out of the rock face and fell hundreds of feet to the valley floor.

"People around here call that mountain Heaven," Father Harold said, pointing at the cloud-shrouded peak, "because it's hard to get to and what's there is a mystery."

Scattered white clouds dotted the blue sky further west while low fog hugged the valley floor. The sky over St. Peter in the Woods, Father Harold said, was clear enough "to see God."

"They talk about God a lot here," Amos said, wearing his dark glasses.

"It is the purpose of their existence."

Father Harold had just heard the monks' confession.

"It is almost a thousand feet to the bottom," the priest said, pointing into the sheer abyss after both men found a comfortable place to stand not too near the edge. "I call this Conversation Point."

"You name places," Amos said.

"Names remind me the abbey and this hilltop are part of the larger world. It would be easy to forget."

"Why don't you wear robes like the brothers?" Amos asked.

Father Harold wore what he called "priest's basic black," with the white clerical collar the only relief.

"My order does not wear robes. Robes separate the wearer from those around him. If you're a monk, that's fine. I need to be more accessible."

"Brother Donato said they wear robes because the fruit of their labor brings them closer to God." Amos looked down at the blue robe of the novice. "I don't like it. It's too hot and gets in my way when I work."

"You'll get used to it. How are you getting along? How many of the monks talk to you?"

"Two. Brother Donato shows me what needs to be fixed. He doesn't have to, but he shows me anyway."

Donato had told Father Harold the first few tools and pieces of equipment the novice fixed worked beyond the monks' needs.

"He lives in the world of man," Donato told him.

"You've given the brothers more than they expected," Father Harold told Amos.

"They don't want to do things better," Amos said. "They want the same tools to do the same things the way they have always done. There is no creativity here."

"That's bad?"

"I don't know what to do."

"John, you said you wanted to be in a place where what you had to do was to understand right and wrong. This is that place. Understanding comes in your head and heart, not in your hands."

"Yes, Father, but how? No one has talked to me about Thomas Aquinas, and most of the books are in Latin. I can't read Latin."

"Let's walk." They moved down hill into the shade of the forest. When they reached the tree line, the priest said, "Have you wondered how all the monks study God, yet do not talk to each other? Each is looking for God in his own way, just as you must find your way."

"Would I know more if I understood Latin?"

"It would be easier. I will arrange for you to learn functional Catholic Latin. Who is the other besides Brother Donato that talks to you?"

"Brother Simon prays with me after Lauds and Mass."

"They don't think Lauds and Mass are enough?"

"Everything's in Latin."

"I'm surprised they haven't thought of teaching you Latin."

"When something is the way it is, it stays that way."

Very true, Father Harold thought. The requirements of this world, a distant second to the world each of the monks created, demanded patience and tolerance, but not change.

"What is God, Father? What if there is no God?"

"That gets to the heart of it," Father Harold said. "Let's sit on a log."

They edged nearer the abyss to a fallen fir. As they sat, Amos saw across the valley to Heaven with its clouds.

"When you think about something, does it fill your head?" asked Father Harold.

"Sometimes, but not for long. I am very smart."

"So when you don't understand something it takes more room."

Amos nodded.

"What fills the space as it shrinks?"

"Nothing until I find an elegant solution."

"And when you find it what happens?"

"I think about something new until it becomes small again."

"Would it make you happy if you found something that would fill your head forever?"

Amos sat very still.

"Yes, if such a thing were possible."

"That is what the search to understand God would do."

"God would never get smaller?"

"No. God is a matter of faith. God exists in everything."

"Thomas Aquinas proved God exists."

"Ah, the five proofs." Father Harold folded his hands together, and smiled. "St. Thomas Aquinas proved God's existence, yes, but to follow the proofs you have to accept some conditions – dogma – of this world."

"You don't think he's right?"

"I don't discount it. God is an empty canvas we each confront. That's me, the man, speaking. Maybe God would be a full tool bench for you. It is the act of evolving our expression that creates our bond with Him."

"How do I understand God?"

"Understanding is a process that never stops."

"I don't know where to start."

"That is your assignment until we meet again. Don't try to make God smaller. Open your head and heart and let anything come in. Think about each thing in relation to right and wrong. We will talk in two weeks. The abbot wants me to come more often while you're on probation."

"It's a long trip, Father Harold."

The priest looked toward the cloud cover of Heaven.

"So is the journey to God."

They started up the hill, picking their steps carefully on the dry hillside.

"How is my friend LaVoy McDaniels?" the priest asked.

"He helped me. Were you looking for me when you found me?"

"LaVoy told me you would come, and the logical way to get to Medford is by bus. There are only two a day you might have taken."

They stopped at the top so Father Harold could catch his breath.

"LaVoy and I have been friends since college. We stayed in touch. Back then, we thought our lives would be so dissimilar, but it amazes us how alike they are. We both try to save and change lives."

"He has sent prisoners to you before?"

"Yes, but none like you. We have a gardener from Crocket, and some who are released find work in the community. When he helped you escape, I was shocked. But the idea of sending you to St. Peters, that was the part of his request I found hard to accept."

"But you did."

"You made a good first impression, but it was the needs of the brothers that made up my mind." They stood at Conversation Point. "When I first came here, I didn't know much about St. Peter's. Then I found some books in the abbey library – in English and Spanish, by the way – about the history. Monks from a hundred years ago started the histories, and others have added their own accounts. There are maps. You'll be interested in this. There are caves all through these hills, even under the monastery.

One of their uses is for food storage during fall and winter. A sort of glorified root cellar."

"I like caves," Amos said.

"Yes, I thought you might."

The phone number listed in *The New York Times* classified would reach Nathan Ferry anywhere in the world. When his phone rang at midnight he knew who it would be.

"What time is it where you are, Marcus?"

"A more civilized hour than yours."

"You know where I am?"

"Wyoming. The Grand Tetons. Didn't your father build that place?"

"Yes. I spend most summers here if you'd like to drop by. Do you always know where I am?"

"Not always, but I pay attention. To what do I owe this summons?"

"No chit chat? No snifter of brandy at your fingertips?"

"A little early in the day. What is it, Nathan?"

"Patience. It took long enough for you to call, so a few more minutes won't matter."

"*The New York Times* doesn't come to my door with coffee. Soon we can use e-mail. Do you have e-mail yet, Nathan?"

"I'm a phone man. Shall we proceed?"

Ferry heard a sigh and took a guess.

"Are you lonely?"

"Ah, still that heightened sense of the jugular."

"Are you?"

"Yes. I miss Eliot."

"Eliot took away my confidant when he killed Ned Greene. *Quid pro quo.*"

"I wonder if the death toll for Bong Sat will ever end."

"Do you still count the dead?"

"Yes. Why did you summon me?"

"The balance. It has changed again."

"How so?"

"I received a photocopied letter from Amos Eliot."

The new silence made Ferry wish he could see Steerman's face.

"I wonder if you know of this letter, Marcus. Shall I read part of it?"

"I know of it. It's from his father."

"It disturbs me. The boy appears to be far beyond your control."

"I never had control."

Ferry closed his eyes, leaned his head back, and let Steerman's reply settle.

"Nathan?"

"I'm trying to understand what is going on."

"The letter is a warning. It is best to leave the boy alone. If you do, he will leave you alone."

"A prosaic interpretation. I consider the letter a threat."

"How?"

"What is the purple bag?"

"Ah! The reason for the call."

"What is it?"

"A Crown Royal bag with a treasure trove of Bong Sat memorabilia."

"What memorabilia?"

After a pause long enough to find Ferry at the edge of his chair, Steerman said, "Here's a devastating teaser. Ho Chi Minh sent his chop to validate the film. The chop and the film leave no doubt as to the film's authenticity."

Ferry shuddered and his hand shook.

"There's more?"

"Oh, yes, but that's enough for now."

"Why hold back?"

"A good question. Let me see. Ah, there is much more than what's in the bag. The most troubling problem tying you to Bong Sat has been why you would do it. Now I have the definitive answer."

"I doubt that," Ferry said, but Marcus heard his tremor.

"Oh, you believe alright, but I feel the need to show off. I have the last known copy of the young McBride's thesis. *Four Justifications for War in Southeast Asia.* It wasn't until I read his fourth postulate that I knew why you made sure he was at Bong Sat."

"It wouldn't fit in the bag."

"No, but it makes a nice package with the film Ho sent and the tape of our conversations. Add the chop and you are a very guilty man for all to see."

"Are you about to raise the ante again?"

"No. I believe our relationship has run its course. Why did you kill McBride?"

"You read the thesis."

"It was 1965. A college paper in a master's program. It meant nothing."

"But others, just as you did, would have read it later and seen the connection. Where did you find it?"

"His professor kept it. He was taken by the scholarship and insight. He said McBride was a brilliant student."

A silence ensued while Ferry remembered the day he read the paper.

"McBride's death was like Bong Sat," he said. "It was a direct and efficient way to solve an unforeseen problem."

"The instant deaths of hundreds and a prolonged war that killed thousands meant nothing."

"Why should they? I work on a global stage and deal in millions."

"Yet you interpret Amos Eliot – one boy – as a threat."

"Yes, and you just said as much. I am advised the boy sent me the letter to make me afraid."

"Afraid if you act against him, but what has he ever done to you?"

"He killed Greene, something I still find hard to believe a thirteen year-old could do."

"The father, not the son, killed your man."

"Still the boy was The Diemaker. Astounding."

"Leave him alone."

"I am as the mother bear with her cubs at her back."

"All he has done is send a letter. How much clearer can I make it than leave him alone?"

Ferry heard Steerman gasp.

"You've stepped up the hunt!" Marcus said.

"And failed, obviously."

"You're a fool, Nathan!"

"I beg your pardon?"

"You heard me! The boy cares for nothing beyond his need to survive. You continue to threaten him, and he will do my dirty work for me."

"A boy will not hinder four generations of plans."

"What is it you fear, Nathan?"

"You think this call is motivated by fear?"

"Absolutely! The mother bear."

"It is risk assessment, nothing more."

"Flummery! I wonder what it is you really fear? Death or the truth?"

"There is no fear in death."

"Leave the boy alone. You cannot defeat him."

"How old is he now? Twenty? Twenty-one? I most certainly can defeat him."

"The boy cares nothing for the world you are so invested in. His world and yours could not be further apart."

"He has backed me into a corner. He possesses the means to destroy me, yet you attempt to convince me to ignore the threat."

"To do nothing is always easiest."

"Certainly true for you."

"Touché'."

"I have a plan to implement. He – and you – are a threat and action will be taken."

"Then here is my second, and last, heartfelt kernel of truth. Amos Eliot will retaliate. He will not instigate. The more damage you do in your attempts to reach him, the greater the damage he will inflict. You were never religious. Has that changed?"

"Why would it?"

"If it has you will appreciate what I'm about to tell you. If you push him hard enough, Amos Eliot is as unstoppable as the will of God."

"Your threats of ethereal retribution sadden me. Have you nothing more substantial than ancient spells to mutter at me?"

"Only this. You are not special. One day you will die. The world will go on without you and you will be forgotten."

"Then I should make the most of what life I have left."

After hanging up, Nathan sat and considered the purple bag. A million dollars for the bag and its contents should make an adequate inducement. Another million for anything of interest found with it. To most people, he thought, one million dollars is a lot of money.

Marcus Steerman hung up the phone one time zone west of Nathan Ferry. As always after talking to his nemesis he felt both wired and fatigued. He'd requested a room well away from the street noise so as not to give anyone listening a clue to his location. He doubted Nathan would tolerate either a tape or a listener, but there was no reason to be careless. He decided a cup of herbal tea would help him sleep. He left his room and walked two blocks to an all-night Denny's. He sat at the counter next to a stack of newspapers.

"Want me to move those?" the waitress asked.

Steerman shook his head, and paged through the papers as he waited for his tea. A cartoon caught his eye. Even without the caption he recognized the caricature of a 19th century Nathan Ferry sitting in a bird nest defecating gold bricks. He glanced at the mast. *Mother's Own*. He'd never heard of it. To his surprise the story was well researched and adequately written. He looked for the writer's name, found it and laughed. Lois Lane. He read the article again and then slowly drank his tea. Lois Lane, whatever her identity, needed a little help. She'd scratched the surface, but Marcus knew the subject well enough to know she would get no further without him.

The next morning he entered the public library and searched the periodicals for past issues of *Mother's Own*. It came out weekly and the library had a year's worth. There was one story on Ferry a few weeks before the one he'd read in the coffee shop. Another cartoon depicting Ferry as a Tammany Hall Boss Tweed gave Marcus a smile. He read the story, also written by Lois Lane, and like the first, he saw her intentions but she came up short. There was gold in the middle of the story when the writer hinted at a tie between Ferry and The Diemaker.

If Lois Lane only knew.

An hour later Steerman placed a call to the number on the *Mother's Own* masthead. When the line answered he said, "I would like to leave a message for the person calling herself Lois Lane. Tell her I know the identity of The Diemaker and why he's left Nathan Ferry alive. As a show of good faith I have a clue for her. Vietnam, November 18th, 1967. She must look deep for the truth. I will call in two weeks."

The voyage of Amos Eliot toward making right and wrong his own started on a kneeling board with his nose less than three feet from a blank wall. His cell consisted of a platform bed, a small wood stove he had not used although the mornings were chilly, and wall pegs to hang his robes. A large window that looked into the central courtyard provided natural light Amos blocked with improvised curtains. Candles gave him light to dress by at four a.m.

Matins started each day. The morning prayers were in the chapel, and since everything was in Latin, they meant little to St. Peter's first novice in twelve years. Brother Donato said the meanings would become clear in his heart. In the meantime, Amos stood silently. He watched as monks rang the bells for lauds. He watched from the side as the rest of the monks arrived in the sanctuary. He watched with head bowed as he listened to the rituals. As the bells tolled the passing of the days, time weighed heavily. He quickly became aware of the "forever" pace of the brotherhood.

Since he was denied the language of God, Amos took Father Harold's advice and thought mostly of right and wrong. Right and wrong, like positive and negative poles, were a dichotomy of equally powerful opposites. By the end of the first week, he decided that thinking in scientific terms did not work. By the second Amos understood that right and wrong, when applied to human beings, lay beyond predictability because they did not apply the same to everyone.

On a sunny afternoon with the blue sky still clear enough to see God and Heaven still lost in its perpetual clouds, Father Harold and Amos stood at Conversation Point..

"How do you know it isn't the same?" Father Harold asked.

"If it did," Amos said, "there would be nothing to talk about."

Talks with the novice demanded an effort. The impenetrable black glasses made it impossible to read his eyes, and he spoke with little inflection.

"A very good beginning, John. But let me add this. Right and wrong are the same for everyone. Every recognized religion says pretty much the same thing on right and wrong. It's wrong to steal, it's wrong to covet your neighbor's wife, and it's wrong to kill. But need and desire dictates how humans practice right and wrong. If you want something bad enough and have the means to take it, you will, regardless of right and wrong. Power, I believe, supersedes any consideration of right and wrong. By the way, the church, which is very powerful, does not agree. They say they are a force for right, but I say right does not require force. There is a very convincing corollary. If power supersedes right and wrong, then it is those with no power who are the most concerned with right and wrong."

"Right isn't the same for everyone. You see? I'm right."

"In Man's world right is not the same for everyone. In God's world, it is. Scripture says the meek shall inherit the Earth. I believe it should read the meek shall inherit Heaven."

"Yes, it should say that. Why doesn't it?"

"It doesn't sell well telling people they have to die to get what they want."

"I don't think the church wants you to say that either."

"No," Father Harold smiled, "there's a good reason I am a parish priest in a small town. I have a mind of my own. I'm even willing to sneak an escapee into a hilltop monastery."

"Father, after thinking about it for two weeks right and wrong are still a mystery."

"It will take longer than two weeks, my son. Be patient. God is everywhere. He exists in all of us, in all we do and all we think. If each of us lives according to the way God would have us live, and if we can do so without forcing other people to do it our way, we can find peace and happiness. Keep looking for the right and wrong God wants you to find. By the way, there are some mighty big ifs in all of this."

The priest stared across the deep, rugged valley.

"This point of land is called God's Finger. The name is perfect if you stand down there, well to the south." He held up a fist and then extended his index finger up at a forty-five degree angle. "This rock points across the valley at Heaven. No one understands the name unless they see it from down there." Father Harold paused. "From here you don't see any of it."

Amos took another two weeks to think. He found little difference between thinking and praying. He liked praying, because the way he prayed he talked to God, not out loud in his cell, but mentally.

On Father Harold's next visit, Amos said, "It is right to seek a bond with God and to do the things he wants me to do. It is also right to defend my life even if it means others might call my actions wrong."

"Give me an example," said the priest, noting the frame of reference remained anchored in clay.

"In prison I did what was asked of me. Other prisoners didn't like what I did, and attacked me. I killed some and hurt others. If I failed to protect my life they would have killed me. Killing them was not wrong. When I was young . . . Father, you don't tell anyone what I say?"

"That's right, John."

"What does a fate worse than death mean?"

"It can mean denying someone what they want the most, but that's an idiomatic explanation rather than literal. In God's world there is no fate worse than death for sinners. They are consigned to eternal torment while the righteous go to the glory of Heaven. We could argue the fine points, but I don't think that's what you want to know. I think your question seeks a secular explanation. For those who do not believe in God, death is the end. It invokes images of the body in the grave putrefying. This often is expressed as going to the worms."

"My father said that," Amos injected.

"So if death is putrefaction, worse differs from person to person. If someone has dedicated their life to achieving a private success, then their fate worse than death could be a public failure, or winning what they sought and being disappointed. The precise fate worse than death would differ for each of us. For you it might be a world where you've lost your hands. For me I would be denied the promise of God."

Amos looked at his hands. He remembered the shop at Crocket and the clumsy-fingered convicts as they worked the lathes and grinders. He shuddered.

"Father, I need your help. I have decided to tell you what I have told no one. My name is Amos. When I was young I made things to kill people. I didn't do the killing, but other people used what I made to kill."

"How do you know they died?"

"I saw magazine stories. They gave me a name and many people were afraid."

In Father Harold's previous conversations with John Nelson, the young man seemed rooted in reality. This was a departure.

"What name did they give you?"

"The Diemaker."

"I know that name. He made all those strange devices – "

"Exploding shirt studs, a comb with poison teeth, a shrinking shirt collar, exploding hearing aides. Yes, I made those. My father picked the targets and I created the elegant solution. I was thirteen when we started and fourteen when we stopped."

Father Harold paced, opened his mouth twice and each time closed it without saying a word.

"Father, can you stay long enough for me to tell you the story of my life?"

"Of course, John, or Amos. How could you make things that would kill people?"

"They killed my mother and best friend. They wanted to kill my dad and me, too. We protected ourselves."

"Is that what he told you?"

"My dad was a soldier and a hard man, but other than about trip wires, he didn't lie. The first man who died killed my father's soldiers. Dad said he cried for joy when that man died."

Amos pushed his glasses harder against his face. He stood still, legs stiff, and after he let go of his glasses, his hands began fluttering.

"Father, understanding my life comes hard. I think if I told you all about me it would be easier."

"Okay, Amos. There is bottled water and some candy bars in my car. Let's get them, and walk to our tree."

As they went down the hill, the priest asked, "Why choose me?"

"You are helping me with right and wrong." As they neared their tree, Amos began. "You said people go against the will of God when they seek power. My story starts there."

After they got settled on their tree, Amos said, "I am not like other boys."

To Father Harold, those six words sounded like Once Upon a Time, but as he listened he found little room for disbelief. It took two hours for Amos Eliot to tell the priest of his father and the far off war where he was betrayed; of Laughland and Marcus; of his early life and what happened to his mother and Bill, and finally to his father. He told the priest of his life Underground, of the carousel and Streaker, but he told it all without names. Amos did not want the priest to "help."

"Now that you know my story I want you to help me answer the question of what I am to do."

"What do you think will happen?"

"Not think, know. My life is tuned to the people who want to kill me. It is only a matter of time before they find me, even here. They have little else to do. I have something they want."

"Do they know you have it?"

"Yes."

"How?"

"I told them. I was honoring a debt to our mutual friend. It was also a warning. If they left me alone they had nothing to fear. But they will ignore the warning." Amos resumed his pacing. "While I was in prison, I saw the world was more than me. When it was just me I never hesitated to do what I had to do, and never considered the consequences of my deeds. I never suffered guilt. But now that I have God to think about, and right and wrong, I do not see my course as clearly. Right and wrong do belong to me. My dad said this would be the day I start to die."

"Why did he tell you that?"

"Because worrying about right and wrong will stop me from doing what I have to do to survive."

Father Harold laid his hand on Amos's arm.

"What is it you want me to help you with?"

"When they come, what do I do?"

Father Harold stood, and now both paced. As they did, they edged closer to the abyss.

"I was afraid you were going to ask that."

The men stopped and stared into space.

"If you had not told me your story it would be easy for me, in the certitude of my faith, to tell you to do the will of God. As a priest I would tell you killing someone is a sin and command you not to do so, and perhaps these words would condemn you to death. The book, be it the Bible or any book of laws, loses touch when death is the price for adherence. This is called martyrdom. There are many precedents, including Jesus Christ."

He stopped and held Amos's arm.

"The world has seen enough martyrs. This is the man talking now, not the priest, and I say we need to find a way to protect God and Man at the same time. Your dilemma is an absolute. It seems, Amos, the appropriate aphorism is do unto others what they would do unto you. Not a Christian sentiment unless you count an eye for an eye, but that's more revenge than a pre-emptive strike. God expects more."

"My father was right."

"No. Life – and death – is more complicated. It isn't kill or be killed. That sounds so chaotic. To live or die deserves more." Father Harold pointed toward the abbey. "There is a monk in the brotherhood you should talk with."

"Who?"

"Brother Sidney, but he talks to no one because the order doesn't talk. His writings on moral dilemmas are well known throughout the church. They are also controversial. They contradict the dogma, which frightens Rome. He would be interested in you. I may be able to entice his interest."

Oscar Mason called Teresa at home to give her the message from the mystery caller.

"What's it mean?" Oscar asked.

"You gotta find something else to ask. It's embarrassing to keep saying I don't know. It's also kind of embarrassing to admit I'm thrilled somebody other than you and me think there's a connection."

"No, you were the only one. I never believed it, but it sells."

"Thanks, Oscar. You thought I was some kind of conspiracy freak?"

"It doesn't matter what I thought. What are you going to do?"

"He left a good faith clue. I'll track it down. If it goes someplace we can decide."

She worried when she would have time to chase the clue, but after her Sunday in the park with Edgar Chiswell, he'd assigned her shorts, stories of fewer words and usually less time in preparation. In her free time she visited libraries, of which Los Angeles has a great number, and when that went nowhere she tried writers who wrote on Vietnam. She tracked down more than a dozen and asked what the date meant. Most said it was three months before Tet; others compared the war to a football game and November 18th, 1967 was in the first quarter while both sides tested the other's resolve. Some said the U.S. had a chance early to take the North Vietnamese out of the fight but blew it. No one elaborated with anything she understood. She did not mention Nathan Ferry.

"Talk to Lois Lane lately?" Chiswell asked, leaning against the side of her desk.

"I wish I could say I was making better use of your generosity with the shorts. You know anybody who's an expert on the early part of the war?"

"How early?"

"November, '67. November 18th to be exact."

Chiswell looked at her and walked away. Two hours later he put a sticky note on her desk. She read a name and a phone number.

"Call this guy," he said. "Use my name."

She called ahead and got an invite. Marty Dunbar lived in a beat up one story house in Compton. Swings and tricycles littered yards and the sidewalk that fronted the modest houses. Cars lined both sides of the street the length of the block except in front of the address the voice on the phone had given her. The voice also told her to give her name at the door. As she parked in the open space she saw faces looking at her from two of the parked cars. On the porch reached both by stairs and a wooden ramp stood a black man in bloused fatigue pants and a khaki-colored sleeveless tee shirt. The sentry waved her in.

The dim interior of the house smelled of cigarettes and sweat. As her eyes adjusted to the low light, a man in a wheelchair entered through a wide doorway.

"You Gill?" the raspy voice asked. When she said she was, he waved her into what had been a dining room, but now the sidebar and built in china cabinets overflowed with loose paper and overflowing manila folders. He pointed at a chair she suspected had been recently vacated for her because it was the only unutilized flat surface in sight.

"You got our attention with the date," the man said. He had long white hair, smudged glasses, and a salt and pepper beard of irregular length. He wore an unbuttoned fatigue shirt with the name tag over the pocket ripped off. He took a cigarette out of a pack on the table next to a computer's keyboard. He lit the smoke and said, "Where'd you get it?"

"What's it mean?" she asked.

"I know more than you do so I go first."

"You wouldn't cheat would you? You are Marty Dunbar?"

"Yeah. Keep it interesting and we can talk all day. Where'd you hear it?"

"Somebody who read an article I wrote. He called and left it as what he called a good faith clue."

"I didn't see anything in *The Times*."

"Not *The Times*. I wrote the article for *Mother's Own*."

"Good answer. Edgar told me you were moonlighting as Superman's girlfriend. You play fair, we do, too. You don't know anything other than the date?"

"It ties to this big shot named – "

"Nathan Ferry, yeah. You got any other names?"

"That's it. Who are you?"

"Still my turn, but that's a fair question. My friends and I run an information clearing house called Peace for Vets. We collect information for the families and friends of Vietnam MIA's of which there are thousands. Pilots who got shot down over the jungles, firefight dead left in unmarked graves, or eaten, or burned depending on who won. The Viet Cong knew our guys dreaded disappearing and leaving their families wondering. The V. C. played these tapes in the night saying how they were going to feed our dead and wounded to the tigers. They had stories about some crazy man-eating fish or crocodiles they would toss our guys to. I don't know if they were true. One way or another a lot of good American soldiers never came back from that shit hole. Since the Saigon bug out Peace for Vets has grown into the place everybody brings their stories. We don't always know what's true and what's not, but we always listen."

"Why Compton?"

"Why the middle of the ghetto? We deal with war - victims and survivors - here. This neighborhood understands. We care about what most people in this country have forgotten. Just like here. Guess what demographic led the draftees for Nam? Young blacks. Gotta serve your customers, right? Easy place to keep people away you don't want to see, too."

"That's a problem?"

"We piss people off. Important people, which brings us back to you." He lit a fresh cigarette and looked at her long enough to make her nervous. "So I tell you what we know about November 18th. What then?"

"It means something? It really means something?" Teresa asked, feeling the adrenaline kick.

It does. If there's one date that's magical in the early history of that fucking war that's it. Let me show you something. Hey, Chuck. Robert. Bring in the board."

Two black men carried in a large blackboard and set it on a low easel. Even mounted low Marty Dunbar wasn't going to reach above the halfway point from the wheelchair. Across the top of the board was printed LOIS LANE. Under her name the chart looked like an organizational tree. One line branched into three. From left to right the names for the three lines read NATHAN FERRY, THE DIEMAKER, and BONG SAT. It reminded her of her own in her notebook, but unlike her's this one had entries in all three columns.

"Those are called myth lines," Dunbar said. Chuck and Robert flanked the board, and Chuck held the chalk. "We added the third line after Edgar called."

"Pardon the interruption," Teresa said, "but how do you know my boss?"

"He said it was okay to tell you. Edgar has a MIA brother. We met seven or eight years ago and we helped him look. Now he helps us even though his brother's still missing. We're gluttons for information."

"So what's Bong Sat?"

Dunbar invited Robert to speak.

"Place my cousin bought it. November 18th, 1967. His name was Terry Dawkins. He was like a brother when I was little. Looked out for me. I was proud of the man when he came home wearing his uniform, standing tall. He told me to always do the right thing."

Dunbar nodded at Robert and Chuck. When they left, he looked at Gill.

"You ever read Conrad's *Heart of Darkness?* Marlowe sailing up that fucking river looking for the seriously psychotic Kurtz?" She nodded. "Gill, you just put a foot on the *Nellie.* Why are you doing this? Edgar didn't assign it. You're looking for extra credit, maybe a career builder. Right?"

"In the beginning," she said. "Now it's more."

"Since when?"

"Since Edgar cultivated my curiosity. I came to him with an idea for a story on The Diemaker, but here I am some place much bigger."

Marty Dunbar smiled. "He'd given up finding anybody at *The Times* to do what you're doing."

"I wanted to get noticed and looked for stories that needed an ending. The Diemaker was the biggest. The tie to Ferry gave me the idea the paper would print it if I came up with some good stuff, you know, new stuff. Edgar told me no way. He told me if I wanted to write that story I ought to find another paper to work for. I thought he meant quit my job, then the idea to ghost write popped into my head. I thought it was my idea, but I know it was his."

"Yeah, that's Edgar. I can tell you, Lois, the guy who called you is paranoid as hell. Anybody who knows that date and isn't dead is paranoid. By the by, I'm calling you Lois because you're going to need a Superman on your side."

"Are you paranoid?"

"Absolutely. South Central works for us. We got more guns than the closest precinct house, we don't get surprised, and no one gets in without calling ahead." He looked at the board for a second. "We saw you coming and opened the parking space. November 18th is damn near the only thing you could've said that gets that kind of service. You put the other foot on Conrad's boat and we'll watch your back, too."

"What do I have to do?"

"Get your caller to meet you here. You can promise him he'll be safe."

"Promising his safety is enough?"

"Don't know. I'm betting it's a guy named Marcus Steerman. He's one of three guys who survived that day, actually two who were there, but a third knew the story, and that's how Robert found out about his cousin."

Dunbar pointed at the chalkboard.

"We're big into myths around here. Myths are organic stories that grow all by themselves. They have a typical mythic structure with heroes and villains and other archetypes. Steerman is the gatekeeper. He has the keys that unlock all the secrets. Most people think he's dead. Not us. What's the point of thinking he's dead? If he is, we're all wasting our time."

"And you want me to get him here?"

"Yep. He's going to call *Mother's Own*, right? Leave him a message with the magic name, your phone number, and when to call. He'll call. He's going to be dying to know where you got Bong Sat."

"What if he still won't come?"

Dunbar drummed the table, then looked at her.

"Yeah, okay. Tell him I'd love to see Eliot's purple bag. That'll do it."

For Colin Truax, the previous three and a half months had yielded nothing, leaving him more than enough time to take care of the necessities. He broke the news to the contractor in Las Vegas who claimed John Nelson was alive.

"Nelson's alive" Truax said.

"He's dead."

"He's alive."

"We paid off and that makes him dead," said the contractor.

"You wasted your money. Nelson's alive and we have proof. We want a refund."

"Our source is impeccable."

"We have a hand written letter saying he's alive. What have you got?"

"Proof?"

"Absolute proof."

"Son of a bitch. Looks like we have a little job to take care of."

"The refund?"

"Check's in the mail."

That was it until three weeks into the hunt a lead materialized. The mug shot of John Nelson was positively identified as someone named William Glint who lived in Sparks, Nevada. It took two wasted weeks to discover that William Glint was both dead and not John Nelson. The mug pictures had either been switched, or a mistake had been made at the time of booking. Either way, they remained nowhere. As a measure of their frustration they followed the William Glint lead to its dead end despite knowing Nelson's real name was Amos Eliot.

Ferry demanded weekly reports. When each report said nothing new, he became irascible. Truax started putting his reports off, but Ferry stopped that by calling him at four o'clock in the morning. As more time passed, Ferry's anger grew.

"I want results, Truax," he yelled. "Concrete results. Not some vague story about the boy disappearing never to be seen nor heard from again. I want him in front of me alive. You copy?"

So it went week after week.

With no leads in the present, Truax combed Matthew Eliot's life again. Records on file in Carson City, Nevada showed the carnival sold not long after Eliot's death to a Canadian company speculating in mineral deposits. The company had all the proper bona fides, although Canadian corporate law made it difficult to dig deep. When contacted, the company said they had no immediate interest in the property, but neither were they interested in selling. The man Truax talked to laughed, and said a couple times a year the big bosses took their kids to Laughland and rode all the rides and ate hot dogs.

Truax and Wilford even visited Laughland in person. They met the same caretaker who was there the first time Truax checked the place out. He was surprised to see five large trucks outside the carnival. One looked like a drilling rig.

"What's going on?" he said to the old man with a gun belt strapped to his hips.

"Drillin' for water. You from the county for the permits?"

"No. We'd heard there was a carnival out here and decided to see if it was true."

"More like the graveyard for a carnival," the old man said, settling his gun belt on his hips. "The new owners bought the valley for the water. They been punchin' wells in for a couple of months."

"Looks like they're about done," Wilford said.

"Gonna miss them," the caretaker said. "Once they're gone nothing to do again except practice my quick draw and trick shooting. Novelty wears off though after a few months. Pretty good, though. Want to see?"

They declined and returned to Las Vegas.

Truax spread the word through the Vesta network they were looking for any information on escapees from Crocket, and bumped the reward for verifiable information to ten thousand dollars, a lot of money to those who had none. It took eight weeks, and two very uncharacteristic pay outs from Vesta for the information that would eventually lead to Oregon.

Marcus Steerman called *Mother's Own* exactly two weeks after his first call. He identified himself as the person who left a message for Lois Lane and asked if they had a message for him. He was put on hold until a man answered.

"My name is Oscar Mason, I'm the publisher. You are?"

"No games. Do you a have a message for me?"

"It was worth a try. November 18th, 1967 is significant for what happened at Bong Sat. She said to call her tonight or tomorrow night between eight and midnight at the following number. Are you ready to write?"

Steerman wrote the number with shaking hands. She'd discovered Bong Sat!

He called the same detective agency in San Francisco he'd used to find Amos and asked them to run the number. At four o'clock he called back. The unlisted number belonged to Teresa J. Gill. She was a reporter for *The Los Angeles Times*. The four hours before he could call passed slowly.

He called precisely at eight o'clock.

"Hello, Ms. Gill. I am most eager to talk to you."

"You checked the number."

"Yes. This is no time for secrets. Does *The Times* know about your articles for *Mother's Own*?"

"A few people know."

"I presume the plan is you stir the soup until it comes to a boil and then they step in. Right?"

"That may be their plan, but they'll take me off it. That's not okay."

"Where did you learn the name Bong Sat?"

"From someone who would like to meet you."

"Who would that be?"

"Names start to be bargaining chips at this point. He said if I mentioned the word paranoia you would understand."

"You can assure him I do. Bong Sat is never bandied about. What else do you know?"

Steerman grew edgy with the long delay before she answered, "I don't want to spook you."

"Spook me? I don't scare easily. Say what you need to say."

"My source lives in the L.A. Basin in a very secure location. He wants you to come to him."

"That will not happen, Ms. Gill. I can not imagine any inducement that would get me there."

"He would love to see the contents of Eliot's purple bag."

If he had not been sitting his knees would have buckled. He had been sure no one other than Amos and maybe Clyde - and now Nathan - knew about the Crown Royal bag. Could her source be Amos? No way unless she lied about the source living in Los Angeles. He started to speak, but had to clear his throat. Maybe it had not been Amos who had cleared out the box at the Stardust.

"How does he know about the purple bag?"

"He would tell you."

Steerman's swings between panic and curiosity started to slow although his fingers still lurked near the phone's disconnect.

"What else does he know?"

"I think I've thrown enough at you for this call. Come see him."

Steerman found himself thinking about it.

"No," he said, as he regained control.

"He knows your name."

Control evaporated, but he didn't see how the claim could be true.

"I have many names." he said.

"Only one you were born with."

"Not even that is true," he scoffed. "You had my interest for a minute."

"How about your name at Bong Sat? Marcus Steerman."

The stab at his chest felt like he imagined being shot felt. His finger broke the connection. Only one person could be behind this. Nathan Ferry!

Steerman sat with his head in his hands. Gill was a pawn, probably unknowing, but still a pawn. Amos had the information, but he wouldn't be in Los Angeles, and Clyde would take no action without Amos. That left Ferry. The timing supported it. Ferry had not known about the bag until Steerman revealed it, and now he was taking action.

Marcus threw on his coat and left his room. He walked in the cool darkness and tried to slow the pinball antics of his thoughts. When his heart rate slowed and sanity returned, he ruled Ferry out. No plan Nathan approved would include the stories in

Mother's Own. Even printed in a small press, the stories were far too revealing. What did that leave?

A new player? Who? So few knew the whole truth of Bong Sat.

Whole truth. They were not dealing with the whole truth! What had been revealed? Bong Sat, but he'd offered a meaningful clue with the date. His name, so who else knew? And Eliot's purple bag. The Marines knew about it but they were all dead.

True, they were dead now, but one had been sent for help. Bill Tagnut. Tagnut knew about him and Laughland.

Thirty minutes later he had no more answers, but no longer felt panicky. He found a Denny's and drank coffee through the night as he mind rolled the pieces of the truth like die in a gambler's hand.

At first light he had a plan.

Amos found books in the library with the abbey's history. The monks that founded the order were half Jesuits and half Russian Orthodox, a partnership not of dogma but of necessity. They were survivors off a sailing ship run aground at the mouth of the Rogue River. In the name of survival, they put religious differences aside, left the rugged, inhospitable coastline, and set out for the interior. They suffered starvation, and native attacks that drove them further inland until they reached the rocky promontory that became known as God's Finger. The inhospitable rock had water, the natives would not climb to the top for fear of angering their gods, and the priests found places in the depths of the caves where they could hide and defend. He found two maps of the cave system under the abbey.

He copied the maps into his notebook and since he rarely spent more than a few hours a night sleeping, he used his waking hours exploring the caves under the monastery. He carried a compass into the caves but it often didn't work. He also took balls of string that he tied at the mouth of a new tunnel. The Trappist did not use many modern conveniences, but they did use electric torches. The second time he used one the battery died. From that time forth, he carried candles and matches as backup.

Water had always been a problem for the abbey. Originally, monks met their needs carrying full buckets from further up the peak where they captured it from a stream before it disappeared into the rock. In the 1930's a pump was installed that pulled water from two hundred feet below the abbey. Over the years, as the abbey's demand for water grew, they needed bigger pumps. During the summer, the pumps ran much of the time supplying the abbey and its agricultural needs, but in the rainy season, which was half the year, collection cisterns on the surface provided most of the load. Amos spent a week improving the pump, then started replacing old iron pipes with plastic. The project kept him deep in the rock while the brotherhood slept.

Amos believed by following the stream he would find an escape route out of the abbey. Mindful of his lesson from Laughland, his explorations carried grim purpose. He didn't mention the fear to Father Harold, but he did warn him someone might inquire at St. Mary's.

One night he followed a promising branch until it abruptly dwindled into a narrow crack. As he prepared to retreat, the battery in the torch died. He lit a candle, and as he stowed the useless torch the candle flame guttered. He put his ear to the opening, heard nothing, then pushed his face in and breathed deeply. Fresh air.

The next night he returned with a pick axe and a shovel. As he opened the narrow passage the fresh air grew stronger. When his shoulders breached the wall, he shown in the light and saw a much larger cavern. He entered the new room six feet up the wall and dropped to the floor. In twenty feet he found a narrow notch to the outside world.

Standing at the mouth, he saw a clear night with no moon. In the starlight, he saw the sheer face of the cliff below him. From his explorations he put Conversation Point two hundred feet over his head and to the left from where the river **exited** the rock.

The next evening, before dusk, he returned. He made sure he had a good hand hold before he leaned out. He felt a tightening in his head and a stiffness in his muscles as the chasm opened below, but he tightened his jaw and leaned further. He scanned the face of the wall and saw a ledge fifty feet down that crossed the rock face away from the waterfall to the tree line one hundred and fifty feet away.

"If I had to, I could slide down a rope to the ledge and move sideways to the trees."

He shuddered. Only if his life depended on it, he thought.

The packet labeled *Personal* and *Confidential* came to Teresa Gill's home by express mail. The manager of her building had signed for it then left a note on her door. From the feel the envelope contained a manuscript. She opened it at her table and read the cover letter.

Ms. Gill:

Bong Sat is the beating heart of all we seek, but let us not get ahead of ourselves. Read the enclosed dissertation. The author was the first to die at Bong Sat, so rest assured I am not leading you astray. At the time of his death, the author, Frank McBride, was a young CIA agent specifically requested by Nathan Ferry for the mission that killed him. Devote your considerable intellect to the following question. Why would Nathan Ferry want Frank McBride dead? Reach the answer and you have your next installment for Mother's Own. Words of warning: Do not idly use the name Bong Sat in print. It is the whistle that calls out the dogs.

M.S.

The initials at the end confirmed the sender, and the voice on the phone, as Marcus Steerman. She read and reread the dissertation. Her mind flared with possibilities, but the density of the paper overwhelmed her. She blamed it on being too long away from academia. Had she been in grad school she would have done better.

She awoke with her cheek on the last page of the dissertation. Judging by the feel of the paper she'd drooled. She sat up, wiped her mouth, and stretched. She walked to the bathroom, peed, and brushed her teeth. As she stared at herself in the mirror, she had what she would later call an epiphany. It manifested itself with an iridescent light in her eyes that at first suggested her brain had caught fire. Given her later description perhaps it had.

She showered, dressed without drying her hair, and drove to the Burbank airport where she caught the shuttle to Oakland. She had not called for a seat, but knew with a clarity that was almost painful she would have a seat. On the ground she called Oscar Mason and asked him to meet her in Berkeley at the Pancake House on University Avenue. Next she called Edgar Chiswell, got his voice mail and left a message saying she would not be in but that it was his fault by starting her on this trail. She took BART to Berkeley and then walked the ten blocks to her meeting. She waited almost an hour for Mason to arrive. While she waited she called the Economics Department at Cal and made sure Dr. Pemberton was in. She left a message that she had to see him on an urgent matter. She would be there by noon.

"Pemberton will see you?" Oscar asked, seated across from her.

"I don't know. He was my thesis advisor and thought I was pretty smart. He told me I could call on him anytime."

"That was what, five years ago?"

"So?"

"He's probably had a lot of smart students since then."

"Today he'll see me." She leaned across the table and took Mason's hands. "I need him to make sure I know what I'm talking about."

"Want to fill me in?"

"Not yet. If I'm right it explains why The Diemaker has a thing for Nathan Ferry."

"And *Mother's Own* will be happy because you do?"

"This story's big, Oscar. Risky big. You get it started and the bigs will try to steal it. I don't know how you can protect it."

"Do I need to call my brother?"

"No," Gill said, shaking her head. "I think the next story will come out looking complimentary to Ferry. After that is the kick to the balls."

"That's when I call my brother?"

"Yes. Let's go see Pemberton. Maybe I'm wrong and there is no story."

Pemberton still had his office in Evans Hall. They found him at his secretary's desk because the office staff was at lunch.

"I didn't want to miss you, Teresa. How are you?"

"Flattered that you would see me on such short – and rude – notice. Thank you."

"Your message said urgent. Not a word often heard in these halls for anything other than late assignments."

She handed Dr. Pemberton a copy of the dissertation with sections highlighted.

"You can keep the whole thing, but I tried to save some time by marking the sections where I'd like your opinion."

The economist read the cover and raised an eyebrow.

"Yale. Interesting. Roger Ormund, the faculty advisor, was an old friend until he died a few years ago. Would have been helpful to see his comments."

"I tore them out," Gill said. "I'll give them to you when we're done."

"Nothing to clutter the thinking, eh?"

"We'll pace the halls while you read."

"Urgent, yes, I see." He thumbed through the pages, glanced at a page or two, then said, "Walk slow."

Two hours later a graduate student caught them and led them to Pemberton's office.

"The date on the front is right? 1964?" he asked.

Gill nodded.

"Very good work. Clear thinking, well written, new ideas. I'm sure this fellow McBride got a good grade. With work this promising, I'm surprised I haven't heard of him."

"He was killed in Vietnam."

"Pity. The paper is clearly about Vietnam. How did he die?"

"He worked for the CIA and was killed on a mission."

"I'm not surprised. Yale. Those folks lost a lot of good minds feeding the clandestine services. Never could see it myself. Must be why I came west. But, you didn't ask me to grade the paper. What do you want to know?"

"The fourth postulate."

"I thought so. Provocative. The author warns against a long drawn out war in the region. He doesn't name Vietnam, but in 1964 what else? A long drawn out war would leave America sick by the end of it and without appetite for rebuilding. During the war it would command full attention leaving the private sector markets open to a few, even one, very well prepared private companies that could work in virtual obscurity."

"What if the war had ended in, say, 1967?"

"In retrospect that seems highly fanciful. It would have been something John Stuart Mill called a black swan because logic precluded the event. But if the war ended, it would have created a very different scenario not addressed in this paper. We, my fellow economists and I, believe America would have adopted a modern version of the Marshall Plan used at the end of World War II to rebuild the markets in the region. People busy working and consuming don't have time to fight wars."

"So no virtual obscurity for one company to get a head start."

"None at all."

"Given the way things turned out, our writer proved himself most prophetic," Gill said. "It was a long drawn out war and when it was over our only view of Vietnam was in the rearview mirror."

"Mr. McBride did not foresee America losing the war," Pemberton said, "but in the context of this paper the nationality of the entity working in its virtual obscurity did not matter. In fact it would have been best if it were not American."

"Dr. Pemberton, has any company, or group of companies, prospered in the virtual obscurity of Vietnam and its neighbors?"

"Yes, but there's nothing obscure about it, not since 1975 or so. Sierra Terrace Holdings. This dissertation is like their business plan."

"But that's an American company."

"It's also a global holding company with a presence on every continent."

"What if the war had ended in 1967? Would they have been hurt?"

"They're huge, so overall they would have still done well, but if the war had ended it would have been disastrous for their strategy in Southeast Asia."

As Mason and Gill walked out of Evans Hall, Mason took her arm.

"You brought me along so I'd know you weren't blowing smoke. Oh, and thanks a lot of not introducing me. I felt like an idiot sitting there."

"You're not an economist. Pemberton wouldn't notice you if I'd taken the trouble, and yes, I wanted you to hear a credible source set the scene."

"You're going to accuse Nathan Ferry of prolonging the Vietnam war."

"Close. I think Ferry had a chance to end the war and made sure peace never had a chance. All we have to do is figure out how to tell it."

"It'd be nice if you could prove it, too. I don't have to call my brother to know Ferry will sue our ass if you can't."

"Being sued might be the least of your problems, Oscar."

Four months after Colin Truax's meeting in Los Angeles, a Vesta informant in Las Vegas passed the word that a doctor whose rounds included Crocket had a gambling problem. Truax and Wilford met the deeply indebted doctor in a fourteenth floor suite at the Flamingo. When the doctor was ushered in he saw two men in suits and hard expressions flanking an open sliding door to the balcony.

"Whatever you want to know about Crocket it's yours," the doctor named Peters said, as he tried to hide his shaking hands.

"No patient-doctor privacy, Doctor?" Wilford asked.

"Prisoner-doctor privilege. I don't worry about it."

"Let's start with John Nelson. Know him?"

"John Nelson? Well, well. The vanishing John Nelson."

Truax saw a shrewd glimmer replace the doctor's fear.

"If you want to talk about John Nelson I want all my paper run through the shredder."

"We'd all like miracles," Wilford said, "but this city isn't renown for them. You tell us, and we'll tell you what it's worth."

"Whisper the magic name, and the price goes up."

Truax saw the glimmer change to defiance, and decided to quash the game.

"Thomas, throw the good doctor off the balcony."

Peters stared at him, then laughed.

"Oh, very good, but bullshit! You're not throwing me off the balcony, literally or figuratively. I'm a prison doctor in debt to every loan shark in the state. My dead body pays no bills, making me worth more alive."

"Tell us what you think is so important and we'll be fair," Truax said. "How's that?"

"I'm more trusting with a scotch in my hand. A double on the rocks."

Truax poured the drink. He took it to Peters who stood in the middle of the room. As he handed him the drink, he saw tears on the doctor's cheeks.

"What's the story?" he asked, softly.

"You're not going to pay up when I tell you what I know."

"Why?"

"John Nelson's dead."

"They reported him as an escapee."

"No other prison in the whole state wanted that poor son of a bitch so they . . . 'let him go.'"

"Let him go. What's that mean?"

"They liberated him. They killed him, then took his body out in the desert and left it for the coyotes. At Crocket, that's called letting a prisoner go. It's the perfect cure for recidivism."

"Who said he's dead?" Truax asked.

"Captain of the guards, a guy named Crane. A hard ass who probably did it himself."

"Did you ask him?"

"No. Crane died in a car crash. Odd, his car went into a canyon on a road he'd driven a thousand times." He took a long drink. "John Nelson was one of a kind."

He held up his empty glass. Truax waved in the direction of the bar. Peters came back sipping a generous pour.

"The late great John Nelson was a reclamation project of LaVoy McDaniels, the assistant warden who usually had two or three cases going at a time. He believes he can spot the cons prison can fix."

"McDaniels care enough to spring him?"

Peters sipped again, and shrugged.

"No. McDaniels played by the book. His thing was everybody deserved a chance. Not easy in a place like Crocket. When Nelson first got there he looked like fresh meat so the queens hit on him. Big mistake. He was a one man execution squad. Supposedly, he almost tore one guy's head off. Nelson's antics amounted to a little housekeeping that offended no one." Peters took a long pull on his glass. "I got to know Nelson because he had a problem with his eyes."

"What kind of a problem?"

"I'm not a bad doctor," Peters said, toasting himself. "I just can't say no to roulette. In Nelson's case, I did a helluva job. His irises were larger than normal. That, and his eyes didn't process ultraviolet properly. When he stood in sunlight his brain misinterpreted a part of the UV range as anxiety, and he lost control. Too much and he could go catatonic. I had these super Polaroid shots made that blocked most of the UV. It worked, too. At least it was working last time I saw him. That's why it pissed me off when Nelson got let go. He disappeared and McDaniels went nuts. He got every guard on the carpet. He even had the usual dumping grounds checked looking for a body. Nothing."

Truax sat on a corner of the sofa.

"No one saw the body, so why are you so sure he's dead?"

"What you said about Vegas not being known for miracles? Crocket's worse. Here," Peters gestured out the window at the city, "some dumb schmuck can hit a jackpot and go home rich. No jackpots at Crocket. The only one who might have a compassionate bone in his body is McDaniels and I can guarantee you he did not want Nelson gone. I'll tell you a story. The head warden, a guy named Stathem, is a politician who wants no trouble. Nelson is trouble so Stathem tells McDaniels to get him transferred. McDaniels passes word under the table that Nelson is bad news so all of a sudden no other house has a spare bed. Nelson stays in McDaniels's class. This sound like the guy who wants him gone?"

Truax imagined how this would play for Ferry and didn't like it.

"Let's pretend Nelson is alive," Truax said. "If we went looking for him, what should we look for?"

"Dark glasses and the world's fastest hands. But if you want to find him - if he's alive - look for someplace like prison. Someplace where he doesn't have to go outside."

"What else?"

"Smart. Like a lot of psychopaths, he'll . . . Hey, I don't want to start retelling rumors of this kid. If I tell you all I heard about Nelson, you'll think I'm crazier than a shit house rat."

Truax shook his head.

"Oh, no, Doctor, I'll believe you. You remember stories about The Diemaker?" Truax saw the connection clicking into place. "That was your John Nelson at thirteen. He killed one of my best friends. Tell us everything."

"The inmates are right then."

"Right about what?"

"They believe Nelson was some kind of ghost. When he disappeared, they said he made himself invisible and walked out the front gate."

"There's nothing magical about him, but he is alive so give us something."

"Well, according to his teacher, he had a thing about St. Thomas Aquinas."

Amos lay on his stomach outside the walls of the abbey three hundred feet down slope from Conversation Point. His eyes followed the ledge across the rock to a point below the cave mouth to see if he could walk it once he reached it. To do so he would need hand holds and ropes. He had to keep the image of him falling from filling his imagination, but even closing his eyes could not drive off the whirling, tumbling images.

He rolled onto his back, shut his eyes and gradually felt better. He normalized his breathing, then visualized crossing the rock face using ropes and hand holds he would cut himself. It would take at least two days to build his path, but he would start that night.

Walked back to the abbey, and saw Father Harold leaning on his car.

"I've made an arrangement with the Abbot. Brother Sidney will meet with you tomorrow after mass." Father Harold opened the passenger door, reached in and came out with a folder. "Read this first. It's an overview of his writings."

Amos glanced through the typewritten pages.

"You will talk in the confessional," Father Harold said. "You will not see him, nor he you."

"That is not much time to prepare," Amos said.

"All night, if necessary." Father Harold took Amos's arm. "This is an event. The order rarely relaxes their rules."

Amos looked out from Conversation Point. In the distance Heaven sat lost in its eternal cloud, and feathery clouds scratched their backs against distant peaks to the north. To the south, gray clouds built up on the Pacific side of the Coast Range. It would rain there. So far none of the storms had made it to God's Finger.

1988

Heaven and Earth

Even with the doctor's information, Colin Truax, Thomas Wilford and his partner of the moment, Hugh Janacek, found nothing. They chased every thin hint as Ferry's screaming got louder.

"You're running out of time!" Ferry warned.

The distance they would go to pursue a lead didn't matter. Truax drove his rental car into Missoula, Montana after chasing a lead into the Bitterroot Mountains of the Idaho panhandle where he'd spent three days under primitive conditions. He'd eaten out of his pack for two of the days, gone without coffee, and his personal hygiene consisted of chewing peppermint flavored gum. The leg he hurt in Vietnam throbbed as it always did when he walked too far, but this time hot nerve sparks shot from his knee to his hip. Saying he felt miserable came up short. He pulled into the first diner he saw and sat at the counter. He was the only mid-afternoon customer. The waitress leaned against the back bar reading a newspaper. She glanced over the top and stared at him.

"Coffee?" she asked. "I'd say scotch from the looks of you, but we don't serve hard stuff. Got beer."

"Coffee and hot food. Steak and eggs. Steak medium rare, eggs over hard."

As he spoke she tossed the paper on the counter and poured coffee.

"It's kinda old. Wanna wait for fresh?"

"That's good enough for the first cup."

He picked up the tabloid. He turned it to the top fold and recognized the caricature above the story. The drawing showed Ferry sitting on top of the world with Vietnam and the rest of Southeast Asia where Alaska would be, and Ferry's ten-fingered hand fondling each of the countries from Hong Kong to Bangladesh.

"Shit," he muttered.

"What's wrong, hon?" the waitress asked, as she set water next to his coffee.

"What is this thing?" he asked, waving the paper.

"It's pro-environment. You know, save the owls, whales, and trees."

"People in Montana are pro-environment?"

"About half of us. The half that rent. You said medium rare and over hard?"

"Yeah," Truax answered. Ferry must be going nuts, he thought, then wondered if Ferry had even seen it. He looked at the mast and saw it was published in San Francisco. Colin never looked at the stack of alternative papers that littered the boxes at most downtown San Francisco intersections. The ones he did notice aimed at the sex trade, so he assumed they all did.

He read the story. His food came and it sat untouched.

"You want me to warm that up?" the waitress asked. "I thought you were hungry."

It was as if the writer had listened to Ferry's explanation for the Vietnam War. It traced specifically Ferry, and by extension Sierra Terrace Holdings, and the profitable strategy used for the long drawn out war. It outlined how Ferry had capitalized on the chaos of the competing ideologies that fueled the wars between Vietnam and the United States, and the limited war fought by China and the Soviet Union. The story went into surprising detail, but he saw it was the kind of detail that once the connection was made the rest could be conjecture. Several authorities were quoted, one an economist at Berkeley and the other a retired army general that agreed the long and distasteful war worked for Ferry and STH. Truax kept waiting for the hook and finally found it in the teaser following the bold letters that spelled NEXT.

The long war worked for Nathan Ferry, but what if hostilities had ceased in 1967? Was that ever a possibility? In three weeks Lois Lane reports the alternative history of the Vietnam War and how the world would be different if a massacre in a small Vietnamese village had never happened.

He left his food untouched, and pushed the tabloid into his pocket. He checked into a motel that had a king room with a big bed and an oversized bath tub. First he called Ferry. As usual the great man was not available. Then he called his office while he ran a bath, and left his number. He stood naked with one foot lowering toward scalding water when the phone rang. He almost didn't answer, no longer being in the mood to talk to Ferry, but duty forced his hand to pick up the bathroom extension.

"We've got him!" Wilford yelled.

"Where? Shit!" He burned his foot and pulled it out of the water, almost falling as he did.

"Southern Oregon. What's wrong?"

"Nothing. Do you physically have him?"

"No, but we know where he is. We would have found him a helluva lot sooner if we'd sweated that damn warden."

"McDaniels? Why?"

"We followed the bus lead to this town, Medford. We had to drive. Place has an airport, but no flights. Can you believe it?"

"Thomas, I just burnt my foot in the bath water. I'm naked. I've been in the fucking mountains for three days. Get to it."

"Okay, okay. We spent some money at the bus depot and a clerk remembered the dark glasses and nervous hands. Said he asked her about the local Catholic church. Turns out the gardener at the church served time at Crocket. McDaniels got him the job with his buddy the head priest. We asked about the kid, and the gardener remembers him. He saw the kid leave alone, but the priest left a couple of minutes later. The gardener said the priest visits a monastery up in the hills. A place called St. Peter in the Woods. Very remote, very perfect for our boy."

"But you don't know for sure he's there?"

"No. We just found the location of the monastery. What do you want us to do?"

Truax looked longingly at the steaming water, and grabbed a towel.

"Okay. No risks, but check the monastery out. What's your story?"

"The usual. Bounty hunters looking for an escaped prisoner. Mostly true."

"When you get to this monastery, stay low. Do not knock on the door, do not be seen. Assume the kid is there, so make sure he doesn't get into the wind. I'll get there as fast as I can. There are no flights to Medford?"

"Naw, I checked. Used to be. United. Out of San Francisco. Now you got to fly to Eugene, a couple hours north. Where are you?"

"Missoula."

"A flight from Missoula to Eugene. Right. Might be faster to drive."

Truax hung up and again started his foot toward the water. The phone rang.

291

"What now?" he said, disgusted and assuming it was Wilford again.

"I need you here now," Nathan Ferry said.

"Can't do it, Nathan."

"That's an order."

"You told me nothing came ahead of the boy. We know where he is and I'm not letting him get away again."

"I've got something more important."

"I doubt it. What's changed between you and Steerman?"

Ferry didn't answer and Truax imagined him mentally running down the reasons for the question.

"You've seen the stories?"

"Story. There's more than one?"

"Three others. They're more important than the boy."

"No. It's the same problem. This story is full of conjecture and history. Even makes you look shrewd. If the teaser leads to more conjecture it doesn't hurt. If she has proof then she got it from the boy. I say she doesn't because the story isn't out for three weeks. She thinks she knows how to get the proof from the boy, or maybe Steerman. So what's changed?"

"Marcus threatened me when he learned we were looking for the boy! He said we would lose, that the boy was as unstoppable as the will of God, or some nonsense like that."

"In a couple of days we'll know."

"Forget the boy for now. I want you here."

"Nathan, we may never get this close again. If Steerman's stepping it up then the boy will, too. I don't want to put Steerman's prophecy to the test. We'll get him. Let's be sure. Forget this bringing him back alive. Why take any chances?"

"I want what he has. I can not be safe until I have it."

"I'll call you in a couple of days."

"By then I will have made other plans."

Truax did not like the idea.

"Be patient for another forty-eight hours."

"No. Colin? Don't bother coming back without the boy. Alive. You copy?"

Teresa Gill took Steerman's call at home.

"You were foolish," he said. "I told you not to put Bong Sat out there."

"I didn't use the name."

"You're splitting hairs. To Nathan, you did."

"So I pissed Nathan Ferry off. What's he going to do? Kill me?"

"Precisely. He will call someone, who will call someone, and so on until it happens."

"You are being melodramatic."

"He killed hundreds with one phone call at Bong Sat. Because of that phone call the war lasted another eight years. How many died because it did? Is your life so special he wouldn't dare?"

"But the paper sold out so fast Oscar is having another press run."

"How will that make you feel better? Your life is in peril."

She sighed, paused, and then said, "I did it partly to get you to call. I need to be able to reach you."

"What could possibly be so important about talking to me?"

"A little matter of proof. Ferry's set up and it's time to stick it to him. I want you to come forward and tell all."

She heard a gasp. She waited for a coherent response but gave up.

"Mr. Steerman? Marcus?"

"I have an alternate suggestion for you. Go where you are safe. Do your job by phone. Do not go to *The Times*. Protect yourself. Will you do that?"

"I have to go to work. How do I explain staying away?"

"If you agree I will give you what you sought in the first place."

"The Diemaker?"

"Yes. In detail. Then in a few more weeks we can come back to the end of Nathan Ferry."

"Oscar isn't going to buy this."

"He has no choice. You will have no proof for your story without me and I will not provide what you need unless you do it my way."

"I'm going to need something explosive to tell Oscar."

"Okay. How about this? The Diemaker was the one who built the weapons. You do understand that?"

"Someone else did the killing?" she asked.

"If by that you mean someone else installed or put into place what killed the target, yes. The Diemaker was thirteen years old when the first target, Ned Greene, was killed. The boy was a genius."

"Was? Is he dead?"

"I don't know, although I doubt it. He has proven a most difficult young man to kill."

"More, Marcus, more."

"His father was a Marine officer at Bong Sat. We escaped together. We were partners for years until Ferry's men killed him."

"What kind of partners?"

"We were in hiding. It was easier for me, a man alone, but Matt Eliot had a family, a wife and a young son. We bought an old carnival, fixed it up, changed the name and he and his family traveled most of the year surrounded by people who all had something to hide."

"What was the name of the carnival?"

"Laughland. Eliot said it was because of something one of his men said at Bong Sat. As the battle carried into the night one of his men said it was like a carnival from Hell."

"How come Eliot was on the run?"

"We saw Ferry order the killing of two of Eliot's men in cold blood. Eliot wanted to charge the killers, but I held him back. I told him dead men don't get a chance for revenge, and that Ferry was guilty of far worse. Eliot didn't care about the far worse. His obsession drove him. He coached his remarkable son into becoming the most creative maker of death the world has ever seen. This is where you should take the story. Everyone has heard of The Diemaker, but nobody knows Bong Sat. One sets the table for the other."

"Can you prove your story of a thirteen year old killer? It's no easier to swallow than Nathan Ferry and Bong Sat."

"Proof of everything exists and is even more dramatic than you could guess."

"What is this giant 'but' I hear?"

"The boy, The Diemaker, is the only one who knows where the proof is, and I don't know where he is."

"That's a big time 'but.' I'll think about your idea, but if we get the proof on Ferry I can't hold off."

"Keep an open mind. To do so you must remain alive. Ferry sent four gunmen to kill the Marine. They shot him dead in a bank parking lot. You are as great a threat as he was. Do you understand?"

"I – I've never felt threatened before."

"You could die before morning. Ferry has had plenty of time to make arrangements."

"I need to be able to call you," she said.

He gave her a number with a Nevada area code and told her it was an answering service. He would check for calls twice a day.

After they hung up, she stood at the window and looked down at the street. Night had fallen. Two cars drove by. Kids ran. A man walked a dog. Her hands shook.

She stepped away from the window. She looked at the phone, then back at her hands. They still shook. She called Marty Dunbar.

"Okay if I come by?"

"Sure."

"I'll have my toothbrush."

"Come on. We've got a room. The sheets are clean, and there's a bath down the hall. Take the same route you took last time. You remember?"

"Yes. Thanks."

"Watch your back, but don't be surprised when you have some company after you cross into our territory."

She packed light. She carried the two small bags to the car, and threw them in the back seat. She drove fast and stayed off the freeway. The San Diego Freeway was tempting but she avoided it finally cutting east on El Segundo. She saw the sign for Compton, and a few blocks later a recent model Buick came along side. The man riding shot gun nodded, then the car dropped back.

She parked in front of Dunbar's house in the only vacant spot on the block and carried in her bags. The house smelled of wood polish and cleaning compounds. Martin Dunbar sat at the dining room table surrounded by file folders. He restacked them when she came in.

"Welcome, Teresa."

Robert came in from the kitchen carrying a pizza box and two bottles of beer.

"You hungry?" Dunbar asked.

"God, yes. Does being scared make you hungry?"

"It does."

She tore loose a wedge and took a bite. She heard voices and laughter from the back.

"How many people you got here?" she asked.

"They come and go. We can mobilize fast."

"All this because I called?"

Dunbar took a bite and shook his head. "We got guys here all the time. Most of them lost friends and relatives in Nam who got drafted. A complicated issue for black men. A military career's got some honor, and fighting proud is good. But these guys were getting drafted while white boys their age sat in college. Add in they were fighting for a country that treats them without respect, so like I said, complicated."

Another hit on the beer.

"Now's a real straight ahead time. These guys have been pissed and grieving for twenty years with no place to put it. Now they do. That war was fucked, and now we're telling them they were getting played by some super rich white guy that wanted more. But mobilizing wouldn't help us. The cops would call out the National Guard and we'd get bottled up in our backyard. Time to play smart. Time for you and me to put all our cards on the table. You first."

By ten o'clock that night, Father Harold and Amos had prepared as well as possible for Brother Sidney. When the priest left, Amos went into the caves and worked through the night on the steel stakes he would drive into the rock to anchor his ropes. He heated the steel, cut and sharpened one end, and bent and rounded the other. He had no experience with rock climbing, but what he needed appeared obvious. He had made soft rubber toe plates for his shoes that would improve their hold on the rock, and to free up his hands he would use a chest harness used for work on the exterior of the monastery.

He planned to space his life savers across the rock face, and attach ropes to create a railing along the narrow ledge leading to the tree line. He worked until dawn, bathed in the cold water of the underground stream, then dried and put on a fresh robe for his trip to the confessional to meet Brother Sidney.

"So you're sure he's there?" Colin Truax asked, after sliding into the booth at the Denny's in Grants Pass, Oregon.

Hugh Janacek and Thomas Wilford, fresh after a good night's sleep, waited while Truax drank his first cup of coffee. Truax had never liked Janacek, a tall dour man with a quick temper.

"Yeah, he's there," Janacek said. He set his empty cup down, and ignored the sugar icing from his raspberry Danish on his upper lip. He wore a light blue dress shirt open at the neck under a black poplin jacket.

"We talked to a delivery driver for a commercial food company who takes a semi up to the monastery once a week. We give him our story, tell him there's a reward for the right information. He says there are about forty or forty-five monks in the place, but doesn't know much about them because they don't talk. He drives his truck, they open the door, and he unloads the order. That's it."

"So how's he know the guy is in there?"

"The doors don't squeak, the hydraulic loading dock ramp finally works, and the pallet jack's been greased. None of them worked then – Presto! – they go from shit shape to ship shape. I say it's our boy."

"Maybe."

"Yeah, but compared to what we've had, this is pure gold!"

"Okay. What's the terrain?"

"Tough. It's up at the end of this road that climbs like a son of a bitch. The truck driver says it's damn near impossible after it's rained. Going down's the worst. Real narrow, no guard rail and a shear drop. You go over, you're dead."

"What about the monastery?"

"It's built out on a rocky promontory called God's Finger. I didn't stick my head over the edge, but the driver says it's at least seven, eight hundred feet to the bottom."

"That the only way in?"

"It's like the cat that climbed the tree. When you get to the top, there's nowhere else to go."

In the morning Teresa stood at the kitchen window drinking her first cup of coffee. She looked into a fenced back yard with more hard pan dirt than grass. Nothing was planted in the borders. Three broken yard chairs sat around a metal table. Beer bottles covered the top. On the far side of the fence an alley divided the block and gave the house access to a garage. She doubted Dunbar ever went into the back since there was no ramp down the three steps. She carried her cup and joined Dunbar at the dining room table.

"What's happening?" she asked.

"You wanna tell her, Robert?" Dunbar asked.

"Last night we counted three two-man teams within a fifteen block radius. A little brother washed a windshield and saw the dudes wore flak vests and had shotguns between the seats. Could have been cops, he said, but they didn't look like cops. Too hard."

"Mercenaries," Dunbar said. "Ferry's behind the scenes of an outfit in San Francisco called Vesta that sends mercenaries all over the world."

"Vesta hires mercenaries?" Gill almost shouted. She imagined Edgar Chiswell's face when she told him.

Dunbar pointed at her, and said, "You're thinking about telling Edgar. Too late. He knows. There's no proof."

"But this is huge!" She stared at Dunbar as his words sank in. "Edgar knows? He didn't say anything when I brought Ferry and Vesta up in the same sentence. This is too big to sit on."

"As huge as making a war drag on for eight years and killing maybe a couple of hundred thousand people? Hiring mercs is small time, Gill. Stay focused." She opened her mouth, but Dunbar held up a hand. "Edgar's got to walk a narrow path. He has all this rage, but if it shows he loses his job and he won't be there when we need him the most. Same for you. Stay alive. Finish the story."

"We need the proof," Gill said.

"Absolutely," Dunbar repeated. "Stay focused and we'll get it."

"I'm talking the war proof. Steerman says it exists. He had it but The Diemaker took it."

A squawk came from the middle of the folders on the table. Robert stepped up and pushed things aside until he found a hand held radio.

"What?" he said, into it.

The reception was scratchy, but Gill got the gist. The three teams had become seven and had pulled back to a thirty block radius. The teams were hard to miss, driving late model SUV's and dressed like paramilitary troops in black fatigues and bloused boots.

"How can they do that in the middle of the city?" Gill asked, surprised.

"Lots of dudes dress tough," Robert answered. "Still got Panthers and they wear fatigue coats in the summer."

"Yeah, but those guys aren't going to attack us in broad daylight?" She waited for agreement and when none came, she said, "Are they?"

"This is South Central," Robert said. "The cops shot up the SLA not that far from here and that was middle of the day. Had thousands of people on the street. TV trucks everywhere. It was like going to a fucking parade. I was there. My auntie took me. A guy sold snow cones out of the back of a station wagon. When the cops started shooting, nobody started screaming. It was real still except for ten thousand bullets hitting that house. My auntie squeezed my hand real hard and kept saying those poor bastards. She meant the SLA."

"We can't have that around here," Dunbar said. "We got families all around. Kids, moms, grandma's. Can't have no war."

They sat silently until Teresa wrapped the table top with her knuckles.

"Let me make a couple of calls," she said.

"The line might be bugged."

"I don't think it makes any difference."

"Who you want to call?" Dunbar asked.

"I'll leave a message for Steerman. Anything we do has to include him."

"Who else?"

"We can use some air cover."

She called Edgar Chiswell and explained their plight. He said he'd see what he could do.

The morning crawled by. Reports came in that the seven teams now numbered ten, but they still kept their distance. Teresa paced.

"Sit down," Dunbar said, "you're making me sick."

"How come in your in the wheelchair?" she asked, leaning against the back of her chair, but not sitting.

"Nothing romantic, nor heroic. I fell off a ladder when I was fourteen. Broke my back. Legs are useless. My father was killed in Korea and my mother's youngest brother was killed in Vietnam. Looking for guys who didn't make it back is as close to being there as I can get."

At noon the phone rang. Dunbar answered, then handed the phone to her saying, "Steerman."

"I'm glad you took my advice," Marcus said.

"Me, too, but we have to make our move now," Gill said.

"Because?"

"Ferry's kicked up the action."

"And you want my contribution."

"Absolutely."

"You know there are no promises."

"Yes. Check your messages on the hour." She hung up and turned to Dunbar. "Whatever we have to do to get out of here, let's do it fast."

Father Harold met Amos at the door of the sanctuary. The priest took Amos's hands and prayed silently. After "amen" he mouthed the words, "Go with God," then, "Meet you at Conversation Point."

The confessionals lined the wall to the left of the altar in a way that made Amos think of Crocket and the cells in solitary. One of the entrance curtains remained open. Amos entered and pulled the drape closed as he sat. He heard a whispered voice speaking Latin, and waited for a signal to begin.

When none came, he said, "I do not speak Latin, Brother."

"Do you believe in God?" a harsh voice whispered.

"I believe there is more to life than what we see," he replied, speaking no louder than the monk. "The design is too elegant to be the work of humans."

"Play no word games with me, Novice." Brother Sidney spoke slowly and with care, but the tone remained sharp. "Do you believe in God?"

"What we don't know is too frightening without a God. I've learned that since I've been here."

"Go on."

"When I was a child, my father left me in the desert. If I died, he believed he saved me from a life of fear and disappointment. If I lived, I had a chance to fulfill his dream." The pain of the memory stabbed him as it had not for many years. It is the pain of truth, he thought. "At night I believed everything was there to hurt me. Now I would not be afraid. God would give me strength against the fear."

"God does not give you strength. Your faith gives you strength. What else?"

"My only job in life has been to survive. I have killed to survive, and I have helped others kill so I would survive. I did not think about why I lived, or what I would do with my life, but I do now. My father was right when he said the day I start worrying about right and wrong would be the day I start to die, but the dying does not have to come quickly." Amos leaned his head against the screen, and closed his eyes. "I no longer wish to live to kill. But if I do not protect myself, those who come for me will kill me. If I hide, they will find me again."

"You are sure they will find you?"

"Yes."

After another long silence, Brother Sidney said, "You can not reach God by evading this life."

"Are you evading this world by seeking God's world?" Amos asked.

"The world of the abbey is not an evasion. It is a bridge. It is a version of Man's world that forces us to confront the plight of Man before we can reach an understanding with God. There are many versions of Man's world. What is yours?"

"In prison, when they put me in solitary, I learned I had lived in solitary my whole life. I do not want to live that way."

"This is your desire?"

"Yes. I want to be more like other people. I want to think of other people and God."

"Why think of God?"

"God fills the emptiness in my head. I have never been part of something larger than me."

"You have always been part of God."

"I didn't know that, so it did not exist."

"If you want God to fill your emptiness," Brother Sidney whispered, speaking even more slowly, "there are responsibilities and laws to live by."

"Are they God's laws?"

"Yes."

"A matter of more faith?"

Another long silence that stretched into many minutes punctuated by more whispering in Latin. Amos grew tired of waiting.

"What came first? God or Man?" he asked.

"God created Man."

"Is all life sacred?"

"Yes."

"Then should I let someone kill me so I can die by God's law?"

"Hiding and killing. Those are your only choices?" Brother Sidney asked. The words came so slowly each found a new space in Amos's head. He had asked the question of himself many times, and found no third choice. Now he saw other possibilities.

"Perhaps," said Amos, "there are others."

"God is a process," the monk said. "God expects you to use the tools he offers you to meet the needs of Man's world in accordance to His law."

"What is Man?" Amos asked.

"Man is marriage of heart and mind," Brother Sidney said. "Too much heart, and emotion overrules God's law. Too much mind, and Man thinks he lives above God's law. God's law guides us to a life of heart and mind lived in harmony, but we may choose to follow his law or to ignore it."

Amos had never lived in harmony.

"Our message to the world is to see the choice God wants us to make," Brother Sidney said. "What is your message??"

"The Diemaker is dead."

"That is your message to Man's world. What is your message to God's?"

"I don't know. I leave here, and there are people who will kill me. If you walked out with me they would kill you, too. Would you knowingly walk to your death at the hand of an evil man who ignores God's law?"

"If that is what God wanted me to do, yes, I would."

"And how will He let you know?"

"You are close to blasphemy, Novice."

"This is my world. If I said, walk with me, Brother, for I fear for my life, would you walk?"

"Are you asking me?"

"No. I would not invite your death."

"But you came here knowing the world would find you."

"I'm sorry, Brother, but I want you to tell me what to do. I do not want you to say it is God's will, or some other phrase men who do not face death use to those who do. What . . . should . . . I . . . do?"

"There are times when God's Church, governed by men, forgets it is a collection of individuals. It attempts to make its teachings universal. There are cases, even though the Church denies this to be true, where that does not work. Centuries ago God was depicted the same way as other ancient gods, male, muscular, old, and wise because it was an image humans would pray to and take direction from. But in our bigger world with a view to the universe, God is a presence. He waits for Man to come to him and to become one with him. Man demonstrates his oneness with God by the way he lives his life."

"You have not told me what to do."

"If you die you will be denied a chance at redemption. Live and demonstrate what you have learned. There is more to Man's world than kill or be killed. The choices you make from here out will determine how close you come to God and fill your emptiness."

"Is redemption more than not doing the wrong thing?"

"Yes. True redemption is filled with irony. It is the understanding of your sin and reforming it to where God would be pleased with what you do with your life."

"Those who pursue me fear me and the death I could give them. They are men who are used to making others afraid. Experiencing their own fear is worse for them than their dying." This insight caused Amos to realize his pursuers would arrive soon putting the order in danger. "I found help here. I am grateful, but if I stay longer you will all be in danger."

"So be it. Go with God, Amos, and find your answer."

The wood door slid closed. Amos sat alone in the world of Man.

Robert ran in from the kitchen with the radio in his hand. "They're moving!"

"That's it!" Dunbar called. "Let's roll."

Teresa lifted the phone and called the *LA Times* while Robert squawked the walky-talky three times. When Teresa got through to Edgar she said they were moving. He wished them good luck and told her the chopper was in the air over downtown. It would be in the area in minutes.

"I put it on the radio we'd received a tip that there was going to be a gang shootout. We gave descriptions of the trucks, too."

"Thanks, Edgar. We won't let you down."

"Yeah, go team."

She started for the dining room then went back to the phone. She got Oscar on the first ring.

"Where the hell are you?" he shouted.

"The shit's hitting the fan, Oscar. We're on the move."

"What shit? Who's we?"

"I don't have time to explain. I just wanted to tell you I'll call when I can."

"We have to talk now. We have to run something this week. We sold out again and the phone's ringing off the hook from the national media wanting to know where we're going with this. They're signing on for big bucks."

"You're going to have to wait."

"No way, Gill. Give all now!"

She saw Dunbar looking at her. He waved for her to wrap it up.

"I gotta go. I can give you The Diemaker story."

"I need Ferry. I need a full length story kicking Nathan Ferry in the balls in thirty-four and a half hours."

"I'm sorry, Oscar. I have people waiting for me right now. We're in trouble."

"Can the melodramatic. I can't think of anything more serious than I'm facing here."

"How about being surrounded by seven teams of armed mercenaries?"

"Sure. Thanks a lot, Gill." He hung up.

When she reached the back door, Teresa saw a wooden ramp now covered the stairs. Dunbar rolled down the ramp then his hands on the wheels. She caught up, took the handle grips and started pushing. He pointed at a gate and she pushed harder. As she reached for the latch, she heard the squeal of tires and the creak of a door opening. A black man she didn't recognize held the gate open and waved to hurry. When she pushed Marty through the opening she saw a white van with the side door open. Robert sat at the wheel.

"They're trying to seal the ally!" he yelled.

She pushed the chair to the open door.

"Come on push his ass," the man called as he pulled Martin erect. Teresa leaned into his back and shoved sending Martin flying onboard headfirst. The man grabbed the wheelchair and threw it past Martin into the empty cargo space. He waved Teresa to dive in and slammed the door narrowly missing her feet. As he got in the front, Robert gunned the van down the ally.

"Shit!" Robert shouted. "They blocking."

"Ram 'em," Martin yelled. "Hit them to the right like a bank shot. We can take the turn faster."

The van accelerated. Teresa reached for anything to hold onto and found nothing but a bare metal frame that sliced into her hand. She heard shots over the roar of the engine just before impact. Both she and Martin bounced and rolled on the bare metal floor as the van recoiled. Her feet came high enough off the floor to send them over her head. As the left side wheels came off the ground her feet came up. The floor leveled and her feet and the tires hit at the same time. She twisted as the van found direction and picked up speed. Two shots hit the rear but didn't penetrate a steel plate blocking the doors.

"The lift gate for my chair," Marty said. "Knew it would come in handy."

"What's that roar?" she yelled, as a deeper throbbing noise layered the racing engine.

"Choppers over head," Robert called.

Teresa reared up to look, but Martin pulled her down again.

"We're in the clear," Robert said. "Nobody chasing us for now."

"Yeah, for the moment," Martin said, and pulled Teresa's arm. "Think you can get my chair bolted into those restraints?"

She slid, bounced, and crawled to follow his instructions. She got the wheelchair anchored and offered to help him climb into the seat, but he waved her off. She watched as his arms carried his weight. He sighed when he got seated.

"Thanks," he said, looking down at her. "It's the only exercise I get."

"Getting shot at?" she asked.

"Yeah. Extreme, but it gets the circulation amped up."

"Where am I supposed to sit?"

"You're young," he said.

For **Colin Truax**, a failed Episcopalian, the ride up God's Finger brought to mind Saul on the road to Damascus. Truax feared the results of a flash of blinding light either literally as lightening flashed on the far side of the valley, or figuratively if their SUV missed a narrow curve. Janacek drove the Ford Scout with one hand and talked to Wilford with the other. He constantly took his eye off the road that Truax felt sure would disappear into thin air around the next turn. Truax considered shooting him to remove the doubt of their end.

"Pull over," Wilford said. "This is the last place to park before the top."

Truax took a deep breath before joining the others and removed his hand from the grip of his weapon. They walked a quarter mile, turned a corner and saw the front gate of St. Peter in the Woods and the priest's parked car.

"What if they don't come out?" Janacek asked.

"How do you feel about shooting priests?" Wilford replied.

"If I was afraid of priests I wouldn't be here."

"We are not shooting priests," Truax said. "The priest will help before we have to shoot him."

As if a celestial hand cued their conversation, the door in the gate opened and a man in a clerical collar emerged.

"It appears," said Truax, "that God is on our side."

Marcus Steerman called his service on the hour and got the message from Teresa Gill. He dialed the number she'd left and she answered on the first ring. Judging by the road noise she called from a booth.

"We're on the run," she said. "Do you have a plan?"

"There is a call I can make that might reach the boy."

"Make it. What do we do?"

"I'm sending you to a place a couple hours east of Las Vegas. Stay in Vegas tonight and head into the desert tomorrow. Leave a number where you can be reached in the morning."

Next Steerman called Crocket State Prison. It took fifteen minutes to reach LaVoy McDaniels because he wouldn't leave a name. When he could get no further he said he had information on an escaped prisoner named John Nelson.

"I don't remember the name I used when we met," he said, when Warden LaVoy McDaniels picked up.

"Ziegler, Larry. I'm surprised to hear from you."

"Is your line secure?"

"You're joking, right?"

307

"Not at all."

"The world is no less paranoid, then? Okay. It's secure."

"Can you reach him?"

"How serious is this?"

"Your life is in danger, as is anyone else you sent Nelson to."

"Let's say I can. What do you want to tell him?"

Steerman looked at the note he'd written.

"Tell him Marcus called. Tell him They are coming and he must come home. Clyde and Streaker will die without him. Got it"

"That's it?"

"No. The purple bag and the contents of the box can save everything. Now, that's it."

Steerman packed up his room. If he drove through the night he would be at the closest phone to Laughland by dawn.

Amos retrieved his life savers and three coils of rope from the cavern and hurried back into the abbey. As he neared the front door of the abbey, Brother Donato grabbed his arm. The monk waved frantically and Amos followed him up the staircase into the belfry. When they reached the top, Brother Donato gasped for breath and pointed to the front of the monastery. Amos saw two men standing over Father Harold.

Amos thought of his life savers and rope and felt a sinking in his stomach. He was too late.

"I'm sorry," Amos whispered, "this is my fault."

Donato opened his mouth again, but Amos held up a hand.

"Is there another other way out of the abbey?" he asked.

The monk shook his head.

"Brother, those men will have a story, but there is nothing they can say that gives them the right to enter the abbey. If you don't see me in three hours, have the abbot call the police."

Colin Truax bent over the priest. The man's face bled from where Janacek hit him after the priest refused to answer their questions. Truax sent Janacek down the hill to watch the car before he could do any more damage. A helpful priest would have made their job far easier.

"I'm sorry, Father," Truax said, and dropped into a crouch, "that guy was a mistake I will deal with later. We have a legitimate reason for being here. Help us, and no one gets hurt."

Father Harold looked at the blood on his hand. His eyes went up to Truax, and shook his head.

"We are willing to overlook aiding and abetting a fugitive," Truax said. "You are worth nothing to us, so we don't care. You were trying to do a good deed. Right? Hooray for you, but Nevada would like to have the convict back, and we want the reward. What do you say?"

The priest continued his silence.

"Tell you what, I'll give you some time to think about it. When I come back, we are prepared to be more persuasive." Truax told Wilford. "Keep an eye on him while I visit our impetuous friend."

Amos stood at the mouth of the opening in the rock a third of the way between the tip of God's Finger and the river far below. He measured off forty feet of rope and marked it with blue tape so he would know he was close to the ledge. With the surplus length, he would start his lateral journey hanging from a rope he could trust. He closed his eyes and pictured himself crawling like a spider on the rock, arms and legs splayed while he groped for purchase.

For ten minutes Amos measured, cut, and threaded nylon rope through the steel stakes. He had two other ropes each of one hundred feet. He planned to set his life savers at eight feet apart, the maximum of his reach. He had sixteen life savers. He quickly did the math and came up three stakes short. The extra length on the drop rope would offset some of the shortage. To make up the rest, he would have to adjust out on the rock.

He hammered his anchor stake near the opening, and tested its hold. He fit his glasses to his face and adjusted the homemade strap made from rubber bands to keep them in place. He put on gloves with the tips of the fingers cut out, stowed one looped rope with its life savers around his neck and the other on a tie to the side of his harness, then stepped to the edge.

The wind blew a soft spray from the waterfall against his bare arms, and ruffled his hair. He had noticed neither before. He didn't know how much water had blown on the rocks, but after a moments worry he reminded himself there was nothing to be done now but jump. He listened for the water hitting the rocks at the base of the cliff. It reached him as no more than a soft whisper.

He looked out into space. Beyond Heaven, massive dark clouds announced a Pacific storm.

"Insanity," he muttered. "Why am I doing this? What hope do I have?"

"Not the point, Amo," said a voice in his heart he had not heard in years.

"Bill! Where have you been?"

"Always here, Amo. Been enjoying the ride as you grow into a man."

"A man?"

"Every inch, and about time. Your pa saddled you with that damn right and wrong idea. He wasn't right to do it, but he did. Amo, you beat it."

"How do you know?"

"Because here you are standing at the edge of life, questioning why. Only a man full of right would be in your shoes."

"Will I go?"

"What do you think? People who stood up for you are in danger for no reason other than believing in a boy from nowhere."

"Will I make it?"

"Long way to come to fail."

"But will I make it?"

"Get to getting and let's find out."

"You coming?"

"I love you, Amo. I'm with you."

"Have I forgotten anything?"

"Give it a think. Last chance."

Amos thought. "I'm ready."

He threw the drop rope into the void, looped the rope under his butt, and stepped back. The rope slipped through his gloves, under his butt, and through his feet as he controlled his descent. A gust of wind pushed him away from the rock and he lost focus letting the rope slide faster. He over-reacted, clamping with his feet and hands and nearly lost his grip as he crashed face first into the rock. He hit his forehead, came close to blacking out, and had to hang still as his vision cleared. The cold mist from the waterfall on his face helped clear his mind. He caught his breath, then slowly resumed the drop.

He stared at long cracks in the bedrock sliding by inches in front of him. He stopped his fall and pressed against the rock with his toes to see how much he could feel through his homemade rubber grippers. He felt no fine definition, but he could detect the gross irregularities in the rock.

The piece of blue tape slid through his vision, and he started feeling for the ledge. When he found it, his feet told him it was uneven and angled slightly down and away from the cliff face, but wide enough to take his foot from toe to heel. He still needed the rope because there wasn't enough room for his chest. He relaxed with his feet holding his weight on the ledge and both hands gripping the rope. He looked across the rock to his destination.

"No further than Laughland's shop to the mess wagon, Amo."

"I can't do this, Bill."

"Piece of cake. What's harder? Killing that rabbit, or taking a stroll over to them trees?"

"This. I need to pick up some distance before I use the first life saver. What do you think? Ten feet?"

"That hunk of rope started out at seventy feet. You came down fifty, but you're six feet tall so you used forty-four feet. If you use that geometry you learned you could figure out how much rope you got left as you move across the ledge."

"Bill, I can't think about that now!"

"You feel safe right here?"

"Sort of."

"You know you don't have enough of them stakes to make it so maybe you damn well better think about it. That smooth running brain can hang on and think at the same time."

Amos closed his eyes and thought about Crocket and his geometry class. He almost always knew the right answer. Proving the answer was the hard part.

"All you need is the answer. The proof is in the doing."

"I can go more than ten feet. More like forty feet."

"What's that tell you?"

"Watch the slack."

He felt exhilarated. With the extra traversing length from the rope he was sure he'd have enough life savers. When the slack played out, he set his first life saver and tied off the rope he carried on his shoulder. He still had a few feet left in the drop rope, so using both secure ropes he resumed his lateral movement. As he prepared to tie off the drop rope, his foot slipped as the rock edge crumbled. Fear raced through his body, but with the ropes he regained his balance.

"Great reaction time, Amo. Regular blur."

He pushed his glasses back to his forehead, took a breath and fed out his traverse rope. He turned his feet sideways and found that by passing the traverse rope to the outside of his body it gave him the sensation of being lashed to the rock.

"What do you think?" Bill asked. "Good time to plan the next stage?"

"Good idea. See that narrow spot? Where the ledge almost disappears? I think I should use the stakes to stand on."

"How you going to do that?"

"I can't reach my toes without losing my balance, but I can reach below my knees. I can make kind of a bridge that goes up slow. After I get over that narrow spot, the ledge is wide and I can step down to it. Right there near the end I might be able to do without the rope around me."

"Go for it, but one step at a time."

He moved across the rock driving each stake deep into the cracks. His steady progress brought him quickly to where he would build his bridge. He set the next life saver with the end slightly elevated so his foot would not slide off. Before he put his weight on the stake, he checked his rope, then held his breath. He moved ahead standing on the stake. He set another, stepped, and made his way across the gap in the ledge. With the bulge in the rock face he had more room to lean into the rock.

The sound of the hammer strikes echoed across the valley.

Hugh Janacek boiled with anger. Truax had reamed his ass for hitting the priest who, rather than answer the questions, wore a smug, shit-eating grin like priests always wore. The look had pissed Janacek off as a kid, and it was worse now. The satisfaction of hitting him had lasted until Truax told him to take a hike.

Now Janacek watched the road with nothing to do but play with himself. He'd always hated authority, and moments like this reminded him why.

Then he heard the sound of a hammer.

"Pointless to doubt, Amo," Bill said, as Amos looked at the stretch ahead. "Keep your head in it. You're long past halfway."

"Better be. I've only got six stakes left."

"How about using those first class hands?"

Amos saw cracks that would take his hands and toes.

"It would save time, Bill."

Out of the corner of his eye, Amos glimpsed dark clouds over the Coast Range already moving into the valley. He smelled rain in the air seconds before the first thunderclap.

"Gotta move, Bill. If the storm catches me out here, I'm a goner."

His hands felt their way across the rock. His feet followed and he had less faith in them, but with each successful move he grew more confident. He came to a place where he found neither hand nor toe hold, and set one of his remaining stakes. He slowly worked his way down to where the ledge widened. When he reached it, he discovered the ledge wider. He slid his feet toward the tree line while still hanging on to the rope.

The flash of lightening reflected off the rock, ozone filled the air, and when the thunder crashed the sound waves shook him. He tried to move faster, but the rope slowed him. He considered dropping it and relying on his feet and hands, but he was too close to make a mistake. The first drops of rain touched his skin.

He looked back. A dark wall of falling water rolled across the valley. Another bolt of lightening ripped the dark sky.

Ten feet to go. Three safe strides. The rain pelted him, each drop on his exposed skin felt like a knife cut. He looked longingly at the tree line and saw a man with a gun.

"I can't decide," the man yelled as he waved the gun. "Should I throw rocks or poke you with a stick? Or I could shoot you. Got a preference? Either way, it's a long way down."

Disappointment crushed Amos.

"Or maybe just leave you out there to get fried by a bolt of lightning," the man yelled. "I hear rock climbers are ten times more likely to be hit by lightning."

Amos stayed glued to his ledge.

"But they want you alive. Pisses me off. Seen a lot of people die, but I never seen nobody fall and fall." He tucked the gun under his arm so he could use the hand to mimic the arc of the fall. In the other he held up binoculars. "I figure I could see you split apart like a fucking watermelon. Probably be dead already, but it would be a mighty sight. But, like I said, they want your sorry ass alive so get off that rock."

Amos moved slowly, rain falling harder, until he was one long, dangerous step away. He leaned into his last step. As his weight shifted, the ledge broke and knew he would come up short. His toes still had contact, he pushed and leaned forward holding out his hand to the man.

The man laughed, waved the gun, and pulled his hand out of reach.

"You fall I hear it's about a six hour drive and one helluva of hike to pick up your pieces. Sure hope you make that tricky little leap."

The wind changed, the rain fell harder, and Amos jumped. His footing slipped and he hit the cliff top with his waist instead of his legs and frantically looked for hand holds as the wet surface slipped away. He flailed his arms and hands to the side, found roots on one side and a rock on the other. The man with the gun stepped forward to see the much anticipated fall.

Amos grabbed his ankles, pulled himself forward, and his attacker fell on his back. Amos reached for the gun, and to his surprise, he missed, as the man slid by on the rain-slicked ground. Amos spun to reach for him. He saw the attacker's surprise turn to horror as he launched into the air above the abyss. A flash of lightening lit the body. Not even thunder covered the scream.

Covered in mud, Amos separated himself from the earth and moved with the awkwardness of a newborn. He stumbled away from the abyss, then used the cover of the trees to move uphill as the wind whipped the branches of the giant firs and the rain beat the ground like a drum.

Lightening backlit the abbey through the trees. Halfway to the gate, he saw two men standing over a third he assumed was Father Harold. In the mud, crouched in the bush, lightning flashes instead of fireworks, he thought of his father outside the cathedral at Bong Sat as his men died.

Amos pulled himself forward on his stomach. The thunder shook the ground and he felt the energy flow into his body. Brother Sidney's words of redemption played at the edges of his mind against the knowledge that the child of his father would not hesitate to kill the men threatening Father Harold. Lying in the mud, the idea of choice grew inside him. He saw the decision as to who lives and dies as being more than his alone. Amos's first responsibility belonged to Father Harold and the monks. Even with his speed, it would be difficult to take both men without Father Harold getting hurt.

In the next flash of lightening, Amos saw one man standing over the priest, not two. He pushed himself deeper into the mud to await the next flash. When it came, Amos saw the other man moving downhill between him and the cliff. The man slipped, then splashed and slid as he tried to pick himself up. Racing on all fours, Amos reached him before he regained his balance, and in seconds lay across him with his hand tight on his mouth. The man fought against him, but when he saw the primitive rain-soaked and mud covered image staring into his eyes, Amos saw the resistance give way to terror.

"Your friend fell all the way to the bottom," Amos said into the ear of his captive. "I wonder if he died before he hit. Are you curious?"

When there was no response, Amos asked again. The man tried to shake his head against Amos's grip.

"Good. What's your name?" he asked, and loosened his hold.

"Wilford, Thomas Wilford."

"Am I worth dying for?"

A brief hesitation, then, "No."

"I'm just a job?" Amos felt a nod. "Do you work for Nathan Ferry?" Another nod. "Your choice is to die like your friend, or go back to Ferry and deliver a message. Your decide. Live or die."

Amos softened the hold on his mouth and Wilford replied without hesitation.

"Live," Wilford said.

"I am going to make your friend the same offer. What's his name? Is he the leader?"

"Colin Truax. Yes."

"I can either knock you out, perhaps giving you a concussion, or tear your shirt and tie you up. Which?"

"Don't hit me."

"If you attempt to interfere in any way, I will find you and throw you over the edge. Do you understand?"

Another nod from Wilford.

"You know what I did at Crocket, don't you?"

The fear in Wilford's eyes answered the question.

"This is my first experiment with mercy. I'm not committed."

Wilford's eyes closed, and he shivered.

Amos tore Wilford's shirt, bound his hands behind him, then tied his ankles, and finally gagged him. He took Wilford's gun and tucked it into his pants.

"Listen to me. If your friend chooses to die, or if he hurts the priest and I decide not to offer him mercy, go back to Ferry and tell him to leave me and those who helped me alone. Do you understand?" Wilford nodded. "If he chooses to ignore my warning, you will die. Truax will die if he survives the next few hours, and Ferry – ." Amos paused a flash of lightening illuminated the future. "Tell Ferry death is not the worst thing that can happen."

Amos leaned closer, pulling Wilford off the ground..

"Are you and Truax responsible for my father's death?" A new terror flooded Wilford's face. Amos nodded and dropped him in the mud.

Amos moved uphill. The time between lightning flashes lengthened, and the rain tapered off, but visibility remained minimal. He slowly worked his way around where Colin Truax still held Father Harold. Amos figured Truax would be watching downhill for his friend, so he circled to come in behind him. The lightning and thunder came as one. Ozone permeated the air and the rain fell with renewed intensity. In the lightening, Amos saw Truax was now within twenty feet. He crouched behind the priest with his right arm out of sight. Amos assumed it held a gun. He edged closer as the rain fell in waves.

"Eliot!" Truax yelled. "I know you're out there. Come in or I kill the priest."

Amos slipped to within arm's reach, waited for a sheet of rain to pass and said, "Then you will die."

Truax jumped at the voice near his ear and let go of the priest. Amos saw Father Harold's arms were tied. He hit Truax from the side and ripped the gun away. Truax screamed as he hit the ground where Amos threw him.

"You'd be dead if I wanted you dead," Amos yelled over a thunder clap feet astride Truax.

Amos dropped to his knees and pressed against Truax's shoulders.

"I am going to release Father Harold. If I feel you move, I will throw you over the cliff."

"I'm not moving," Truax said. "What about Wilford?"

"I haven't decided yet. The other one is over the edge."

As Amos spoke he worked the bonds on Father Harold's arms loose.

"You're loose, Father. Are you hurt?"

The priest shook his head. He rubbed his arms and hands, then wiped the water from his face.

"Father? You decide Truax's fate" Amos leaned closer to Truax. "Should we leave it up to a priest? Did you threaten him? Do you fear what he will decide? Life or death, Father?"

Another wall of rain hit them and more of the slope slipped away.

"There is little time," Amos said, gun still in Truax's face. "His friend has already chosen to live, and I gave him instructions to take back to their boss. They are not to bother you. The moment he breaks the arrangement, I come back. Do you understand you will be taking any promise this man makes on faith?"

The priest nodded again, eyes wide despite the water streaming off his forehead.

"If these men live they know where to find you. They have only my word that you know nothing of the man behind them. Are you willing to take the risk, or should I kill them?"

"Would you kill them if I asked you to?"

"Without hesitation. I will not kill if there is a choice, but that is the extent of my redemption."

Amos saw fear, hope, and resignation all play across the downed man's face.

"Risk or not," Father Harold said, "I cannot ask you to kill."

"Would you pray for me if I killed them regardless of what you want?"

"Of course, although I see you have learned a better way."

Amos thumbed the hammer down slowly on the gun. Truax's eyes closed as Amos pulled him to a sitting position.

"Do you understand what you are to do and the message you are to deliver?" Truax nodded. "Father Harold offers you mercy. What about you? Would you rather die than be the bearer of bad news? Can you give your word to uphold the agreement?"

"You have my word," Truax said, the relief plain on his face.

"You understand the consequences of breaking your word?"

"I do," Truax said.

"So be it. Can we leave, Father, or will the road be washed out?"

"It will be dangerous."

"Please go into the abbey and tell them they are safe, and get my bag from my cell. I will take these men to their car. Meet me there."

After the priest left, Amos brought the gun back to Truax's face.

"Wilford said you and he were responsible for my father's death. Is that right?"

Fear returned to Truax's face washing away the newborn hope.

"I wasn't there," he said, teeth chattering.

"But he died because of you."

Truax's lips moved, but no sound came out.

"Did you kill my mother?"

Truax shook his head, eyes wide.

"But you know who did."

"Yes. We knew nothing about a woman I swear to God. The Marine was the target. The same guy who told us about him set up the hit. He was supposed to be alone."

"I want a name."

"Martin Dunbar. His name is Martin Dunbar."

Amos pulled Truax's face close.

"Do not take my mercy for granted," Amos whispered. "It is something new and will not be offered again. Deliver the message to Ferry as I gave it to your friend."

"Listen, please," Truax pleaded. "Ferry wants you alive."

"Why?"

"He says you have something he wants."

"I do. He need not worry as long as he does what he's told."

"No one tells him what to do."

"I just did. Try hard to get him to believe."

"He won't pay attention."

"If you cross me again you die. I can see in your face you believe me."

"I don't want to die!"

"Can Ferry kill you as easy as I can?"

Father Harold came running down the hill. He slid in the mud to a stop.

"There is a message for you," he said.

Amos watched Truax but moved away to listen to the priest.

"It's from Horatio. He says someone named Marcus called him and said you must come home immediately. *They* are coming and Clyde and Streaker are in danger. He also said the purple bag and what was in the box will save everything."

Amos returned to Truax.

319

"In prison they said I twisted a man's head off. Your life is again is at risk. What is Ferry's plan?"

"I swear I don't know!" Truax said. "He told me he had other help."

"Who?"

"He has lots of mercenaries."

"They are soldiers who like to kill?"

Truax closed his eyes, then said, "They will kill."

Amos looked to Father Harold.

"What should I do, Father? I thought I would have time to find my answer."

"There will be others who you must protect?" Father Harold asked, placing a hand on Amos's shoulder. "Just as there were here?"

"Yes."

"Here you gave me and these men the choice of life and death. Seen by the rules of this world that was fair."

"I don't know if I can control what happens."

"An answer exists. As long as you live you will seek it. If you die others will die, too, without the choice you gave me."

"Is that the priest or the man talking?"

"It is the priest whose feet are held to the same fire as yours."

Amos searched Truax and Wilford's truck. He found a rifle and another hand gun. He also found a telephone, and placed them on the ground. Under the passenger side front seat he found a newspaper. He started to put it back but he saw a cartoon and the name Nathan Ferry. He stuffed the paper under his arm, and before releasing his captives gave it to the priest.

When he had the men in the Ford, he gave Truax the keys.

"If you make it down the road, remember my instructions."

Neither Truax nor Wilford looked at him.

"Go with God then," Amos said, and stepped back.

Father Harold walked to Amos's side. The two men watched the car slowly disappear around the corner of God's Finger.

"What does your message mean?" the priest asked.

"I don't know. These men know about Warden McDaniels but I don't see what advantage they would have by killing him. He would be difficult to reach. You, father, are vulnerable." The rain had slackened, but now that he was out of immediate harm, Amos felt the water running down his back and over his face. "We must begin our journey."

They came to a near stop before venturing around any blind curve in case Truax and Wilford found the courage to ambush them. When they reached the bottom, Father Harold drove quickly over back roads. As the priest drove, Amos read the article in *Mother's Own*. Before he finished it he understood why Ferry looked for him.

"Father, I liked living alone better. Too many things happen now beyond my control. Would you drive me to Nevada, please?"

"Now?"

"Yes, Father, now. As soon as we change clothes and eat. Could I have some pancakes, please?"

"Amos, I have a parish to run. I can't leave because you need a ride."

"You are not safe. You saw the humiliation of those men. They said what they had to say to get off the mountain. Your church will be safer without you."

"I could find you a car. Perhaps rent one."

"I can't drive, Father."

The priest looked at him. "Not at all?"

"I could become a very good driver, but it would take practice, and we are in a hurry. I can drive where the road is straight and there are few cars so you can rest. We can drive through the night."

"Nevada?"

"We have to stop in Las Vegas, then go to my home. You will be safe there."

"You said no one knows where you live."

"I did not lie. Things are changing. I think the message means others will be there, too."

The priest parked in the church's lot. He turned off the ignition, then leaned his head on his arms that rested on the steering wheel. Amos thought he was praying. When he finally lifted his head, he sat straight.

"It is time for me to resolve the differences between the priest and the man." He opened the car door. "Come, let us put on dry clothes, then pay tribute to Mrs. Rafferty's cooking. A long journey starts on a full stomach."

Mother's Own took up the third floor of an old brick warehouse north of Candlestick. It wouldn't stand the next eight point anything earthquake, but in the meantime the building provided lower rents within reach of smaller enterprises. The windows leaked and the chill of foggy nights near the bay seeped in from thousands of cracks left behind by previous tremblers.

Oscar Mason's hands shook with fatigue. He'd had no sleep for two nights as he worked on a way to keep the Nathan Ferry story alive without Teresa Gill. Just thinking her name made him angry. The ridiculous story she'd told him about mercenaries threatening her and being on the run only made it worse. He figured she had a story for *The Times* and didn't want to admit they came first.

He picked up the fax he'd sent to all the inquiring media for a preview of *Mother's Own* frontal assault on Nathan Ferry. It read:

Mother's Own has irrefutable proof that Nathan Ferry prolonged the Vietnam War for personal gain.

Over the next few weeks we will detail the role of Bong Sat, a small village at the heart of the war, and how Ferry used the cover of the war to give his businesses a chance to prosper amid the chaos of eight more years of the deadly war that took so many American and Vietnamese lives.

As part of this investigation we have uncovered the truth behind the mysterious killer known as The Diemaker and his connection to Ferry.

Sign on to the releases now. Those who delay will not be included in pre-release and will pay more.

Oscar Mason, Publisher

In the first three hours after its release, every national television network called as did all the wire services. Their questions centered on proof. He had to call his brother for wording to satisfy the callers, and the lawyer complained bitterly at Oscar's black and white wording that offered little wiggle room and could come back to haunt him. He set the fax aside.

He could not put out the feature length story without Gill. Since his return from fish tacos and a beer, he'd worked on a teaser that would also keep him out of court. He'd settled on a cartoon with a shadowy figure screaming attack and pointing at soldiers huddled around an American flag. The cartoon figure was not Nathan Ferry but it took the space on the page that for three of the last six weeks had carried Ferry's caricature. Minus the teaser he stared at, the whole edition had gone to the printers – a different printer than they usually used due to a mechanical failure.

How did it come to this, he mused. Gill, of course. Before she came along, he was still pushing whales and spotted owls. He believed in green. He was no opportunist. There wasn't that kind of money, anyway, but he felt he'd taken the environmental press as far as it was going to go without a big influx of cash. That was the Ferry story. A springboard to a bigger and better *Mother's Own*.

As the fax transmitted to the printer, he looked around the office with its cubicles and partitions, its posters and slogans, and thought it couldn't look anymore dated if the posters were for the Grateful Dead and the New Riders of the Purple Sage. The fax dinged signaling it had gone through and he reached for his feed sheet. He died before he touched it.

The gas explosion took out the third floor in one massive blast. The concussion crippled the already compromised building. What didn't get blown a block away collapsed inward on itself.

PART V: The Return

1988

With full stomachs and wearing dry clothes, Father Harold and Amos Eliot journeyed south on Interstate Five. Within thirty minutes they crested the Siskiyou Mountains and entered California. Even though it remained overcast with intermittent showers, Amos wore his dark glasses.

"Do you regret your decision to leave the men alive?" Amos asked.

"No. I feel bad leaving my parish so abruptly, but it's time." The priest checked his mirror and changed lanes to pass a slow truck. "I learned from our conversations. While you were trying to resolve right in your life, I tried to resolve the man and the priest in mine. Relying only on faith is no longer enough. I saw my faith had become like my mother when I was a child. She would pick up behind me so I didn't have to do the hard stuff. I did the same thing with God. I left the hard answers up to him. Your search is difficult, and mine will be, too."

"Where will you go?"

"Monastic life will give me the chance I need. Not St. Peter in the Wood, but there are other monasteries in other countries. I speak Spanish and French, so I have choices."

By Redding, darkness had fallen and the priest started to yawn. He stopped at a rest area south of Red Bluff.

"It's straight for many miles. Can you drive?" he asked Amos.

They traded places. There was nothing smooth in Amos's entrance to the freeway. He mistimed his merge and drew the ire of other travelers, but he stayed in the slow lane until he felt more sure. He discovered that without the driving gear of his youth, everything came easier. Their progress became smooth, and soon the priest slept. Amos drove gradually faster. They would be in Las Vegas before dawn, and Laughland by mid-morning. He looked forward to being home, and not even the shadow of Nathan Ferry could change that.

After talking to Steerman, Teresa Gill and Marty Dunbar, driven by Robert and Chuck, traveled to Las Vegas and checked into adjoining rooms at the Budget Inn on the outskirts of town. She slept until the phone woke her.

"Turn on CNN," said Marty Dunbar. "Stay on the line."

She caught the end of the story from San Francisco with pictures of what was left of *Mother's Own's* offices.

"What happened?" she asked. "Anyone hurt?"

"Get dressed and come over. Robert's getting coffee. I'm calling Steerman's service and leaving this number."

In five minutes she stood watching a local channel with the story of the gas explosion that so far left at least one dead.

"Did you print the paper in that building, too?" Dunbar asked.

"No, Oscar used a printer off site. Oh, please don't let it be Oscar."

"Call the printer. Let's see if we can rule out coincidence."

It took her a few minutes to find the number. They answered on the first ring.

"We're not printing this week's edition," the man who answered told her. "We had two presses break down. Never had two go down the same week. Do you think Mason's the one who died?"

She said she didn't know and asked who had this week's job. He told her and she made the call. Preswick Printing said they would start the run in about an hour. They'd received the last piece from Oscar Mason a little before eleven the night before. She suggested they add some security.

"What time was the explosion?" she asked.

"A little before eleven."

"It's Oscar," she said to Dunbar after hanging up. "The printer said Oscar faxed the last piece to them a little before eleven. This is my fault."

"Maybe, maybe not. Why last night? You aren't even there to write a story."

Teresa shook her head and called *The Times*. She gave her name and the switchboard put her through to Edgar Chiswell.

"Where are you? You okay?"

"Yeah, fine. They blew up Oscar Mason. Why?"

"Yesterday, he sent out a release to the media. It said *Mother's Own* had proof that Ferry prolonged the Vietnam War for personal gain. It said the paper had the truth about The Diemaker."

Teresa pounded her fist on the bed. "Oh, Christ! I told him to sit tight!"

"I guess he couldn't do that. He was making more money than he'd ever dreamed and wanted to keep it going. No story from you so he hyped it for next week and trusted you would come through."

"This is my fault," she said again.

"Keep your perspective. The day you walked into my office was the day the ball started rolling. It rolled over Mason last night and it's picking up momentum. Don't let it roll over you. Are you going to get the story?"

She straightened her shoulders.

"Edgar, I'll call you back. I'm waiting for a call from the guy who says the proof is out there. I need to know what it is and how hard we can kick."

She paced outside the motel room as the Nevada morning dawned clear with a slight desert chill. Ten minutes later the phone rang, and she ran into the room. Even though it was within arm's reach of Dunbar, he made no move to answer it. He held her eyes as she stooped to lift the receiver.

"Lot riding on this," he said.

"I know, I know. Hello?"

"You've heard?" Marcus Steerman asked, on the phone.

"Yes. The body is probably Oscar Mason's. He put out a press release yesterday saying he had proof that Ferry prolonged the war for personal gain."

"You should have warned him!"

"I did! I told him he had to wait until we had the proof to run the story. He didn't listen."

"And it killed him."

"I have to know what the proof is."

"I don't know when I can get it."

"I need to know. You keep teasing me, but now it's time to show your cards."

"Why?"

"Ferry's going to take some shots today about *Mother's Own* being blown to hell and the next story hyped to tell all. Oscar died for that story and I'm not letting him down."

The silence stretched.

"An attack on Nathan," Steerman said, slowly. "I've waited for this day for twenty-one years. I gave up thinking it would happen."

"I won't let the moment slip away. I promise."

"How will the story get out?"

"The story's gone national. All the big guys are waiting for the blood to start flowing before they jump in. But if we if have the proof *The Times* won't wait." She waited through another long silence. "Can we make Ferry bleed?"

"Part of the proof of Bong Sat is a film of Ho Chi Minh offering peace."

Gill almost dropped the phone.

"Jesus Christ! For real?"

"Matthew Eliot and I carried it out of the jungle. Originally, tt was to be delivered to Lyndon Johnson by Nathan Ferry. We received the film from a team of influential North Vietnamese including Ho's cousin. He carried Ho's chop for authenticity. The chop is in Eliot's purple bag. Instead of accepting the film, Ferry called in a gun ship to sterilize the site."

Steerman paused. As bad as she wanted to ask questions, Teresa sat the silence out.

"I wore a wire," Steerman's voice came softer, lost in the moment. "Ferry's words are very distinct as he orders the death of Frank McBride, and the Marines, including Matthew Eliot. The gun Ferry used to kill McBride is part of the cache. There's more, but that's the big stuff."

"How could you sit on this for twenty years? This is the crime of the century!"

"Who would I take it too? The United Nations? The CIA? My voice tapes, as damning as they are, could be faked even back in the sixties."

"What about Ho?"

"He wouldn't have admitted the film. He was not in absolute power at the end of 1967, but he ran the military. He considered peace because he didn't think the North could win if we decided to bomb them back to the Stone Age. But he still kept the film quiet, even in Hanoi. After Bong Sat he drove the war into high gear. I think part of the reason for the Tet offensive in February of 1968 was for something Ho could point to in case the film ever surfaced. By the time I could go public he would have repudiated the film."

Teresa's mind flew through the possibilities. "The problem is what to charge Ferry with."

"Exactly. Every war has been prolonged for one reason or another. Mass murder on the other hand . . . "

"Okay, I get the idea. Did you reach The Diemaker?"

"I think so, but please do not call him that. It demeans a remarkable young man. His name is Amos."

"How do I meet this Amos?"

"I'll take you to him. We can meet on the road. If there is a God and he cares enough to make the world right, we are going to the place where he will settle Bong Sat."

They arranged time and place to meet.

"How is your relationship with your editor at *The Times?*" Steerman asked.

"He wants more than I can give him."

"Maybe I can help. There is a motive in the present that explains why Ferry would want to silence *Mother's Own*. Ask your editor what Maine, Louisiana, Colorado, and Montana have in common with the death of a Minnesota congressman? Tell him to follow the money."

After she hung up, Gill tried to make sense of what she'd heard but the enormity of it threatened to drown her. Steerman promised even more than she'd dreamed, more than *Oscar* had dreamed, and he had just handed her the entree for selling the story to Edgar.

"So?" Dunbar asked.

"We're on," Teresa said. "I need to walk and get my head around everything that's happened. I'll be back before we need to leave."

"Where are we going?"

"He didn't say. He just gave me a place to meet him."

"Steerman will be there?"

"Yes."

"Where?"

"Give me a chance to think! I'll tell you when I get back."

She walked out to the street, turned away from the looming casinos of downtown Las Vegas, and walked slowly into the desert. The wind ruffled her hair; a ripple in the sand almost tripped her, but she wandered on. Her mind operated at full throttle and she spoke aloud.

"Let's say Steerman - love the name - has everything he says he has. Sounds great, but how do we put Ferry in jail? No idea. Can we pin a twenty year old murder on him with no body and no witness? Never fly. Prolonging the Vietnam War? Should put him in front of a firing squad, but Steerman's right. It's not a felony. Morally reprehensible, but no way to prove. Maybe the film wouldn't have brought peace. How about getting him on a murder charge for the friendly fire bombing that killed, among others, a squad of Marines? Even with a tape of him giving the order it might not win at trial. It's not fair!"

She walked for a while.

"Change the story. Steerman says Ferry's involved in elections. Not a crime, but why those states? Link the above to the elections, then what do we have?"

She jabbed her fist into the air.

"A Watergate moment! We can't get him in a court of law surrounded by lawyers, but we can bury him in every newspaper in the world."

She jogged out of the scrub to the road, and turned toward town. She trotted on the shoulder and stopped at the first phone booth to call Edgar Chiswell.

"Gill, before we can use anything the proof has to get past the lawyers."

"I know, Edgar. I really believe Steerman has the goods, but he gave me something you can use now." She recited Steerman's question. "You find the tie, build it up, and in the meantime I can get the backstory that ties Ferry's Vietnam atrocities to what you get."

"Elections today sound a lot better than war atrocities twenty years ago, Gill. I'm taking this to the meeting today. We might get a story out of the explosion, the election tie, and a mystery informant. I'd like to get us out in front of the competition. I'm sending some help."

"You can't! I don't know where I'm going, and I don't know when I can get back to you."

Chiswell said nothing, but Teresa heard him whistling to himself.

"Okay, Gill, but if Ferry was willing to prolong a war and bomb the shit our of a church twenty years ago, what all's he willing to do today? He already blew up Oscar Mason."

She walked the last two blocks to the motel and saw Dunbar's door was closed. Robert said he was on the phone. She told Robert to pass on the word it was time to go.

Father Harold awoke south of the Fresno exit and they stopped at the next rest area. Trucks, but few cars, pulled in and left, at two AM.

"It seems you drive quite well," the priest said, looking at his car and seeing it undamaged.

"It is well you slept," Amos said. "There were several times when only my reactions saved us. I learn fast, but I am happy it is your time. I need to sleep."

The priest drove through the last of the night. Father Harold shook Amos's arm as they neared Las Vegas. When they parked at the Stardust, dawn lit the eastern sky.

"I've never been to a casino before," the priest said.

"We won't be here long."

It took both of them to carry out the contents of the safe deposit box. Father Harold drove until they reached the edge of town. Even with the daylight growing stronger, Amos said he would drive. He got settled behind the wheel, adjusted his dark glasses, then aimed the car at Laughland.

Nathan Ferry did not arise until after eight Los Angeles time. He walked to his morning room where his breakfast, newspaper, and the night's communiques awaited him. He sipped his juice standing at the french doors to the veranda and admired another glorious California day. He ran a hand through his hair, noted he felt more scalp, and smiled. Even with his hair thinning, he did not look his age of almost sixty. He had the erect posture of a man ten years younger, and his stamina still tired his aides.

He had worked until two, coordinating the last few months of the four senatorial campaigns Sierra Terrace backed. In two of the races the leads were three points. So much depended on winning all the races that he would take no chances, especially if a few well-placed millions would remove the doubt. Before going to bed he arranged for the flow of more soft money to the right places.

He returned to the table and rang the ceramic bell by his place setting. Frank, his domestic assistant who served his food, managed his wardrobe, and kept matters in Nathan's various houses in order, brought coffee and a covered plate. As he poured the coffee, Frank said, "Sierra Terrace in New York has called twice in the last thirty minutes. They say it's quite urgent."

"Did you inquire?"

"Yes. I agree that it's urgent. Would you like me to dial while you have your coffee?"

Sixty seconds later Nathan listened to a recap of the last twenty-four hours beginning with the background on the articles in *Mother's Own*, then their news release with the claim of proof, and finally the gas explosion that destroyed their office and apparently their managing editor.

"I presume you are dealing with the coincidence," he said.

Sierra Terrace's managing partner in New York, Sir Christopher Blackstone, only displayed his British accent when under stress.

"Our public relations people are overwhelmed. Networks, syndicates, and cable news – all demanding statements."

"Blackie," Nathan interrupted, "your vowels and umlauts are showing."

"Yes, well, I should say with cause. Nathan, our usual denials failed to slow them one iota. The longer we go without a strong statement the more water we'll take on. Not the best of time this close to our primary goals."

"Send me a draft of what you think is an adequate response. I'll look it over, and make the necessary changes. Who's screaming the loudest?"

"*Newsweek*. They've never liked us."

"Set me up on a conference call with them and *US News and World Report*. They should balance each other out. Make it for nine-thirty, that's a little over an hour. You copy?"

Blackstone said he would see to it himself.

"And, Blackie, take another look and be sure our involvement in the campaigns is well shielded. If there are any doubts, move us back another step."

Precisely at nine-thirty the phone rang. Nathan sat in his office where he could see the portrait of his grandfather. The phone introductions were terse.

"I have a prepared statement to read," he said. "Recorders running? Here goes. 'Sierra Terrace Holdings, and me personally, have been the object of a series of baseless attacks written in a tiny press known as *Mother's Own*. We were unaware of what this street corner exercise of this country's right to a free press, had written about us. I am told they had little or no distribution outside of a small pocket of radicals. Our interests are world wide, and there is always somebody making unsupported charges. If we gave time to deal with each it would limit pursuit of our lawful and gainful interests. We know of the articles now only because the media has bludgeoned us with demands that suggest we must defend ourselves against the ridiculous idea that whatever act of God destroyed this muckraking press was our doing. This is ludicrous. We have no need to respond to rumor and innuendo.

"'My personal record to my family, my company, and my country has been exemplary. If such a day ever comes that I am confronted by proof of wrong doing I will deal with it openly. I make this statement knowing none exists.'"

He stopped, drank from his coffee, and said, "End of statement."

"Do you wish to clarify that last sentence?" *Newsweek* asked. "Do you mean there's no evidence of wrong doing, or that you have never done anything wrong?"

"You have my statement."

He hung up.

The value of their cargo made Amos vigilant. They saw no other car as Amos drove eastward into the morning.

"You're better," the priest noted.

"Yes. Do you think I will ever be normal?"

"I pray you will."

They drove through the abandoned town of Mercy. Amos saw one car and that was parked next to what had been Clyde's store. He didn't slow.

After they turned on the road that led up the hill, the car bounced on the deteriorated paving, a victim of time and wear. Amos felt sure the heavy trucks that had worked on Laughland while he'd been away had done most of the damage. He knew the work had been done, because he saw the well tower on the ridge line before he made the turn. At the top of the hill, he stopped at the turnout that overlooked Laughland.

"Amazing!" Father Harold cried. "It looks ready for business. You should have told me you lived in a carnival."

"Not in," Amos answered. "Under."

He opened the window and breathed deeply. He had missed the smell of the valley. Mesquite, mostly, but there were under notes of sage and Pinon pine. After the confined smells of prison and the damp forest aroma on God's Finger, the familiar notes of home eased the tensions he had carried since crossing this ridge in the other direction nearly three years ago.

He pushed his dark glasses against his forehead, now more a habit than a need, and drove down the hill. He saw Clyde walk out to meet them as he parked. His old friend settled his hat square on his head, hooked his thumbs in his gun belt and stood with his feet apart. Amos saw his surprise when he recognized who drove.

"I'll be damned," Clyde said, when Amos stood beside the car. "Driving out here in the light of day like you owned it. Care for a sucker? Got purple and yellow."

Clyde stood his ground as Amos walked to him.

"I missed you, Clyde."

They looked at each other, both at a loss.

"You going back in the hole or should I make up a bed in the house?"

"I will sleep in the house tonight if that's alright. Tomorrow I'll decide. Do you have a way to reach Marcus?"

"Good to get the mushy stuff out of the way," Clyde said, and resettled the gun belt on his hips. "Who's your friend?"

"This is Father Harold."

"Nice to meet you, Padre. Any friend of Amos's is welcome. Sort of a miracle, too."

"Clyde, can you reach Marcus?"

"Don't have to. All I got to do is sit on my butt. He's on his way."

"How do you know?"

"If that's your way of asking if I took care of business, I did. We got radio here and a sort of phone service. Not as secure as you wanted, but technology's been sort of slow getting to us. Could have put in a satellite dish, but that would have tipped our hand."

"We need that today."

"You are one lucky son of a buck, pardon me, Padre, because I knew you were going to say that. It's in the shed, but you're going to have to make it work yourself. I ain't got a clue."

"Then I will be busy," Amos said, and walked away.

"Amos, I'll make the padre at home," Clyde called after him. "I see you're all worried about that. Oh, one other thing. There's a map to the Underground on the table by the stairs. Putting in the sub-basement and re-enforcing everything made lots of changes. I don't want you getting lost."

"Clyde, don't be silly. I don't get lost."

Clyde watched the man – no longer a boy – walk toward the shed that still housed access to the subterranean world beneath Laughland.

"He may drive and have a friend," Clyde said to the priest, "but it don't seem all that much has changed."

A few minutes later, Amos walked into the wasteland toward the spot where Amo died and The Diemaker was born. He wondered who he was now. He found the site where he'd first buried his supplies, dropped to his knees, and dug with both hands. He uncovered a khaki-colored rubber-lined bag, then lifted it out. It was heavier than he expected. He opened it. The purple cloth bag with "Crown Royal" stitched in gold sat on top. He bounced it in his hand and thought of all the death the bag and its contents represented. He wondered if this would have been his first thought if he hadn't gone into the world.

Near the bottom he found a large manila envelope closed with tape. Amos ripped it off. He found a copy of the letter from his dad, and letters from his mom to his dad. From their dates they were sent during the war. One letter felt thicker. He opened it and saw a photo of a baby. He turned it over. On the back he read, "Our beautiful boy's first picture." He thought of his mother and felt engulfed by a profound sadness, then remembered the name of the man responsible for her death. Martin Dunbar. This man had killed Bill, too.

He chopped off the memory and held up the purple bag. If he had not gone to the Stardust how would he have found what his father had left? He looked back toward Laughland. He saw Clyde leaning against the wall of the shed.

"The man has to pay," Clyde said. "I was supposed to tell you when I thought you were ready."

Amos pointed at the rubberized bag.

"Did you look?"

"Matt talked about what was in it, but it wasn't my job to dig it up. All I was supposed to do was make a judgment call on when and, like that faithful old hunting dog, point you in the right direction."

"After I left, were you sad at what my father and I asked you to do?"

"Kind of a complicated answer. There were times I wondered what the hell I was doing. I was never cut out to live in no city, but seeing no one for weeks wore on me. I remembered about you forgetting how to talk, so I walked around talking to myself. It helped, but it didn't make up for nothing. All the work you left took longer and cost more than I thought, but I sure loved being busy. Kept me going. Since then life here has been one heartbeat ahead of dead."

"I'm hungry, Clyde."

"Got flapjack batter and a pound of bacon."

"What will you eat?"

"Did you just tell a joke?"

"I don't think so. Should I learn to tell jokes?"

"Someday."

Colin Truax stood at the picture window of his Sausalito condominium. White sails dotted the blue water off the yacht club pier complimented by the white of sparse clouds floating on the same wind that pushed the boats. When he and Wilford had reached the bottom of God's Finger, they drove to the freeway and turned south. There had been no discussion. They split the driving and reached the Bay Area in less than seven hours. Wilford dropped Truax at his home, and then headed for downtown San Francisco. Truax slept a few hours and got up at daylight. He drank his coffee standing at the window.

He turned on the television news and within minutes saw the story of the gas explosion north of Candlestick that destroyed a building and killed at least one. The dead body was identified as Oscar Mason, editor and publisher of an environmental weekly called *Mother's Own*. Truax remembered that the paper had been in the news since it started running a series of articles written under the byline of a mysterious 'Lois Lane' about Nathan Ferry. Yesterday, Mason had sent a press release to the media claiming he had proof of major wrong doing by Ferry. Earlier today Ferry issued a blanket denial. He said in a later interview it was an insult to have to respond to such a scurrilous attack by a sensation seeking muckraker. Investigations pointed at the identity of the writer of the articles as Teresa Gill, who also worked for *The Los Angeles Times*. Mason and Gill had gone to UC Berkeley together.

Truax called Ferry and left a message. He waited almost three hours for a call back.

"What happened?" Ferry demanded.

"Thomas Wilford, Hugh Janacek and I went to a remote monastery in Oregon called St. Peter in the Woods. The monastery sits on a cliff that drops almost a thousand feet. There's only one road and no trail. We felt it was the perfect place to corner Eliot."

"Was he there?"

"Yes. Inside the walls, but we had leverage with a priest who had helped him."

"Then?"

"He beat us."

"Three of you, plus a hostage, and he won."

"Yes."

"What else?"

"Consider this carefully. Eliot chose to go to prison. When he thought it was time to leave jail, he left. Then he goes to the literal edge of the world and gets admitted to a monastery that hadn't had a novitiate in years. When he had Wilford's and my life in his hands he said mercy was something new to him and he wasn't committed to leaving us alive."

"If he left you alive he must have changed."

"No. He decided to give it a try."

"Is that it?"

"He said to tell you that as long as you left him alone he would do the same. When you come after him or the people who helped him, he will kill me and Wilford. Then you."

"Should I be afraid?"

"I won't speak for you. I am afraid, but not broken. I think he broke Wilford. He dropped me off here and the way he looked at me, I think he's gone. Nathan, when Eliot had me on the ground with a gun in my face, I told him I could not control you, and that you would come. I told him I didn't want to die. He told me to live by my wits."

"Meaning?"

"He knows you won't stop. When you come he intends to close the book on his father."

"You make it sound as if I'm already dead."

"No, sir. Dead is up to you. What do you want me to do?"

Truax held his breath waiting for Ferry's answer.

"He's right. I'm coming for him. Do you want another chance to do your job, or do you wish to run?"

"He humiliated me. I want another meeting and this time mercy will not be on the table."

"Get as many men as you think we'll need. It will become clear where and when we will need them."

Truax hung up. If Ferry had equivocated when asked what he wanted Truax to do, Truax would have known it was his death sentence. He would have then called *The Los Angeles Times*.

Instead of him making a call, his phone rang.

"This is Martin Dunbar. You remember me?"

Truax remembered. As he listened he began smiling. The rematch with Amos Eliot would come sooner than he'd thought.

Nathan Ferry spent a sleepless night. Most of the time he lay there with his eyes open. When they did close and he thought he might drift off, distant whispering brought him awake. A phrase of Marcus's tickled his memory: The Ghosts of Bong Sat. He shivered, then hit his pillow with a fist. The whispering came and went until dawn.

Frank handed him coffee as Nathan passed through the kitchen on his way to his office. His desk light burned and the television displayed CNN as it did every morning. He set his coffee on his desk, sat and then looked up to the screen. As the network broke from a commercial, he saw his own face looking back at him. Beneath his picture ran the headline "Ferry Allegedly Prolongs Vietnam War." His eyes bulged as he used the remote to turn the sound up.

" . . . reports *The Los Angeles Times* in their morning addition. They say they have an informant who has proof in the form of a film of Ho Chi Minh offering peace in November of 1967, eight years before the end of the Vietnam War. The film was to be delivered to Lyndon Johnson. Ferry, who worked at the State Department at the time, allegedly intercepted the film.

"*The Times* informant said Ferry allegedly prolonged the war in Vietnam to help his business interests. Ferry is CEO of Sierra Terrace Holdings, a company that owns many subsidiaries around the world that specialize in petroleum, precious metals, and food stuffs. The holding company did prosper in southeast Asia in the 1970's and since. Ferry has recently been the focus of a series of articles in a small alternative press that seemed to be leading to where *The Times* says they are now. The editor and publisher of *Mother's Own* died just days ago in a explosion that is still under investigation. Neither Ferry nor any of his spokespersons have responded to the story."

Ferry stood and leaned over his desk, weight on his arms. His legs shook as he screamed. He hurled his coffee at the fireplace, sucking air through his open mouth.

"Sir?" Frank stood in the doorway. "Colin Truax on line two."

Nathan waved Frank off, then picked up the phone.

"What do you have?" Ferry asked.

"A claimant for the million dollars."

"Someone knows where the purple bag is?"

"He says he can deliver more than that."

"How much more?"

"The whole Bong Sat nightmare package. Ho's film, Steerman's audio tape, Steerman himself, and the boy with the purple bag. "

"Don't tease me, Colin. It sounds as if *The Los Angeles Times* already has it."

"Not yet. They're talking about an informant and withholding details until *after* they have the source material."

"Do you think he's telling the truth?"

"He's the one who gave us Tagnut, the Marine."

"What else did he say?"

"He's helping the reporter, the one calling herself Lois Lane, and she bringing Steerman who saw the stories in *Mother's Own*. Steerman's going to lead them to Eliot and the kid will have all the stuff his father left him."

"And you think it's possible he's telling the truth?"

"This guy's in it for the money and he isn't getting a dime without the goods. Yeah, I'd say he's telling the truth."

"What's next?"

"He said he needs twenty-four hours to get things set and have the goods in hand, then he'd call with instructions. I'm getting the crew together. I'm going to stage them in Vegas."

"Why there?"

"Because that's where the caller is and he's driving. I think Eliot is right under our noses again. I'm going to what information is available on the property."

"So I do nothing for twenty-four hours."

"Try acting like you don't have a care in the world."

After hanging up, Ferry looked at the television and saw himself again. Acting as if he didn't have a care in the world would not be easy.

Teresa Gill refused to ride in the back of the van another day. She had the men wait for her at Budget rent a car. After she had her car she led the way. Steerman's instructions took them south on I-15, then east on Hwy 62 to a sign pointing toward Mercy. She slowed as they entered the town. Tumbleweeds and signs hanging by a single hook announced the town had run dry years ago. She saw a blue car parked in front of a faded but still legible sign that read CLYDE'S STORE. A slender man with graying hair and wire rim glasses sat with his legs crossed on the covered porch.

"I'm Teresa Gill," she said, walking slowly toward the man.

"Yes." He stood and looked at her then at the van. "Your friends?"

"Yes. Martin Dunbar, Robert's the driver and Chuck's a helper. Martin's in a wheelchair."

"Tell them it's only about fifteen more minutes. I'll ride with you."

She did as instructed while Steerman threw a bag in the back of the rented Pontiac.

"Where to?" she asked.

"Same direction. Drive slowly because we have to talk. Did you talk to your editor?"

"Yes. I told him about the elections. He was excited. Said it was easier to work on a story happening now than one twenty years ago regardless of what happened. He'd take it to the editorial board and they would move fast. He said they want to get out in front."

Steerman looked at her.

"You are seeing the end phase of a plan concocted by Nathan's great-grandfather," he said. "The Ferry family creed is control what people need, and you will be both rich and powerful. As the world grew, so did their ambition. Their goal is to control at least 75% of the world's supply of key consumables. That includes energy and food. Your stories failed to imagine the scope of their ambition."

"How do you know this?" she asked, keeping the speed under thirty miles per hour.

"I am a rare breed. A Nathan Ferry insider who left him and lived. My leaving was his decision and he had no intention of my living, but I did."

"Tell me about Amos Eliot?"

Steerman told her one hard to believe detail after another. She held her questions until she could wait no longer.

"How did his mother die? That seems like the turning point for him."

"It was. For Matt, too. Matt believed Ferry was responsible, but I didn't."

"Why?"

"How could Jessie Eliot be killed, and Matt and Amos not? That question has bothered me since it happened. It's hard to believe it was an accident. Bill Tagnut, her bodyguard and driver, and Matt's trusted old Marine buddy, was too good to accidently miss a turn, especially since where it happened had no turns.

"I think they were after Bill, and Jessie was collateral damage. They didn't know who she was and didn't care. It's the only explanation that makes sense. Tagnut survived Bong Sat because he wasn't there. Matt had sent him out for help, but he knew about Ferry. Bill didn't make it back with help and his failure haunted him. After the war he went looking for other survivors. Even after Matt told him nobody else had made it, Bill kept looking. He must have asked the wrong person."

"Who would he have gone to?" she asked.

Steerman looked over his shoulder at the trailing van.

"How well do you know Martin Dunbar?"

"I don't. I trust the person who gave me his name, and Dunbar has been open and helpful. Why? Because this is the kind of guy your Bill Tagnut would have gone to?"

"Yes. I've known about Peace for Vets for years. I've even helped anonymously a few times by sending them leads. I tried to stir their interest in Bong Sat, but curiously nothing ever came of my efforts. Dunbar's group always seems better funded than their filings explain."

"How do you know?"

"My dear, I've been on the run from the most powerful man in the world for twenty years. You would be astounded to know how good I am at many things. Being suspicious of Martin Dunbar goes with my territory. On the other hand I don't trust anyone." He pointed out the windshield. "Up here on the left. A hundred yards. Turn, and take it slow. The road needs work."

Amos watched the car and van arrive from where he worked mounting the satellite dish. The other part of the communications package, the antennae array, was already in place. Next he would wire in the data cable from the Underground, and Laughland could communicate with the outside world. The tower that held the dish looked like the others scattered around the edges of Laughland that were built during the hunt for water, but this tower had no functioning pump. A slit trench at the foot of the tower reduced the profile of the dish to keep it out of sight from any direction other than overhead. When he finished, he walked down the trail to Clyde's. He had a headache and felt slow from his long day outside with only his glasses to protect him from the sun.

Despite the late afternoon chill, people stood and sat outside the house. One sat in a wheelchair with a blue bag hanging from one of the arms. Amos found it strange to see so many people where he usually saw only Clyde. Amos recognized Marcus Steerman, but none of the others.

"Hello, Marcus," he said.

Steerman had been seated on a plastic patio chair, but stood.

"Hello, Amos. It's been a long time."

Clyde stepped out of the background and joined Amos.

"How about I do the introductions?" Clyde said. "This young lady is Teresa Gill. She's a reporter for *The Los Angeles Times* and wrote the articles in *Mother's Own* as Lois Lane."

Amos watched her examine him. The direct stare of a woman was a novelty.

"This here fellow over here," Clyde said, "in the wheelchair is a friend of hers named Martin Dunbar and these men are his driver and helper."

The name hammered Amos. He tried to move but his muscles would not respond after his day in the sun.

"Martin Dunbar?" his voice managed. "You killed my mother and Bill!"

He got halfway to Dunbar before the man's hand holding an automatic came out of the bag.

"I got no idea how you know," Dunbar said, "but I'm too smart to bluff it out."

Amos stared into a gun for the second time in two days. He knew he'd been lucky on the rock when the man lost his footing on the wet ground, and could not count on being lucky twice. He saw surprise on the faces of Dunbar's driver and helper. Whatever Dunbar had done he'd done alone.

"Okay, old man," Dunbar said, waving the weapon at Clyde, "drop the gun belt. Use your left hand."

"Can't. Got arthritis in that one. I can hold it up, but that's about all."

"Slowly then with the right."

Clyde's right hand slowly untied the rawhide thong that strapped the holster to his leg. Then, still slowly, his hand came up to the buckle. He worked the buckle and tongue of the belt free. As the belt started to drop, Clyde's right hand blurred to the big .44 that came free as the holster fell. The gun fired. Dunbar's weapon flew into the air. Two more shots so close together they sounded as one, separated the bag that had held the gun from the chair.

The shots released Amos from his torpor. As he covered the ground to Dunbar, he saw the man's face go from shock to pain, and then to fear. No hint of mercy slowed his hands as they closed around Dunbar's neck. Steerman tried pulling Amos away.

"Stop, Amos!" Marcus yelled. "We might need him."

Amos loosened his grip, but did not let go. He felt hands pulling on him and again he heard Marcus calling his name.

"He can breathe," Amos said, then he looked at Clyde who still held the smoking revolver.

"Very good," Amos said. "I didn't know you could do that."

"You'd be amazed what you can do with lots of time for practice. Pretty good at throwing cards in a hat, too."

"You are very close to death," Amos said, turning his attention back to Dunbar. "Do your friends know what you've done?"

For a moment Amos saw defiance flare, but just as fast it dimmed.

"No."

"You did it for the money," Amos said.

Dunbar tried to look away but Amos's hands brought his face back.

"Yes, for the money on Tagnut. I didn't know anyone else would be hurt."

"You told Truax and he told you to take care of it. So you did." At the name Truax, Amos saw Steerman stiffen. "How do you know Truax, Marcus?"

"I paid him for information. He was supposed to let me know if Ferry ever picked up our trail."

"Was he supposed to tell you about Bill, too?"

"He didn't."

"Teresa Gill?" Amos said, looking around and finding the reporter. "Are you getting this? Liars and cheats. Two of them."

"Oh, come now!" Steerman yelled. "You kill to save your life. I tell lies to save mine. Which is worse?"

"I do not betray my friends. Being loyal takes courage, and as you have said many times, you are a coward."

Clyde still covered Dunbar's friends as Amos approached them. "Did you know your friend betrayed you?"

"No," Robert said.

"I didn't betray you!" Dunbar shouted. "It had nothing to do with us. I was almost broke and we weren't getting any donations. I did what I did and we had money for months."

"That was the only time you dimed out?" Chuck asked.

"Yes. I swear."

"You're lying," Steerman said. "I gave you hints and leads on Bong Sat and not once did anything happen. You killed those leads and got paid for it."

"So what? It wasn't about us, the people who fought your fucking war! It was about fat cat white guys. I got a chance to fan their flames and make money. Yeah, I took their money and used it closer to home. I'm sorry about your old lady, man, but it's not my fault. Blame the guys who made that war. Blame Nathan Ferry."

"Why are you here now?" Amos asked.

"One million dollars." Dunbar said. "You got a purple bag? One million dollars. That's what Ferry will pay."

"There are too many of us for you to kill all by yourself. What were you going to do?"

Dunbar looked at his useless legs and pounded the arm of his chair.

"What kind of a place doesn't have a phone? Uh?"

"Still you had a plan."

"Drop the girl off, say glad to help, and get the hell out of here. Get to the nearest phone and call Ferry. He comes in, finishes you guys off, and I get paid. I didn't have to have the bag. Just lead him to it."

Amos pointed at Robert and Chuck.

"Dunbar will not need your help. If he needs a ride when we finish, we'll get him home. You can go."

"Robert! Chuck! Don't leave me! I've never let you guys down."

Robert lowered his hands.

"That's how you see it, Marty, but you didn't talk to us. People would have helped until we got back on our feet. You sold our honor, man."

Dunbar watched them walk to the van then leave. Amos knelt at the side of the chair.

"Steerman says that he and I will do anything to stay alive. Let's find out what you will do. Who were you dealing with?"

"A guy named Truax."

"And when was the last time you talked to Truax?"

"A couple of hours ago."

Amos shook his head and looked at Father Harold. "How did you leave it?"

"I'd call tomorrow morning with instructions."

"And so you shall." Amos stood and looked at everyone. "Bong Sat will end here. Each of you has a role if you're all willing to help. Are you?"

All the heads nodded, and he said, "Good. Let's get started."

Teresa Gill stood on the ridge line next to a satellite dish mounted on a pumping tower. She watched Amos Eliot's mesmerizing hands fly as they connected a phone into a junction box.

"All I have to do is dial the number?" she asked him.

"Yes," he said, without looking up.

The sun had set below the horizon but the sky remained red. She carried a flashlight. Earlier she'd had her moment of wonder staring at a table top covered with two film canisters, three audio cassettes, a plastic bag with a handgun, and a bulging purple Seagram's Crown Royal bag.

"Here," he said, and handed her the phone that looked like a phone repairman's with the dial on the back and the ear and mouth pieces on the other.

In less than a minute she got through to Edgar Chiswell.

"Gill! Reporters call in! First rule!"

"Edgar, yeah, I know, but there are no phones out here."

"What are you talking on?"

"Okay. One phone. As of a minute ago. Edgar, we need somebody on the line to take down what I'm going to read. It's a transcript of a of a very famous film."

"A film? Are you on task here, Gill?"

"Yes, and please be patient. There are things you need to know."

She read by flashlight. It forced her to read the words of Ho Chi Minh slowly and with reverence, as they should be. On the first page, Edgar interrupted twice with exclamations, then fell silent as the import of what he heard sank in. When she switched to the transcript of the audio tape and read Nathan Ferry's words that condemned so many, her throat caught. Edgar managed an "Oh, God," but that was it.

"You have the source material?" Edgar asked, when she finished.

"Yes, but seeing how we're a newspaper I thought the words ought to come before the film and the soundtrack."

"Yeah, good call. You got confirmation?"

"That's going to be hard. I think the only living people who know what it says are right here, and now you."

"Okay, but don't lose the film. This is the day I always dreamed about. A story that shakes the world. Guess I'll quit tomorrow."

"Edgar, there's something else I have to tell you. It's about Martin Dunbar."

She hung up five minutes later. As she handed the phone to Amos, she said, "You betray somebody, it hurts."

She watched him stow the phone in the control panel.

"I have another job for you," Amos Eliot said. "Do you know how to use a frequency scanner?"

"I've used a police scanner. Close enough?"

"The day after tomorrow they will come. We will be outnumbered. You can leave, or you can be in at the end. It will be dangerous, but I am very good at this sort of thing where people die."

"People will die?" Of course, they will, she thought. This is a war. "I'm in."

"I'm sure they will come by helicopters and you will be our spotter. I want you to find their frequency then play them a tape you and I will make. It's a warning. We will give them a chance to leave before we destroy them. Can you do that?"

"You're asking me to help kill people?" She wondered about her quick "I'm in" now that she knew there would be blood on her hands. She wondered if war correspondents ever fought.

"Yes. People who will kill you if given the chance."

"What if I can't do it?"

"Marcus Steerman is such a person. You do not want that to be you."

She held his eyes, then slowly nodded.

He took a walkie-talkie off his belt.

"Clyde? Are you there?" he said into it, as they started down the trail.

"Where the hell else would I be? Somebody's got to look after this guy. He keeps moaning about his hand hurting where I shot him. Told him if he didn't shut up I'd push him outside and he could bitch to the critters."

"Okay, Clyde. Please turn Laughland on."

Amos held out an arm and they stopped. Moments later the night came alive.

For Teresa Gill watching a carnival spring to life deep in the wasteland of the American West became the exclamation point to a day filled with emotions that reached from wonder and awe to fear and disappointment, . The midway blazed with light, the roller coaster car made its steep climb, and at he far end the carousel turned while raising and lowering its horses accompanied by what she felt sure was a Bach fugue rich with its thundering organ notes.

"It's beautiful," she said.

"Laughland was born at Bong Sat. The battle was fought because of Nathan Ferry's ambition and heartlessness. My father told me about the rain, the jungle, and the giant cathedral."

The carnival glowed, every detail etched in crystalline clarity against the darkness of the surrounding desert.

"Clyde says Laughland is the conscience of Bong Sat. What happened was so terrible that God will close the books here on the midway, or if Clyde had his way, in the fun house. Father Harold says Laughland is the moral scab of an evil so profound it cannot heal without an exorcism."

"What do you say?" she asked, and felt the intensity radiating from the young man beside her.

"I am the heart and soul of all who have died," he said.

Teresa spent the next day alone prowling the corners of Laughland. Clyde and Amos worked together and when she inquired Amos said it had something to do with trip wires. She heard Clyde say he'd found all the stuff buried by Amos's father and there was enough to fight a small war which was just about right. Dunbar sat in his wheelchair near the front door. Father Harold and Marcus Steerman walked into the wasteland at sunrise. Later she saw them talking and walking slowly among the tumbleweeds. Once, she saw Steerman on his knees in front of the priest who held a hand over the kneeling man.

She walked Laughland's midway, explored the rides, peeked into the tents but didn't enter because their interiors were dark. By afternoon, she saw Clyde and Amos coming and going from the fun house. She tried to follow but a draped cord across the aisle stopped her. Instead, she explored the outbuildings. In one she found a map labeled "Underground." She looked at it, then around the shed, and found a trap door. She opened it, flipped a switch and turned on lights that lit the stairs into the nether world. She dropped to a knee and looked into the hole, thinking of another girl who had done more than look and traveled down the hole.

"And so shall I." she said. She reached the bottom of the stairs and consulted the map, then walked from hall to hall, and room to room.

Time in the underground seemed a viscous liquid that transported her through a child's trip to young adulthood. She saw one miracle after another, and with each her curiosity and admiration grew. As she walked, she decided she needed to write a book about the boy who had lived here.

Night had fallen when she returned to the surface. Laughland lived bathed in artificial light, and this time happy organ music accompanied the carousel. She saw a rider and walked toward the flashing lights of the beautiful carousel with its brightly painted facade and lighted poles between the horses. Amos rode upon a glowing, golden horse. He sat calmly, rising and falling, as his head swayed with the music. She watched him, wondering what must be in his mind and how many times he'd ridden the horse. Clyde rode a black stallion on the side opposite from Amos. Clyde did not look at her when he glided by. The expression on his face suggested to her he dwelt in another time, if not another place.

Amos saw her as she stepped into the light. He stopped the horses, then walked to her and offered a hand.

"Care to ride?"

"Thank you, sir. My favorite place to think in Los Angeles is near the carousel in Griffith Park. It's a nice carousel, but not this nice."

"You can have any horse but Streaker."

"The palomino?"

"Yes, he was my only friend when I was a boy. Other than Clyde."

She wanted to reach out and touch him, but nothing invited her other than her pity. She chose a roan with a white mane. He started the motor again, and they rode until Clyde stopped them. As the horses slowed and the music died, Clyde went to Amos. He put his arm across the man's shoulder.

"Are you sure about this, son?" Clyde said.

"Yes, Clyde. It's time. My father, Bill, my mom, and all the others. They're waiting."

Laughland

"Nobody Gets Out of Here Alive"

Marcus walked into a morning with high clouds turning the sky white, while a chill morning breeze ruffled the canvas flaps on the tents on either side of Laughland's abandoned main street. He found Amos on the midway.

"Did you know your father was superstitious?" Marcus asked him. "He had this idea the color of the sky could foretell the kind of day it would be."

"I don't believe my father was superstitious," Amos replied.

"Believe what you wish," Marcus said. "I want to tell you about Bong Sat."

"I know about Bong Sat."

"No, you know only what you've been told, and since no one but me knows what I am about to tell you, you don't know. I am going to tell you why I wouldn't let your father die."

"Because you couldn't get out of Vietnam without him."

"Yes, that's true. But that isn't the main reason."

"Is this another lie?"

"No. This is a day for truth. I admit that I would most likely have died without Matt's help, but it was a death I could have accepted. The death I could not accept was his. He had the one thing I wanted above all else and he was about to throw it away. He had family."

Marcus saw the boy's eyes meet his.

"Everybody wants what they can't have," Steerman said. "You know I grew up in an orphanage. I wanted a mother and a father so much I would have done anything, but by the time I understood that was what I wanted it was too late. No one adopts a twelve year old. When I left the orphanage I promised myself I would become educated, I'd get a good job, and marry and raise a family. I'd be like all the people I envied."

"You wanted to be normal."

"Exactly."

"Why didn't you?"

"The other thing I'd never had was wealth and power. I met Nathan, saw his and all he could do with it, and decided I wanted that more than family." Marcus held his arms wide. "This is the result."

"Why are you telling me this?"

"We stood right here six years ago when I told you your father was dead. I told you I was sorry. You said not to say that again because no one had believed me for a long time. If sorry meant keeping your father from getting killed at Bong Sat, then I wasn't sorry."

Marcus rubbed the ache blooming in his chest and looked to the dawn of the new day.

"For over twenty years I have walked the Earth as a pariah because I forsook my dream of family. Today is the end of the world as you have known it, one way or another. Be clear about what you want in your new world. Don't trade it lightly no matter how much you're tempted."

"What if I die?"

"Then make your final thought one of joy and thanks for what you've done."

"But you don't think I'll die."

"No, not today. Today is like that day at the cathedral. Before all the death, I knew I would survive while many others died. I knew your father would live, too." Marcus pulled a fine silver chain from inside his shirt. He held up the medallion suspended from it. "This is Frank McBride's St. Christopher's medal. He wore it when Nathan killed him. Your father found it where Frank fell. His medal belongs here today."

As he handed it to Amos he saw Clyde approaching.

"Will you survive today?" Amos asked Marcus.

Steerman chose not to answer.

"I have no more 'I'm sorrys.'" Marcus said. "Instead, thank you. You are as close to family as I ever came. You brought me joy more times than I can tell you."

"Will Clyde survive?" Amos asked, when Clyde joined them.

"I have no gift of prescience beyond myself and your father and you."

"What if I fail today?" Amos said.

"You ain't gonna fail," Clyde said, then pointed at Marcus. "That's what failure looks like."

For the third time Martin Dunbar pushed the wheels of his chair over the hardened ground of the path where he would lead Nathan Ferry. When he emerged from the exit of the fun house tent, he saw Amos Eliot standing in the midway with the priest.

"Eliot!" Dunbar called. "One question. Your revenge or my redemption?"

"Do you want redemption?"

"I've been listening, Eliot. You're calling in all the people who've done you wrong. Why?"

Eliot pointed at the priest who had stopped at a respectable twenty feet off.

"Would you answer, please, Father?"

"None of us are innocent, Mr. Dunbar. We all choose redemption . . . or not. For those of us who choose redemption some must climb a sharper peak, but despite the climb, the hardest part is dedicating the will to reach it."

"I don't climb so well," Dunbar said.

"Look around you," Father Harold said, opening his arms and turning in place. "Everyone who ever went to a carnival made it what they wanted. The fun house, the fortune teller, the carousel, the roller coaster, the bearded lady, everything to awaken your feelings and change your perceptions. You are being offered one more chance. You can change from a man who has dishonored himself to a man of honor."

"The mystical carnival."

"Mystical?" the priest said, and made his turn again. "Yes, ethereal, spiritually significant, all of that. You know what will happen here today. A place born in death will die to offer rebirth."

At the sound of laughter the men all looked to see Teresa Gill walking with Clyde. They both carried canvas bags.

"Got to have enough food, don't we?" asked Clyde. "What if we have to stay buried for a couple of days?"

Teresa hefted one of the bags.

"Good chow. Won't be terrible if we do."

"Clyde," Amos said, "have you checked everything?"

"Twice, but this is the last load and I ain't coming out again. Already made my good-byes."

The priest took the bags from Gill and kept Clyde company as they headed for the underground where Clyde went sit at the command center and Father Harold said he would pray for everyone. Teresa waved at them as she headed for the ridge line.

"Eliot," Dunbar said, "when I'm alone with Ferry how do you know I won't give away the plan?"

"He wouldn't save a witness. He'd leave you here to die, unless he killed you himself. Besides, I'm sure Truax will be with him, and Truax has figured it out."

"Do I still get to choose between revenge and redemption? If I do, then I choose redemption."

Sierra Terrace Holding's 737 landed at the private arrivals terminal at Las Vegas's McCarran airport. Ferry saw three helicopters waiting. One was an executive chopper that would carry both him and Truax. The other two were modern versions of the durable Vietnam era Huey for the men that would close the book on Bong Sat. Ferry liked the nostalgic touch.

As Nathan walked across the tarmac he thought of how he had matured over the twenty years since Bong Sat. He remembered his nerves that day. The flash of fear for the instant he thought Marcus would shoot him, his exhilaration as first the gun ship than the Phantoms raced in to fulfill his plan, and finally his anger at Greene and Brinks for not getting him what he wanted. None of that today. His cool, well planned agenda would go without a hitch. Fate owed him that much. He laughed at such an archaic concept as fate.

He joined Truax in the chopper and they took off.

"I don't want any hitches and no surprises," Truax said.

"What are you talking about?" Ferry demanded, irritated at the tone.

"Do you have anyone else out there to do your dirty work that I don't know about?"

"Do I need more than what we have?"

"No, but I wanted to be sure. You have a decision to make. We're going to that carnival. To Laughland. We'll be there in about thirty minutes. We'll bring the other choppers in unseen, but I swore never to underestimate Eliot again. There's a fallout shelter under the carnival. It's been there since before Eliot bought the land. I think the kid lived there, off the grid, until he went to jail. The prison doctor we saw in Vegas said the kid had grown up underground so it fits. The shelter's not deep so we could cave it in with enough firepower. I think the goods are there."

"So what's the problem?"

"If we blow the place to hell you may never be sure the stuff's gone. I think Eliot's counting on how much you want that stuff intact, so he's waiting to take us on."

"So if I say I don't care, you blow it up, I never know, but it would seem safe."

"And we all live. That's as good as it gets without letting that maniac Eliot and all his toys loose on his home ground. We've only seen him on the road. Taking him on there might be bloody. Some of ours, too."

"I want the goods in my hand, and them on their knees."

Truax sighed.

"In that case, you have to go in with me. Dunbar says he'll only deal with you. You hand over the money, he hands over the goods."

"I don't have to leave the chopper! What good would my going with you do?"

"Nathan, this is not Bong Sat revisited, and I am not Marcus Steerman. Dunbar is not negotiating the end of the Vietnam War, although, I guess, in a sense, he is. There is no gunship to wipe the place out. This is Nevada, not Vietnam in the middle of a war. Play the game, get the goodies, and we'll call in the troops."

Ferry felt the excitement. So close to all these problems ending, so close to realizing the dream of all the previous three generations. Was it worth stepping onto the field of battle and changing his role?

"Let's get started."

Once they were in the air, Nathan Ferry removed his headset. He closed his eyes and rested until Truax touched his leg. His eyes opened as Truax pointed out the window. He saw the empty scrub of the desert give way to a burst of color as the carnival appeared below. He saw rides of different shapes and colors; and tents that would hold hundreds of people, and multi-colored wagons. Not normally given to flights of fancy, it didn't take much to imagine it with people walking the midways and laughing and happy. He could almost smell the popcorn and sawdust, and hear the music. He had never been to a carnival.

"What's happening to me?" he thought. With the question, the carnival-inspired fantasy melted into a misty jungle scene and the calliope became the whisperings that had kept him awake.

"Quiet!" he demanded.

"What?" Truax asked.

"Nothing, it's the feeling of all this ending. I'm turning maudlin. Get us down there."

The chopper circled lower.

"That's got to be Dunbar," Truax said, and pointed at a single seated figure surrounded by Laughland.

"Where is everyone?" Ferry asked.

"Yeah," Truax answered, "where are they?"

The chopper settled to the ground fifty yards from the nearest building and about seventy yards from the carnival. Before Truax got out Ferry saw him check his weapons, one gun in a shoulder holster and another at his back. When Truax was on the ground, Ferry joined him.

"What did the chopper do at Bong Sat?" Truax asked. "Did the blades shut down?"

"No."

Truax leaned back into the chopper and Ferry heard the whine of the engine shutting down.

"What are you doing?" he demanded.

"Playing the game. You can bet Steerman's watching this. If this is *deja vu* for you it sure as hell is for him, too. Let's break some of the images. Come on. You got the money?"

Ferry picked up the satchel, looked inside and saw the automatic on top of the stacks of bills, and followed Truax toward the gate of the carnival. Ferry heard the calliope music start, sending a chill along his spine. As the music played, the rides started turning, lifting, spinning, and bouncing. Laughland lived. When they entered the entrance, the music stopped and Ferry heard the sound of a helicopter on the ground, then his own voice saying, *"There is a reason for everything, Right Hand. Focus on all the lives saved by ending the war. You will be a hero."*

The voices came out of the air. "Out of the past," Ferry thought.

Teresa Gill lay on the ground under the tower on the crest of the ridge line next to the phone that led to the outside world. Besides the phone, she had a map of Laughland Valley with a grid imposed on it, binoculars, a military field radio, and a walkie-talkie. Clyde had the other one in the bunker where he sat with the detonators to the mines and booby traps that weren't tripped wired. Her job was that of spotter to report when and where the choppers landed, but she had another job first. Find their communication frequency, and play the tape she and Amos had made. The minutes crept by.

Over the distant hills she saw a lone chopper appear. It moved fast and low, and her heart rate picked up. Through the binoculars she saw it was too small to hold many passengers.

"Clyde, we have one chopper coming in. It's too small to have attackers."

"Roger that."

The chopper swung wide then approached to land outside the main gate.

"On the ground," she said, and told him where.

"Watch for the rest of them," Clyde said.

She watched the lights on the scanner, then she heard voices. From their conversation there were two pilots. She watched the sky and then she saw them. She pressed the send button on the tape player wired into the radio.

"You have entered a monitored defensive perimeter," her voice said in a matter of fact tone. "You have entered an area with automated defenses against unauthorized traffic." The choppers slowed, and she heard the pilots asking for directions. She heard a voice other than the pilot's command them to move ahead. The warning repeated, but still the choppers came ahead. "Clyde, the star burst please."

She saw the liftoff of the firework and watched its trail as it climbed. It detonated in brilliant color against the steel gray sky. She repeated the taped warning again, but the choppers came on.

"They're still coming," she told Clyde. "Two of them. They look like the one you showed me last night."

"Good job," Clyde said. "Play the other tape."

She changed tape cassettes.

Nathan Ferry's voice yelled, "*No one get's out of here alive, but me!*"

It had been recorded at Bong Sat, cleaned up, and copied to the tape. They had it on a loop and it would repeat until she stopped it.

"*No one get's out of here alive, but me!*" Then again. "*No one get's out of here alive, but me!*"

"*There is a reason for everything, Right Hand. Focus on all the lives saved by ending the war. You will be a hero.*"

"Steerman's tape?" Truax asked, pointing at the conical speakers scattered around Laughland.

Ferry nodded.

They saw Dunbar waiting for them. He remained alone.

"Ah, Truax," Dunbar called. "Eliot said you'd be here."

"So he knows," Truax yelled.

"Of course. You and him and me, Truax, we're just pawns on the big board. Come along, boys. They have quite the show for you."

"Why should I?" demanded Ferry. "I'm no one's pawn!"

"You're here aren't you?" Dunbar said, and laughed. "Come on. Get over yourself."

"No, we're leaving!"

"Bullshit," Dunbar called over his shoulder. "You've waited twenty years for this. Inside that tent is everything you've wanted. It's like the crown jewels. You can walk away from all that? I doubt it."

"Come on, Nathan," Truax said. "We still have the upper hand. Let them have their little show."

"We go in there," Ferry pointed, his voice getting more shrill, "they'll kill us."

"If they wanted us dead, we'd be dead. This is the price for holding Bong Sat in your hand and having them on their knees. It's not too late to bomb the shit out of this place. We can get back on the chopper and watch from a distance. That's what you did at Bong Sat wasn't it? That didn't work out so hot, though."

Dunbar had slowly rolled closer to the tent. When they followed, he went faster. As they neared the tent's entrance, Ferry saw the sign. FUN HOUSE. He heard Truax say, "That figures."

"Why aren't you afraid?" Ferry asked. "You know what Eliot will do to you if he wins."

"I'm not afraid because Eliot is not going to win. Come on."

Dunbar swiveled his chair in the entrance to face them.

"Eliot's not going to win?" he said. "Bit optimistic, don't you think. I'm responsible for his mother being dead, Truax, you did his father, and you, Ferry, you caused the whole fucking thing. Here we are, walking – so to speak – into a dark tent on his home turf. 'Not going to win.' Hold that thought."

Ferry felt his resolve melting. Bong Sat wasn't a failure. He could run back to the chopper, lift off and wait until it was done. He would have more time to sift the ruins than he had at Bong Sat, and he wouldn't have that incompetent Greene whining at him.

Greene! Blown to pieces by The Diemaker!

He shook off the rogue thought. With less destruction he had a better chance to find the purple bag and be sure.

"Come on, boys," Dunbar said, "soups getting cold."

Ferry's hesitant steps followed Dunbar and Truax into a dimly lit, canvas-sided passage. The sound of beating helicopter blades filled the air. The rotors faded and he heard Steerman's voice.

"Who are you?"

"Eliot. Recon, 2nd Battalion, 3rd Marines. Who are you?"

Had to be the voice of the long dead Matthew Eliot.

"None of your business," Steerman again. *"What are you doing here?"*

The sounds of Bong Sat, and a sound bite he'd never heard, filled Ferry with dread because he knew what he would soon hear.

"Could use a ride. Been out two weeks."

"No way. You picked a bad time, Marine."

"Bad for us, too."

"Captain, I got no time. Get your men and head back where you came from."

"Not an option, sir. We're pursued."

Ferry waited breathlessly through a pause.

"How'd you happen here?" Steerman's voice asked.

"You can see the steeple from the hill over there. We saw the chopper."

"No hope here. Last time, Captain, there is no room on that Huey, and you do not want to be here." A long pause then more Steerman. *"Okay, Captain. Wait one."*

Ferry saw back through the years and Steerman running toward him as he stood in the open door of the helicopter, the huge cathedral lurking in the background.

"Recon patrol," Steerman said to the much younger Ferry. *"He's looking for a ride."*

"Well, that isn't very practical, is it? Forget him. Get your fucking job done!"

"He's not taking no for an answer. He's an old Captain name of Eliot."

"Old? A loser if he's still out here. He won't be missed, will he?"

The *"He won't be missed, will he?"* repeated, echoed, and faded.

"Sort of sings as the epitaph on your headstone, doesn't it?" Dunbar said, and laughed.

"Not subtle, Nathan," Truax said. "If Steerman didn't know what you had in store before, he sure as hell did after that little slip."

"Let us not forget the context," Dunbar said, more heard than seen in the near darkness. "Ferry, you just condemned Amos Eliot's father to death and here we are playing his game. Still not scared?"

Ferry felt Truax grab his arm. He tried to pull away, but the grip tightened.

"Come on, Nathan. This was your play. Time to do your own dirty work."

They moved ahead. Out of the darkness a bright light erupted. They heard the clacking of film running through a projector. A large face, the thin, ascetic face of an Asian with a goatee, stared down at them. The face spoke to them in Vietnamese.

"He spoke nearly perfect English, you know," Ferry said.

"Ho?" Truax asked.

"Yes. He worked in New York, Brooklyn, when he was young."

Ho looked off screen and the translator began.

"President Johnson, my message to you is not to be taken as weakness. It is a humanitarian attempt to save many thousands of lives that could ruin both of our countries. If America has any honor you will respond in kind."

The face faded.

"And you bombed them to pulp," Dunbar said. "So much for honor. How much did you make having the war drag on?"

"You wouldn't understand," Ferry said, hearing the defensive whine in his voice and hating it.

"No doubt. The explanation for thousands of dead has got to be too complicated for me."

"Don't take that tone with me, you pathetic creature! You took my money."

"Shut up! Both of you," Truax said. "Eliot has to be listening. He's waited his whole life for this and here you are giving him exactly what he wants."

The frozen face of Ho lit the room, but instead of the audio from the film, they heard Steerman's voice.

"No!" Steerman yelled over the helicopter sounds. In his remembering, Ferry saw Frank McBride dead on the ground. He had just thrown down the gun he had used to kill him.

"*Listen!*" Steerman again. "*Two minutes and this place will be . . . gone. Save yourself. Shooting me will do you no good. You might even be doing me a favor.*"

"*What's coming down?*"

"Steerman knew exactly," Truax said. "How?"

"I don't know," Ferry answered.

"*Bad luck, Marine,*" Steerman's recorded voice interrupts them. "*If you want to live follow me. I can get you out, if we're lucky, but just you.*"

"*My men.*"

"*Dead and don't know it.*"

"*Bullshit! None of my men die that easy.*"

"*Save yourself or die. No one's supposed to get out of here alive.*"

"Ambush! Ambush!" came a voice from the background. No doubt one of the Marines. "*Three o'clock!*"

"*Last chance, Eliot! You and me, or death.*"

"*Fight with us, Steerman. Tell me what's happening.*"

"*Betrayal, Marine! Betrayal, and it's my fault! I could have killed the devil and failed.*"

Ferry remembered the moment when Steerman's gun passed his chest.

"*Fight with us!*" Eliot yelled.

Gunfire erupts and the roar of the Huey lifting off almost covers the voices. Then, distinctly, over the sound of the guns and death, Nathan Ferry called from the past, "*Nobody get's out of here alive. Nobody but me!*"

"*Who the fuck – ?*

"*The devil, Eliot. The devil!*"

As the helicopters approached, dropping as they came, she read her map for the correct coordinates to tell Clyde.

"They're landing!" Teresa Gill called into the walkie-talkie. "Grid C-126, hundred feet in altitude."

"Watch this," Clyde said. An explosion sent dust and dirt into the air. The upheaval rocked the nearer chopper and it climbed. The other chopper pulled back. On the scanner, she heard more conversation, then gasped.

"They're going to use rockets or something. They aren't going to land."

"Keep watching."

The choppers came closer but kept altitude, and hovered. She saw the side doors open and men sitting in them holding tubes. She watched them fire and a second later an explosion shook the carousel. More explosions shook the carnival grounds, but none came near the center.

"They're staying away from the tents!" she said, as two more shells struck. This time the roller coaster frame buckled.

"No payday if they kill the boss," Clyde answered.

Two more rockets struck on each side of the midway starting fires.

Clyde's voice said, "Warn the one to the north that they will be shot down in ten seconds unless they withdraw. Tell them now."

"The chopper to the north," she said, and was surprised her voice remained calm, "you will be destroyed in ten seconds unless you withdraw. Nine, eight, seven," they didn't move and fired another rocket. "Three, two, one."

From out of the heart of Laughland, a *whoosh* and a trail of fire raced into the designated chopper. It erupted in a ball of flame. To her horror, she saw the door gunner fall and pin wheel to the ground. The machine hung in the air a few seconds longer, then as awkward as a child of all arms and legs, it fell to the ground. A new blast bloomed on impact.

"Warn the other one," Clyde said. "Keep it calm just like you did."

She took a deep breath and let it out before she keyed the mike.

"The remaining helicopter. You will be destroyed in ten seconds. Ten, nine, eight, seven . . ." The chopper wheeled away.

Explosions, louder now and of a different timbre, and felt as well as heard, pulled Ferry out of the past.

"Come on," Truax called. "It is a trap!"

"I don't think the help you counted on is going to make it," Dunbar said, as more explosions shook the ground. "Just like those Marines waiting and praying!"

Ferry stared as Truax dropped to a knee in front of Dunbar.

"What did Eliot promise you? Money?"

"The same thing he promised you. A second chance. Looks like I'm smarter than you."

A second chance! The idea galvanized Nathan. The reason he was here was to give others a chance to redeem their failures. Dunbar had called him a pawn and he saw they were. Eliot had created a diorama to amuse and fulfill others at Ferry's expense.

"Nobody does that to me!" he said, and the others looked at him. He opened the bag of money, took out the gun. "Second chance? There's no such thing."

He stepped in front of Dunbar and shot the man in the head.

Truax fell backward as the spray from the wound hit his face.

"No second chances, Truax. Bomb this place to dust!"

"You fool!" Truax screamed, wiping at his face. "Bomb it? What do you think is happening out there?" A much bigger explosion shook the ground. "They just shot down one of the choppers! We're on our own here, and if we don't work together neither one of us is getting out of here alive."

"Fool? How dare you!" Ferry's gun moved to Truax. "I should have done this years ago."

"Right! Go ahead and shoot me. Who's going to get your miserable ass out of here if you shoot me. You're the same as Steerman at Bong Sat. You need me the way Steerman needed Eliot to get out of the jungle."

"Wrong, Truax." Ferry fired twice, both shots hitting Truax in the chest. "You're no good to anyone now. And I never needed you. I've never needed anyone!"

Amos heard the shots inside the tent. He looked at the purple bag in his hand. He hoped the brothers at St. Peter in the Wood were right about Heaven. He wanted the Ghosts of Bong Sat watching. The smoke and dust of the destruction of Laughland swirled around him pushed by the wind blowing off the wasteland. Flames burned from the crashed helicopter as well as from the wounded Laughland.

Amos walked slowly along the midway toward the fun house, the smoke blocking the view in waves. He stepped out of a heavy cloud and saw Nathan Ferry, gun in hand, standing in front of him. Ferry's gun came up as Eliot lifted the purple bag.

"Do you want this?" Amos called, and held up the Crown Royal bag. "I'm through with it."

Ferry raised the gun, then hesitated. "Through?"

"Bong Sat's over. No more magic of any kind."

"It won't be over until you're dead," Ferry yelled, and raised his gun.

"Hello, Nathan."

Marcus Steerman materialized out of the smoke to Amos's right.

"What are you going to do with that gun, Marcus?" Ferry asked, with a laugh. "Think you'll have more courage to kill the devil this time?"

"This is your gun, Nathan. The one you used to kill Frank McBride. It's been cleaned, and repaired by an expert. The Diemaker. It's waited a long time for this moment."

Ferry's gun moved back and forth between Amos and Steerman.

"You have always been a failure," Ferry said, and the aim shifted to Amos who still held the purple bag.

"That's twice I've been called a failure today!" Marcus yelled.

"Here!" Amos called, and tossed the purple bag high toward Ferry. He watched as Ferry's eyes traced the bag's arc. He saw Ferry's fingers reach, splayed, ready to pluck it from the air.

Marcus screamed as he pulled the trigger. Ferry stumbled back, and dropped the bag with his million dollars. His eyes stared in disbelief at Steerman, then his gaze fell to the purple bag as it landed near his feet. His knees gave way and he fell, hand reaching for the prize. He died, fingers still scrapping at the dirt, still trying to reach that which lay beyond his grasp.

Marcus walked slowly to his fallen enemy, squatted, gun dangling from his hand. He looked back at Amos then lay beside Ferry nose to nose.

"He's dead," Marcus said. "It took less than a second to pull the trigger. Amos, I watched the light go out and I didn't feel a thing. No sense of revenge, no righting of my wrong, no rebirth for all those who died because I couldn't do this when it mattered."

Steerman reached out his empty hand and Amos helped him to his feet. Steerman held the hand, then squeezed it.

"The Ghosts of Bong Sat are waiting, my boy. I am tired of this life. Yesterday, Father Harold helped me with my preparations. I will die now with a sense of where I am going." Marcus still held Amos's hand. "Father Harold helped me yesterday. Technically he shouldn't have given my last rites, but he did. Well he recited them all I could think about was the death of the young Marine at Bong Sat when I couldn't think of the words for his last rites. Another failure, another death."

He dropped Amos's hand a last time before walking slowly into the fun house. Amos waited. The sound of the shot rang with a finality that echoed across Laughland Valley. It was the last shot of the battle for Bong Sat.

Amos picked up his father's purple bag and felt the memories of the dead. With his other hand he picked up Ferry's money.

Teresa Gill hurried down from her post on the ridge and met Father Harold and Clyde as they came out of the underground. They walked through the drifting smoke until they saw Amos standing in the midway surveying the ruins of Laughland the body of Nathan Ferry lying near by.

"What happened?" Clyde asked.

Succinctly, Amos told them.

"You know what you did?" Father Harold asked.

"Yes," Amos said. "It was like The Diemaker."

"You didn't do the killing," Father Harold said, "but you enabled it."

"How would you have done it?" Amos asked him.

"We are not the same."

"If we were?"

"The man would most likely have done the same thing."

"What about the priest?" Amos asked.

"The priest would be dead."

Teresa scribbled the exchange in her notebook and underscored the priest's final quote.

"What now?" she asked Amos, moving slightly as the wind shifted. "What about the other chopper?"

"Soldiers without leaders do not fight," Amos said. "What about you? How will you write your story?"

"I don't know. With Ferry dead, the stakes have changed."

"His body is dead," Amos said, "but his business survives. Marcus said their political agenda could still succeed with significant long term consequences. He also said to tell you this could happen again. Any war should be analyzed for who profits. He said always follow the money. You would understand."

"I still need proof."

"Everything from Bong Sat is intact, and this is a million dollars." He held up the black bag. "Ferry thought he was buying my father's bag. I want you to use if to find the families of my father's men. He kept the bag to have something of the dead for each of those who loved them. He never got the chance to find them. I'm sure there's a story with each item."

"I want to tell your father's story, too. He was a hero."

"He would be angry if he heard you say that, but if you find the families it would ease his pain."

"What do I write about you?"

"Whatever you wish. I will cease to exist long before your words are printed. Officially, I have never existed."

"You have had your fingerprints taken, and a mug shot."

"As John Nelson, but I'm sure they have been removed."

They walked until Teresa asked, "What do you want to do?"

"What I've always wanted. I want to be normal."

"There's nothing normal about you."

"I will practice," Amos Eliot said.

She flipped her notebook open and across the top of the page she printed in uppercase THE RETURN OF THE DIEMAKER.

Later, Teresa Gill and Father Harold stood by her rental car. They watched Amos Eliot and Clyde walk west into the wasteland while the fires of Laughland burned behind them sending black smoke tinged with orange high against a white sky.

The black smoke slowly became gray, then white, as Bong Sat's doorway to Hell screeched closed.

THE END

ACKNOWLEDGMENTS

This book would not exist without the initial help and guidance of the late Michael Kasner. His help with the Vietnam scenes in everything from equipment and order of battle, to language and strategy, is gratefully acknowledged. Eric Marcoux shared his first hand knowledge of life in a Trappist monastery. Harvey Gurman did a remarkable job of line editing and continuity.

Rae Richen read early versions with pencil in hand and provided grammar and encouragement as needed. My brother, Steve, offered a comment that led to a scene that fueled the middle of the book, and Dana Dee Little's "cut, cut, cut" came at just the right time. Other readers who all offered help of one kind or another include Jay Harris, Rick York, and Joyce Gifford. Thanks to you all.

A special thanks to Don Treadwell for solving the problem of the right words in the right place, and to Harvey Gurman for being sure they were spelled and punctuated correctly .

My most special thanks are to my wife, Meg, who over the years has always been supportive and encouraging, and keeps at least one of my feet on the ground. She has read this book too many times, but with each reading she found ways to make it better.

Ken
2010

NEW! From Ken Byers

NOW AVAILABLE ~

The Weight of the Journey

In Banner County, Oregon, the trees grow taller, the marijuana grows stronger, there's gold in the creeks, and there's even a feud that's lasted more than a century.

Out of work ex-cop Dewey Farrell hasn't been back to the scene of his youth in twenty-three years, but when childhood friend, Thatch McPherson, calls and says he "needs" him and "please" come back, Dewey goes because Thatch never said need or please.

Dewey arrives too late to save Thatch and finds all the mysteries he left behind still waiting for him. Pearl Banner threw him out of her bed and her life, but now is glad to see him. There's a chance the mother he never had is alive and manipulating his life, and what is his role in the future of Banner County that has everyone so concerned? And the biggest mystery of all is what happens inside the Cloud, Banner County's most obvious and oldest secret?

The Weight of the Journey is available from Lloyd Court Press and Amazon.

36702562R00224

Made in the USA
Charleston, SC
11 December 2014